ELLA'S CURSE

BOOK TWO OF THE LOST WARRIORS

CHRISTINE PRIESTLY

To Mr Lee, I promise there's no sewing or shopping in this one.

To Kelly, who helped shape the future.

And to all my readers and supporters, who make it all worth while.

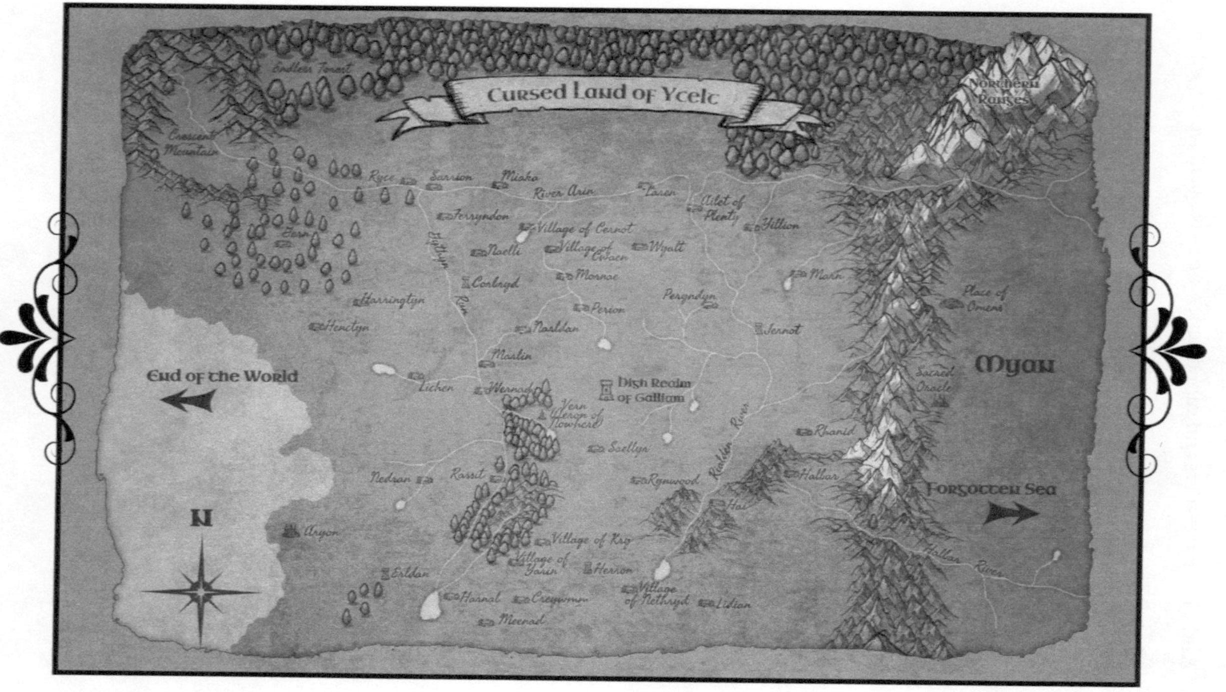

Cursed Land of Ycelc
Endless Forest
Northern Ranges
Crescent Mountain
Ryce
Sarrion
Miaho
River Arin
Taren
Ailet of Plenty
Ferryndon
Village of Cernot
Yillion
Fern
Naelli
Village of Cvaen
Wyalt
Mann
Corbryd
Mornae
Place of Omens
Harringtyn
Perion
Pergndyn
Henctyn
Naaldan
Jernot
Maslin
End of the World
Lichen
Wernad
High Realm of Galliam
Sacred Oracle
Myan
Vern Village of Nowhere
Rhanid
Saellyn
Kralten River
Nedron
Rassit
Rynwood
Hallar
Hai
Forgotten Sea
Aryon
Village of Kay
Erldan
Village of Yanin
Herron
Hallar River
Harnal
Creywmm
Village of Nethryd
Lidian
Meenad
N

Author's Note

Before embarking on this magical journey...

A note on language:

I invite you to embrace the spellings peculiar to the Australian (UK English) dialect of its author. Readers more used to US English spellings may be unaccustomed to the quirks of UK English, such as the additional 'u' in words like 'colour' and 'honour', but trust this will enrich your reading experience as you become immersed in the author's world.

A note on content:

Certain content contained within this novel may be sensitive to some readers. As specific content warnings are not spoiler-free (nor without their own perils), I invite readers seeking content advice to head to christinepriestly.com/content/ to learn more. Or to enjoy your read spoiler-free, simply begin your journey.

Map

To view a full colour map of Ycelt, visit: christinepriestly.com/map/

ELLA'S CURSE

BOOK TWO OF THE LOST WARRIORS

There are those who ask for whom is the Curse a punishment?
Borne of anger and betrayal, is it not a double-edged sword? To
those I answer, only if you let it be.

The Lost Warriors by Ynad of the Gern

PART ONE: RESIGNATION

The Temple of Aryon, Order of Xenon of the Black Moon

Spring 796 A.S.

ONE

'There's a reason it's called the dawn homage, *Princess*.' Ella woke to prodding hands, shaking her amid disgusted groans.

Bleary-eyed, she rolled from her bed onto the cold stone floor, her back aching and stiff. She stood, and the world lurched, her morning queasiness churning. Ella grabbed the nearby chamber pot and heaved. The other priestesses left her, their revulsion burning in her mind.

Now alone, Ella glanced around her small, partitioned cell. With scattered tears, she set the pot aside and sank onto her slat bed in the endless, windowless dark. Her hands splayed across her abdomen. Sensed the murmur of her unborn child.

Ella hadn't bled since the morning Gohran brought her to Aryon, the babe stirring in frequent protest, as though it had no wish to be trapped inside her, either. If only Lynden listened instead of fetching Gohran, she would still be at Nedran with Venn.

Venn.

She closed her eyes, stretched her mind, and reached for him, for the love she harboured before her passion corrupted and reduced him to a husk. She imagined him yearning for her as she ached for him. But the moment she sensed the faintest echo, the feeling slipped away.

Another stir within her womb, from that creature who rendered her powerless. *Like its father.* Even with their relationship soured, remaining with Venn must be better than being trapped with these priestesses, unwillingly pregnant, and utterly alone.

A familiar tug at her mind. Her former tutor, Amber, hovered in the doorway. In the dim corridor light, Amber's saffron-coloured braids appeared almost ochre, her eyes glowing as a cat's by moonlight. Without uttering a word, she settled on Ella's bed.

'Come, let's comb out those tangles.' Amber ran tender fingers through Ella's knotted hair and began the painstaking process of braiding and securing it against her skull, winding and fastening each strand, until she looked like one of them. 'You should learn to do this for yourself.'

Ella bristled. She didn't choose this. To be like them. Why should she be complicit in making herself resemble them?

Amber sucked on her lip. She must have known Ella's thoughts, but didn't acknowledge them, running her fingers through Ella's hair and twining.

'Oh Ella, I wish I could have waited and taken you with me, but I could not delay or neither of us would have got away.'

It wasn't the first time Amber had uttered this apology, as though if she said it often enough, or found the precise words, it would make things right between them.

'When I saw you with Lord Venn at Nedran through the god-sight, I assumed you would be safe...'

Amber's hand brushed her cheek. Soothing. Quiet. And warmth! Is that what Venn experienced when Ella used her powers on him? Pure and tender, it would keep Ella safe. To give in and lose herself in that peaceful bliss! She longed to curl into Amber's arms, shrug away the lies, and unshackle her shame. Yet against the warmth, ice might have melted down her spine.

Her former tutor continued to stroke her cheek and, with it, her mind. 'When I saw you back at Erldan with your brother, the king—'

'You saw me with Gohran?' Ella flinched. *What had she seen?* She clamped her thoughts down.

Amber nodded. 'Please know I never imagined Lord Venn would... Well, that you would end up like—*this*...' Amber glanced at Ella's softly swelling abdomen.

Bitter relief. Much as it pained her for Amber to blame Venn, who was honourable beyond measure, it was safer for them all this way.

'You must be angry at your brother for bringing you here. But Ella, Aryon is where you belong, with people like you—people like us.' Amber clasped her hands.

There was a yearning in her Ella had never observed at Erldan. A craving that hovered beneath the surface. 'You don't need to keep your guard up here,' Amber said. 'You're safe now.'

Ella sensed her longing to connect, to reestablish the bond they shared before Amber fled Erldan, leaving Ella behind, but Ella's mind shied away. The priestess was so different here at Aryon, wearing plaits and a robe, mousing around her superiors. She seemed more at ease than Ella remembered, but Ella knew her ease came at a cost—a price she wasn't willing to pay.

Most of all, Ella feared letting Amber in because she didn't trust herself not to reveal the truth. That her brother raped her, and that she felt responsible. That he misunderstood and misconstrued her longing to be close, and her deeper fear that she led him to it. Now here she was, carrying the product of that shame in her womb.

Letting Amber in would cause everything to tumble out. How she manipulated the man she loved to harbour her, convinced him the child was his, all the while whittling him down until her will subsumed his. She might as well tell Amber she was right to leave her behind, that she was a monster. She didn't deserve freedom, love, or happiness.

A bell clanged. The dawn homage had begun. Amber quickly finished braiding Ella's hair and helped her off the bed.

'Don't forget the chamber pot.' She nodded towards the now-full ceramic bowl.

Ella's nose wrinkled, but she did as Amber directed, holding the pot away from her. Its contents sloshed, and she almost vomited again. Face pressed into her sleeve, she defended against the smell, and hid her ever-present tears.

She had known the priestesses lived as virtual slaves, in humble service to their heretical god, but never imagined they would treat her no better than the lowliest servant at Erldan. Amber was wrong when she said Ella belonged here, but perhaps being here was exactly what she deserved.

Two

Late into the night, Venn stared through faded light at his bedroom's vaulted ceiling. He ached. *Gone. Ella's gone.* Gohran's words tore through him. Once, he imagined he could live without her. He hadn't known then what it meant to experience the stars melting into her eyes, his flesh dissolving into hers. Now he knew, and nothing would be the same.

Eyes closed, he remembered her sweet voice whispering beside him, jasmine scent on her skin. He reached to wrap his arms around her, scoop her against his body, and bury his face in her hair. An icy void greeted him, and he choked off a howl.

Sleep came, only for him to wake moments later in a fit of realisation, the agony beginning again.

The previous day, Gohran had despatched a courier to his older sisters at Erldan, and at Lynden's insistence, to Jonas in Lichen. Gohran told them he held Ella as hers and the babe's life bled out, but they agreed he would declare his sister died of a fever, conceiving no other way to explain her sudden passing that preserved her honour.

As Gohran described the scene, Venn tried to picture her, achingly beautiful, even as she drew her final breaths, but the image slipped away, and his vision flashed white. Back in Erldan, he and Ella danced, her warmth flooding him for the first time. Strolling at Nedran, her smile twisted and tugged. Then he recalled the agony of finding her on solstice morning, limbs draped across his brother—nothing compared to the devastation of losing her from this life. A sob escaped.

'Venn?' Lynden took his hand.

Another flash. Ella in her mud-soaked dress, terror in her eyes, as he told her he must send her back to Erldan. Her distinctive warmth wrenched, so intense it was painful, and all reason slipped away. If only he'd devised a way to protect her at Nedran without taking her to his bed. But he had craved her, as he wanted nothing before. Now, his carnal urges had cost Ella her life.

His breath stabbed in his chest. 'We—I—should have waited,' he said. 'She was so young…'

Lynden's hand squeezed his. 'This isn't your fault, Venn. You once told me the goddess will take our loved ones when She sees fit and not a moment later. Remember?'

Gohran's palm rested on his shoulder, reaching out with a warmth too much like Ella's. 'Let me take you to her.'

Venn shrugged him away. 'I can't…'

To see her grave would bear witness to her passing, and he couldn't accept she was gone. Wasn't ready to believe. She had been by his side, in his arms, in his bed, only one day earlier—vibrant, healthy, glowing. He could hear her still. Smell her. Feel her.

Days passed before Venn let Gohran lead him and Lynden to her resting place. They rode out before dawn. The town was eerie and quiet, as though the entire populace mourned. Nedran's guards opened the gates to allow them through, and they continued south towards the woodlands and pastures outside the city's jurisdiction.

The early morning fog glowed a preternatural pale vermillion, as if rust powdered the sky. Leaving under the light of uhtan was for their privacy, but Venn imagined the thick mist might bury him.

His stomach lurched. 'Stop the carriage. Stop!'

Gohran knocked to his driver, and they pulled up.

Venn barely made it outside before his nausea besieged him. Hunched over a patch of grass, a biting ache gripped his joints. His entire body trembled, his skin damp and feverish.

'Shall we turn back?' Gohran rested a hand between Venn's shoulders, and with the other, held Venn's cloak away from his face.

Venn shook his head. 'No—No, I need to do this.'

Gohran nodded.

Venn wiped the drool from his mouth with his sleeve and looked up into Gohran's eyes—so like hers.

'Come.' Gohran helped Venn back into the carriage.

There was warmth in that voice—Ella's distorted echo. It was all he had left of her.

The carriage jerked into motion, and by the time they reached a small clearing on the edge of a steep valley, Elnora climbed over the horizon. The glade peeked through the now-white mist, so it seemed they stood amid a moat of clouds. It was here Gohran had buried his sister and built a cairn.

Such an odd location.

'When it happened, I couldn't bear to carry her with me.' Gohran's voice caught, and his jaw stiffened. 'Besides, to where? She no longer had a home...'

In defying her brother and seeking to marry Venn, Ella's actions bordered on treason, so Gohran had every right to deny her a burial in his kingdom. The marriage contract would have established Venn as Ella's husband and overlord, but Ella had died before the priests could seal the betrothal.

He shaded his eyes from the morning glare, squinting at the vacant, rolling grasslands and fog dissipating in every direction. Gohran had been taking Ella to get help for the babe, but there was nothing and no one out here. Sealed or not, Venn would have housed her body in his family's plot, rather than at this midpoint to nowhere.

Beside him, Lynden sniffled into her handkerchief, her shoulders shaking. She would mourn properly later, in private. He wondered if, like him, she was remembering their parents' graves in the family plot at Nedran. He recalled the great headstone built for his father beside the grey, weary stone erected for his mother years before. Priests had chanted and wailed, people whimpered and snivelled in a horrid cacophony, offering their condolences in one breath and congratulations in the next. Venn remembered his anger. Fury that the gods had taken his father, too, but more—that duty denied him indulging his grief.

Now, staring at this pitiful cairn, sprinklings of grass and dandelions sprouting atop the grave, he longed to be that angry again. Instead, he experienced nothing—less than nothing. It didn't seem real. She wasn't in there, beneath that pile of dirt and rocks. He sensed her still.

A hand squeezed his shoulder. Gohran. Blue eyes misting as they met his, their heat melting into him, trying to fill her void. In grief, they were brothers once more.

THREE

Gohran felt torn between staying on at Nedran to mend his relationship with Venn and wanting to escape the disbelief and bewilderment in the dryhten's bovine eyes. Venn had questions he could not answer—that he dared not think upon.

He hoped showing Venn Ella's mock grave would convince him and give him a focus for his grief. In truth, it was as much for himself. He would never be free of Ella's hold, but imagining her down there, beneath the ground, he might mourn what the gods forbade.

When they returned, Venn did not linger, excusing himself to attend to his duties. No doubt he wanted privacy to grieve.

Their bond felt strained, and Gohran realised part of that strain came from him. When Venn took Ella to his bed, he betrayed them both. Gohran couldn't fault Venn entirely. He understood the hold Ella had over his friend—the grip she had over him still. How could Venn or anyone defend against that? But Ella did not belong to Venn. She never had. She belonged to him.

Gohran stifled his desire to keen.

Lynden's adoring hazel eyes sought his. She sat beside him in the drawing room, where a maid served tea with a side of distilled spirit made from fermented hallit, a specialty of the region.

'I can't imagine your pain right now, Your Highness.' She squeezed his arm.

Pressure crinkled the scabs beneath his shirt. He clasped Lynden's fingers, then stroked her cheek. 'I must return to Erldan.'

'So soon?'

'My sisters expect me.'

'Of course.' Tinged with disappointment. 'If you need anything at all...'

He could have her again, he was certain. Those tantalising lips curved with desire. She was lovely.

Ignoring the tea, he downed the spirit and stood to leave. 'Please send my regards to the dryhten.'

He spoke truth. Raeyn and Jaydyn would be in shock and mourning, and he should relieve Raeyn of the duties of his realm. But a greater truth was his eagerness to flee his web of deceit and the strained relationship of the only genuine friend he'd ever known.

Though the sky threatened a storm, he ordered Jarrod to drive their carriage home. By the time they reached Erldan, rain pelted, wind howled, trees swayed and creaked as lightning forked above.

Indoors, Gohran tossed his drenched cloak to a waiting servant and trudged upstairs to his bedchamber. Eyes closed, he sank to his knees before the remnants of his personal altar. He had not rebuilt it since the night the goddess had forsaken him, but habit drew him to Her now, staring into the void where once Her statue perched. He reached for Elnora's echo, but found Ella's.

Entangled with the goddess, she stood before him in his mind, arms thrown around his neck, body pressed against him. Her azure eyes sought his, as they looked up to him during those last moons when she'd been home—his alone for that brief glimmer of time. He recalled the warmth that flowed between them, knowing with her he never had to hide what he hid from the world, and from himself.

But it was against the laws of the gods, and when he took her... Her terror and disgust flooded him, and he stifled a cry.

Part of her must have wanted it, needed it, as much as him. The burning ache that was not even lust, but a longing to be seen—to be known.

Taking Lynden was not like that. With her, there was physical desire, heat flowing from him to her. But with Ella, he sought that fire to surround him, in turn. He knew somehow that it would. It had. If only the goddess didn't forbid it, they might live as they needed—a matched pair, their tainted souls mingling as their bodies entwined.

Though he'd placed her safely away from him—away from any man—he would never be free. His breath quickened and his flesh trembled as Ella's image replayed: her yearning, like his. Her need to connect, to be whole. A constant throbbing in his mind and bones, his longing burned. Placing his sister at Aryon should have freed him, but her tentacles strangled and clawed and his hunger intensified.

Wretched desperation engulfed him, followed by the familiar stirrings of an ice-fire passion, hot and cold at once, almost like acid, coursing through his loins. Without her to contain and balance his energy, he needed to find a release.

He knew only one way to make the craving stop. He peeled off his shirt and stared at the row of scabs and scars, some fresh, some healed. Revulsion filled his throat. He crouched beside his bed and hefted a heavy locked chest from beneath, then reached between his mattress and bedframe and retrieved an old brass key. Sweat beaded his forehead and clavicle. Hands shaking, he slid key into lock. It clunked free, and the lid groaned open. Gohran rifled through layers of worn linen until he found his dagger. With a jagged inhale, he drew it out.

The ice-fire surged. He gripped the knife so hard his knuckles turned white. His hand hovered, pale flesh taunting, damp hairs prickling between old scars. Revulsion fused with desire until desire won. He had no choice.

Breath held, he sliced. Sharp, fiery pain. He waited for the relief as blood leaked down his forearm. A surge, almost unnoticeable, escaped, and Ella's image wavered before him. Lust mingled with regret. It was not enough. He needed to numb, to banish her entirely.

He loosened his grip, and the dagger dropped to the floor. He swallowed, reached into the chest, and retrieved his leather strap. Sweat poured off him, pressure throbbing through his temples, his breath labouring between tightened ribs.

He faced the wall, shoulders braced. Swung forward, then back until the leather bit, and he flinched. Teeth gritted, he drew and swung again, eyes watering as it landed. Another bite. He imagined his naked back as a slab of meat, pictured the edges around each bite splicing and opening, the blood leaking.

And then it came. Pain. Numbness. Euphoria.

He let the strap fall and collapsed face-down on his bed. The burning pulsed and oozed, finally set free.

Four

When Gohran first summoned Raeyn and Jaydyn home from Rynwood with the approaching spring, he informed them that following Shiana's trial, some angst in the nearby villages took him patrolling Erldan's outer fringes.

'Where's Ella?' Raeyn had asked.

'At Nedran,' Gohran dismissed with a wave, then closed the matter.

It was Lyrra who later revealed Ella had left during an altercation with their brother. The lady's maid overheard whispers the princesses were not privy to.

'I heard she and His Highness exchanged all kinds of words,' Lyrra told them, wide-eyed. 'And afterwards, the young princess fled.'

Raeyn looked heavenward. Why were her siblings so impulsive?

Earlier, Raeyn convinced Lyrra to take up her old post at Erldan. She dared not return following her cousin Shiana's Cleansing.

'I promise no one bears you any ill will, only sympathy.' Raeyn's eyes said, *We have shared your fear, your pain.* Lyrra had known the princesses most of their lives. She was there when Gohran denounced their mother.

'What about His Highness?' Lyrra scrunched her pinafore with her fists.

A gentle squeeze. 'Leave Gohran to me.'

In the end, Lyrra agreed. While the princesses welcomed the extra help, especially now Serrah was toddling, Lyrra welcomed the coin.

Gohran didn't even notice their maid's homecoming—he rarely paid attention to those so far beneath him. And when he returned, his stay was brief.

Almost immediately, he had headed back out to Nedran, because Ella and Venn had taken it upon themselves to declare a betrothal.

This news stabbed like a knife through Raeyn's sternum, but she swallowed her anguish, and took the reins of the kingdom as duty demanded. She had long accepted the dryhten was smitten with her youngest sister, but she didn't have to like it.

Now, as she ran her fingers over her brother's letter bearing word of Ella's passing, she felt guilty for begrudging Ella anything.

Gohran's study appeared darker and more forbidding than when she was a girl, peering around the door, judging if it was safe to bring the king accounts of her doll's latest ventures—the fondness she longed for, elusive. She'd not witnessed her father's affection until Ella was born. How he doted on his favourite little princess!

And now Ella was gone. Just like that. Gohran said she died of a fever, but Raeyn didn't believe that for a heartbeat.

She put the letter aside and wiped her tear-stained cheek. She and her youngest sibling were never close. There were times she wanted her family to send Ella away to Aryon as Erldan's treaty demanded, but never would she have wished her an early grave.

Raeyn sniffed and blew her nose upon her handkerchief. She realised she was weeping for losing her parents more than her sister, and if she were honest, at least some of those tears tinged with guilt for the affection she'd never quite felt. Ella was always so *different*. If anything, Raeyn envied her that difference. Their father's favourite, their mother's protégé, and their brother's confidante. And now she was gone.

When Gohran's carriage pulled up a short while later, his stomping footfalls told Raeyn he was in no mood she cared to encounter. She gave him time to get settled and calm. Then she steeled herself, and, clutching his letter, pursued him to his chamber.

'Gohran.' She pounded on his door.

Muffled shuffling before footsteps approached. Her brother opened the door and moved aside to let her in. His mussed hair looked as if he'd just dressed. Was that blood soaking through his sleeve? A soiled shirt lay crumpled on the floor beside the charred area where his altar once stood. Thank the goddess he had not reconstructed it since almost burning the keep down with his ridiculous obsession. As if Elnora cared one way or another if a candle remained aflame in a single room of the entire High Realm.

Raeyn shoved the letter at Gohran's chest. 'By the goddess—what happened?'

'A fever took her...' Gohran reached out, comforting, but Raeyn shrugged him off, arms crossed.

'A fever, Gohran?'

Gohran's eyes narrowed. 'That's what you will tell anyone who asks.'

'And when people want to know how a healthy young woman succumbed to a fever, what am I to say?'

Gohran drew a slow, deep breath, but remained silent.

'Was she ill? Was she weak? What aren't you saying? Speak the truth, brother. I'm not a fool.'

Gohran stepped in close, voice low. 'Yet it seems your sister was. Ella did not learn from Jaydyn's shame, nor her own over the summer. When I arrived at Nedran, she was already with child.'

Another stab. Venn had taken Ella to his bed. She swallowed her hurt as she might consume mouldy bread—begrudgingly, for politeness. 'Go on.'

Gohran's expression hardened. 'Ella miscarried, and she bled out.'

Raeyn exhaled. That made more sense, but she wondered... Had Gohran caused her to miscarry? Lost his temper like when he'd discovered Jaydyn was with child?

'If you dare tell a soul...' Gohran's threat dangled.

'Who would I confide in besides Jay?'

'You'll not whisper a word to anyone. Not even to Jaydyn.'

'You can't ask me to keep this from our sister.'

'I can, and you will. Jaydyn has proved herself brash and foolish. Her tongue is as slippery as her sense, and we both know the local gossips enjoy nothing more than to tear this family down.'

'What does it matter at this point? We've hardly a thimble of honour left between us.'

Gohran's voice came out as a growl. 'It matters, sister, because I will not preside over a degraded kingdom, and if you want to make a decent match, you'll do whatever it takes to preserve our remaining integrity.'

Raeyn pursed her lips to stay her words. Arguing would get her nowhere. In the end, did it matter why? Ella was still gone.

'Very well, brother. I've arranged an intimate memorial as you requested. No priests, no proclamations, just the three of us, and the servants who knew her growing up.'

Gohran softened, running his hands through his dark hair. He looked broken. 'You have my thanks, Raeyn.'

Raeyn mellowed in turn. Gohran was her overlord and a stubborn brute, but he was still her younger brother. Her voice cracked. 'Gohran? I am sorry for your loss. She held a special place in your heart. I'm sorry for you and for us all.'

FIVE

Jonas savoured Vera's warm hands against his bare chest, breathed in her sweet, rose-scented skin, shoving down that hollow void and dissonance from where his body and senses sought Ella. Vera edged nearer to kiss his lips, but he pulled her back and kissed her forehead, keeping her nuzzled against him so she couldn't read his face.

Dim light peeked through the silk curtains covering the latticed windows of the groundskeeper's cottage, where they lay on an old daybed. The keeper didn't mind, provided they left the place tidy. At night, they sneaked between rooms, but too many pairs of eyes roamed the castle keep by day. Much as Vera's father, Lord Teegan of Lichen, admired and respected Jonas, he respected his daughter's reputation more.

Had Ella agreed to elope with him, they might exist tucked in such a cottage, cosily furnished, idling afternoons in each other's arms...

He sighed. 'Sometimes I wish I was born a groundskeeper. Or a farmer.'

'Apart from the hard labour that would require, of course,' said Vera.

'Apart from that, yes.' He chuckled. 'I could live comfortably in a cottage like this... Though perhaps with more stylish drapes. Did Lady Selmyra choose these?' He tugged at the garish emerald fabric.

'Jonas! Ma's taste isn't *that* bad.' Vera laughed. 'Once settled on your own plot, you may dwell in a hovel with no window coverings at all, if you please.'

'Ah yes, the day I am out from under my brother's hoof, and can shoe and stable myself.' Another sigh. 'That little dream must wait. I travel to Creywmm in the morning.'

Vera frowned. 'You only just arrived.'

'I promised Princess Ella moons ago I would smooth relations with Sheevan, and with her wedding on the horizon…'

Vera tensed, as she did whenever he mentioned Ella. He twined his fingers through her flaxen hair, as much to soothe himself, and pulled the soft ilak's wool blanket snug around them.

It was unfair to daydream about Ella, and usually, he gave each lover his full attention, but that day, every small thing reminded him of her. Vera was lovely, his affection for her deep, but she wasn't the princess. More than their pleasure, Jonas missed Ella's friendship. He let her down. She was right to be angry. And now she was marrying his brother. After everything. He still couldn't quite believe it.

Something altered when Gohran dragged Ella away from his arms to Erldan the last summer solstice. She was brittle, part of her shattered. What had Gohran done to her?

'Curse it!' He perched on the edge of the wood-framed bed.

'What is it?' Vera's hand rested on his shoulder.

'I'm going to be trapped with His Highness King Gohran at that wedding, aren't I?' He tugged at the overgrown ends of his hair.

'We all have to breathe the stale air of people we don't care for, Jonas.'

A sigh. 'I told Ella I had no desire to encounter her brother again unless he was at the other end of my sword, and I meant it.'

'Jonas!'

'I've never liked him. I'm certain he hurt Ella badly. When she returned to Nedran, she was fleeing him.'

'Surely not. Lyn would have shared fruit that ripe.'

'El might have asked her not to.'

'I dare say she would tell me, anyway. Though, I haven't read her last letter. Someone has me a little preoccupied.' Vera's naked breasts pressed against him, her warm palm tracing his chest and abdomen, continuing downwards to slip beneath the sheets.

A stiff inhale as heat tingled through his groin. 'Vee…'

Her lips traversed his shoulders, breathing in the moisture of his skin as she stroked him. 'You don't feel threatened by him, do you?'

'By Gohran? Why would I?' Another gasp as his muscles flexed in response to every stroke. It was difficult to concentrate. 'He doesn't seem creepy to you?'

Vera laughed and withdrew her hand. 'He can be ferocious, but for a king, he's quite charming. And he certainly inherited his mother's looks.'

Jonas pulled a face.

'If it wasn't for all that trouble over Queen Prya, Ma and Pa would have set their sights on him for me.'

'And I thought they loved you.'

'Don't mock. And don't underestimate the charm of a throne, especially to a lady's parents.' Vera sidled back, hand sliding beneath the sheets once more. 'Are you certain I can't take your mind off all that?'

Afterwards, they lazed in each other's arms. Jonas yawned. 'I should go before I fall asleep.'

He grabbed his shirt and trousers, hurriedly dressed, and headed to the main keep, giving Vera time to dress and follow at a discreet distance. Eventually, he would formalise their betrothal. There would be no cottage refuge, only a lord's duty. At least with Venn's wedding on the horizon, his could wait.

A knock at his door. Jonas groaned, shuffled out of bed, and opened it. He'd only just got to sleep.

One of Lichen's pages hovered. 'A letter for you from Nedran, my lord.'

Jonas took the scroll and ruffled his hair. 'What does my exacting brother want now?' But the wax insignia wasn't Venn's; it was Gohran's. The priests must have sealed Venn and Ella's betrothal. A weight settled in his chest and gut. Until that moment, he hadn't realised part of him still hoped the king would refuse them.

'My thanks.' He dismissed the page, closed his door, tossed the unopened letter aside, and crawled back into bed. He needed to rest up for the following day's trip to Creywmm.

Six

I nside the high-ceilinged hall of prayer, the priestesses curved themselves around the pulpit, the highest ranked nearest the front. Ella slinked to the nave's rear beside the other novices, the weight of fifty pairs of eyes upon her.

In Ycelt, the women's coarse figures would have blended into the brown and grey of peasants, except almost all bore some distinguishing attributes that would have aroused suspicion. Unique coloured eyes or hair, marked skin, or peculiar features.

Behind the altar, the stone idol of Xenon oversaw the congregation. The tall, foreboding statue was strangely familiar, as she imagined the god would appear—sad, wielding his shattered and bloodstained sword. Was that genuine blood? A sharp inhale. The god's anguish seeped into her bones, forcing her to look away, as if the priestesses charged the statue with pure pain.

Their adulation unnerving, the women poured past the replica of the god, and knelt to kiss His cold toes. Ella stooped, but her neighbour jerked her upright. *Only those sworn may touch Him.*

Until sworn, they forbade her from participating in the rites or using magic during worship. Standing apart from her peers, she wished she could dissolve into the walls.

Amber had described the ritual of summoning the god to swear her vows. Poverty, passivity, and celibacy. 'We forego worldly goods. We commit no violence, but also none can be committed against us. And any act of lust is forbidden.' An anxious glance at Ella's belly. Another thing to set her apart.

Towards the hall's front, high-ranking priestesses wore robes bearing subtle but distinct sigils—the marks of their status. She noted their relative positions, who sat closest to her aunt, including Breeyan's apprentice, Shira, and Meela, the woman Amber said allocated tasks.

Ella hovered beside the other novices, trying not to draw attention to herself, as they stepped through each ritual, at once alien and familiar. The service was too recognisable, a distortion of Elnora's priests' worship. Some prayers were almost identical. Only the archaic dialect of certain words—and that women, not men, led these rites—reminded Ella she was not back home in Erldan.

As High Priestess, her aunt, Breeyan, stood behind her altar in the exact manner of Davith, Erldan's head priest, recounting the history of the Great War—a tale told as often here as the birth of Elnora in Ycelt. The story droned, heard a thousand times before, until one line caught Ella's attention.

'...When King Myrhan's subjects arrived in Ycelt from their homeland, the Ancient Ones embraced these new people with their cult of the Dark Sun. At last, another deity to worship...'

Was it true? Did people inhabit Ycelt before the old king? What had happened to them? Ella assumed the 'Ancients' were the first colonists, not some other race.

'King Myrhan's people settled, but they were not content to live alongside those whose ways they did not understand. The king outlawed speaking in the Moon Tongue and practising the Ancient rites. Time passed and Myrhan's subjects moved farther across the new land, where the Ancients' worship persisted. Myrhan's men could no longer ignore Xenon's powers. Some even questioned the king's authority. Why should they answer to a mere mortal when a power so much greater existed within the realm?'

The women exhaled their adoration, and a slight breeze touched Ella's skin. That sigh had genuine power behind it, the surrounding air stirring as its energy shifted.

As the story unfolded, pictures forming in the women's minds became manifest. Each thought joined, creating a diorama made from shadow and translucent light, hanging like a chandelier above them. A primitive king knelt before a goddess. Colours thickened, becoming opaque as each priestess added her embellishment—the king's stylised armour, his leather sandals, the flame-flickering yellow hair of the goddess.

Breeyan's narration continued: 'A prickle lodged in the king's heel, this god made of flesh grew into a bunion which blistered, itched, and burned. Why should a king of mortals answer to a celestial being, yet one of temporal form? They must stop this blasphemy, this heresy. Myrhan was the rightful king, appointed by the gods to rule upon the mortal plane, not this immortal yet corporeal being.' She paused, her words landing like stones sinking into a pond.

'Thus, he summoned the goddess, Elnora of the Dark Sun. But Elnora would not help him. Xenon was not of her world. He was the God of the Silver Moon and all its magic; she the Goddess of the Dark Sun and all its fire.' The goddess's image swelled, huge and bloated, while the king's likeness wavered and paled.

'"King Myrhan," said She. "You reek of mortality, and it pains me. What can you offer that I might desire from a temporal being?"

'And he replied: "Souls, My Lady. I offer you the souls of my people." But it was not enough. They worshipped other deities alongside Her.'

Light gathered, flickering.

'"Then let my people renounce them," said he. "For no one exists who is as mighty as you. Your fiery power shines more brightly than any other. Who are these but false gods and demons? Help me oust Xenon to the Afterworld, and all who follow this weak Moon Bearer will prove themselves heretics."'

The women gasped in unison, and the light extinguished.

'"An offer I can accept," said She, and so revealed The Way. "Take the Sacred Stone of the East and fashion a sword to hold it. I will fuse stone to metal, and you shall have the means to destroy the god of flesh." Thus began the Great War, the most horrific, most bloody, most devastating conflict of time itself.'

The picture shifted again, displaying a battlefield strewn with corpses, thousands of faceless warriors felled by a handful of robed women on horseback. At their head towered a giant warrior who must be Xenon. He wore a mask of grief, as though he felt responsible for each death.

Ella had known nothing like it. Power pulsed and throbbed. Through half-closed eyes, it resembled a summer haze on tiled rooftops. In places, the power peaked, beacons of fire cast by the most distinctive individuals. Breeyan was one such, and Amber another. In others, the energy dulled, as bland as its creator.

'The sworn priestesses of the Silver Moon fought beside their god, but the losses they suffered horrified Xenon.' The diorama showed endless tides of dead and dying atop parched land. 'Xenon surrendered. His worshippers recognised His mercy, but Myrhan declared him a coward, without honour, and that night, the Silver Moon turned Black, stained with bloodshed.'

A chilling chant stirred and swelled, ink-like blood pouring across the moon until the magical scene became an endless pool of grief, an ache so palpable it might swallow her. Tears glistened in the women's eyes and Ella wrenched her mind free to save from drowning. So many minds uniting in a pure, awe-filled joining. There was pleasure in that pain, she realised.

'Before Xenon left, he swore to avenge those who crossed him. He cursed Ycelt to be always at war and took away their power by shattering the Sacred Stone. Shame and dishonour followed. Myrhan's men forced the sisters from their homeland. Exiled. But the day will come when Xenon's people return, when they live and worship without fear of persecution. Until that time, our vows protect us, the gift of the Curse that falls on any who dare violate Xenon's decrees.'

Absurd to frame a curse as a gift, Ella thought, yet it offered protection. For anyone who dared touch a sworn priestess in violence or in lust would die an excruciating death.

'The Curse hurts not only the violator—it touches those around them. It's said to bring horror thrice over.'

Breeyan used the exact words Amber taught back at Erldan, and several uneasy minds hovered Ella's way. The Curse. What they smelled upon her. Lust and its product: her unborn child. Ella wanted to slap those minds away. Why would she be Cursed? She was not a sworn priestess, and it had not been her lust, no matter what her brother believed.

The ceremony ended, and the women dispersed, jostling into the hum of their gruelling workday. Tension eased from Ella's shoulders and her jaw relaxed. With their focus elsewhere, she could breathe.

Seven

'She can't stay, Your Worship,' said Pyrina, a dark-haired priestess in her middle age.

The council had convened at Pyrina's insistence. Usually, she kept her opinions to herself, but on this matter, much to Breeyan's chagrin, Pyrina insisted they hear her.

The women holding the posts of Elder, Wise, and Veritatis, who made up Aryon's sacred committee, took their usual places around the long table. The high ceiling loomed. A rarity within the citadel, this chamber remained almost unchanged since its original construction.

Breeyan settled into position at its head, and pictured the historic king, once sitting as she did now, presiding over his advisors, their troubled frowns seeking guidance, or conniving smiles trying to persuade. The chamber's staid walls sighed under the weight of accumulated history, pressing in on her.

Pyrina wasn't the only one agitated. A writhing undercurrent passed between the women.

Chin raised, voice steady, Breeyan peered at the sisters. 'The treaty binds Aryon as it binds my family.'

'Then have the king send another of his siblings. One who isn't with child,' said Shaena, whose peculiar aqua eyes exposed her magical inheritance from infancy. Shaena was a stranger to life outside the order.

Breeyan drew power to shield and calm. Her councillors could be insufferable. 'Neither of Ella's sisters has any magic. The oldest holds a royal title, and her middle sister already has a babe at her breast. Need I remind you; the treaty exists for all our sakes. If we send Ella away, Elnora's priests will uncover her soon enough.' She didn't reveal that Gohran had threatened to denounce her himself.

Breeyan wished Gohran had said more. Having seen her son in the flesh, a full-grown man, her ache intensified, followed by a twist at his petulance, even belligerence. A monarch's arrogance. Was she any different?

'People denounce sorcerers all the time in Ycelt,' Pyrina dismissed with a wave. 'What about the Curse? Are you willing to risk us all to save one life?'

The women fell silent.

Breeyan sighed. 'Two lives, if you count the babe. And Ella is not just any sorcerer.' How could she explain Ella's potential? If her niece had a fraction of the strength Prya described... Imagining that much power tingled.

You favour your family over your duty to us. An unvoiced thought slipped through.

And another: *Your judgement is clouded.*

You put your desires above our safety.

Breeyan's voice cut through the silent chatter. 'Ella's powers can only benefit our order. The princess remains unsworn—she was not a priestess when the lust occurred, had not even set eyes on our sacred walls.'

More objections: 'But we intended her to be.'

'She was supposed to be here already.'

'She will swear to Him while carrying the product of lust.'

Breeyan held up her palms and shook her head. The priestesses' wariness around her niece was trying. She was wise to stay in Ycelt all those years ago. If an unsworn novice made the superstitious among them nervous, imagine their terror had Breeyan returned to Aryon with Rohan's seed growing in her belly. Back then, she had started her training but had not yet taken her final vows, a fact she clung to whenever her own doubts about the Curse surfaced.

Her thoughts drew to Gohran and his strangely churning aura that buckled and shifted, as though expanding and contracting. Did he know he possessed magic? Or was he so adept at suppression it remained hidden, even from himself? Was this the price he paid for her failings, forever living in denial about his true self?

No, she thought, this could not be the Curse. Still, she was grateful no one at Aryon knew her secret, not even her erstwhile High Priestess, or she could not have returned. Would not be here now, presiding over all these souls.

She pulled her attention back to the women and their expectant glares. 'I took my final vows only after I completed my apprenticeship.'

'You suggest she remain unsworn?' Pyrina asked, arms crossed.

'Ella can delay her vows until after giving birth. There is no rush. Let us wait until she weans the child, if that comforts you more.'

'She is to forgo the rites?'

'When necessary. As she has been, she can attend homage and worship, but refrain from participating.'

'What of the babe's father?'

'Amber claims the dryhten is honourable and law-abiding, but not pious.' She had queried Amber earlier that day. She dared not ask her wound up niece directly. Ella wouldn't just unravel if Breeyan pushed too hard, she would explode. Breeyan wondered again what happened to her back in Ycelt. She had asked Amber to learn more, as she reestablished her bond with Ella. Breeyan knew they had one. Amber need not tell her that. It seeped from the energy between them.

'Even those who aren't pious fear the Curse, Your Worship.'

'And honourable might not be to our advantage. What if he feels honour-bound to protect his unborn child—and future heir—from so-called heretics?'

'Honourable might also mean he considers a royal treaty sealed by robe-bearers sacrosanct.' Breeyan shook her head. 'I am not concerned about the dryhten. If nothing else, we can count on King Gohran to keep him away. It is in the monarch's best interest not to have his sister uncovered.' The guilt she smelled upon Gohran assured her of that. Did he feel responsible for her becoming pregnant while unwed, for not bringing her to Aryon upon his mother's death, as he should have done?

'And will she birth her babe here?'

Breeyan considered taking Ella to a nearby village with a midwife, but then pictured the pallid faces of the villagers spying a pregnant priestess. She might not fear the Curse, but the villagers would, and they would do more than sign their warding. They would string her up and burn her.

'Indeed, she must.' Breeyan ran an absent hand across her belly and the other over her breasts. It had been over eighteen years since she carried a babe, and she had remained in Ycelt until after Gohran was born, aided by an experienced midwife, with King Rohan's personal chirurgeon available had she needed. Ella would not be as fortunate.

More objections toppled: 'Who will assist?'

'We've no expertise....'

They were right. Besides aiding pregnant refugees, the priestesses had little understanding of birthing. Ella would be safer among the poorest peasants in Ycelt than at Aryon.

'Can we not send her north to the sisters at Crescent Mountain? They might have more experience with *fecundity*.' Shaena spat this last word as though it contained sour ilak's milk.

'Yes! And should her man come hunting her, she will be far from here,' a further priestess added with enthusiasm.

Breeyan stood and planted her palms on the table. She had waited too long for this. To fulfil the only legacy she would ever know.

'Ella stays. She belongs to this order.' She did not add, *she belongs to me.* 'My apprentice shall search the archives for lore on gestation and birthing, and I'll speak to Felda to prepare medical supplies.' If her niece was going to remain at Aryon while pregnant, the priestesses needed to gird themselves with all haste. 'Then together, we can decide upon the timing appropriate for Ella to take her vows and join in the rites.'

Eight

When Amber saw Ella for the first time in seven seasons, her breath caught. Devoid of childhood naivety, Ella had grown even more captivating. Amber yearned to reach out, but the more she probed, the more Ella clamped down, trampling any hope of resuming their relationship.

What happened to her over those seasons? She guarded herself like a hound kicked and then kicked some more. Her nightmares were incessant, and she startled at the least provocation.

But when Ella looked her way, Amber experienced the preternatural pull of her smile, recognised the thrall of her longing as Ella's beguilement, an expression of magic so rare she had never encountered it until meeting the princess.

At least Ella was among Aryon's powerful women now, scholars who knew more lore than Amber could learn in her lifetime. Women who might help her understand the destructive potential of her power, help her heal from whatever rendered her brittle and broken.

Her peers were also wary of Ella. Few kept abreast of events in Ycelt, but the council members who knew of Erldan's treaty expected Ella to come to Aryon as she approached sixteen summers, under the guise of being sent away to marry. Instead, she arrived approaching seventeen, while pregnant, and they were making their disapproval known.

It pained Amber to see Ella struggle to settle into the priestesses' routine. She was often clumsy and fatigued, yet the sisters lacked patience and compassion for her. How much easier it would have been if, like the others, Ella were common born, used to working, to waiting upon herself. If she'd never hoped for, or expected, a life outside the order. *If I'd taken her with me when I fled.*

Ella looked miserable as she ate her supper that night. The women on either side of her were chatting and laughing. No one wanted to include the newcomer. Now, as Amber approached the washbasins, a group of her sisters turned away to form a huddle, as though their distrust of Ella spilled over onto her. Their wariness reminded her of when she'd first returned from Erldan. Apart from Amber's beloved Nykki, the others remained suspicious of her for an entire moon-cycle—some for longer.

Amber dipped her hands into one of a row of wooden buckets atop a trough that served as their washroom. No tub, no fire, no privacy, and no different to the servants' quarters at Erldan. It was all Amber had known, yet each time Ella came here, Amber noticed her hugging herself, shrinking away from prying eyes.

To anyone else, the princess's pregnancy might have passed unnoticed. But to the women, who sensed the babe's aura, smelled the fleshiness growing within, her body held a dark fascination. She was grateful Ella retreated early to her sleeping cell that night, so she did not have to cringe from the women's curiosity, thick and hostile upon the air.

She spied Nykki among the other women; her loose chestnut hair kinked around her shoulders. 'Nykki?' She caught Nykahlia's shoulder, sensing the rift between them. *Nykki, please...*

Nykki faced her, arms crossed. The others made a show of pumping water into the trough, giving the illusion of privacy.

'What did Her Holiness want today?'

Earlier, Breeyan summoned Amber from the fields and into her private study. Amber shrugged. 'She wondered how Ella was settling in.'

'And she couldn't have asked the princess herself?'

The pumping stopped.

Their curiosity was as intense as Breeyan's had been. The High Priestess queried whether Ella revealed anything more about her circumstances, why her brother waited to bring her to Aryon, and what she knew of Lord Venn of

Nedran. What kind of man was he? How devoutly did he worship the goddess? Was he likely to come after Ella?

Amber wished Breeyan would leave her be, and not just for the sake of her relationships. If she was being tapped for information, Ella was right to keep her distance. Foresight was not one of Amber's strengths, but it was one of Breeyan's, and one of Ella's, as they discovered too late through the tragedy of Queen Prya's denouncement. Ella must have a reason for shying away from sharing with her.

'Perhaps it's too much bother for the precious princess.' Sallyn, the next closest in age to Amber and Nykki, twirled and flicked her tresses to mimic Ella's mannerism, concluding her parody in a mock pout.

A pink stain covered half of Sallyn's face. Her remaining skin was milk-white, and her hair moonbeam-pale. Sallyn's aptitude for magic was slight, and Amber wondered if that birthmark was the only reason she'd ended up here.

Amber slowed her breath and stood firm. 'Have any of you considered that perhaps the princess is afraid? Maybe she doesn't feel safe to open her history to a sworn priestess. You forget, Ella watched her mother die for her magic, for being like us. Can you blame her for being cautious?'

Nykki's mind touched hers, soothing, but beneath she sensed hurt, resentment, and something else, deeper, of which even Nykki wasn't aware.

Mind-melding had its snares. Intimate and exhilarating, but once joined, it was difficult to untangle. Nykki could hide specific thoughts, but the undercurrent of emotion remained, and Amber's stronger psyche pushed past her barriers with ease.

The other women shuffled and shifted, but Amber's gaze continued to challenge them. 'Was it any different when you arrived, Sal? Or any of us? Well, was it?'

Sallyn shrugged. 'I suppose not...'

Nykki's mind still prickled, but gentler. *This is different.*

Amber sensed the women's web of emotions. Few had worldly adult lives in Ycelt, and they pictured Ella's swollen belly grown huge, and later, holding a suckling babe, and then a child—experiences denied them. Others pictured her wearing fantastical ball gowns and lavish jewels, being waited upon, and fussed at by an army of faceless servants. Beneath it all flowed a greater resentment: envy at Ella's raw power.

NINE

Ella leaned on her hoe, shaded her eyes, and kicked at the dirt. So strange to see farmsteads beside the citadel with no walls or fortifications. She worked alongside the priestesses, who grew crops of all kinds—fruit, vegetables, grains, herbs, and spices. To the north sprawled a patchwork of square paddocks and fallow fields where ilaks and bovine grazed, while poultry peck-waddled through caged pens. Eastwards rose the occasional tangle of peculiar trees, like misshapen monsters. Further west and south, barren brown stretched forever.

Gohran was right, there was nothing out here. Not that it mattered. Even if she fled and hid somewhere habitable, her brother would find her, she was certain.

'What is it?' Beside her dug one of the few priestesses who hadn't shunned her. She introduced herself as Nykahlia, but the others called her Nykki. The name sounded familiar, but Ella couldn't recall why. Perhaps someone Amber had mentioned.

A fiery cramp shot across the side of her ribs, adding to the deep ache that had settled in her shoulders and lower back. She didn't want to admit how fatigued and sore she felt. How useless. She motioned to the expanse of land surrounding the fields. 'Why is this landscape so parched?'

Cat-green eyes grudgingly faced her. 'The lore tells us the Upheaval caused it during the Great War.' Nykahlia traced a semi-circle with her arm. 'It decimated most of this region.'

'But those pastures?' Ella pointed to where the grass grew verdant.

Nykahlia shrugged. 'The channel beneath the ground irrigates our fields and feeds our wells.'

How little she understood of agriculture and farming.

'Hush, both of you,' an older priestess, Pyrina, called from where she dug alongside a group of women.

Ella's cheeks burned. She was about to scold the woman's insolence, then remembered it was she who had no standing here. Not a princess to be waited upon, not even a noblewoman, but the lowest ranked member of the entire order. A deep inhale. She soaked up power in a cloak of calm.

You've hardly the time to stop for chitchat. For once, someone—she couldn't tell who—avoided humiliating her by sending their rebuke privately, mind-to-mind.

Ella surveyed the fields. A relentless fire-ache consumed her, yet she churned a fraction of soil compared with her companions. Out here, her delicate frame was no asset. It made her weak.

Nykahlia looked towards the citadel, to where a dark-haired priestess waved. Nykki's eyes shifted out of focus and her mouth slackened. She was thought-sharing. Ella shuddered.

Nykki turned back to Ella. 'You're being reassigned. Shira will take you.' She took Ella's hoe and nudged her to where the High Priestesses' apprentice waited.

The other women's thoughts stalked her. She stood tall, chin raised—her mother's likeness.

Shira led her across the open fields and alongside Aryon's only river. Like the others, she wore her tight braids close to her skull in a style Ella had only ever seen in the tapestries depicting the Ancients.

Women washing linens stopped and stared as they passed.

Further downstream, they reached a long, narrow trench, cut into the side of the river, which veered westwards and beyond. The man-made tributary fed a trickle of water, reed-clotted and choked with algae, before the channel took a sharp turn. A putrid stench. Ella's stomach lurched. Ahead stood an old hut that housed a row of wooden benches suspended over the ditch. The privy.

'The stream usually runs strong and flushes out our excreta, but with so little rain...' Shira shrugged. 'See these pails?' She pointed to a pair of yoked buckets hanging from a hook on the privy wall. 'Fill them, and use the water to clear the waste.' She motioned to the ditch below the hut. 'Anything that sticks, dig it out and flush again.' Shira set a shovel against the privy wall and left her to work.

Bile rose. The forest of cobwebs and foul odour inside the privy had been horror enough. But this? Ella spat to get the stench out of her throat. There was no evading it.

She balanced the yoke awkwardly on her shoulders and hooked her hands over each wooden arm, as she'd seen the other women do. Buckets dangling, she shuffled towards the stream.

At the junction where the ditch began, the ground sloped like a giant soup bowl, and she edged nearer the water. Braced, she stepped in. Cold struck her open toes and seeped into the fabric of her vestment. She tilted and dipped one bucket below the surface, and then the other. When she raised the second, the contents of the first spilled over.

She tried again, with the same result. After a few more attempts, each pail was barely a third full. It would have to do. She climbed out and shuffled along the embankment, her sodden robe dragging.

Near the privy, she halted and released the yoke on one side, pulling the front of her robe over her nose. The yoke slid along her shoulder and sloshed water onto the ground. Breath held, she let her robe drop, steadied the yoke and crept nearer the ditch, her chest aching. Exhaling, she lowered the pails, trying not to spill. She unhooked the first, took another breath from beneath her robe, and sluiced its water along the trench wall. Liquid splashed up and over, but the muck barely moved. With held breath, she hefted the second, refastened the pails and returned to the river, gasping the cleaner air.

On her third or fourth trip, a woman washing linens called out. 'You had best get a move on, *Princess*.' Laughter followed.

Ella ignored them. She reached the privy and repeated the process, hurling her bucket's pitiful contents into the ditch. At least now the dried waste was budging. The shovel leaned against the privy wall, mocking her. She refused to get down and dig.

She picked her way back across the bank and fetched the second pail. Mud squelched between her toes and sucked at her sandals. Another step left her sandal bogged. Her bare foot slipped free, and her pail flew from her fingers and splattered in the ditch. She kicked off the other sandal and tiptoed to the muddy bank. Crouched, she groped for a handhold and reached down to retrieve the upturned bucket, begging every god not to let her fall.

Again, the hateful laughter. They were spying on her.

She hauled herself up. Muck clung to her cheeks and filth filled her nostrils until her guts wrenched. Hunched over, she vomited.

Once her stomach stilled, she stumbled to a patch of nearby grass and ripped out a handful to wipe her mouth. Her eyes and throat burned. She returned to the river, upstream from the excrement. Still wearing her vestment, she plunged into the chill water and sloshed towards the gaggle of priestesses, ignoring the slap and scrape of rock along the bottom.

Ella peeled off her soiled robe. 'Here.' She tossed it on top of the clean laundry, piled up and ready to be hung—a full day's work. 'You'll need to wash this as well.'

The women gaped like startled ilaks.

Ella helped herself to a chunk of their soap and scrubbed her skin pink and hair to a squeak. She swam further upstream and ducked to rinse off the last of the gunk. Cold ached her limbs. She paddled to the bank and climbed out, spied a patch of clean, dry grass, out of sight of the others and sat. Knees clutched to her chest, she wept.

It was sometime later when Amber found her, still curled up, naked and shivering. Wordlessly, she handed Ella a fresh vestment and sandals. Ella pulled on the shapeless, coarse robe, then tied the stiff leather shoes over her blistered feet.

Amber's mind touched hers with soothing warmth as her arm slid around Ella's shoulders.

'I finished flushing the privy. Her Holiness says there will be rain soon, so if the god smiles upon us, it won't need clearing again this season.'

Ella nodded, unable to speak. She met Amber's gaze. 'Why? Why do they hate me? Don't tell me it's the Curse. If it was, they would fear me. This is something more.'

Amber sighed. 'Your power—Ella, it is what every priestess desires. You have it in abundance without trying, without even wanting.' She frowned, as though struggling to put her thoughts into words. 'It's more than that... It's not that you don't *want* it. You want *not* to have it.' *And our power is all we have.*

'But I haven't even used it here, not really...'

A sly smile crept across Amber's face. 'No, you haven't, have you?'

At supper, Ella queued silently before an iron pot perched atop a blackened fireplace. A fair-haired, stout priestess, called Shaena, dipped a ladle into the mixture. It splodged unpleasantly. When she looked up, Ella noticed the peasant-crevices etched into the skin surrounding her eyes, which, when the light caught them, were a startling aqua.

Ella took her bowl. Cold, unseasoned gruel stared at her like twice boiled glue. Her resentful stomach growled.

She sat at her place along a bench in the stark refectory. A former warrior's mess, with long wooden benches and no honour table, dance floor, or entertainment stalls. She tried to pretend she wasn't ravenous as she brought the first spoonful to her lips. Her skin prickled. She peered around. Eyes crawled all over her, malicious and eager, and then one pair opposite, cautioning and sympathetic: Nykahlia.

She followed Nykki's gaze back to the table, to her bowl. Something inside it wriggled. She clanged her spoon on the bench top. The women on either side of Nykahlia shared a glance. Ella caught and held the focus of the priestess closest to her, a woman named Meela, who she recognised from the riverside that day—the woman who allocated their tasks.

She kept thinking about what Amber had said earlier. Cursed or not, she was stronger than the others. She knew it, and so did they. Yet when she thought of using her powers again as she had on Venn, Lynden, and especially Gohran, her throat clogged.

Someone smirked. She sensed it before she saw it, followed by an audible snigger.

Anger rose, the flood of raw emotion crowding out her hesitation. She let its full force rise. Little by little, she allowed the priestesses to feel it, too. As if they had provoked a caged animal inside her, it paced, raging, clawing. It was a heat that whipped and stung.

The woman before her, Meela, winced. Visibly fighting her discomfort, she pushed her half-eaten meal across the table. With a smirk, Ella took it, swapping it for her own tainted bowl. The others didn't budge, instead watching the silent exchange. Ella released her gaze. The priestess sank into her seat, rubbing her temples.

Ignoring her, Ella ate the remaining gruel, which went some way to easing the biting hunger deep in her belly, but more to satisfying her sense of vengeance.

Ten

Venn was relieved when Gohran left him alone with his grief and returned to Erldan, but he didn't realise how lost he would feel. Ella hadn't just been his beloved and his lover, she had been his mate. He kept going to share some minor detail with her, only to find her place beside him bare. He had come to rely on consulting with her on matters of state, confiding in her about the minutiae of his day. Thinking of her, his hands shook, and sweat curled the hair at his temples and his unshaved upper lip.

For days he paced his chamber, his study, the hall, the grounds, but it was no good. He sensed her still, as though she weren't gone at all, and yet, he couldn't escape her absence.

Jonas hadn't arrived home, so he asked his steward Mykan to hold over significant matters until he gathered his head and heart enough to ride back out to Ella's grave. A lone guard accompanied him. To one side of his saddle, he hitched a spade. To the other, he fastened a burlap sack carrying a jasmine seedling he would plant to honour her, and the pearls that had been a gift from her brother. They were all he had to offer.

When he reached the cairn, he sat atop his steed, hugging himself against the cold, inhaling the heady scent of jasmine, and exhaling puffs of white. He closed his eyes, searching for her upon the wind.

Venn dismounted, passed the guard his reins, and approached her grave, spade in hand. He knelt facing her cairn. His free palm traced the tips of the grass and weeds, following the outline of the cairn's rocks. He stood, chose a patch where the ground appeared newly turned, and dug. With each *crunch*, *hurl*, and *thud* of soil, he felt lighter, freer.

His shovel hit hard-packed clay. Another *crunch*, and then a *ting*. Venn set the spade aside and crouched. A metal object poked through the dirt. He brushed the soil away to reveal a coin-sized pendant on a broken neck-chain. It must be Ellas, but Venn had never seen her wear it.

The pendant called to him, urging him nearer, but as he approached, a numbing cold seeped into his fingers. From behind, a whisper. He swung around. No one was there. A chill ran the length of his spine.

Venn's steed snorted and stomped impatiently.

He reached to retrieve the chain, but hesitated. What if it was a grave gift? Perhaps something from her childhood, or a family keepsake. Venn withdrew his hand, with the sense of peeling back a curtain during an intimate moment. He pushed some soil to cover the pendant. The opening was deep enough, anyway.

He fetched the seedling and pearls from his saddlebag, placed the pearls inside the hole and spread the plant's roots on top, careful to avoid its thorny stems, peculiar to this breed, which he'd chosen for its sweet scent—Ella's favourite. He covered them both with the remaining soil.

Satisfied when the seedling was in place, he tugged at a single white flower, pinching the stem between thumb and forefinger to sever it from its branch. A thorn bit into his finger, but he did not pull away. He squeezed and pushed it further into his flesh. Blood dripped onto the cairn and over the grass and dirt. Like the ritual he and Gohran performed upon the forest floor when their friendship was first forged, Venn shed his blood in honour of the gods, in honour of her.

This time, there was no euphoria. Instead, Venn hungered for Ella's warmth. Through the haze of his tears, he imagined her before him, yet she appeared as distant as the surrounding mist. The blue of her eyes called, bright as a midday sky, yearning, her mouth forming soundless words. She floated nearer, getting closer. Her arms were outstretched, becoming fleshy, solid.

So close now.

He moved to catch her, but where flesh should have met flesh, his arms passed straight through.

The jasmine flower lay crushed between his palms. He let it fall to the ground. She was gone.

F or once, nightmares did not plague Ella's sleep. Her brother's weight trapping her, his hungry mouth violating. Instead, as dawn approached, she heard someone call her name: Venn, standing before her, appearing so solid she might touch him.

He stood atop a mound of dirt that poked through the clouds. She moved closer, but it was like swimming through an oily, violet pool, its billowing tide tugging her this way and that. There was no horizon, just an endless depth extending in every direction.

It seemed she drifted for hours, though it could only have been a few seconds before his voice broke through the mist. The sound tore the space between them as he wept tears of blood. Jasmine scent tugged at her flesh, and a sweet metallic tang touched her tongue.

Falling. She was falling towards him, his arms outstretched, ready, but as she neared, his figure wavered and warped like water, and then faded.

'Venn—Wait!' The ground hit her, sudden and hard.

She jolted awake, gasping. Sweat and tears soaked her pillow, and her bones ached as if she had fallen through the sky, the taste of blood upon her lips. She looked around, her body pressing into the chill. It had only been a dream. She closed her eyes, trying to resurrect the image, picturing the mound amid the clouds, but the spot where Venn had stood was abandoned, the defiant grass standing upright.

A sharp pinch at her mind, and a thought slipped directly into her awareness: *The High Priestess wishes to speak with you.*

She loathed these minds invading hers. Amber would tell her to shield if she didn't want her thoughts trampled, but as now, the hateful women often caught her unawares.

Ella sat up, smoothing the strands of hair that had come loose from her slept-in braids. She took a few steadying breaths and headed to her aunt's private study.

Whenever Ella moved through Aryon's dark corridors, she felt she was stepping back in time. Where she expected to see rich tapestries, the citadel's stone and brick walls were bare. But in other places, adornments appeared more decorative than functional, like the embossed iron bars that crossed heavy arched doors, and the coloured glass welded inside disused arrow slits to resemble the figures from old manuscripts. Some spaces looked opened and widened, or partitioned and closed off, yet a musty odour clung to the passageways as though they remained untouched from their original construction centuries before.

Ella hovered outside Breeyan's study, waiting to be invited in. After a moment, Breeyan's apprentice opened the door.

'Her Holiness will see you now,' Shira said.

Ella stepped inside to find Breeyan perched behind a broad, ornately carved desk.

'Sit.' The High Priestess nodded to the empty chair opposite.

Ella took her place, the stool's heavy legs dragging against the stone floor in a weighty echo. Ella sensed the murmur of silent thoughts passing between Breeyan and her apprentice before Shira stepped outside and closed the door.

Breeyan was an imposing woman. Not tall, but striking, her comportment making her as commanding a presence as Ella's mother's had been. She appeared several summers older than Prya. Ella always assumed Prya was the eldest, given she was the sibling to stay in Ycelt and marry King Rohan. If Breeyan was the older of the two, might her family have sent her sister Raeyn, a Princess Elder, to Aryon after all?

Ella sensed Breeyan's curiosity nagging and gnawing, as much as her own, though her features remained composed.

'How are you settling in?'

She thanked every god her aunt spoke to her aloud instead of ravaging her mind for answers.

'I understand it has been trying for you...' She let Ella see images of incidents relayed to her by the other priestesses. Distorted depictions of Ella's tools trailing as she fussed over her delicate hands and dirt-crusted nails, worrying at strands of hair flying out of place: a spoiled princess waiting to be waited on.

Rage boiled. Was there any use trying to explain? 'What would you like me to say, Aunt? It was not my choice to be here.' Ella drew what power she could to barricade her thoughts.

Breeyan sucked on her teeth, eyes narrowed. 'Indeed, it wasn't. Nor was it mine when I first arrived.'

Ella looked up.

'You seem surprised.' A smirk. 'I suppose your mother never told you. Our family intended for Queen Prya to be a novice here, just like you.'

Ella recoiled from the edge she heard in Breeyan's voice, the bitterness behind her eyes.

'I believe your mother harboured worldly ambitions for you as she had for herself. Luckily, King Gohran saw sense and brought you here, where you belong.'

Was that a slight waver when Breeyan mentioned Gohran? Did she suspect something? Ella redoubled her efforts to conceal her thoughts, focusing on her memory of her mother's face, so like Breeyan's, so like hers. She pictured her mother twisting her royal ring around her elegant fingers whenever she was nervous—her only tell. For until the moment her son denounced her, Ella had seen Prya look nothing but poised.

'Let me share something my predecessor told me,' Breeyan said. 'Your existence here can only be what you make of it. If you decide to see it as a punishment, then penance is what it will be. If you decide to embrace everything this life affords—safety, collegiality, power—with your abilities, you could rise through the order's ranks. I have appointed my apprentice, but there are other posts—posts that offer access to our most treasured lore—power beyond your imagination.'

Breeyan's eyes illuminated as she described this imagined future, while Ella kept her expression neutral, almost bored. She had no intention of staying long enough to take up any post. Once her body rid itself of this parasite, she would leave.

Breeyan continued. 'The seasons following your mother's death may have given you very different expectations. But Ella, though you might not have pretty clothes to wear or parties to attend and servants to wait on you, this is the life Xenon intended for his blessed ones. Here, powerful women surround you. You can practise your magic in the open—you need not live in fear.'

'Not even in fear of the Curse?' Ella pictured the women's agitation as they thought of her pregnancy.

'The Curse of War is something every man, woman, and child in Ycelt must endure.' Ella could sense Breeyan choosing her words. 'Here at Aryon, we reside in peace. Our vows provide a greater defence than any sword anywhere in the realm. Who would dare touch us, in violence or in lust, with the threat of the Curse hanging over them? Yes, the Curse is to be feared, but for us it is a blessing—the ultimate protection. Here, our bodies are sacrosanct.'

'But my body has already been touched with lust.' Ella detected the faintest shudder ripple through her aunt as she uttered these words.

Breeyan waved a dismissive hand. 'You are not yet a sworn priestess.'

'Indeed, I am not.'

Breeyan stood, her brow as ferocious as Gohran's could be. 'I realise you are used to being treated with deference, but you should view your superiors at Aryon as your overlords. Part of our vow of passivity is obedience.' Breeyan paused, eyes narrowed. 'Of course, you won't take your vows until... Well, until after your babe is born. In truth, it's probably already safe, however there are other factors to consider.'

Relief. She would have a period of reprieve before vows she could never uphold trapped her soul, as she pledged to a god in whom she did not believe. For how could she love and honour any god now?

Breeyan looked Ella up and down, her mind reaching, probing. Ella clamped down.

'Stand,' Breeyan commanded.

Ella stood.

'Turn.' Breeyan motioned for Ella to rotate in a full circle, and she complied. 'You're further along than I expected.' She tutted, and let Ella experience her disgust at the lusty weakness of men.

Ella's stomach churned.

'The queasiness should leave you soon. Until then, allow Xenon to guide you to counter the waves when they arise.'

Ella was about to ask how, when a calming sensation bathed her in blue light, accompanied by an image of still water against a level horizon. A moment later, the image, light, and sensation withdrew, and her nausea returned.

'Close your eyes, reach for your power, and replicate what I just showed you,' Breeyan said.

Ella searched for a source of energy to draw on, but found nothing, save the quiet murmur of the babe ripening within her womb. The desk before her stayed a stubborn, vibrationless grey, as did the brick walls and stone floor. She couldn't even sense the power arising from her aunt, whose life force should have blazed.

A pinch at her mind. 'You won't find my source, nor should you search for it.' Breeyan's words landed like shattered ice.

'I wasn't—'

Did Amber teach you nothing? Breeyan's chastisement whipped across her psyche.

Ella winced and opened her eyes, meeting her aunt's gaze. 'Amber taught that the god forbids us drawing power from living creatures, especially humans, but—'

Breeyan held up her hand for silence. 'You will not find my source, as I keep it shielded. One day you shall learn to do likewise.' Breeyan clicked her fingers. A blast of chill, before a fire ignited in the hearth behind Breeyan's desk. Ella hadn't noticed it before. 'Try again now.'

Ella closed her eyes. The blaze grew and warmth caressed her skin. She opened her mind's sight and perceived the flame's source vibrating with life. As Amber had taught, she reached for the fire's power, scooping and tugging the energy as though made of corporeal substance. She imagined the force cascading over her, soothing and flowing, to form a cooling body of water that calmed and settled into a perfect horizontal line against a pastel sky. She absorbed more, waiting for the rushing sensation as her imagination transformed into something more...

But it never came. Any power she drew bled out, leaking as if sucked from her.

Startled, Ella opened her eyes. 'What's happening? Why can't I hold on to it?'

A stab deep in her abdomen, and with it, the last of her strength evaporated. She ran her hand along her belly. It was that creature growing inside her; she was certain. Extracting every iota of energy for itself the way its father warped everything to his will.

Breeyan's eyes narrowed, her mouth forming a grim line. 'How long has it been since you practised your skills?'

Ella was about to blurt the truth—that she had been using her magic without meaning to for several moons, and before that, despite her best efforts to stop it, her power poured unbidden. She bit down on her lip to keep silent and shook her head. 'I couldn't say, Aunt.' She pictured studying with Amber in her old tower room at Erldan, hoping if Breeyan read her memories, that's all she would find.

Another frown. 'I'll have our medic mix you a tonic. We can't have you constantly nauseated. It's unsettling enough for the sisters to have you here in this state.'

This state. She meant pregnant. A state that evidenced the lust forbidden to sworn priestesses. Ella shuddered. She had no desire to discuss the Curse any further with her aunt. 'A tonic would help. My thanks, Aunt.'

'It would be in your best interests to call me Your Holiness.'

Ella frowned.

'If you would like to draw less attention to yourself.'

Another rush of images, this time of Ella disrupting work schedules, sleeping late, standing apart from her sisters during their worship. 'My thanks, Your Holiness.'

'On a separate matter, your brother said I should ask you about the babe's father…'

'Did he?' Ella tossed her head, challenging her aunt's gaze.

Breeyan sighed, a rueful smile playing on her lips. 'Amber tells me you were supposed to marry Lord Venn of Nedran. Does the dryhten know where you are and why Gohran brought you here?'

'How am I to know what the dryhten knows, Your Holiness?'

'What did Gohran tell you?'

'Gohran told me nothing. Lord Venn and I were to wed. Then Gohran learned I was pregnant, and he dragged me here.' Ella's voice choked off.

Breeyan's brow creased. 'You may take your leave.'

As Ella slipped out the door past Breeyan's apprentice, a final thought slid into her mind. *Neither of us chose this, Niece, but if you follow my example, you could one day wear my robes.*

ELEVEN

Raeyn might know Ella had not died from fever, but she did not suspect her sister was alive, and so far, no others had queried Gohran's tale.

Those around him offered condolences and pity, and at times, he swore he heard their thoughts: *Poor lad, and those poor girls, losing half their family.* He dismissed his mind's whispers as imagination—their sloped eyes and mouths, heads tilted in hateful sympathy, warped into words. The only person whose thoughts he ever heard and believed were Ella's, because he *felt* them.

Ella. His nightly dreams of her tormented him. Each morning, he woke as wretched as if he'd drunk a skinful of mead on a hollow stomach.

Once, he would have sought solace from Davith, but moons had passed since he visited his High Priest beyond what was required to fulfil the sacred rites. Davith's disapproving words from one of their last conversations trembled through him: *You allow them to live like falcons when they are mere sparrows.*

The High Priest was right. Raeyn did not hesitate to confront him, Jaydyn regularly disregarded him, and Ella had manipulated and betrayed him thrice over. If he could not contain his sisters, how did he expect to rule his kingdom?

These vigilante Cleansings were further evidence of the cracks in his authority. He needed to regain control, assert his rule and command the respect his mother lost when she exposed her heresy before a crowded hall, using magic where everyone this side of the Gythyn Run could see. There must be a way to salvage this situation.

He sighed. He would need Davith's aid to restore order. The vigilantes flouted them both.

That morning, following Davith's service, Gohran stayed behind, kneeling at the priest's feet. Once, musty damp would have clung to the temple walls, invading the cracks and crevices in the brickwork, but now the closer odour of wooden pews, ilak fat candles, and vellum scriptures—all funded by Gohran's generous contributions—kept the scent of approaching rain at bay.

Davith drew himself up to full height, his shadow falling over the prostrate monarch. 'You look troubled, Your Highness. I dare say you haven't been sleeping. Do your dreams continue to trouble you?'

'Since Ella's passing...' Davith knew him too well. He yearned for the comfort of his touch, his soothing tone. Yet he hesitated. Experienced a hardness, as he always had around his mother, whose affection could never slake his thirst.

'Losing the young princess must be trying for you.' There was a sour note to Davith's voice whenever he mentioned the women in Gohran's family. He paused, then continued in his sermonic, lilting tone. 'There are those who say heretics send such dreams to torment us. The stain of your mother's heresy makes you vulnerable to the Afterworld. Witches sense this. Their mind powers call when you are defenceless. It is the devious way of the Moon. You must pray to Elnora to keep you safe.'

'Is that not why I keep Her priests close by?' He had not come to receive empty platitudes.

The faintest curve at the corners of Davith's lips. 'The safety of the soul rests with the purity of its bearer.'

Heat rose and sweat prickled as Gohran's stomach turned to water and his chest to lead. Instead of being nurtured, he felt judged—accused. Gohran grunted and spoke through clenched teeth. 'The only thing I value more than my kingdom is the goddess.'

Davith was about to leave Gohran's side, but the king stopped him. 'I seek your council on another matter, Your Holiness.' If he could not heal this rift with his erstwhile mentor, he would leverage it.

'Go on.'

'You once offered me the use of your priests...'

'"Use," Your Highness?'

Gohran waved an impatient hand. 'Help. Assistance.'

Davith rocked back on his heels, rubbed his chin. He nodded for Gohran to continue.

Gohran straightened to his full six feet. As he approached his nineteenth summer, his chest had deepened and broadened, and he now stood with eyes level to the head priest. 'I'm sure I don't need to inform you of the growing number of vigilante Cleansings in this region...'

Davith stiffened. 'I'd hardly call them Cleansings, Your Highness.'

Gohran exhaled, eyes narrowed. Something scurried across the floor towards the atrium. 'Barbaric ritual killings, then. My people honour the goddess, and the rule of law should reflect that.'

'Rodents will infiltrate the holiest of harbours, Your Highness.'

'I want them gone,' Gohran snapped. He paced. 'Your holy men have done a thorough job rooting out heretics within Erldan proper. I should like them to do likewise throughout Greater Erldan.'

'Go on...'

'Let us establish royal outposts with Erldan's vassals. Hold localised hearings, so the people do not need to take matters into their own hands. My subjects must see their king and priesthood united on this front. Know we will not tolerate vigilante activity.'

Davith sneered. 'This requires additional resources, Your Highness.' He appreciated as well as Gohran that Erldan's coffers were more than stripped bare. Already Gohran had borrowed money against the trade deal he was supposed to strike with Nedran—a loan he did not know how he would repay without a marriage to seal Erldan to Nedran. While the negotiation Gohran made with his aunt to cover Ella's dowry was enough to see his people starve through the next three winters.

Gohran stopped pacing, caught Davith's gaze, and held it. He let the heat of his anger churn between them. Davith's jaw pulsed where his teeth ground, and Gohran sensed him longing to break away.

'It is in Elnora's priesthood's best interest to strike hard and stamp these vigilantes out,' Gohran said. 'Do you want their ongoing presence undermining your authority for decades to come?'

Davith shook his head.

'With my men and their arms to assist, I don't doubt you can furnish the campaign with holy volunteers to oversee hearings and conduct the raids of which you seem so fond.' Gohran released the priest's gaze.

Davith stumbled as though Gohran had held him by force, not will.

Gohran surveyed the temple, eyed off the gold leaf mosaics, fingered the newly scribed and bound scriptures. He looked the priest up and down. With one hand, he tugged at Davith's silk brocade robe and ran his other along the sacred jewels sewn into his vestment.

'It would be a shame to sell these to raise the funds for the campaign, but I would as soon see the royal coffers put to better use now that the priesthood's glory flourishes.'

For the first time, Gohran witnessed Davith pale. 'I'm sure we can come to an arrangement, Your Highness.'

'Then it shall be done. I trust I have your backing on this matter, and that you value peace and order in Erldan as much as a head priest should.' He took a breath, waiting for his implied threat to land. Davith nodded slowly, his torso swaying as though his weight shifted.

'I plan to take an escort to call on the chief of the moneylender's guild in Halbar. Upon my return, I look forward to hearing your plans for how we execute this crusade to restore religious order.'

Davith bowed. 'As His Highness commands.'

Twelve

Elnora's rays warmed Jonas's back as he journeyed east towards Wernad. The breeze carried the baking flour and tilled soil scent of purple flax blooming alongside golden wheat and copper hallit. Where woodland thickened into a rising crag, he veered south, following the Gythyn Run to Harnal, then zigzagged east, passing farmers, merchants, and the occasional mercenary, heading home from one hire or scrounging to find another.

Normally Venn insisted he take an honour guard when travelling this way, but Jonas didn't care to inform his brother of his comings and goings at this moment, nor request Venn's men for an escort. Instead, he hugged the main trail that wound between river and forest and camped beside the road. A slower route than cutting through the forest and rock-cliffs on the other side of the Run that avoided the bandit-filled woodlands.

A full week passed before he approached Creywmm's trenched moat and drawbridge, which the town relied on in place of an outer wall. That day, the bridge was down, and people had spilled onto the street on either side. They mobbed a wicker cage atop a horse-drawn cart, waving hats and shouting.

Jonas slowed his steed and pulled up along the track's edge before the moat to dismount. Guards struggled to push the spectators back, using their shields to inch and shove.

'Stand clear!'

'Coming through!'

Peeking between heads, Jonas glimpsed a woman inside the enclosure. Hooded, arms tied behind her, she leveraged the cage walls to keep steady as the cart's motion flung her.

'False-godder!' someone called from the mob.

'Demon-worshipper!'

'Witch!'

Hurled stones thudded against the enclosure. The prisoner jerked away, overbalanced and toppled.

Across the bridge, the guarded cart picked up speed and left the mob and village behind.

The displaced crowd milled, watching the wagon disappear into the distance.

'What was all that?' Jonas asked a nearby spectator.

The man looked him up and down. 'Passing through, are you?' Then he recognised the insignia on Jonas's shirt. 'My apologies, my lord.' He gave a curt bow. 'The wardens are taking away another witch.' He spat on the ground.

'For trial?'

The man shook his head. 'Execution.'

When Jonas reached the gates of the main keep, the guards, who usually let him straight through, made him wait while a page sent word of his arrival. He pointed out his insignia, but they shook their heads. He caught his unwashed and unshaven reflection in a glint of shield. Beside him, the guards also held up a couple of well-dressed men Jonas recognised as local merchants.

The page returned, and the guards finally let Jonas pass. He handed over the reins of his steed to be stabled and followed the page to the main keep.

Wood-panelled walls splashed with cerulean tapestries and matching drapes lined the central corridor. Where older keeps wore representations of their histories and dynasties, Sheevan's family had chosen a solid theme that continued through the main hall to the drawing room, reminiscent of their far eastern ancestors.

'May I present Lord Jonas of Nedran?' The page bowed and allowed Jonas through.

Sheevan stood before a pair of plumped up cerulean settees. The wall sconces created a halo around him, making his ruddy cheeks pale. In this light, the bluish tinge in his complexion hinted at his Myan heritage. 'By the hells, Jonas, you look as if you've just returned from battle. What brings you here, unannounced?'

'You know me. I never go anywhere I'm expected.' Jonas sat, limbs sprawled. The page presented a tray of canapés and poured them wine. Jonas surveyed the food on offer. 'Besides, I find a good stink an effective disguise.'

'Are you in hiding?'

'Only from my brother. Oh, and yours and my most favoured friend, His Highness, King Gohran of Erldan.'

Sheevan rested a hand upon his shoulder. 'I feel for you with him always hanging around your brother. I'd as soon not cross paths with the king again in my lifetime.'

'Soon he'll be hanging around even more.' Jonas drained the remainder of his glass.

'It's true then—Venn is to marry the Erldan princess?'

'By every demon, how does gossip travel faster than I can spread it?' Jonas held out his glass for the servant to refill. 'That's why I'm here. I promised the princess I would put in a good word for her. See if there's a way to repair relations between your two families—and in turn, between yours and mine.'

'Oh Jonas, I wish I had better news. If the priests have sealed that betrothal, you'll have to leave tomorrow. Father will be back, and he won't want to be seen hosting one of Erldan's allies.'

'That's absurd.'

'Our situation has changed.' Sheevan leaned in, voice low. 'It's the priests. These days they don't trust us to Cleanse our own.'

'That caged woman...'

Sheevan pushed his hair from his face and ran his palms down the front of his shirt. 'I swear it's spilled onto everything. When they realised anyone could be a heretic in hiding, even a monarch... You know Gohran made a claim against my family to maintain Jaydyn's child? Father refused him. Says he only wants the coin to bribe the priests. Of course, he told Gohran it was because the child's not mine.' Sheevan tugged at his sleeve. 'I admit I wasn't keen on marriage, but I never wanted Jaydyn to end up like this. And now I have a daughter I'll never declare.'

Jonas buried his face in his glass. 'Have your parents someone else in mind for you?'

'They do. It won't be long before Father proclaims it. That's why he's not here to greet you. He's gone to the High City to seek permission from High King and priests alike.'

'Then why don't I clean up? Let's venture into town for some entertainment before I head home.'

Sheevan grinned. 'Now *that* I can drink to.'

Thirteen

Venn hoped time would act as a salve and that his grief would ease. But as each day passed without Ella by his side, the hurt intensified. Once, he would have thrown himself into his duties, but concentration failed him. He sickened for her, skin burning, muscles trembling.

The only thing offering peace was visiting her grave, so each morning he rode and knelt before her cairn, calling to her in his mind. Some days, he spent hours out there, his patient guard waiting for him to return to his steed. He hadn't sensed her as acutely as when he'd planted her seedling, but he continued to reach for her, willing her to reappear.

Often, he missed holding council, returning too late, while his courts went without a presider, for Jonas had not returned from Lichen.

'Venn, you need to stop riding out there.' Lynden rested a palm on his shoulder. 'It's only hurting you more.'

Venn shrugged her concern away.

'Don't you recall how it was when Pa died? I know it seems impossible, but I promise you'll feel better for attending to your duties and finding normalcy.'

'This is different. *She* was different...'

Lynden shook her head, eyes soft, and squeezed Venn's hands in hers. 'Please try, Venn. For me. For Nedran.'

His sister must have written to the king, because afterwards he received a letter from Gohran beseeching him to move on. He wrote: 'I understand your loss more keenly than you could know, but urge you not to let your province wither with your grief.'

After that, he took to sneaking out before dawn, ordering his guard to stay behind—a risk he'd not taken before.

Unobserved, he lay atop her grave, pressing his body to the ground, inhaling grass, soil, and jasmine, which grew taller and stronger as though nurtured by his pain. He reached for it, closed his fist around a thorny stem as he had the day he imagined seeing her. As it bit and his blood welled, he called her name.

For the briefest moment he saw her, hair strangely braided, wearing some kind of drab vestment, as if she had joined the Ancients in the Afterworld. Her voice grew louder, closer. He smelled her, almost tasted her as her warmth wove around and through him. Energy thronged through his limbs. He felt alive again.

'Why?' he called into the darkness. 'Why did She take you from me?'

Ella's replies faded in and out. Something about being taken beyond, as she begged him to follow her into the Afterworld. How he ached to do just that, to end this torment, fall upon his sword, or weigh himself down with stones and sink to the river floor. He could join her.

He imagined crossing over, but pictured Lynden weeping, begging him to stay. He heard Jonas cursing him for abandoning his duties. Last, Gohran's blue eyes beseeched, carrying a tantalising echo of Ella's warmth.

Venn cried out. 'I can't... Gods, I'm sorry...' He sat up, let the crushed jasmine fall from his hand, and she was gone.

As he rode back to Nedran, his ache was worse than before. Sweat dripped from his hair, soaking his shirt, and his body shook. He sensed the shadows circling his eyes, heavy and sunken. He had intended to see to his duties, but by the time he reached the main keep, all he could manage was to crawl beneath the blankets of his bed.

For weeks, in the early hours of each morning, dreams of Venn replaced Ella's old nightmares. Often, she heard him call to her, sensed his longing.

In her dreamscape, the pair strolled through her favourite places at Nedran. The trees, meadows, streams, and sky appeared even more beautiful, shot with light, refracting and crystalline, as though seen in vision, water the colour of turquoise, and the horizon an endless twilight. Occasionally, as they sprawled on the emerald grass, Ella almost felt Venn's touch, flesh upon flesh. The tang of blood accompanied those times, as that first night she'd dreamed of him. These moments with Venn seemed pure, untainted. He chose her, no matter the truth of it.

But that evening, sleep eluded her. She closed her eyes and willed him into her mind, trying to ignore the intermittent snores and snuffles that punctuated the dark. She built an image of the night they met. He appeared fresh-faced and portrait perfect. Tears welled, and she imagined him reaching for her cheek. She caught his hands in hers and brought them to her lips. The tang of blood filled her nostrils and the back of her tongue.

Why? Venn called in her mind, his voice faint and clogged like sound passing through water. *Why did She take you from me?*

Another moment and she saw him. Not as she had just pictured, but bearded, sallow-cheeked, his limp dark hair clinging across his brow. Amidst the bloody tang, he reeked of fever-sweat, his fists balled.

Why did She take you from me? he repeated. His lips moved, but his words slunk into her mind the way the priestesses' often did.

Venn! Venn, Gohran took me west, to a temple beyond Erldan. She thought her reply, but could not know if it reached him.

Beyond, yes. Where She took you, he thought back.

Not 'She'—Gohran. Venn, I'm to the west. Come for me.

Venn's reply echoed in her mind: *I'm not ready to follow. My city needs me... Lynden, Jonas, they need me...* A crumpled vine dropped to the ground. Venn's palm bled. *Gods, I'm sorry...*

She tried to take his hands in hers, but she couldn't get a hold. She cupped where his cheeks ought to be, but they were cool and clammy, akin to her childhood visions of her dolls brought to life.

Venn's hands sought hers, but the sensation was as ephemeral as walking through mist. He was fading, his image breaking up—a wind-torn fog.

Wait—please! she called.

Too late. He vanished, his words a mere echo. *Where She took you.*

Who? Venn—Who? Ella thought into the void.

The blood-scent was gone, along with the sour stench of Venn's sweat. She collapsed back onto her pillow, stuffed a corner of the blanket into her mouth and silently howled.

FOURTEEN

Vera's stomach fluttered when she heard Jonas return. He always liked to bathe before he presented himself, so she didn't greet him, but hurried to her chamber to preen. She brushed out her flaxen hair, fastening it with a jewelled silver clasp, then reddened her lips with the juice of sour berries squeezed into melted ilak's fat and sweetened with a drop of honey. Thinking of her beloved, her wide blue eyes lit up.

There were days she had to prick her skin in case this was all a dream. She had desired Jonas for the longest time, and now it seemed a betrothal was imminent.

'Our handsome lordling is a wanderer at heart, my darling,' her mother Selmyra warned.

She sighed. 'I know.'

Selmyra looked pained.

'I don't need your pity, Ma. My eyes are open.' *So long as he comes home to me,* she thought.

Selmyra cupped her daughter's cheeks between her palms. 'I know they are. I just wanted more for you...'

She meant more than her father's wandering heart and meandering loins had provided Selmyra. But if her mother made a comfortable life loving such a man, so could she.

When she located Jonas at last, he stood before the window of the sunroom, clutching a parchment. Her heart thudded. His knuckles appeared ghost white. She hesitated, then laid a gentle hand on his shoulder. Jonas swallowed, drawing a sharp breath as he scrunched the message and faced her.

'You're shaking,' she said.

'I have to go home to Nedran.'

'You only just got back from Creywmm…?'

'It appears my esteemed brother has need of me.' He thrust the crumpled letter into Vera's hands. 'Please offer my apologies to your father. I won't be joining his hunt this stay.'

'Of course, but—'

He drew Vera to him and pressed his lips to her forehead. 'I'll return soon enough. I can never keep away for long.'

His words sounded hollow, and while his brow quirked in its usual front of bravado, his smile never reached his eyes.

Vera sat by the window and watched him retreat. With a knot in her stomach, she smoothed out the message and read.

When, a short while later, Vera's handmaid arrived with her tea, Vera was still there, her own knuckles now white and her forehead creased. Vera took the tray without looking up.

'Shellyn, could you fetch some fresh parchment? I need to send a letter of condolence with Lord Jonas when he leaves.'

'He's already gone, my lady. I passed him only moments ago. He was in a terrible hurry.'

Vera pursed her lips. 'Pa can see to it, then.'

'Young Jonas might have stayed for his meal before rushing off,' Vera's father, Teegan, lamented.

It was just three of them at supper, Vera being the last of Selmyra and Teegan's brood at home. Vera's eldest brother, and their father's namesake, had settled with his wife, while Stevyn, her youngest and the only other surviving sibling, was in fosterage with a distant cousin. Vera liked to call him the heir in reserve.

Teegan was as dark as Vera and her mother were fair. His once-black beard grew up and over his ruddy cheeks, and his thick brows crowded his black eyes.

The sky outside had clouded over, and the darkened room turned Selmyra's irises grey, making her appear every one of her forty-odd summers. 'Gan, he needs to be with his family.'

Vera knew she found her husband's lack of empathy astounding.

Teegan's eyebrows formed an unbroken line. 'What nonsense, Sel,' he said. 'Had Princess Ella been our lordling's sister, his concern would be admirable, but she was no relation at all, was she? Leaving my beautiful daughter pining.'

'Pa!' Vera slathered butter across a hunk of bread.

'Humph. I was hoping for an extra pair of eyes on the hunt.' Teegan pushed his dinner around his plate with disdain. 'We could be feasting on venison instead of fowl.'

'He'll be back soon enough. He gave me his word.' *And now there was nothing to keep him away.*

Teegan rubbed his greying beard, frowning at the rattling shutters as thunder sounded. 'When Our Lady takes someone so young, it makes you wonder.'

'Listen to you. As superstitious as an old farmwife,' scoffed Selmyra.

'Well, after that nasty business with her mother...'

Selmyra turned from her husband and motioned for her daughter to pass the bread. 'What do you think, Vee?'

'Hmm?' She pushed the trencher closer. 'Oh, yes, a terrible business.' She stuffed her mouth with the last of her bread to hide her satisfied smile.

Fifteen

'By the hells, Venn. You look like a demon swallowed you down and spat you out again,' Jonas said when he arrived home from Lichen. How long since Venn slept? Since he'd shaved? His hair resembled the fur of a sick cat, his pale skin glistening beneath the shadow of a beard.

Jonas took Lynden's arm and led her beyond Venn's hearing. 'You should have sent word that he was this unwell,' he hissed.

Lynden shrugged him away. 'I thought you'd be back weeks ago. Did you not receive our letters?'

Jonas puffed hair from his eyes. Didn't acknowledge the messages he'd ignored. 'I was in Creywmm—'

'Creywmm?'

'Trying to smooth Erldan's rift with Sheevan—a lost cause.' Jonas signalled to a nearby servant. 'Head to town and fetch a medic for his lordship.'

'A medic?' Alarm crossed Lynden's face.

'Lyn, look at the state of him. How long has he been like this?'

'It's hard to know… I thought he was pining…'

Jonas frowned.

'He spends each day beside Ella's grave.'

'How morbid.'

'Don't jest. And before you chide, I've tried to stop him. So has the king.'

Jonas soured. 'Let's await the medic's advice.'

Hours later, a crinkled, slack-mouthed man arrived to attend to Venn. His brother lying sweat-slicked atop his bedclothes, the dim light, and sour smell, reminded Jonas of their father sickening abed during his final moons.

The physician ran his hands along various parts of Venn's anatomy, holding his ear to others. He soaked Venn's fingers in a flask of green-tinged water, a jasmine bower floating at its bottom like a spider with too many legs.

He pulled Venn's hand back out, pressed on each nail, then peered at the whites of Venn's eyes. 'I detect a mild fever from an imbalance in humours, but no excess moisture to cause alarm.' He rummaged through his bag and handed Jonas an indistinguishable satchel of dried herbs. 'Take three pinches, boil it in a quart of water and let it steep. Recite the *Ballad of Fyora and Zar*, add another pinch, then have the dryhten drink.'

Grateful, Jonas took the offered medicine, Venn's breath rasping in the background.

The medic bent and leaned in close to Venn. 'Try to sleep, my lord.'

Out in the corridor, Jonas pulled the physician aside. 'What's wrong with him?'

'I cannot be certain, my lord, but I surmise grief is at the root. The mind plays upon the body in peculiar ways, ways hidden even from the greatest medics in the High Realm, under whom I have studied.' He cleared his throat. 'I have seen nothing like it without some *external* cause. Such is out of the question here.' Chin lowered, eyes peering upward. 'Therefore, grief it must be.'

A cause like white smoke, Jonas wondered? Or witchcraft—if you believed that sort of thing. 'Will the herbs help?'

'Not truly, my lord, and I won't charge you for them. It is good counsel, however, to never leave a man with nothing for hope. If naught else, they should aid the dryhten's sleep and settle his stomach.'

For his silence, if not his service, Jonas handed over a silver coin.

Afterwards, he joined Lynden in the dining hall.

'We were so excited about the babe, and then—' Lynden choked off. 'She wasn't even two moons along. How can that happen?'

Jonas squeezed Lynden's hand. He couldn't curse his brother for getting Ella with child. He had no voice in such matters.

But if Ella was pregnant, that would explain the changes he noticed when he saw her last, and her insistence on marrying Venn against her brother's wishes. Her sister Jaydyn's fate would have loomed.

Why hadn't Ella told him? He might have helped her.

A strangled sob. She would share nothing with him again. He threw his napkin over his uneaten supper, refilled his wineglass, and gulped its entire contents.

'I found her curled over, blood on her nightdress.' Lynden relived her memory through glassy eyes. 'As soon as I could, I fetched help...'

Jonas could almost hear his sister's unfinished reflection: *not soon enough.*

He was about to reassure her it wasn't her fault when she said, 'The king took her to find a medic right away. But when he returned, she was gone...'

'You left her with Gohran?' He swore.

'Yes, but—'

'Curse it, Lyn. Why him?'

'He was the first person I thought of...'

Something in her tone gave him pause. 'Lyn, you realise he beat Ella, that she was here to escape him?'

Lynden swallowed. 'Only after you dishonoured her. Gohran is her brother, and a king. He did everything he could, Jonas. Her death—it devastated him...'

Eyes still glassy—dreamlike—Jonas recognised her expression: complete preoccupation. The same face Venn wore as he doted on Ella when he'd last seen them together.

'Please tell me you did not take him to your bed, Lyn.'

Lynden's cheeks and neck flushed scarlet.

Venn's steward, Mykan, entered and cleared his throat. 'My lord? Several matters came up while you were away that his lordship requested I pass to you. Guild master Jethryn asked how we'd like his hallit dues, in coin or in kind?'

Still studying Lynden, Jonas shook his head.

'My lord?'

'My apologies.' He turned to the steward. 'Tell him in coin. No—in kind.' Would it ever be his turn to grieve?

Jonas answered Mykan's queries and took the rest of his drink to the warrior's refectory. It was preferable to sitting alone with his sister. He'd never been so disappointed in her. Gohran? The man creeped Jonas's flesh in ways he didn't care to dwell upon. Lyn must have been acting from the heat between her thighs, though Jonas had never understood the king's appeal. Vera argued he was handsome, and a monarch, but... Jonas shuddered.

He recognised he was fixating on Lyn and Gohran to avoid thinking about Ella. But in truth, it hadn't struck. Didn't seem real.

He focused on his fellows. Ribbed them about their latest quests and love affairs. Raucous laughter echoed off the bare floors and walls as he swigged any drink he could lay his paws on. Eventually, the men retired to their barracks, and he slunk back to his chamber in the main keep.

Half drunk, he sprawled atop his bedclothes. The moonlit grey cast shadows across his walls. Down below, the night watchmen carried lanterns. Their shadows travelled back and forth, overlapping and intertwining. His mind grasped at the familiar in the unfamiliar, and Jonas could have sworn he saw Venn's silhouette through the muted light. The shadow-figure loomed, then shrank away, sickening for what was forever gone.

The watchmen must have turned, because two figures now made their way along the wall. *Bedposts. Distorted bedposts forming head and shoulder shapes.* But in Jonas's imagination, he pictured Lynden fawning over King Gohran, all reason beyond her, as Ella had beguiled Venn once they shared a bed.

Meanwhile, his drink-addled mind imagined Gohran returning to Nedran with news of Ella's death. Jonas wouldn't have put it past the king to have dragged Ella to an abortionist to keep her dishonour contained. It might explain her untimely passing, considering how dangerous that could be.

An owl cried. '*She wasn't even two moons along. How can that happen?*'

Another replied. '*Only after you dishonoured her.*'

Eyes shut tight.

'*Everything's different now.*'

Jonas sat up. Was he going mad? He groped for his trousers, slipped on a shirt, and pulled on his boots.

Outside, he meandered through the city's winding alleys with the thick fog covering his tracks. After dark, Nedran might be another place entirely. A new set of darkly painted night-time faces replaced the sunny daylight ones. Everything took on a lurid hue, hanging lanterns casting eerie shadows.

Peddlers transformed their open wagons into covered ones, offering wares for which the town wardens had not issued proper permits or that promised tantalisingly forbidden sensations. The men and women who walked the streets were peddlers of a particular kind, advertising their merchandise as though the chill wasn't biting bared flesh. Doubtless, one mind-numbing tonic or another aided them.

Jonas pitied their goose-pimpled bodies and bloodshot eyes, but not enough to offer coins from his purse; he had no desire to have a knife pulled on him the moment he let down his guard for what remained.

He pressed past the clamouring traders and wretched nightcats towards a corner tavern. Its door hung open and the boisterous crowd spilled onto the street. Jonas stepped inside. He avoided the crammed bar, and slipped through the haze-filled room to a small corridor out back, where a narrow ladder led to the roof.

As he climbed, light and sound fell away, until he reached a trapdoor embedded in the ceiling. He knocked thrice in a precise pattern and waited.

A moment later came the reply, a corresponding *rat-tat-tat.*

He pushed the lid up and over to reveal a cramped, poorly lit attic. Within, atop a reclining chair, sprawled a sultry woman, all piled-up hair and kohled eyes.

'Alina,' he greeted.

Lips the colour of blood curved into a sleepy smile. 'I was hoping it would be you.'

Jonas climbed inside and lowered the trapdoor behind him.

'Come, take a seat.' Alina patted the silk-covered stool beside her.

Jonas complied, ignoring the straw poking through its fabric.

She worked her hands into his shoulders, kneading out the knots with practised ease. 'You're troubled, my lord.'

He nodded, grunting with appreciation.

'I feel it here, and here.' She leaned into the hollow of one shoulder blade and then the other. 'It's been a while, Jonas. I can honestly say I have missed you.'

'Missed my coin, more like.'

'Is that all I mean to you?' She pressed the soft flesh of her breasts against him. Her left palm found its way along his chest, while the right massaged the back of his neck, fingers twining his hair. 'You haven't saddled up another lass, have you?' Still kneading. 'You know I don't offer those services anymore.'

'No, no, Alina. Nothing of that sort.'

'Then are you here for some...?' She pointed to a series of pipes atop a sideboard that stretched the room's length.

He shook his head. 'It is tempting, but I won't, my thanks.'

'There's few like you. Most who come through that door are back within weeks, days, even...'

'And eventually hours, and then not at all. I've no desire to end up in that state, I assure you.' He shifted in his chair, pulling at a tuft of exposed straw. 'This may sound daft, but do you recall sharing a tale of a man using your potions to see into the future—or was it the past?'

'Hardly. Are you sure you haven't been at the white smoke already?'

'Alina.'

'If it's a fortune-telling shaman you're after, you'd do better searching the marketplace.'

'Don't pretend to misunderstand me.'

Alina ceased massaging and stepped around to face him. A black curl fell from the pile pinned atop her head. Jonas caught it between his fingers. Close up, though her deep Myan skin was supple, Alina appeared a decade older than he. Probably she was more. She had a peculiar aura about her, dark eyes that promised and threatened.

She pulled away. 'It won't work.'

'What do you mean?'

A shadow passed over her.

Those eyes. The way she looked at him reminded him of Ella.

'For a start, you're filled with anger,' she said. 'Anger and this brew are not a pleasant combination.'

'The truth, Alina. You said it *won't* work—what did you mean?'

'It's difficult to explain.' She paced. 'Something in the way your mind reacts. I see it when you resist the smoke. This potion acts in the same manner.'

'But I mean to resist. If I let go, this other potion...'

'No, my lord. I tell you, nothing good can come of it.'

'I must know what happened. You don't understand how important this is—'

'And you don't understand what you ask.' Eyes coal-dark and hard. 'That fellow I told you of? Not two weeks after he left here, his corpse washed up on the riverside, forcing his wife and four children to mourn him.'

She made her way over to her sideboard. Between two pipes rested an ornamental glass sphere. In Alina's hands, its surface reflected murky water. A man drinking one of Alina's potions, then sucking at the blood of a freshly maimed animal until he was all-seeing, all-knowing. Then later, skin slick, body quaking, he sickened for more, a thirst he could not quench.

Like Venn.

Alina put the ball down. Its ordinary glass mocked him.

'How did you do that?'

Still facing away, she said, 'Some things should stay buried.' When she turned, she held out a vial of sickly liquid. 'Here, this will calm your nerves for tonight.'

He reached into his purse, but she stopped him. 'Take it.'

Her scent and the touch of her flesh against his, was electrifying. He caught her fallen curl in his fingers, tugged it, then traced her neck and brushed the brown skin at the top of her breasts.

Alina snatched his hand away and placed it around the vial. 'Take it and go.'

I t was almost noon when Jonas woke to pounding at his door. The room lurched, and he groaned. *Damn Alina.* Doubtless, she calculated her draught would put him off asking her for another thing. A second knock. He scrounged for his shirt.

'Enter!'

It was Mykan, Venn's steward. 'Pardon my interruption, my lord. You're needed downstairs, at council.'

'Did the medic's prescription not help the dryhten?' Jonas ran fingers through his hair.

'I believe it did, my lord, but his lordship rode out before dawn. When he returned, he retired to his chamber, and left instructions not to be disturbed. My apologies. I assumed he'd arranged for you to attend today's hearings.'

'No apology needed, Mykan.' Jonas slipped on his shoes and followed the steward downstairs. 'I should apologise to you. You have done more than your share of late.'

Even before they reached ground level, the restless crowd's clamour pressed into Jonas's skull. He stepped inside, and some two scores of angry citizens, some of them farmers, others merchants, turned his way, ready to swarm. He groaned.

'There he is—My lord! My lord!' someone called.

'When are you going to do something about the barges?'

'We need to transport our hallit.'

A man in a farmer's hat pushed past the merchants. 'Shut it, false-godders. I've a family needs feeding.'

Jonas held up his hands for order. 'One at a time.' He took his place as adjudicator to the citizenry's gripes. 'You.' He pointed to a dark-skinned fellow with a thin beard. 'We'll start with you.'

When the complaints finally eased, night approached. Jonas could not recall Nedran's mood being so tense. This year's harvest had been exceptional, but instead of bringing relief, their newfound prosperity inspired greed.

Jonas thought he understood why. The latest contracts negotiated between Erldan and Nedran gave Erldan extended access to the trade routes north and south, and while the hallit market should not have been affected, competition for barges had increased, forcing up the hire price.

The citizens would have worn the increase if it meant greater security, which Erldan's army should have brought. Ordinarily, merchants paid exorbitant fees for guards on their journeys, but the penalty for meddling with royal cargo was deterrent enough to forgo that cost. That was with the promise of a betrothal between the two provinces on the horizon.

With the princess gone and no formalised kinship-bond, the contract terms between Nedran and Erldan had become murky. From what Jonas gleaned, farmers and traders alike were vying to secure their share of the swollen profits before the ground shifted under them once more.

In sheer exhaustion, Jonas bypassed supper and went straight to bed. He aimed to rise before dawn and catch Venn. He needed to understand his brother's fascination with Ella's grave.

Sure enough, when Jonas woke the next morning, Venn was already sneaking to the stables. Jonas followed, saddling his steed alongside his brother without saying a word. Even in the faded light, Venn's eyes appeared bloodshot. When he mounted, so did Jonas, and together, they headed towards the castle gates.

The entire ride there, Venn shifted in his saddle, fidgeting with the bridle, stopping to check the horse's hooves for stones, until Jonas thought they would not reach the gravesite before noon.

Finally, they arrived at the remote spot far from the main path, in the middle of nowhere. There was nothing remarkable about it, save the scenic view of the surrounding landscape. Jonas shivered. He wanted to ask why here, buried away from her family, without the priests' blessing, but the words caught in his throat.

He stared at the mound of dirt, the cultivated jasmine bush and the cairn. Shouldn't he feel something? Anything? He was numb. It was like standing outside his body, peering down over his own shoulder.

His brother wore a curious expression, as though he were holding a private conversation in his head, awaiting a reply that never came. Jonas squeezed his arm.

'When I am here, sometimes I sense her,' Venn said.

Jonas frowned.

'Right here.' Venn pointed to the jasmine growing around the cairn.

Jonas watched Venn lose himself in memory, in grief. They stood for a long moment until Jonas broke the spell. 'Come, Venn. We need to return.'

'Lynden wants me to stop coming here,' he said, as though Jonas had not spoken.

'Lyn's right. It isn't helping. Ella's gone. Pining won't bring her back.'

'Then why do I still feel her?'

'You're not ready to let go.'

Venn shook his head. 'Sometimes—Jonas, it's like she's here, standing in this exact spot. Even now, the feeling is faint, but I can sense her.'

Jonas hesitated. If he were honest, he could sense a part of her, too. As much to convince himself, he went on. 'You're remembering—longing—that's all. It's the heart's way of coping, Venn. Look at your city crumbling. It needs you. We need you.'

Venn shook his head, but this time, when Jonas urged him, he returned to his steed and allowed Jonas to lead them home.

Sixteen

A hand-selected escort accompanied Gohran to Halbar. Named for the picturesque headwaters fed by snowmelt from the Halbar ranges, Halbar sat east of Rynwood across the Rialdon River. Further east ran the great north-south range that divided Ycelt from neighbouring Myan. The Halbar River cut through the great divide, giving Halbar unique access to the prosperous eastern land. Only the River Arin in the far north was comparable.

For this reason, the Myan moneylender's guild had established an outpost in Halbar. The outpost kept trade constant between the two peoples while the guild profited from providing this convenience.

'This will be a lengthy trek, Your Highness. Are you certain such a long absence is wise?' Jarrod asked when Gohran told him of his plans. Gohran had recently promoted the royal driver to the post of steward. One of the few people he could trust, Jarrod understood the value of his silence. 'Could you send someone in your stead?'

Gohran shook his head. 'I dare not. It might insult the guild if I don't make my request in person.' The gods knew he needed this loan. He still had to pay Ella's dowry, and now he had to furnish the priests with enough coin to support the henad outposts and extended surveillance.

Jarrod was right. The trek took them some weeks, as they followed a circuitous route that avoided Creywmm, Herron, and the High Realm of Galliarn. As Gohran's party rounded the final bend of the switchback that led into Halbar proper, Gohran's tension seeped from his shoulders.

Gohran had expected Halbar to feel sub-tropical, being so close to Myan, where the humid jungle tangled and clogged the towns and cities. But the perennially snowcapped mountains surrounding Halbar seemed to suck the moisture from the air. The lower slopes remained barren and dry, littered with shale that flanked the river, which oscillated from a seasonal trickle to snow-fuelled rapids.

Set into the craggy inclines, the city's architecture hinted at its proximity to exotic Myan. Multistorey tiered rooftops, whose eaves sloped and curled up at the ends in peaked corners, topped red lacquered rectangular buildings. Beneath, the supporting columns bore green and yellow paint, embossed with copper and gold.

Gohran and his escort rode through the bustling town centre. A sprawling marketplace surrounded the main cobbled street on either side. Vibrantly dressed customers meandered, a kaleidoscope of peacock feathered hats and fur-lined cloaks topped woad vests and saffron-dyed shirts.

'Find us somewhere to stable our steeds, will you?' he called to Jarrod, who hastened ahead, leaving the remaining riders to amble along the wide thoroughfare.

When Jarrod returned, he led them to the public stables, a common feature of larger trading cities throughout Ycelt.

Gohran directed his men to settle into a large trader's inn, which housed wealthy lords and merchants en route to or from Myan, then took Jarrod with him to find the moneylenders. As they strode the streets, Gohran pulled his cloak around his shoulders to hide his insignia. Outside the guild's outpost, they travelled incognito.

Gohran and Jarrod passed wagons carrying exotic plants—vegetation unlike anything Gohran had seen: pink, yellow, purple, and cinnabar-tinged blossoms against verdant green. The peculiar foliage was as vibrant as the flowers, whose elongated stamens and horn-shaped petals resembled beards. Carts advertised animated creatures inside wicker cages, who leapt and swung from curled tails. Others contained pointy-nosed scaled rodents or rainbow-coloured birds that squawked like someone had pinched them.

Gohran scoffed. How long would any of these survive in Ycelt's temperate clime, tended by wealthy fools?

Gohran drew his cloak further around him, nose wrinkling, as he pushed through the milling crowds, wishing the moneylenders' station wasn't in the centre of this milieu.

Finally, they spotted the red flag bearing the guild's gold coin icon flapping in the breeze. A converted temple, the outpost was one of the few permanent buildings in the marketplace. Gohran and Jarrod ducked inside.

A fine-boned man whose dark, bluish complexion spoke of his Myan heritage greeted them. Myans traditionally bore skin like the night sky, hair like the moon, and twilight eyes, while artist's renderings depicted the Ancients as their inverse, with midnight hair, moonbeam skin, and the azure eyes of a noontide sky. Gohran had witnessed neither in the flesh, for generations of cross-border exogamy had rendered the complexion of many Myans more ruddy or bronze than indigo, just as the tone of Myrhan's descendants' skin ranged from milk white to tanned leather.

The man bowed from the waist, gaze lowered, hands crossed with jewelled fingers splayed, as was the Myan custom. Long nails filed to a point accentuated each elongated finger. When he straightened, the irises of his monolid eyes shone violet.

Jarrod stepped forward and bowed, introducing the king.

'We have been expecting you, Your Highness.' The fellow pursed his thin lips, his wispy tapered moustache and pointed beard dancing with each word.

Gohran recoiled from the man's spiced-meat breath.

The fellow ushered them through a cloth screen to a back cubicle where they perched on silk-covered stools. Servants arrived with local fare: a clear heated spirit, served in a smooth lacquered cup, and jellied titbits.

Opposite, the man's gold-embroidered sleeves gaped across the tray, somehow managing not to dip low enough to touch the food.

'How does your family fare, Your Highness?'

He wished they could forgo the insufferable chitchat and get down to business, but etiquette demanded he play along, sharing news, and asking the same from his host. He supposed it was to build rapport, but he did not doubt the guild's representative was squirrelling away knowledge to be leveraged at some point.

'The untimely passing of my youngest sister has left an unfortunate debt hanging over my kingdom. You see, my ancestors forged a treaty generations ago...'

The guild master held up his hand. 'The Erldan treaty. Yes, we know of it.'

Gohran stiffened. *What did they know?* 'The details of any such treaty are irrelevant to our business, save that my sister's untimely death does not relieve me of the burden of paying her dowry.'

'I understand. You require funds to honour the terms of the treaty.'

'There has also been unrest since Queen Prya's denouncement...'

'Indeed, you seek resources to restore order.' The guild master's expression did not change. 'My guild is happy to lend much-needed coin, subject to assurances.'

'You want collateral.'

'We would honour His Highness's word alone, but promises can grow hollow without tangible security behind them.'

'Of course. Never would I expect you to offer a loan with nothing to back it. That is why I am offering the hand of my second sister, Princess Jaydyn, as surety.'

All the air seemed to be sucked out of the room.

'A husband of your guild's choosing, and a betrothal that guarantees passage along the length of the Gythyn Run.' Those cool eyes watching, judging. These men could censure him all they liked. He had nothing else to offer, and without this loan, his people would starve while his kingdom descended into anarchy.

'A generous prospect provided the proposed trade agreement between Erldan and Nedran proceeds. Given your youngest sister has passed...'

How did this man know Ella was ever to be wed instead of Raeyn? 'That deal was first forged between Lord Venn of Nedran and the Princess Elder, Raeyn of Erldan. Once the dryhten is out of mourning, the arrangement will proceed as intended.'

The guild master ran his slender fingers along his gold weave cincture, the points of his fingernails sliding between its fringed edges. 'I am sure His Highness is correct in this matter; however, the second princess is already over twenty summers, is she not? And I understand she carries a babe in arms.'

Gohran steadied his breath.

'Our merchants prefer their new spouses unsullied. Many enter pre-contracts from infancy, to guarantee the purity of their future consorts.'

The tang of bile filled the back of his throat. Those same merchants took on multiple wives as they tired of the elder ones, forever seeking fresh, youthful bodies to satisfy their putrid lusts.

He held the guild master's gaze, a pressing heat surging through him. 'A princess of royal descent down both lines of her ancestry is a prize for any merchant. And with that trade agreement...'

The guild master blinked and cocked his head to one side, unruffled by Gohran's rage.

Gohran's heat subsided, petering away.

'A royal infant—a babe in arms, barely toddling—now, *that* is a prize, Your Highness.'

The skin around Gohran's neck reddened as a storm brewed inside him. Jarrod's soothing hand rested on his arm. Gohran shook him away and turned back to face the guild master. 'You reject my sister and propose a contract with my niece?'

The guild master blinked again, unswayed, cocking his head the other way. 'A pre-contract, yes.'

'And in this pre-contract Princess Serrah will not wed until—?'

'Eleven summers, Your Highness, for the betrothal ceremony. To be wed at twelve.'

'So young...'

'A customary age for subsequent wives, Your Highness. And she would need to be raised with her future family. To ensure her purity and school her in Myan customs. A pre-betrothal adoption is conventional in these cases.'

Gohran sat, stunned.

'Why don't I leave you to get settled into your accommodations, and we can meet again tomorrow to discuss the terms of the agreement?'

Gohran stood and strode outside, Jarrod shuffling after.

'Your Highness, what they are proposing... You can't be certain Serrah won't be married off before—'

Gohran met his gaze with hardened sapphire eyes. The telltale twitch in his jaw was enough to warn Jarrod that an eruption was imminent, and he fell silent.

Passersby kept their distance, parting to let them through. When they reached the inn, Gohran shut himself in his room. A short time later, the innkeeper's servant arrived, carrying a ceramic bottle of Myan spirit. Gohran shoved the offering aside. 'Take this foreign swill away! Bring wine or ale or mead.'

The servant stammered an apology, all colour draining from his youthful cheeks. He bowed, then scurried off like a frightened mouse.

Myan was another world, with different morality and customs. He pictured his niece in that world, then shrugged the thought away.

Seventeen

'Here, let me...' Nykahlia said, breaking away from a group of priestesses crossing the field. She picked up a fallen corner of a blanket and passed it to Ella.

'My thanks,' Ella smiled. Tasked with retrieving clean, dried linens, she had wrangled that oversized beast single-handedly for longer than she cared to contemplate.

Warmth slid between them as they folded. Nykki's cheeks flushed, and she returned Ella's smile. Ella hid her relief that while her babe was still, her power flowed without hesitation.

She placed the blanket in her wicker basket, and reached for the next, but Nykki had already scurried after her companions. One turned and snickered. Nykahlia shushed her and they continued towards the citadel. Most of the women had avoided Ella since she countered them in the refectory, but their hostility stalked her as the weeks ground past.

Tedious prayer, mind-numbing lessons, and the drudgery of never-ending chores consumed each indistinguishable day, punctuated by insufficient sleep and meagre meals. Ella wondered about the prior lives of each priestess, that they endured this perennial monotony.

She hefted another blanket from the grass, her back creaking, sweat moistening her braids, their strands clinging to her brow and cheeks. The air was crisp but dry as the days grew warmer and longer. A single bout of rain fell as Breeyan predicted, but there was no sign of the heavy seasonal showers Ella experienced at Erldan.

How she longed to be rid of her growing babe so she could flee. She would travel far to the north or east, perhaps close to Myan, somewhere no one would recognise her.

'There you are.' A stout, blonde priestess named Samian waved as she neared. 'Once you've finished here, Shaena wants you in the kitchen. She needs eggs, so you can start by clearing the nesting pens.'

Her back twinged, and she massaged her aching shoulders. She still needed to cart these blankets inside.

A deep breath. She met Samian's gaze, forcing a heat-smile. Samian's expression grew velvety-soft. Her desire to have the priestess think well of her flowed like stream water. Samian bent and grabbed the basket's handle and helped Ella carry it back to the citadel.

Ella hid a smirk. The priestess seemed unarmed and oblivious to Ella's unexpected influence.

With the blankets stowed for the summer, Ella heat-smiled again and thanked her, then answered Shaena's summons. Within the citadel, she passed roomfuls of priestesses poring over lessons. Gasps and giggles floated atop the steady drone of the instructors. One room contained a great fire which puffed and smoked, flaring up and dying down at intervals as the women drew on its power for their workings.

At the main landing leading to the yard, Ella encountered a couple of novices scrubbing the cold floors, plonking rags into soapy water, then sloshing them across the wooden boards. Neither looked up as Ella tiptoed past, but their whispers followed her like a pair of hissing snakes.

When she reached the bird coops, Ella braced against the pungent stench and collected freshly laid eggs.

Her basket was half stacked when an older priestess joined her.

'Are you here to fetch eggs, too?' Ella asked.

The woman shook her head. 'Just sending these messages from Her Holiness.' In one hand, she held a rolled parchment. With the other, she opened the pen beside the poultry coop. Inside were several speckled carrier birds. Their awkward bodies waddled back and forth.

Ella frowned. 'Does the order normally send letters this way?'

'Sometimes the Ancients' ways are best.'

Her companion sealed the parchment within a metal tube attached to the bird's foot. She clutched the creature in both hands and peered into its eyes. The bird cocked its head at her, panicked. She cooed, and it relaxed, neck lolling, before perking back up. Arms outstretched, she tossed the bird into the air. Beating frantic wings, it soared, gliding on the wind, circling and turning in the distance.

Ella felt its excitement at flying free. And yet it wasn't free at all; bound to undertake its journey to one of the other orders at Crescent Mountain or the Gern, or to wherever the priestess enchanted it. The woman picked up a second bird and repeated the process. Ella watched it fly in a slightly different direction before her companion secured the remaining birds.

Conscious that she was there to collect eggs, not gawp, Ella stacked her basket with as many eggs as she could carry and hurried back to the kitchen.

Not looking up, Shaena motioned for her to place the eggs in a large crate. 'Not many, is there, *Princess*?'

Ella tried to force one of her special smiles and reach out with warmth, but the desire caught in her throat. A murmur within her belly. She fought the urge to choke and gag. Her babe was awake.

She exhaled and let go. 'I'll fetch more.'

Daylight brought the aches and strains of days running together, but also perspective. In mundane physicality, Ella saw tools she had previously ignored: carrier birds. Creatures free to roam where she could not, trained to contact the world she reached only in dreams.

Weeks passed before Ella found the opportunity to try, however. Meela mostly assigned her to strip and change bed linens, but finally, sent her to the scriptorium. Ella spent the morning preparing parchment, ruling lines, and mixing ink, ready to replicate an old, faded manuscript, *The Lost Warriors*. She had left Amber's copy in Ycelt, and Breeyan wanted her to replace it.

As usual, Ella worked alone, as if her aunt wished to minimise contact between her and the other women. She arranged her desk with two loose parchments, one for her allocated task—in case anyone walked in—and another for her letter. She lay them flat beside the manuscript and posed a magnifying glass as though scribing.

Mind engaged, she listened for her sisters. Silence.

She sharpened her quill, dipped it into the well, then bled the excess ink. Her knuckles white, she brought the nib to the taunting blank space of her parchment. *Breathe.* A crooked blot formed where her arm shook. She gripped her wrist to steady it and wrote:

Venn, my beloved, I need your help. Destroy this letter and tell no one I have contacted you. I will write again. Yours always, E. E.

It was done. She blew on the page to dry the ink, rolled and tucked it beneath her robe, safely hidden. Freedom was a step closer.

Heart thudding, she returned to scribing. She arranged the second sheet of parchment and flipped the manuscript's pages, looking for the scrap of vellum that marked her starting point.

The manuscript was immense and detailed. Entire spreads depicted stylised battle scenes and the lives of the Ancients, with illuminated initials and marginalia scattered throughout. Amber's copy had been a cut-down version, barren text containing selected stories and precepts. Both versions claimed single authorship by a man named Ynad, but it was more likely works compiled and refined over generations by multiple contributors.

Past readers had singled out favoured passages using flattened twine and vellum, leaving marks on the manuscript. Ella struggled to find her marker among the years of debris. Someone had even left a loose parchment between its pages.

About to flip past it, something caught her attention. *Was that a picture?* Ella retrieved and smoothed the parchment. It bore a series of lines sketched like two drawings stacked atop each other. Sometimes scribes practised drawings to include in a manuscript, but this was no illumination. It was a map.

She recognised the various buildings and surrounds as Aryon, including the old lookout post where the priestesses met beggars and refugees. But someone overlaid the citadel and grounds with sweeping, shaded arcs resembling rivers. Perhaps a priestess had re-used the same scrap without bothering to scrape it clean.

The images blurred into each other, and she blinked. These drawings had an intimate connection.

Her fingertips traced the faded ink as her mind explored. Through the reading glass, the pictures wavered. One reached towards her while the other fell beyond the page's surface, appearing in three dimensions. *Tunnels.* The second drawing showed a network of passages beneath the citadel. One started in the library behind the scriptorium and ended all the way out at the lookout post. Another linked off west, connecting to an underground cellar amid the order's grounds.

Footsteps. She recognised Amber's thought pattern, stuffed the parchment back between its pages, and mimicked scribing when her old tutor entered. 'There you are. You've missed the bell for supper.'

Ella followed Amber to the refectory. She ignored the women's sneers and took her place along one of the hard wooden benches. She kept her mind alert, checking her chair, the floor, and her plate for signs of tampering before settling down to her meal. Deep within another mental compartment, she stored the knowledge of her discovery and her newfound hope: the parchment tucked beneath her robe.

The following day was much the same. Ella hadn't solved how to deliver her letter. Asking to send messages was too risky, and not something Meela had entrusted her to do. She could request kitchen duty, but Shaena may not need eggs, and she dreaded being trapped with her rival's undisguised animosity. In the meantime, she scribed and hoped.

The strange hidden passages she'd discovered nagged. One of those tunnels would take her from the library to the grounds, close by the pens, unseen. She set her work aside and tiptoed through the connecting door into the library. The drawing showed the passage beginning on the north wall, now covered with overcrowded bookcases.

She removed some books from the left, but found no opening. Dusty book edges scratched and rubbed, forming red welts along the delicate skin of her arms. She ignored their itch and tried the next shelf. Still no opening.

Ella returned to the scriptorium to re-examine the parchment. She angled the reading glass until the surface caught the light from her lantern, just as it had when she'd first uncovered the hidden drawing. She squinted, focus drifting until the map's edges shimmered. Her mind slid into the picture, then through it, to the other side, eyes viewing the diagram as it appeared on the page, while her mind saw the drawing in full relief, as its mage-drawer had imbued. The passage blazed. No wonder she couldn't find an opening. The entrance wasn't through the bookcase; it was behind it.

Excitement tingled. She was about to withdraw, when she realised her mind had floated away from her body, weightless, travelling through the tunnel. The passage twisted and turned. Cool clay walls and dirt floor appeared as a curious blend of sketched and physical reality. The tunnel was dark and dank, putrid in parts.

She paused. A little further along, a pair of human-shaped shadowy forms huddled against a heap of fallen rock. Beyond, the tunnel became blocked.

Ella shuddered. Her mind backtracked through the passageway until it reached the fork that veered west towards the underground cellar. Here, the air was musty, but milder than in the other direction. Clay compacted against the walls, in parts no wider than her shoulders. She arrived at a solid door, likely the one leading up to the cellar. Ella imagined pushing on it, but it wouldn't budge. Her psyche refused to travel beyond this corporeal barrier.

Ella's flesh tugged. A dull ache wrenching as her simulacrum grew leaden. The surrounding image wavered alarmingly. She pictured travelling towards her body, struggling against its insistent pull. It became harder to maintain control, to resist letting her vision-body spring back unrestrained, damaging her simulacrum.

Her senses quivered in painful discord between the physical and ethereal. She had to merge the two, transfer her sight from mind to eyes, compel her ears to hear only what surrounded her, her nose and mouth to smell the dust of the scriptorium. Like the first time she'd learned about the chambers within her mind, its edges grated and ground.

Cold touched her skin, hard boards pressing in. She focused on the sensation, on her body's solidity, forcing her mind to fill its boundary. She blinked until she saw only the room in front of her. Used the last of her strength to banish the sketched quality of her vision.

Sweat-drenched, she couldn't lift her arms. The scriptorium spun, and she sank to the floor. Purple splotches of dark light closed in before turning black, and then to nothing.

Eighteen

The men were rowdy when Gohran joined them the next day to break their fast. He allowed them their jests up to a point. This had been a tedious trip, which could end up as a boiling pot blowing its lid if he didn't release his hold occasionally.

'Did you see that Myan lass seated at the table across from us? Skin like satin...' Ganno, the youngest of Gohran's riders, said.

'As if she'd let your filthy paws near her.' Tarraen cuffed the back of the lad's neck.

'I tell you she did, and if we weren't on the king's business, you wouldn't have seen me before dawn.'

Eyes rolling. 'She was doubtless too old for the men of her ilk.'

'Well, she wasn't too old for me, not by half!'

'For once, I wish you had tethered your wagon elsewhere,' another of the riders joined in. 'I don't know what you feasted on last night, Ganno, but it was like sleeping with a horn blower's trumpet dipped in sulphur.'

Ganno grabbed his fellow in a headlock and farted. 'Lucky escape for the lass, then!'

The rider choked and sputtered. 'Gods, Ganno!'

'Come now, settle, all of you,' Gohran said. 'I need to return to the marketplace to conclude my business this morning, and then we can head home. Stay near where they dock the barges, and Jarrod and I will meet you before the noontide.'

As they approached the moneylender's temple, Gohran sensed Jarrod's uneasiness. His brows pinched together, and his lips pursed as though he were trying not to voice his thoughts.

With a solid hand pressing on Jarrod's shoulder and a warm, steady gaze, Gohran assured him the loan was sound, that this was right for Erldan.

Jarrod nodded slowly, his mouth slack. 'A wise decision, Your Highness.'

'Good man.' Satisfied, Gohran released his hold upon the driver, noticing an abrupt chill in the air surrounding them.

Jarrod stumbled, as though the king's hand had pushed him, before he found his footing again.

'How much of that Myan spirit did you down?'

'A cup, no more, Your Highness. It must be stronger than it seems.'

When they reached the temple entrance, Gohran steeled himself and stepped inside.

As he waited to see the guild master, he fidgeted with his ring, circling it around his finger, back and forth, as he'd watched his mother do for many years. He wondered what she would think of this strategy.

A servant in the reception area offered refreshments, but he waved them aside. The thought of food or drink curdled his stomach.

Directed to the same cubicle as the previous day, Gohran took a few steadying breaths and sat opposite the guild master, flanked by a pair of witnesses in matching white robes. All would be well. At worst, Serrah would join an illustrious household and enjoy a more comfortable existence than he or her mother could provide. The arrangement would simultaneously liberate Jaydyn to pursue the life she'd always wanted, wedded to a noble family. And it may never come to that. Should he repay that loan, neither his sister nor his niece need ever know they were part of these negotiations.

Instead of presenting the contract for Gohran to sign and seal, the guild master cleared his throat, his spindly fingers winding around the ends of his wispy beard. 'After much consideration, Your Highness, the guild has declined your request.'

'What! Why?'

'The guild has concerns about Erldan's ability to service the loan. In its current form, your proposal is contingent on a trade agreement that is tenuous at best. And should you fail to repay, as time passes, the promised collateral decreases in value.'

Heat rose within.

'However, we will make the offer provided we set out and seal the betrothal contract and pre-betrothal adoption this day.'

Gohran stood, his chair dragging along the hard temple floor. 'Are you proposing I sell my niece?'

The guild's witnesses stepped forward, knives at the ready.

The guild master released a breath but remained seated. 'Never, Your Highness.' He motioned for Gohran to resume his seat, and then faced his men and raised his palms for them to stand down. 'My guild does not engage in such immoral practices.'

Sweat beaded across Gohran's forehead and upper lip. 'I mean no insult, but you insult me. Erldan can and will pay that debt.'

The guild master's brow twitched. 'Over what time frame, Your Highness? This is not an indefinite offer...'

'Again, you insult me.'

The guild master bowed his head, gaze lowered. 'Not my intention, Your Highness.' He looked back up and met Gohran square on. 'We have calculated the precise terms of the loan considering the offered surety. The greatest repayment term we can grant is thirty-six moon cycles.'

'Three summers?'

The guild master nodded.

'For a loan this size?'

The guild master smirked. 'Hence our concern about Erldan's ability to repay. The difficulty, Your Highness, is the child. The pre-betrothal adoption is to ensure a suitable upbringing... She is useless to us once she has passed her fifth summer.'

Gohran seethed.

'Without the babe as surety, I am sorry to say, we cannot offer the coin...'

Gohran heard tales of what happened to rulers during the Great Famine that befell the early settlers in Ycelt, when floods deluged the sparse crops that survived seasons of successive drought. When the starved populace perceived their overlords' excesses were to blame, they took to the streets and strung up their leaders, butchering lords and kings like ilaks in a slaughterhouse. What choice did he have?

'Then it must be done. I will take the three-year term.' Without that coin, their lives were forfeited.

'Very well, Your Highness.' The guild master signalled to his men to bring the contract. He amended the time to repay as thirty-six moons, then pushed the parchment towards the king. All the while, the guild master's expression remained calm and even, as though this were routine business. As though Gohran weren't signing over the life of a child.

Solemn, Gohran scrawled his initials across the deed that would further indebt his kingdom, and pressed his seal alongside it. It was done. The coin would be his. He could deliver Ella's aunt her dowry and begin his crusade to restore order.

Yet as he stepped out into the clear blue day, instead of a great weight lifting, thunder rumbled through his limbs, like a storm brewing.

His unease heightened as he and Jarrod neared the docks. They found the others crowded around a circle, peering in its centre to a row of four-legged scaled creatures carrying shells on their backs. The creatures were unlike anything Gohran had seen. Someone had painted symbols on their shells to identify them. The men shouted and jeered as the shelled beasts waddled towards a line drawn across the dirt on one edge of the ring.

'I've a silver on that three-stroke tortoise! Look at him go!'

The critter was leading by the full length of its elongated neck, but then paused near the finish line, peering over at something. It turned and waddled sideways. The crowd roared.

Behind them, a strangely covered barge caught Gohran's attention. Muffled weeping, then a mother wailing. A girl of perhaps four summers was being ushered onto the barge, a chain around her ankles and another yoking her neck. He saw a handful of other such youngsters being rounded up and herded on board, many wearing torn rags, with dirt-crusted skin and hair. Some bore obvious cuts and bruises, visible across the backs of their legs, and peeking through the sleeves of their tunics. He felt as though bugs crawled all over him until a leaden sensation settled in his stomach and chest. For a moment, he couldn't breathe.

'What say you, Your Highness?'

'Hmm?' Tarraen's question drew Gohran back to his surrounds.

'I asked if we were heading out.'

'Let me collect my winnings first,' Ganno said.

'Can you believe Ganno's critter won after all that?'

'I swear Elnora's rays shine on you more than most.'

'Fetch your coin, Gan, and then we'll head out.' Gohran peered past the crowd towards the docks once more. The barge was gone. Perhaps he had only imagined it. 'Jarrod?' Where was his driver?

Jarrod stood apart from the others, eyes squinting in the same direction as Gohran's moments before. He turned, met Gohran's gaze, and swallowed. 'Right when you are, Your Highness.'

Gohran was relieved to leave the trading hub and all its peculiarities behind. But as they reached the open road, he could not rid his mind of those children being transported like herd beasts. He fingered the contract and promissory note tucked beneath his shirt. By every god and demon, what had he just done?

Nineteen

Ella lay sprawled across the wintry scriptorium floor for hours before Amber found her. Her old tutor's arms encircled, rubbing her limbs to warm them.

'Ella, what happened? This room is like a sheet of ice.' Ella drank in that warmth. 'Let's get you near a fire.' Amber slipped an arm under her and helped her stumble to her sleeping cell.

Tucked into her bed, Ella's shivering eased. Amber ignited and stoked a brazier, but the contrast of sudden heat itched, like something crawled along the insides of her arms. She scratched and rubbed.

Amber caught hold of her wrists. 'Your skin is red raw!'

She was right. Welts covered the inside of Ella's forearms where the vellum and dust had inflamed her skin.

'Stop scratching,' Amber said.

Ella stayed her hands, trying to ignore the worsening itch.

'I need to fetch food to restore your strength.'

Ella nodded, but her old tutor seemed so far away, her mind not quite connected to her body. She stared at the bedclothes, hands tucked beneath to keep from scratching, and waited.

When Amber returned, she held two bowls, one for each of them, and a tub of ointment wedged under her elbow. She rested the tub beside Ella's bed. 'Just rub a little onto the rash.' She pointed. 'Now, are you going to tell me what happened back there?'

Shaena and her close companion, Meela, watched Amber leave the refectory, tray in hand, and ointment tucked under her arm. She had gone to hunt for Ella when the princess hadn't arrived for supper.

Shaena rolled her eyes, smirking. 'Poor precious princess needs something to soothe her soft princess hands.'

Meela sniggered.

Breeyan peered their way, and they fell silent, focussing on their meals.

'She says she drifted to sleep while she was working and has no memory of what happened.'

Breeyan's eyes narrowed as Amber relayed her story of finding Ella unconscious in the scriptorium. 'You don't believe her?'

Amber frowned. 'There's something she's not—'

A piercing shriek cut Amber short.

'That's Ella.' Breeyan gasped.

Amber sprinted towards the sleeping quarters.

Breeyan sucked on her teeth, then let out her breath. Wondered again if she should have turned Gohran away instead of taking Ella in. Since arriving, her niece had caused nothing but disruption.

Pain broke across her psyche. Lashed through her mind's barrier like fire. *Ella.*

She hurried after them.

Perched on the bed's edge, Ella's face contorted, her hands splayed awkwardly.

Breeyan helped Amber take Ella's weight and usher her to the washroom.

'Fill the trough with cold water,' she said.

They doused her flesh until the stinging eased—until the shriek of Ella's mind quietened.

'She had just applied the salve I left for her,' Amber said, turning Ella's wrists face-up to examine them. The irritated and inflamed welts had blistered, the surrounding skin flamed a violent red.

Breeyan's throat clogged. 'The ointment. Where did it come from?'

'Felda was busy, so Shaena offered to fetch some from the infirmary.'

Breeyan recalled Shaena and Meela huddled at supper. She shook her head, lips pursed, left Amber with Ella, and went to find the culprits.

Hours passed before the stinging subsided. Amber stayed by Ella's side, and they eased her pain with magic as much as water.

'Why would they do this?' Ella's voice a half-choked sputter.

Amber didn't respond, her arm resting around Ella's shoulders. Ella sensed her struggling to explain the myriad reasons the others resented her.

Ella shrugged her away. 'I need to see Aunt Bree.'

'It can wait until morning, Ella. You should rest.'

She shook her head. '*Now.*'

With a sigh, Amber helped Ella along the winding corridor to Breeyan's study. As they approached the High Priestess's room, they paused. Voices inside. Amber caught Ella's arm, but Ella brushed her off and pushed open the door.

Shaena knelt at Breeyan's feet. The High Priestess's hand rested on her head. A blue line of force emanated from Breeyan and wound around Shaena's psyche. The priestess's face contorted. The force twisted and contracted, and Shaena cried out.

Ella sensed Shaena fighting her aunt, but again, the force constricted. Every muscle tensed as the lightning of Breeyan's strength surged. Power tore at her mind until part of it snapped clean away. Shaena's mouth slackened and her body grew limp. Satisfied, Breeyan released her hold and the line of force faded. Shaena looked up, her gaze chillingly vacant.

Whatever Breeyan had done, it was permanent. What kind of people was she living with? And if these were, as Amber had said, 'people like her', what kind of person was she?

Before Breeyan noticed her, she turned and fled, pushing past Amber and clambering towards the kitchen. With sickening dread, she stuffed a sack full of food and hurried to the library to finish what she started. She grabbed random tomes and tore them from the shelves. Her blisters scorched and oozed.

She blinked away her tears. There must be another way to escape. She abandoned the library and shoved past Amber, who trailed behind.

'Ella, wait!' Amber reached out, but Ella didn't stop.

Breeyan called, 'Leave her. We can't keep her against her will.'

Amber let Ella go and she scrambled to the main corridor.

Outside, rain fell, but Ella barely noticed. She ran to the stables, ignoring her blistered hands, and mounted one of the shorter steeds. With a kick, she urged it east, towards Ycelt, gritting her teeth as the reins bit her raw flesh.

They galloped into the night until her steed wearied. The drizzle had eased, but the ground was still wet. Ella dismounted and searched for somewhere to camp. The few scattered trees bore sparse branches, providing no shelter. She gathered fuel to lay a fire but couldn't keep it alight. The moist wood smoked and smouldered, petering out.

Biting air seeped into her bones as her steed stomped and snorted. Ella offered it food, and ate a little too, but it would not settle in her stomach. More than herself, she wanted to rest her horse, but in the end, gave up, the cold and damp driving them onward.

She let the steed pick its path through the meandering paddocks, always heading away from Aryon. Once or twice, she dozed, jolting awake before she slid from the steed's back. She needed to find shelter, to give her time to think, to plan. Already she suspected she'd travelled too far east; she would reach the outskirts of Erldan if she kept on.

She considered turning around and riding further west, but recalled the stories of endless desolation, of explorers who headed that way and never returned. Aryon was on the edge of civilisation. North wasn't an option either; she might run into someone from the other orders. South was where King Myrhan's people had come from, fleeing for their lives. There was nothing for her there.

She looked up. The moon had ducked behind the clouds again. After a moment, it reappeared, and with it the caw of a raven carried across the night. She followed the sound but instead of a bird, saw a bird-shaped shadow crossing the moon as the clouds transformed. They changed shape once more to form giant shadow-eyes. It must be the cold, the pain, her fatigue, addling her mind. Or perhaps her simulacrum drifted outside her body once more, but Ella swore Gohran's thoughts and eyes were on her. He knew where she was. She felt it in her bones. By the hells, would she never be free of him?

Panicked, Ella turned her steed back around. She nudged him to a gallop, no longer caring if he foundered.

Hoofbeats in the distance. *Gohran!*

'Ella!' It was Amber. 'Ella—wait!' Ella's mount slowed but didn't stop. 'Death will catch you out here. You don't even have a blanket.'

Ella urged her mount onwards. Another step and it stumbled, throwing Ella forward. She landed with a *thwack* on the ground. Every part of her stung, but it was nothing compared to the sharp pain deep in her abdomen.

'Ella!' Amber caught her up. She dismounted, grabbed a pair of blankets from her saddlebags, and wrapped them around her.

Ella saw herself through Amber's eyes, pathetic and shivering. Amber rubbed heat into her arms, letting warmth flow between them.

Another stab. Ella winced.

'What is it? Where are you hurt?'

'The babe...'

'Hush,' Amber soothed, drawing her close.

A second set of hoof beats neared. 'Get me away. Now. Amber, help me. *It's Gohran—!*' Ella gritted her teeth as her womb spasmed.

'It's only Breeyan.'

Her aunt joined them, for once, not hiding her concern behind a mask. She knelt and pressed a hand against Ella's forehead, and the other to her torso.

Soothing warmth flooded. Everything turned hazy, and Ella's muscles relaxed. First, the fire in her hands extinguished and then her womb settled. In her mind, she could feel her baby calm, resting once more, secure in its cocoon. 'Come, let's get you back to safety.'

Ella burst out sobbing, but it was with relief as much as disappointment.

TWENTY

A dark cloud settled over Gohran as they left Halbar, and with it, a sense of foreboding he could not shake. His men's spirits remained high, jesting and singing along tedious stretches of open road, the shadow of the Halbar ranges looming. At least they knew to leave Gohran to his sullen silence. Only Jarrod appeared similarly subdued, as if succumbed to the contagion of his master's mood.

Gohran's uneasiness grew as he led his men through Hai's township towards the river crossing to Rynwood. One of the few points where The Rialdon River was shallow enough to ford year-round, frequent travellers had widened and flattened the river's banks, carving a passage between the ranges. Half-trampled and seasonally drowned vegetation clawed its way along the rock face, grappling to thrive between dirt and stone.

The party crossed without incident, but as they approached the sea of maize and barley surrounding Rynwood proper, lads playing in a fallow field beside the road drew Gohran's attention. The boys kicked a small, sagging object back and forth with flexed feet. As he neared, Gohran discerned the carcass of a grey rat with a long, thin tail. Ice rippled along his vertebrae.

The youngsters paused their game and looked up, nudging and pointing, as Gohran and his men approached.

'Son of a false-godder!' one of them shouted through cupped palms.

Another yelled, 'Witch's spawn!'

Fire scorched Gohran's chest and stomach.

The tallest lad stooped to pick the dead rodent up by the tail. He lobbed it towards them, and it thudded to the nearby dirt.

Gohran's steed reared. He steadied it, signalled to his men to pull up, and dismounted, then strode nearer to the huddled lads.

'Who threw that?' His words growled in his throat.

Awkward shuffling, eyes cast down.

'Who!' He grabbed the lapel of the nearest, an acne-pimpled lad with greasy brown hair and a sprinkling of moustache. Fire roared along his limbs, and he throttled his hands around the lad's neck, teeth gnashing in his face.

'Your Highness!'

A multitude of arms restrained him, voices soothing.

'Please, Your Highness—'

'He's just a boy.'

'Don't do something that can never be undone.'

That final caution penetrated, and his internal fire waned. He loosened his grip, but towered over, glaring.

Older and more experienced than Gohran's other men, Tarraen stepped beside him. 'Come now, lads. Do any of you realise the king might consider your actions treason?'

Colour drained from their pimpled faces, and the boys dropped to their knees.

'Any other lord would have your hands and feet if not your heads for that, but our King Gohran is a forgiving man and knows you meant no insult.' A sideways glance at Gohran.

Their apologies toppled over one another: 'We were just fooling about, Your Highness. No harm intended. I swear it on the light of Elnora.'

The heat subsided, but remnants throbbed through his muscles and core. Tar was right to stay his hand, but how dare these miscreants dishonour him? If his men had not been there...

Gohran addressed the eldest among them. 'What's your name, lad?'

'Stevyn, Your Highness, son of Tygon the silversmith.'

'Well, Stevyn Silversmithson, you and your friends here best make a formal apology to my subjects in your lord's next people's court.'

'Highness,' Tar said under his breath. 'Are you sure that's wise?'

Eyes on the boys, Gohran said, 'If I hear you weren't there, my men will be back, and you'll be making your case in my court for why you shouldn't be charged with treason.'

They left the lads slinking to their homes and resumed their journey. The sooner Gohran collected his loan, the sooner he could stamp out the recalcitrant element under his dominion.

By the time they approached Rynwood, Gohran's outrage settled into his bones. He had not planned to stop, but as they neared the portcullis, Jarrod took him aside, his voice low.

'Your Highness, I think it wise to take shelter behind city gates tonight.'

Maybe Jarrod was right. He was in no mood to entertain sycophants, but his disquiet intensified following the sour encounter with those lads. At least Kerr would no longer pursue him like a hound after a bone, seeking Ella's hand.

Unannounced, he directed his men to Kerr's barracks while he imposed upon the lord's hospitality.

Lord Kerr's sister, Lady Layla, greeted him in the parlour, wearing her usual widow's cowl over her dull yellow hair. His unexpected arrival meant she had not even rouged her cheeks.

Layla curtsied. 'Always a pleasure to have you call, Your Highness.'

Gohran acknowledged her greeting with a nod, then scanned the room. Servants scrambled to ignite wall sconces and candelabras as Elnora's light faded beyond garish, peacock-coloured curtains.

'I was expecting your brother?'

'Kerr is in Creywmm, Your Highness.' Layla appeared flustered, fussing at her cowl and the loose waist of her modest day dress, a stark contrast to her usual figure-hugging attire.

'Oh?'

'Yes, Your Highness, for Lord Sheevan's betrothal...' Her voice trailed off, cheeks blanching.

Gohran sucked in his breath. 'Betrothed to whom?'

Layla swallowed. 'My apologies, Your Highness. I assumed you knew. Lord Sheevan is to wed the Princess Elder of Herron.'

Gohran swore. 'After defiling my sister, King Sardin would deem that lordling worthy of his eldest?'

Layla's hand inched across her chest, as though to put something, anything, between her breast and the king. 'The decisions men make are beyond my comprehension, Your Highness. Come, let us take some refreshment.' She invited him to sit on a gold-winged settee and waved a servant over.

Gohran forced his breath steady. Did his sister's honour mean nothing?

Someone must have served mead, for the next Gohran knew he was staring into an amber-filled goblet. Through the swirling liquid, he pictured the young lord sitting opposite his betrothed, and beside King Sardin, that arrogant sod. Grey-bearded and gruff, a faded echo of the handsome prince he'd once been.

The image altered, and he envisaged his last interactions with Sheevan's father, Lord Samwwl, refusing to pay a copper to maintain Jaydyn's child. Gohran relished Samwwl experiencing the weight of his displeasure. But afterwards, Samwwl broke with Erldan, seeking direct fealty to the High King in Galliarn, an ugly precedent for the surrounding villages, who paid their taxes to Erldan.

Samwwl could have changed allegiance more readily to their neighbouring king, Sardin of Herron. But allying with the High King now made sense, strengthening the appeal of a marriage to Lord Sheevan. And wedding his son to a princess of Herron, Samwwl established a financial and military stronghold between all three provinces, while reuniting Herron with the High Realm.

A sudden chill. He swigged his mead to erase the image, wiped his mouth on his sleeve, and swore again.

'Your Highness?'

'My thanks for your hospitality, my lady. I'd best retire. Travel has made me weary. Have my supper brought to my chamber.' Gohran stood and strode towards the door.

Layla set her drink down and trailed after.

At the doorway, Gohran paused. 'When Kerr returns, please inform him of my visit. With my youngest sister passing, I had hoped to discuss Princess Jaydyn's betrothal.'

'Princess Ella? Are you saying she's passed to the Afterworld? Oh! Your Highness, my deepest condolences.' Layla squeezed his arm, her flesh pressing against him. When Gohran flinched, she stepped back. 'The pain of losing a loved one... Tragic.'

'Tell your brother, if Jaydyn's daughter deters him, I may have a path around that.'

Layla looked puzzled, but Gohran ignored her.

'Good eve, and farewell, my lady. I will be out from underfoot at first light.'

That night, Gohran dreamed he marched through Erldan's streets. Each step crumbled the paving as gravel gave way, and the ground buckled beneath his feet. A cold, grey damp soaked into exposed dirt and left a moist film across every rooftop, wagon, and carriage. Oppressive smoke-filled fog pressed in around them. Tattered peasants crowded, shouting with stained and gap-toothed mouths, their stale breath puffing curses through the putrid air.

False-godder! Son-of-a-witch! Demon-spawn!

The mob hurled rodent carcasses, animal remains, and finally the half-rotting stiffened corpse of a stillborn child, each landing with a sickening thud.

Amid the horde, King Sardin of Herron sneered, one arm resting on Shee-van's shoulder, the other patting Lord Samwwl's back.

The peasants neared, their miasma clinging, arms waving, spittle flying, while the king and lords laughed, pointed, jeered.

He tried to shout, to flee, but his legs remained anchored in place, limbs and torso paralysed.

Then, in the distance, a familiar call: Ella.

His dream body turned towards the sound. Ella sat robed and on horseback. Beneath her hood, moonlight revealed the glistening sheen of wet cheeks.

A fire-ache twisted in his core, radiating through his limbs.

Pain pierced her like shattered glass, hot and raw as her bitter determination thundered through him, so much stronger than the yearning for freedom he sensed from her now and then. She was trying to escape. He was sure of it.

A raven cawed, and he faced the angry mob, his fire-ache steeling, mounting, throbbing. Freed from his paralysis, he stood erect, arms raised, and thrust his palms forward, to topple them like game pieces with his will alone. They scrambled as if his phantom blow landed, and his chortle followed them.

Another caw broke through his dream, and he woke, covered in sweat, Ella's name upon his lips.

He ripped off his drenched bedclothes and gripped the nearby wash basin. Unchanged from the previous day, its cold, soap-scum coated water goaded him. His stomach churned, and he hurled the bowl against the wall. It smashed, streaking a tapestry and soaking the carpet, now peppered with jagged-edged ceramic fragments.

A startled and bleary-eyed servant entered. 'Your Highness?'

'You!' Gohran grabbed the lad's shirt front and smacked him across the face. The boy cried out. Gohran shoved him towards the floor. 'Clean this up.'

The crawling servant resembled Gohran's dream populace, clambering away from him. The lad wiped his nose, smearing blood on his sleeve.

An exhilarating thrill surged like a static charge amid a storm. He could bask in that sensation forever.

He wrenched himself back. 'Once you're done, fetch a courier.' He must speak to Venn with all haste.

He would send his men home while he and Jarrod journeyed to Nedran via Rassit. With his neighbours forging potent alliances, he needed to solidify his own. If Ella felt tempted to return to Ycelt, he would make certain she had nothing to return to.

PART TWO: RESISTANCE

THE KINGDOM OF ERLDAN, YCELT

Summer 797 A.S.

Twenty-One

D awn. Ella woke in an unfamiliar bed, her arms and wrists swaddled. Eucalyptus clung to the air, stale and oppressive above the smoke from the burning hearth. Beside hers, three companion beds lay stripped of linens, while across the room sat a pair of wicker baskets used for transporting laundry.

She propped herself upright, avoiding her scattered bruises, and swung her feet over the bed's edge. Someone had dressed her in a fresh robe and shoved moon-time rags between her thighs, though she stopped bleeding the moment Breeyan laid her hands upon her.

The letter!

She scanned the room for the lost parchment, in case it had fallen loose when they stripped her. Then, leveraging her elbows, she stood and shuffled towards the baskets on wobbly legs, using the empty beds for support.

She ignored the first basket, which contained clean and folded linens, and reached into the second, the one that housed soiled laundry. Wincing, she rifled through it, gripping garments between bandaged hands. She lifted, shook, and tossed each item on the floor until she located her bloodied robe, but there was no sign of the letter. An omen-shiver wriggled along her spine.

'Are you looking for something?'

Ella turned.

Her aunt stood in the doorway. 'Something like this?' A scroll rested on Breeyan's upward-facing palm. Ella dropped her soiled vestment back into the basket.

'Reckless! Selfish!' Breeyan's face appeared shadowed in the windowless chamber. 'Don't you see? Your message puts us all at risk.'

The room spun, closing in.

'Thank the gods your brother has some sense at least.' Breeyan handed Ella the scroll.

She unfurled the worn and thin parchment. Not her letter to Venn.

Colwani of the High Order at Crescent Mountain sends greetings to Her Holiness of Aryon. News of great import has reached our borderland. It is with sincere condolences and genuine sadness that I write of the passing of Her Holiness's niece, Princess Ella of Erldan...

Breeyan's hand rested leaden on her shoulder while Venn's words echoed in her mind. *Beyond. Where She took you.* Ella sank to her knees. Of course. How utterly vindictive of her brother. No one would think of searching for a dead person.

Ella's aunt hovered, and she tugged her emotions back in.

The corners of Breeyan's mouth curved. 'Come. Sit up. We need to change those dressings.'

Breeyan urged Ella to her feet and sat her on the bed. She fetched a bowl of herb-infused water and rested it in Ella's lap. Pungent eucalyptus stung her nostrils. Her aunt unpeeled the bandages. Beneath, blisters wept and oozed. She dipped Ella's arms into the cooled liquid and Ella sucked air in through her teeth.

Breeyan's grip tightened. 'I need you to relax. I can't help you if you fight me.'

Rough and determined, her aunt's power shoved against her barriers, until finally, she broke through. Relief came in waves as numbness seeped into Ella's hands and forearms, creeping its way along her shoulders and down her back. Her muscles weakened like porridge, and she slumped, eyelids drooping, head swimming.

Breeyan let go, and pain pierced her. Ella bolted upright, almost spilling the water. Her aunt clasped her again, and the soothing returned, this time just enough to blunt the fiery outer edges. Ella had no choice but to accept the offering in whatever measure Breeyan saw fit to give.

Breeyan's eyes narrowed as she upped the dosage of her power. Ella sank back, calm. 'Good. Good.' Breeyan smiled, but it was cold and hard. 'You can trust me, Ella. More than you realise, we are alike.'

Ella pictured Breeyan's hands upon Shaena, the whip-like fire of her mind's ministrations as she tore and severed, and Shaena's stare afterwards, chillingly vacant. She shook her head back and forth. They were nothing alike.

A weight sank across Breeyan's chest as she left her niece to convalesce and retreated to her private study. Itching, gnawing, Ella's defiant gaze was a haunting echo of Prya's.

When Ella arrived at Aryon, Breeyan avoided asking too many questions. Hadn't wanted to push. But she drove her niece further from trusting her, nonetheless. Given the malice she witnessed in her priestesses, was Ella's distrust justified?

She hated resorting to such severe and absolute discipline, but she could not tolerate cruelty in her order. Why they took to Ella with such spite was beyond her. The sisters had not treated her so malignly upon her arrival at Aryon, though their circumstances were much the same.

Another enigma was Ella's power. Prya boasted of her daughter's incredible raw strength. Breeyan sensed Ella's potential churning, but observed her struggling to draw and transform her source. When Breeyan opened her god-sight, she noticed Ella's aura weakened and scarred. Perhaps from the loss of her mother, perhaps something more.

Recalling her sister's terrible death picked at that old scab, making it bleed anew. To think she begrudged her sister her freedom. Prya had never been free.

The gods handed Prya everything Breeyan wanted. King Rohan, a kingdom, a family, while Breeyan's role as matriarch within an order of exiled priestesses was being presented with a gosling when you were owed a pheasant. But in the end, it was Rohan and then Gohran who held the genuine power. What little reward the gods gifted Prya, the freedom she experienced she paid for with her life. At least Breeyan ruled Aryon in her own right. There were no men here to control her fate.

She longed for Ella to experience that freedom. But when she examined her niece, she sensed that a part of Ella feared her magic. Another part despised it.

Curse Elnora's priests, spreading their poisonous lies. Amber's schooling should have gone some way to countering those beliefs. But then Ella witnessed her mother's denouncement and murder for her gifts. And now this disturbance had driven her further away from her power, from her sisters, and from her.

In time, she hoped that, like her, Ella would appreciate the freedom a life at Aryon afforded. Would recognise she was safe here and embrace her power's blessing.

Breeyan wished there was someone she could contact in Ycelt to find out what happened. Wanted to be certain no one would come looking for Ella. That Lord Venn would not employ his large army and hunt his mistress down. The dryhten might not be pious, but he ought to fear the Curse. However, he may not realise Aryon was a haven for sworn priestesses, and she needed to know if her niece tried to run away again that she had nothing and no one to run to.

Once, her sister would have kept her informed, but now she depended on the titbits of news from refugees or the other orders—gossip, no more, and almost no reports from the southern provinces.

Her reluctant scrying of her lost son revealed little. Despite dismissing the council's concerns over the dryhten, Gohran may have brought Ella here for his safety rather than hers.

'Your Holiness?' Shira interrupted her musings. 'I found those parchments you asked about...'

Steady and obedient, Shira perched before her, awaiting instruction. Breeyan motioned for her to bring them over.

She had delayed apprenticing a priestess for as long as possible. When it seemed Ella may never arrive, she took on Shira, a sound choice with her reliable magic. Breeyan counted on her loyalty, but wished she was sharper, that she had some sting to her.

Though Ella's power appeared less potent than Breeyan hoped, a volatile current writhed beneath. With the right provocation, her niece could bite. Shira might be her apprentice, but she had not named her successor.

Shira pushed a parchment across her oversized desk, pointing to a passage in elaborate calligraphy. 'Here, Your Holiness, this scholar refers to energy wastage and fatigue in gestation...'

Breeyan snatched up the parchment and squinted until the letters came into focus. She thought back. Had her pregnancy impaired her magic? She recalled it fatiguing her body. But the forbidden and intoxicating thrill of seducing King Rohan energised her, and then fuelled the negotiations that followed.

She continued to read: *Innate source is diminished only to the degree required by the gestation...* Was this scholar saying the level of diminishment depended on the strength of the babe's latent powers?

Breeyan wondered about Ella's babe's father. Lord Venn of Nedran wielded no power, but if the child was as powerful as Ella was supposed to be, strong enough to diminish her magic...

'Is the new novice to birth her child at Aryon, Your Holiness?' Shira asked, disrupting her thoughts.

Breeyan nodded. 'It is as I agreed when we took her in.' No midwife. No chirurgeon. Only Felda, the order's so-called medic, trained in basic herb-craft, and what sparse knowledge the priestesses mustered between them.

Shira swallowed, looking as nervous as Breeyan felt. She pursed her lips as if she wanted to speak but let out a breath and remained silent—precisely why Breeyan chose her.

'We must study all we can and prepare. Ella and the babe's life are in our hands.'

Meanwhile, she would locate her family's genealogy map. See if she could uncover why Ella's unborn child would be strong enough to weaken its mother to that extent. Perhaps some magic lurked in Lord Venn's ancestry she wasn't aware of. Or perhaps the father was another of her niece's acquaintances.

Regardless, she hoped Ella's power would restore once the babe was born.

'I never realised our sisters could be so nasty,' Amber said as she braided Nykki's hair that morning. It seemed an eternity since they shared an intimate moment. *I can't blame Ella for trying to run away.* That last thought she slipped silently into her beloved's mind. She didn't add she was more disturbed by the cruel retaliation of the High Priestess. 'I wish I knew what to do.'

'Me too,' *my love*, Nykki replied, her endearment silent.

'Thank you for being kinder to her. I'm glad she has someone.'

'No need to thank me. I've rather warmed to her.' The corners of Nykki's mouth curved, eyes wistful.

Amber's heart skipped. Their relationship felt strained since Ella's arrival. When she wasn't watching over Ella, Breeyan had her running so many errands, and she scarcely saw Nykki alone.

She shoved her uncomfortable suspicion aside and continued to weave the strands of Nykki's hair. The backs of her fingers lingered at her beloved's nape, sliding down her back between her shoulder blades as she savoured their meagre time together.

She sensed Nykki responding, a twinge in the small of her abdomen. A twist of longing. An ache. She drew the ritual out until the bell rang, and they had to scramble to the dawn homage.

Twenty-Two

Once Jonas heard Gohran was on his way to Nedran, he packed his saddlebags and headed to the stables. He had no desire to encounter the king, and now that Venn had resumed his duties as dryhten, he could leave in good conscience.

But as he was tying off the last of his packs, Venn called, 'Please—stay.' His brother's bovine eyes entreated. 'Until I find out what he wants.'

Venn had never begged him for anything. Jonas sighed. 'Very well. But help me untie these, will you? I just got them fastened.'

When Gohran strode into Nedran's foyer that afternoon, Jonas had joined his siblings to welcome him. Venn had stood motionless, while Lynden fussed at the low-cut dress she'd slipped on the moment the king's courier arrived. She'd kohled her eyes and painted her lips, too. Jonas rolled his eyes towards the gods.

The king's heavy steps neared, and Gohran lobbed his cape to a nearby servant, greeting the trio with a toss of dark hair. Jonas couldn't help but see an echo of Ella. Gohran's eyes were the same shade and shape, framed by long, black lashes, and there was a similarity in the bone structure of their faces. Apart from their looks, the siblings were nothing alike. Where Ella had been warm and alluring, Gohran was cold and determined.

Gohran clasped Venn's arms as if nothing had soured between them. Jonas's gut sank when Venn perked up in response, as though sunlight warmed his brother's veins.

Before the king could address Jonas, Lynden stepped forward and curtsied. 'It's good to see you again, Your Highness.'

The corners of Gohran's mouth curled as he captured Lyn's hand in his. His lips lingered on her fingers, displaying a kind of charm Jonas wouldn't have imagined possible. Is that what Vera described?

'My heart goes out to you and your sisters, Your Highness. We feel the loss of the princess every day.'

Gohran stiffened. 'My thanks, Lady Lynden.' The king's voice was tight, more like the man Jonas remembered.

Gohran turned his way, and Jonas steeled himself. He owed it to Ella's memory to confront her brother. His treatment forced her to flee to Nedran and the safety of Venn's arms—his bed—and an early grave. He also owed it to Venn to stay his hand and tongue. These past weeks, overseeing Nedran while Venn mourned, exposed the disarray their ongoing instability caused. Nedran might not withstand another round of turbulence between their provinces.

'Your Highness.' His flourishing bow was almost parody.

Gohran's eyebrow twitched as he acknowledged the gesture with a slight nod.

'Come, let's get you settled in, Your Highness.' Lynden linked Gohran's elbow in hers, as though he were a familial guest and not a ruling monarch. 'You must be weary from your travels.'

Jonas perched his forearm on Venn's shoulder as they watched Lyn lead Gohran upstairs. He leaned in and whispered, 'You will let me know when my presence is no longer required, won't you?'

Gohran pushed the parchment forward. 'Amended, as we agreed. A year and a day to mark her passing. We can be true brothers under the law.'

Seated in his study, Venn hesitated, quill in hand, as wind whistled through the corridors.

'There is no shame in this. You are a great lord. A dryhten. Don't let your city and your people decay for the sake of misplaced pride.'

Venn flinched. It wasn't a matter of pride. Signing that contract was placing the final rock upon her cairn. Though Jonas urged him to stop visiting Ella's grave, he sensed her still, ached for her, and in weaker moments, thought about joining her in the Afterworld. At times, his father's memory was the only thing keeping him rooted in this world. He would not shame his legacy by abandoning his post and his people.

Gohran's hand rested on his shoulder. Reassurance came in waves, as soothing as Ella's touch had once been, and the tension eased from his shoulders and jaw.

A lucid thought slipped into his mind: *This contract will be the first step towards recovering your old life, to moving on.* He could have sworn the words belonged to Gohran, yet the king's lips remained sealed in a downward curve. He had spent too long pining after Ella, imagining conversing with her spirit. Imagining voices.

Whatever its source, the words resonated. He needed to move forward with his life. For himself, and for Nedran. This alliance with Erldan was crucial. His merchants' angst was spilling onto the everyday dealings of his people, while the fallout between Creywmm and Erldan had clawed its way into neighbouring Herron and the High Realm.

With Erldan and Nedran sealed as allies, Nedran's robust hallit trade and large army would keep the villages loyal to Erldan, to Gohran. Meanwhile, greater political stability would enable his merchants to settle into the more mundane concerns that allowed their commerce to prosper.

Gohran patted his back. 'This is the right thing.'

He gripped the quill and signed, feeling strangely weightless.

Afterwards, Gohran suggested they spend the afternoon sparring. 'You need to get in shape, especially if you are to be my champion and defender.'

'That I do.' Venn's reputation as a swordsman was as much from hard work and determination as natural skill, and it had been many moons since he trained.

The pair headed to the open square of the courtyard beside the water garden—perfect for confined sparring. Time had worn cracks between the uneven pavers, a test of their footing, while large planters around the border tried their agility. An oversized ceramic pot against one wall held a handful of practice weapons and some light armour.

'Blunted swords or sticks?' Gohran asked.

'Best we start with sticks until I see how I fare.' Venn picked up a pair of wooden poles.

'No armour, then.' Gohran stripped down to his loose undershirt and trousers.

Venn did likewise, tossing Gohran a stick.

Gohran's stance was wide and firm as he assumed a fighting crouch, while Venn's stayed looser and lighter. Poles raised, they circled. Gohran made the first move, lunging forward. His strike was vigorous, but Venn side-stepped it with ease, then retaliated with a high strike of his own. Gohran didn't manoeuvre out of the way. Instead, he focussed on deflecting the blow.

The rhythm was familiar, an awkward dance. Venn, graceful, agile; Gohran, blunt, hostile. Unfit as he was, Venn's reactions remained quick. Gohran did not share his speed, but anticipated Venn's moves and repelled each strike fiercely. He struck again, hard. Too hard. Venn slipped out from beneath him, exposing Gohran's right side. Venn sliced in and up, resting the end of his pole high on Gohran's chest, at the gully of his throat.

'I call game,' he shouted, breathless.

'Curse it!' Gohran dropped his weapon and stepped back, panting. 'One day I will best you,' he breathed, wiping his sweaty brow with a sleeve.

'It had better not be with a real blade if you do. By Our Lady, you hit hard!' Venn said, peeling off his shirt to wipe his face.

Gohran smirked. His shirt clung with sweat, but he did not remove it.

'Let's get some supper,' Venn said, as his hunger awakened for the first time in months.

Twenty-Three

'We have an announcement to make,' Gohran said at supper, and the table fell silent. 'At the completion of his mourning, Lord Venn shall wed Princess Raeyn of Erldan.'

Jonas swore under his breath. He understood wanting to smooth relations between their provinces, but for the king to leverage his sister like this... He refrained from swearing again.

Poor Raeyn. It would not be a love match. She would exist in the shadow of her dead sister. *As he would have lived in Venn's had Ella eloped with him.* At least if he'd got Ella away, she might be alive.

They were raising their glasses. Jonas reached his forwards, barely discerning the *chink* of his neighbour's drink, then downed its contents, and signalled for a refill.

'Here's to a long and prosperous future as brothers under the law,' Gohran said.

'Brothers-in-law,' Venn echoed.

'I'm so pleased for you both!' Lynden squeezed Venn's arm, and then Gohran's, masking any disappointment, the slight tautening of the muscles around her lips, her only tell.

'And now you can give Nedran the surety of *legitimate* heirs, my lord.' Gohran spoke to Venn, but his hard eyes fell on Jonas, watching, watching.

Jonas kept his expression neutral as if betting his life on a game of tiles. He fixed his attention on his roasted fowl wrapped in pastry, washing it down with copious mouthfuls of wine, until he wasn't sure if his stomach churned from over-indulgence or seeing Gohran fawn over his brother, while Lynden fawned over the king.

Jonas woke before dawn, grabbed his still-packed saddlebags, and tiptoed down the grey corridor. Behind him, a door creaked open and then clicked shut. He turned to see Gohran leaving Lynden's room, his shirt loose as he held his trousers in place with one hand. The other smoothed his tousled hair.

'You were right not to trust your sister with a hot-blooded male,' Gohran smirked.

Jonas dropped his bags and faced the king. It was a good thing his sword wasn't within reach, or he might have drawn it. 'Ella may have taken to Venn's bed before he pinned a betrothal brooch to her dress, but that was only after she fled here to get away from you, *Your Highness*,' Jonas spat the king's title.

Gohran's face flushed scarlet. 'It was you who laid your filthy paws on her first. She would still be here if it wasn't for you.'

Jonas sneered. 'If that's what you choose to believe. But it wasn't my doing that put her in that grave.' He stepped nearer, his broad torso casting a shadow over the king. 'Your sister left my arms with her maidenhead intact—despite my best efforts to convince her otherwise, I'm not ashamed to admit. If there is some crime in following one's natural desires, one's instincts, then let the wardens arrest me.' He held out his wrists, palms facing the sky in mock surrender. 'Clearly you think not, given you've succumbed to yours.'

The king seized his wrist before Jonas could retreat. Gohran caught and held his gaze, and he had the strangest sense the king was trying to mesmerise him the way a shaman in the marketplace entrances unsuspecting clients for coppers.

Jonas snatched his hands away. He needed to get on the road before he did something he regretted. 'Don't let me keep you from your rest after such a tiring night, *Your Highness*.'

Jonas fumed the entire journey to the stables. Wished Venn had not asked him to stay, so he didn't have to witness this charade. The king's hypocrisy was riling. Before Venn could convince him to stay longer, he left word of his departure with Mykan, and rode out the moment the guards opened the city gates.

Though tempted to ride to Rassit, Leesa was adamant Jonas kept away. And where Vera always welcomed him at Lichen, the idea of taking to her bed while trying to mourn sat like an overfull goblet on an unsteady table. Even disappearing into the bustle of a township offered no comfort. He needed quiet, removed from the yoke of others' desires, their expectations, and so he headed west.

Riding this way made him uneasy. The landscape became increasingly arid, the trees more misshapen, and the air drier, while those he passed ignored him unnervingly. Usually when he travelled, locals eyed him as curiously as he observed them, but out here, people didn't want to notice him.

By mid-afternoon, the surrounding vegetation grew sparse. Jonas loped towards a scatter of unnamed villages and the makeshift camps of semi-nomadic pastoralists he'd stumbled upon years earlier. Where Lynden wore their mother's disappearance like a cage, Jonas refused to let fear bind him, sneaking out to explore townships and wilderness alike.

These villagers living on the periphery of civilisation fascinated him. An odd collective of unfortunates, misfits, and loners, who foraged seasonally to supplement their meagre crops, herding beasts and flocks to wherever feed thrived.

One villager he counted on to shelter him was Tymot, a widower who loved company but distrusted authority. Settled far enough from every major town and village to keep to himself, Tymot had no ties of note, so Jonas could lick his wounds without scrutiny.

Tymot once explained the villagers' lack of curiosity over a skinful of mead. 'These folk don't want to be seen,' he said. 'And if they don't notice you, you're less likely to scrutinise them.'

Invisibility came as a relief as Jonas pulled up outside Tymot's farmstead, dismounted, and tethered his steed.

'Ty?' he called, ducking his head through the low door. Inside the cool circular mud-brick building, straw and clay filled Jonas's nostrils, along with the distinctive odour of beasts, fowl, and swine that clung to every farm he'd ever visited.

Still high above them, Elnora's light barely penetrated the wedge-shaped room. Jonas rapped his knuckles on an exposed beam and called out again.

A clamour from behind a cloth partition, followed by a grunt.

'Ty? Is that you, groaning like an ox back there?'

Another grunt, and then a snort. 'Can't a man have some peace?'

The musty tang of stale shrillan clung to the walls. 'Are you still smoking from that rusted old pipe?' Most provinces outlawed the herb, but folklore of the Ancients maintained the covert tradition. 'Get out of bed and join me for some ale. I've a trinket for you.' He moved further in, leaving the door ajar to let in some light.

More shuffling, and then clomping from behind the curtain.

Jonas loosened the tie on a saddlebag and rifled for a spherical glass bowl with a mouthpiece and spout. He set it atop the nearby bench and searched for a chair or stool.

Finally, a bleary-eyed Tymot pushed the curtains aside. 'Oh, it's you.'

'That might just be the warmest welcome you've ever offered,' Jonas said.

'Ha!' Tymot scratched his unkempt beard.

'That's for you.' He motioned toward the smoke-bowl. 'Now you can stop shredding your lungs with that old rusty contraption.' Copper rot was common among peasants who couldn't afford glass pipes.

'Generous for a younger lordling, aren't you?' Tymot rubbed the pipe between callused hands.

'It's easy to give away someone else's coin. Though this didn't come from my purse. It's a gift from our good friend, Alina.'

Tymot nodded. 'She wants another supply of shrillan, I suppose.'

'I don't ask after her business, and she doesn't offer,' Jonas said.

Shrillan only grew on the outskirts of the desert, but more importantly, would only be grown beyond the watchful eye of town wardens. Out here, Ty could grow, harvest, and smoke dried shrillan leaves as often as he cared to. And now it seemed, supply them to clandestine markets.

Jonas didn't get involved in such matters. He figured citizens could take their own risks. After all, shrillan caused less harm than the opium smuggled from Myan.

Priests warned of shrillan-induced visions that drove men mad, but Jonas surmised they were half-mad to begin with. More likely, laws forbidding shrillan derived from its use in arcane rituals by so-called witches and sorcerers.

'Shall we head outside where it's light?' Jonas did not care to sit on the grotty straw inside.

Once Ty got smoking, he plied Jonas with ale and stuffed his ears full of wild theories and suspicions about priests and their henads working to undermine temporal rule. Once Jonas had his fill, he faded out Ty's gloomy prattle and sank into his own dark thoughts.

Twenty-Four

Sun baked their backs as Jonas helped Ty plant beans, beets, and carrots in their communal plot. Villagers tended fields alongside them, pulling weeds, watering, and mulching with pea straw. Further west, not even these kinds of crops would grow. It felt good to disappear for a time. Experience the burn of labouring muscles, smell tilled soil and open air, with no one expecting anything of him.

Jonas straightened to arch the creaks from his back and surveyed his surroundings, his hand shading his view. A trio of ravens circled above. He turned towards the sound of a distant wail.

A mother wearing a tattered dress and matted braids led three small children—two lasses and a lad—hobbling by some villagers. Jonas winced at their hollow eyes and sunken cheeks. The woman's extended palms begged, pleaded, but every person they passed turned aside or shuffled on, some signing to ward against witchcraft.

Just beyond the last villagers, the boy collapsed. The mother stooped to pick him up, crying for help.

'By every demon!' Jonas tossed down his hoe, stepped over the row they planted, and towards the fallen child.

Tymot gripped his arm. 'Leave them.'

Jonas shrugged him off, glaring. 'They need help! We should—'

'I said, leave them.' Jonas had never heard Ty so grim. 'See that disc graved with an "X" around the lad's neck? When you see that mark, you stay well away. Trust me. Cursed—the lot of them.'

'You can't be in earnest.'

'If you help them, you're consigning yourself to an early grave.'

Jonas wondered if the shrillan made his old friend paranoid. 'If I don't help them, I'm consigning myself to the torment of a wronged conscience.'

'Your conscience won't be nagging for long if someone reports you to the henads.'

'Curse it!' Jonas sank back on his heels. 'Would someone do that?'

'It would surprise me if they didn't.' Tymot patted Jonas's shoulder. 'Come, lad. The gods know you mean well, but it's better not to take risks in these troubling times.'

'I don't give a copper what the gods think. I won't stand by and do nothing.'

'Be it on your head. But wait until the cover of nightfall, will you? Then there's at least a chance you'll go unseen.'

But by night, it was too late. The woman and her children had moved on.

'**H**elp me fit these onto the pannier.' Breeyan signalled Ella to grab the other end of her bundle.

After weeks in the infirmary with only Amber, and sometimes Nykki, to keep Ella company, her aunt released her.

'Meet me in the stables,' Breeyan said. 'I've received word a party of refugees is arriving, and we need to deliver them supplies.'

Refugees from what? 'How do they know about Aryon?'

'The way our family knew.'

Whispers passed from mother to child. Ella helped heft sacks into the basket one at a time, wincing, her burns still tender. With the pannier loaded, Breeyan untethered the beast and led them outside.

Elnora's rays brightened the cloudless sky, and Ella raised her hand to shield her view. 'Are we not riding?'

'Not in your condition.'

They walked, Ella's laboured breathing settling between them, until they spotted a copse of shrubs and trees. Ella recognised the northern grove from the scriptorium's map. Once part of the order's defences, the former lookout post had functioned as a fortress rather than a refuge.

Breeyan retrieved some scrunched fabric from a basket and handed it to Ella. 'Put this on.'

Ella shook it out—the dress Amber wore at Erldan, with the side seams let out. Its bodice hugged her swollen breasts, with room to expand into the ample waist and skirt. Breeyan stowed her robe in the pannier, and they continued towards the grove, picking their footing through oversized trees until they reached a fire pit surrounded by flat-topped stones—chairs and a table.

'Help me tether the pack beast. Then I'll light a guiding fire,' Breeyan said.

The blaze was long established when the figures approached—straggly, emaciated sticks. A woman led two small children with jutting bones whose hollow eyes were too big for their sunken faces. The mother wailed, a horrid, rusty sound. She sank to her knees and brought a coin-sized metallic disc that hung from a chain circling her neck to her lips. It glowed, and her weeping intensified. The youngsters clung to their mother's skirts, watching warily.

Breeyan ushered them to the fire and helped them eat and drink while Ella shifted awkwardly, unsure what to do, or where to look.

Breeyan poured water into a wooden cup and offered it around. 'I expected another of you.'

'Weeks it has taken, Your Worship. Weeks. No one would help. Not one person!' She wiped her nose on her sleeve.

'You should have left this behind.' Breeyan pointed to the disc graved with an 'X'.

The woman shook her head. 'Never. He showed us the way. If we'd abandoned His mark... Never.'

Breeyan examined them with narrowed eyes. 'Your son?'

'Kahl. My poor Kahllee...' The woman's voice broke, and she clutched her two living children, one snivelling, the other owl-eyed and silent.

'He was the blessed.' It was a statement. Breeyan extinguished the fire now the refugees had found them. 'I am sorry.'

Another wail.

'Hush!' *I hear something.* Breeyan held up a hand for silence.

Ella reached out her mind, but Breeyan had sucked the remaining heat from the fire's coals. She followed her aunt's gaze in the direction the refugees had arrived, and tried to sense something, anything, but her mind and ears met with quiet.

'Were you followed?' Breeyan asked.

'No, Your Worship, I swear it.'

'Camp here tonight. We shall watch over you. At first light, take these supplies and travel north, then west past the desert. Make sure you avoid Henctyn. The food should last until you reach the Gern.'

'Kahl promised you would look after us.'

'You won't be safe at Aryon. People know you travelled this way, carrying the mark of Xenon. Leave the mark with me. We will ensure any trackers find it south of here.'

Eyes wide, children close, the woman nodded.

'It worsens all the time,' Breeyan said to Ella later across the dark. 'Once the villagers would have helped that family, Xenon's mark, or no. But now...'

Images rushed behind her eyes, of henads dragging women and children through the streets, some caged like animals, the horrid cacophony of desperate grief, knowing what was to come. Like the trial Ella witnessed at Erldan, once accused, no one could intervene.

'This is Gohran's doing, isn't it?' The rest of the letter Breeyan showed her contained news of a further three Cleansings and recruitment of additional henads across Greater Erldan.

Breeyan's eyes narrowed, but she remained silent.

Ella struggled to sleep. Stones and twigs jutted through her sleeping mat, poking her awake. Worse was the whimpering that broke over the darkness in waves. When morning came, Ella was relieved to see the refugees go.

Having imposed on Ty's hospitality long enough, Jonas rode out at first light. The villagers ignoring that poor woman and her children soured his sojourn, and he needed to get away.

For a time, he wandered west, curious if he would catch them, far from prying eyes. The sun scorched, and he removed his sweat-soaked shirt to wipe his temples and hairline. The only clean shirt left in his pack was his father's—the one Ella helped him mend. He couldn't face wearing it, so draped the damp one back over his shoulders and continued riding.

Rhythmic cicadas thrummed. Across the horizon, an illusory haze shimmered like running water as he neared the desert's edge. Settlers aptly named this wasteland the End of the World.

A cry. He squinted and looked up. Ravens circled to the south. Another few cawed and joined them, circling and diving, then circling once more. Likely, an animal had met its fate up ahead. As more carrion birds joined the procession, Jonas felt queasy.

He steered north, away from the commotion, then hesitated. Curiosity nagged. Perhaps he could ride south far enough to discover what excited the birds before moving on.

Approaching their frantic activity, he slowed. Something child-sized lay unmoving. *Please let them be sleeping*, he thought.

Birds scattered and squawked, and the now unhampered view confirmed his fears. 'Ah, curse it!' Not sleeping, but lifeless, the abandoned boy lay half-covered by a worn blanket, which the birds had pecked, waiting for his decay to ripen. 'Poor lad.'

Someone, presumably the child's mother, had crossed his arms over his chest. A wreath of twined grass lay on the ground nearby, no doubt tossed from the body by the impatient birds. Jonas couldn't dig the lad a grave without heading back to borrow a shovel from Ty, and he didn't trust himself not to let every one of those villagers feel his condemnation.

A distant wail to the south. He squinted. Was that smoke coming from a copse? He shook his head. Another heat-haze illusion. He was becoming as paranoid as old Ty! The boy's family would have veered north by now—no one could survive south of here.

Jonas crouched and patted the grey-tinged body as though the boy were still alive to receive it. 'Apologies, lad. May you have a better fate in the Afterworld.' Jonas stood and dusted himself off. 'Go on then,' he called to the birds. 'Have your feast.' At least this death would offer something. He untethered his steed, mounted, and galloped north.

Twenty-Five

After their trip to the grove, Ella resumed her regular duties. Remarkably, Meela assigned her to work unobserved in the scriptorium. If Breeyan believed her niece would give up trying to escape, she did not know Ella at all. Tucked away, with the musty tomes her only witness, she plotted.

Someone removed the parchment containing the hidden map, or she might have explored those tunnels further with her mind. She wondered if, with sufficient power, she could transport her physical body to where her simulacrum reached. She sighed. The priestesses forbade lighting fires in this wing of the citadel, and with her belly swelling, she didn't dare navigate those narrowed passages in the flesh.

She would have to try the birds again.

The priestesses working in the summer fields made it difficult to traverse the grounds unnoticed, but with a newly scribed scroll hidden beneath her braided hair, Ella watched and waited.

That day, when Ella stepped outside to stretch her aching back and inhale the fresh grassy air, she spotted Shaena heading towards the pens, carrying an empty basket.

Shaena passed Ella without acknowledgement, and Ella called, 'Here, let me.' She reached for the basket.

Shaena nodded, her aqua eyes drifting as she handed it across. 'My thanks.'

Ella shuddered. Accustomed to the shift and murmur of thoughts exchanged and the sudden chill when priestesses employed their power, this recent change—wills that warped and melted, displaying vacant eyes and slack mouths—was something she would never get used to.

Though unsettling, Breeyan's interventions were an unintended gift, for Shaena and Meela did not hesitate to acquiesce to Ella's desires.

Ella made one trip from the enclosure carrying eggs. On her second, she bypassed the poultry coop and opened the cage to Aryon's messengers. Wings fluttered and wriggled, beaks scrounged and scratched, until she enchanted them quiet.

With a coo, she reached into the pen while curious birds craned their necks and pecked at her. She gripped the calmest and retrieved the empty message tube from its leg, tucked her parchment inside, then re-fastened it around the creature's foot. All the while, her thoughts soothed.

With the bird in both hands, she hesitated, unsure how to direct it to travel where she wanted. She summoned a mental image of Nedran and slid her picture into the creature's tiny brain, feeding each remembered detail, but the transference squeezed and pinched, like when Amber first taught her about the chambers of the mind. The bird's psyche was unlike a person's, and its chambers made little sense to her.

She pulled away, breathing deep, then forced the image again. It crunched and ground, and the bird squirmed, pecking at her marred hands. With a sigh, she eased her mind off, recovered the tube, and let the creature loose in its pen.

Perhaps it wasn't a concrete image she needed to lodge in the bird's awareness. She relaxed her thoughts and allowed the bird's experience of flying to come to her. A rush of yearning. To be somewhere safe, with food, shelter, a mate. Freedom. Oh yes, she understood that longing.

She selected another bird and replaced its tube. Instead of picturing a location and a place, she imagined Nedran, and all it represented. Each emotion became a compass, a lodestone, a yearning for home. The bird cooed, eager.

Your letter puts us all at risk. The whispers and mind-murmurs that stalked her, the callous stares and the twisted sneers overshadowed her aunt's words.

She raised the bird, her scarred hands resembling the knots and gnarls of ancient tree roots, and set it free.

Let them all burn.

Venn drafted a formal missive welcoming Raeyn to his family, which Gohran delivered when he returned home. Polite and perfunctory, his letter acknowledged Ella's loss, and finished with, '*Your brother and I agreed the wedding should wait the customary year and a day to mark her passing.*'

Knowing Ella had been his first choice, Raeyn would still agree to the match. The Princess Elder understood her duty to her kingdom and her family as much as he understood his. In that, they were alike.

Once sealed, the priests would deliver formal decrees to Nedran and Erldan's citizens and neighbours, which should help settle the growing unrest.

Something in him shifted once he signed that contract. A weight had lifted, leaving a hollow. Having Gohran by his side for a time helped—some small connection to Ella. But in his absence, a detached gloom settled in his bones.

That night, as he undressed for bed, he heard a tapping sound at his window, followed by a bird-like trill. Probably wind rattling the pane. Perhaps the servants hadn't closed it properly.

He pulled on his nightshirt, grabbed a lantern, and moved closer, studying the frame. The window was firmly latched and unmoving in the still air.

Another trill, followed by a *tap-tap-tap* and a flurry of wings. Head tilted, a white and grey pigeon peered through the glass. He hoped it wouldn't decide his windowsill was a cosy place to roost.

He unlatched the window and pushed it open. The bird fluttered, and then waddled nearer, eyeing him almost expectantly. Had Lynden taken to feeding stray animals, as she'd done as a girl? Creatures had pursued the servants for weeks, begging for scraps, until their father put a stop to it.

'Go on then.' He waved at the pigeon. 'Away you go.'

It fluttered off the ledge, and then settled straight back down, undeterred. He tried to shoo it again, and it pecked him.

'Cursed creature!' He sucked on his finger where the bird's beak had nipped.

The bird peered sideways as though it wanted something from him. If it wasn't Lynden, perhaps one of the servants' children fed it. He had nothing for the bird, didn't want to encourage it, but it would not leave. Another flap of wings as it pecked at the ledge.

Venn raised his lantern. A glint. Was that a metal ring around the bird's foot? Venn squinted. An old-fashioned message tube. He set the lamp aside and reached out his hand, cooing.

Tame as a caged pet, the bird let him clasp its torso and hold it snugly in the crook of one arm, while he unclasped the ring around its foot. The tube flipped open, and a scroll dropped onto the ledge. He retrieved it cautiously and refastened the tube.

Satisfied, the bird turned, waddled a few steps, and took flight, beating frantic wings, leaving Venn staring at the curled parchment atop his palm.

Ella mostly avoided scrying on her old life—it was far too painful—but she needed to know if her letter made it to Venn. She judged when enough time elapsed, angled her reading glass to catch the lantern light, and peered through its shimmering surface. Faint at first, she saw Venn pacing, turning her message over and over, searching for truth in its very texture. His eyes were narrow and his mouth tight. He knelt before a hearth and Ella's breath caught. He seemed to look directly at her. After a long moment, he raised the parchment. Flames licked until it ignited, blackening and curling. From opposite sides of the fire, worlds apart, they watched it burn.

TWENTY-SIX

'Ki ng Gohran is getting what he always wanted, then?' Vera sat opposite Jonas in the richly furnished parlour with her mother and her aunt, who spent more time visiting her sister in Lichen than with her ogre of a husband in Corbryd.

'It appears that way.' Jonas traced his fingers along the burgundy velvet seat of his chair. He hadn't mentioned his journey out west, but brought news of Venn's betrothal.

'Poor Lyn must be devastated. She's absolutely smitten with the king,' said Vera.

'Don't remind me,' Jonas said.

'Not to speak wrongly of those passed to the Afterworld, but I never understood why your brother didn't settle on the Princess Elder instead of fish-flopping about from princess to princess,' Selmyra said to Jonas. 'What was so special about the younger princess, besides a pretty face?'

'Ma!' Vera cried in mock outrage.

'Well... It seems rather mercurial to me.'

'Mercurial is not a word I have ever used to describe my brother, my lovely Lady Selmee,' Jonas said.

'That's what made it so peculiar. Quite out of character for the dryhten.'

'I wonder why King Gohran pushed poor Venn into a marriage he clearly didn't want, instead of asking Lyn for her hand,' said Vera. 'That would have given him his alliance and pleased everyone.'

'I was like you once, Vee. Forever dreaming of ballad-worthy love.' Vera's aunt, Leena, shook her head with a wistful sigh. 'Sadly, we all must contend with the practicalities of the Cursed Realm.' Leena was a few years older than Selmyra, but where age padded and softened her sister, it had made her spindly and gaunt.

'You'll forgive me for holding onto hope, Aunty Lee.'

Jonas felt three pairs of eyes on him. 'Please excuse me?' He stood. 'I promised Lord Teegan a hunt.'

'Oh, Jonas, so squeamish!' Leena chuckled.

'My apologies. I was thoughtless,' Selmyra said. 'I know you cared for the young princess. Sometimes we get carried away with our—*speculations*.'

'The word you're looking for is "gossip," Ma.' Vera faced Jonas. 'Ma's right though. Apologies. As you see, little else holds our interest when you men abandon us day after day.' A mock pout.

'We can't keep the young lord hostage simply for our amusement. Even if he is rather pleasing to the eye,' Selmyra said with a wicked grin. 'Off you go, my lord. My Gan will be overjoyed if you join him.'

'**G**ohran, no!' Jaydyn screeched. 'I won't do it. Lord Kerr is short as a goblin and his breath stinks worse than a rat-eating hound!'

Raeyn barely had a moment to take in news of her betrothal when Gohran dropped this weight upon their sister.

Jaydyn halted her rant long enough to wrestle her skirt from Serrah's prying fists. 'Stop it, Sess!' She peeled her daughter's fingers off her fabric, then re-crossed her arms to confront her brother.

Serrah filled her lungs and howled with the outrage of a dozen banshees.

'Gods, Jay. Take her outside, would you? My head is pounding.' Raeyn pressed her hands to her temples. Jaydyn's daughter was becoming as wilful as her mother.

Raeyn waited until her sister and niece were out of earshot. 'She's right, Gohran. Lord Kerr has no interest in Jaydyn—he made that clear when we visited with Layla—and Jaydyn will make all our lives unbearable if you force her hand. Besides, he won't want to take Serrah in. Assuming he can plant his own seeds, why would he choose to raise another man's seedling?'

'There are ways around that.' Gohran ran his hands through his hair, pacing. 'But there aren't ways around what will happen if one of King Sardin's brood secures that alliance in our stead.'

'Then ask for Layla's hand. I can't imagine her refusing. If you adopt her daughter, there will be no qualms about her honour. She birthed that babe in her marital bed.'

Gohran grunted and paused, his back to her.

'You know I'm right.'

Another grunt.

'We don't always get our foremost desires, Gohran. I've accepted that. You might do likewise. If you'll excuse me, Your Highness, I should help our sister with Serrah.'

Poor Layla if he married her. Raeyn wouldn't wish her brother on any woman.

Gohran knew the prospect of marrying Kerr wouldn't thrill Jaydyn, but he didn't expect her eruption to be volcanic. Perhaps Raeyn was right. Forcing a match between two people who clearly disliked each other was futile. He'd hoped Jaydyn's friendship with Layla might sway her. And it would offer Serrah a playmate, for the goddess knew how lonely it was to grow up without one.

A memory stirred. Gohran standing in a clearing by the old temple, surrounded by lads teasing and jeering. Rage simmered as tears welled. An imagined whisper as Ella waved from behind the wheel of a cart. He turned from the village boys and ran to where his sister hid. She took his outstretched hand, and they ducked through the alleyways as the boys chased after.

Ella tugged him through a small door at the back of the smithy, and signalled to crouch, her finger resting across her lips for quiet as they listened for the procession of footfalls racing past.

They stayed hunched together, eyes locked, until long after the sounds faded. He met her gaze and a soothing calm washed over him. Ella had always offered a refuge.

He shrugged the reverie aside and addressed the matter at hand. If Kerr did not desire Jaydyn, and Jaydyn would not tolerate Kerr, he needed to consider other options. He would not contemplate marrying Layla. Not yet. He would take a wife eventually, but attending to his wedding plans might delay settling his sisters, and they had waited long enough.

Apart from Jaydyn's furore, it felt good to be home. His relationship with Venn appeared restored, though he wished he had not encountered Venn's miscreant brother. Whenever he saw Lord Jonas, he pictured Ella waking twined beside him, and an icy fist clenched around his stomach and heart. It was the moment that set him on an inescapable path, a reminder that for every stride he made forward, the gods clawed him twice as far back.

To punctuate that thought, a courier arrived with a letter from his aunt. Breeyan wanted to collect her due. He had the promissory note now; he could deliver the dowry. Breeyan suggested she send her priestess in plain clothes to meet him on the outskirts of Ycelt, presumably to minimise the risk of exposure if he headed to Aryon a second time. This way suited him, too, keeping him away from Ella.

As he contemplated the task's logistics, a chubby youth he recognised as one of Davith's neophytes knocked on his door.

'Your Highness! His Holiness begs you to come assist him. There have been stirrings afoot.'

A summons from Davith set Gohran on edge, a tightness in his chest and a queasiness in his stomach. His aunt would have to wait.

Gohran found Davith inside the temple sanctuary, polishing and positioning a newly acquired gold chalice, gilded cruet, and a set of brass censers.

Davith looked up the moment Gohran entered. 'Your Highness! It's good to have you home.'

'Your Holiness,' Gohran bowed. The warmth of Davith's greeting quietened his unease, as it had since he was a boy grieving for his father. 'Your man said you needed to speak with me?'

'Yes, yes. Come.' Davith set his task aside and ushered Gohran to approach the sanctuary. Light streaming through the stained glass formed a halo around the head priest.

As Gohran neared, his need for Davith's light to shine upon him intensified.

'I understand the dryhten of Nedran is soon to wed your eldest sister.'

'As I have long hoped for.'

'Are you aware people suspect your future brother of harbouring a witch and her family?'

Gohran tensed like a deer spying a hunter. 'I am not. Who would cast such an ugly allegation?'

'This was some time ago, Your Highness. After discovering a band of outlaws—presumed heretics—hiding in the forest, the dryhten placed them on one of his vassal's farms, rather than denouncing them. A visitor to the farm suspected heresy and reported them, but when my men arrived to investigate, the trio had abandoned the farm and moved on.'

'*Your* men?'

'Holy men, Your Highness. Neophytes under me.'

'I see.'

'At the time I didn't pay it much mind. Better they be gone from our midst, but reports of a further group of heretics passing between your two territories reached me. Now people are questioning whether the dryhten has been too lax and word is spreading.'

He had barely recovered his relationship with Venn. Was he to accuse his friend of concealing heretics? 'Even with an alliance afoot, Nedran lies beyond my jurisdiction, Your Holiness. Indeed, I wonder why your men were on the dryhten's lands investigating...'

Davith's eyes narrowed as a cloud passed overhead, dimming the light until his face was in shadow, the halo gone.

The priest's disappointment gnawed, and he wished he'd stayed silent.

'You must talk sense into the dryhten, Your Highness. You are special. Powerful. He will listen to you.'

Like a half-starved plant kept in the shadows, Davith's praise poured over him like sunlight. 'Of course, I shall speak to Lord Venn, Your Holiness.' He needed that light more than ever.

Twenty-Seven

Since Breeyan's interventions, Shaena readily had Ella fetch eggs for her, while Meela was happy to assign her to the scriptorium. It required no exertion on her part to persuade them, their loose minds wedged open to her machinations.

Her influence over them differed from the few priestesses she'd swayed, like Samian and Nykahlia, who appeared congenial, almost friendly.

Sometimes, even that level of persuasion eluded her, and, thinking about using her magic, Ella pictured her aunt pinching and tearing at her priestesses' minds. Or worse, her brother responding to her persuasions in all the wrong ways. Bile rose, her flesh puckering, damp with sweat, and her power slipped away.

In sleep, she remembered her and Gon playing in the glade, hiding from Mother, or from Ren and Jay, laughter and understanding shared between them. Before he'd realised what she was, and before she forced him to realise that he was like her. Following those dreams, Ella roused to dew-covered grass upon the air and tears wetting her cheeks, the babe awake and demanding inside her.

Weeks passed in this manner, and Ella sent a further three letters to Venn. The birds grew accustomed to her visits. In their peculiar avian way, they looked forward to her charms, lapping up her soothing warmth like drunks lining up for free ale.

Ella always gravitated to the calmest. On this day, the chosen bird hunched its tawny feathers, burrowing neck into body.

'That's the way,' she whispered, and the bird trilled.

With the message fastened, she blew on its side, feathers puckering. She sensed the concordance between them and let it fly, as close to freedom as it would ever get.

Ella was returning from the pens carrying a basket of eggs when Amber caught her attention.

'I need to discuss the upcoming festival,' she said, holding up a wax tablet. 'A fast that marks the Autumnal Equinox.'

When Ella's babe was due.

'The festival lasts five days and nights. We do not eat, we do not sleep, we do not practise any magic. Her Holiness has arranged for you to camp out at the grove during the festival.'

Where she had met the refugees.

'As you are not sworn, it's not safe for you to be present during the order's most sacred rite.'

Unsworn and pregnant.

'Someone will fetch you when the fast is over. But Ella, during that time, you shall be entirely out of contact, even by magic.'

'Breeyan isn't worried about leaving me there on my own?'

Amber studied her tablet. 'She assures me she's had no omens to concern her.'

Ella wondered if Amber had as much confidence in Breeyan's foresight as the High Priestess herself.

Another glance at her tablet. 'The next little while will be hectic, with every-one preparing for the fast, so Breeyan suggests you continue your scribing.'

An oddness gnawed as Ella delivered her collected eggs. She ought to feel ter-rified. She would be alone in the wilderness, unreachable even by magic, when her babe was due to be born. Instead, she experienced the tickle of anticipation, like the night before a ball. Hiding a smile, she headed to the scriptorium, pulled out a clean parchment, and scrawled.

When Venn read Ella's first letter, delivered by a carrier pigeon like some fanciful saga of the Ancients, he assumed it was a prank. But who would be so cruel?

A torment, he slid the parchment between his fingers and fancied he could sense her. He grasped at the feeling, longed to absorb it into his body, his soul, before remembering she was gone, and destroyed it.

For a time afterward, his ache to ride to her grave returned. He yearned for her ghostly presence, but no good could come from pining. It only prolonged his grief.

The letter instructed him to tell no one, but once he might have confided in Jonas. His brother had stepped in to care for him in his darkest moments of sorrow. But Jonas hadn't returned to Nedran since his betrothal announcement, and he feared their relationship wouldn't recover from the past year's betrayals.

It didn't seem right to tell Mykan, and he did not wish to trouble Lynden. Instead, he pushed thoughts of Ella aside, and hoped whoever thought to mock his pain would leave him be.

But then one morning, in the early hours, he woke again to something tapping against his window. He crawled from beneath his covers and opened it. That same bird perched on the sill, cocking its head at him.

With a sigh, he retrieved the message tube.

Satisfied, the creature cooed and flew into the dull light of uhtan. It circled, then flew south and west, as if heading to the End of the World.

Venn should throw the cursed scroll away without unfurling it and save himself the heartache. But he hungered for the barest echo of her memory, even if it was a lie. He closed his eyes and inhaled. Imagined he could smell her amidst the tang of metal, birds, and ink.

Another sigh. He was a fool. She was gone. He struck a light against a flint and set his lantern ablaze, then brought the parchment to the flaming wick.

E lla wanted to scream, to howl. Venn burnt her letter without opening it. The telltale tingle of magic rumbled through her, ready to erupt. A moment later, it abated, as the babe sucked power away from her.

That night, she waited for the constant snuffling and eerie quiet in her mind that told her the sisters slept, before summoning Venn via her dream state. Briefly, she pictured him, but her magic lacked fuel.

She wished he would return to the hill where the jasmine plant grew, and let the thorns bite his flesh—a source for her to draw upon. To reach him.

Another thing forbidden.

What did it matter now? The sisters already believed her Cursed.

F or the first night in weeks, Venn dreamed of Ella. As he walked near the Leaping Lake, he sensed her beside him, but when he turned, his vision misted over. He reached for where she should have been, but his arms passed straight through, and she merged with the fog between them. Her voice faded in and out, like a horn blaring across a windy field, becoming louder and more distinct, before dwindling to silence.

'Venn, please don't destroy my letters—I'm still here, Venn. I'm alive...'

His dream image fogged back over, until Gohran's arm rested on him. 'You need to recover your old life, to move on...' The fog thickened, and Venn realised it wasn't fog, but smoke. Gohran's touch grew hot, as if his flesh was on fire.

Venn bolted awake, heart racing, drenched in sweat. Ghostly images hovered in the recesses of the dim room, but he blinked them away. Gods, if that grief-fever started up again...

He slipped on a shirt and trousers, pulled on his riding boots, and headed out to the stables. It was irrational, but he had to see her grave.

Heart pounding, breath jagged in his chest, he rode. But when he arrived, he found vacant grass growing atop an abandoned mound—nothing more. Her jasmine climbed along the rocks of her cairn. He reached down, tugged away a sprig to carry with him, but sensed nothing of her there now.

Twenty-Eight

G ohran was eager to share news of his loan with Davith. For his mentor to acknowledge the lengths he would go to fulfil his wishes. 'Soon, these stirrings and rumours will belong in the past, as we spread Our Lady's word through this entire region.'

'I knew I could rely on you, Your Highness.' Davith's words slipped through a crack in Gohran's shell. How he thirsted for his mentor's approval.

Establishing the henad outposts involved long hours together, planning, liaising with Gohran's vassals, negotiating access to lands and buildings. He hadn't worked so closely on an endeavour since Ella helped him survey Erldan's defences.

Their first stop was Harnal, where Gohran felt confident of a ready welcome. Davith had close oversight of the local priesthood there, and the villagers attended worship in its small temple. Installing a henad's court should cause minimal fuss.

They left Jarrod to attend to other business in the town while they met the local priest inside the temple's atrium. Unlike Erldan's newly renovated building, Harnal's wooden temple was dim and musty. They sat on a timber bench opposite Sornad, who perched on a small stool.

Given his pre-existing relationship with Sornad, they agreed Davith should lead the discussion, but it was not going well.

Davith delivered his proposal in the same lilting tone as his sermons. '... and so, we invite you to incorporate hearings into your regular services to minimise disruption,' he finished, his voice oozing.

Sornad paled, then flushed beet-red. 'Are you suggesting, Your Holiness, we're not trusted to try our own?'

'Not at all. But this will ease the pressure for your good self, and others, who do not wish to jeopardise your *community*.'

Sornad frowned, arms crossed.

'Your Worship, may I?' Gohran asked. If they could not persuade Sornad, they would not sway the others.

Davith nodded.

Gohran turned and spoke gently to the priest. 'We find, Your Holiness, that some citizens are reluctant to come forward before their peers and loved ones. When this happens, and heresy goes unchecked, certain individuals can take matters into their own hands.'

'I see.' Sornad rubbed the stubble of his shaved head, leaning back on his stool.

'Each time a man plays blind, deaf and dumb to heresy, these false-godders infiltrate. And when people flout Our Lady's rule and mete out their own savage justice, they flout *our* rule,' Davith added.

Gohran moved forwards, catching and holding Sornad's gaze. 'Do you wish to see people suffer while heretics thrive and mock the goddess?'

The priest swayed in his chair, his jaw slack, head shaking back and forth. 'Never, Your Highness.' He faced Davith. 'Your Holiness, use my temple as your own.'

Gohran patted the priest's shoulder. Thank the goddess! 'You have the gratitude of my kingdom and all my subjects.'

Outside, Davith raised his eyebrow, his lip curving. 'Excellently done, Your Highness. You certainly have the gift of persuasion.'

Gohran couldn't speak. Davith's praise bathed him in light and warmth, as if in that moment, he was the sun.

'Shall we return, Your Highness?'

Gohran shook his head. 'I have an errand to attend to first.' He needed to send word back to his aunt with instructions for the delivery of Ella's dowry. 'Let us find Jarrod.'

They pivoted and headed towards the town's main street.

'I don't know how I would have managed these past moons without Jarrod,' Gohran said, contemplating. Still basking in Davith's light, he slipped easily into his old habit of confiding in his mentor. 'One of the few things my late father taught me, was when a king finds such a man in his service, he should hold on tight.'

'Indeed, such servants are rare. You are fortunate to have found one. After all, no one knows you as I do, Your Highness.'

That last remark left a sour aftertaste. It contained a reminder that at any moment, Davith might withdraw his light, leaving Gohran thirsting, craving, once more in a dark void that no one could fill. Not anymore.

'T he king insists this is the only suitable time, so you'll have to miss the festival.' Breeyan would have guessed the timing was a ploy, but Gohran may not have realised how sacred this period was to the priestesses when he suggested it.

Amber glanced up, and Breeyan tightened her thought-shield.

'Perhaps this timing will be fortuitous. We'll have so much happening here, the others might not notice your absence. You can drop Ella at the lookout post. If anyone asks, I'll tell them you're staying with her, while you continue onwards to meet the king.'

'Aren't you worried about leaving her alone out there?'

Breeyan shook her head. 'She will not try to leave again. Not in her condition, and not after what she has seen.' If meeting those refugees didn't deter her, nothing would.

'What if the babe comes while she's out there, cut off from everyone?'

'I've had no omens to indicate such,' Breeyan said, noting the crease forming across Amber's brow and tight twist to her mouth. 'We must trust in the god,

Amber. We have no choice. She can't stay here. The god's laws forbid it. And I won't ask another of you to miss the festival. You forgoing it is sacrifice enough.'

Amber winced as though something pained her.

'What is it? Are you unwell?'

'Not unwell… It's hard to describe. Like someone taking a hammer to my temples. I can't shake this sense of unease, this lingering darkness.'

Breeyan inhaled. Amber rarely received omens. She tucked her hands beneath her robe to hide her nails, which were chewed to the quick. 'And the feeling developed now, when we were discussing leaving Ella at the grove?'

Amber nodded.

Breeyan sensed nothing. 'I would know if she was in danger.'

'Never would I question it, Your Holiness.'

Her eyes narrowed. 'You should meditate on it, and so shall I.'

Breeyan retreated to her private study and bolted the door. A large oak barrel rested in one corner. With a sharpened block of wood, Breeyan levered it open. The stench of sweat-soaked leather, like closed-in shoes, wafted as the aroma of fermenting shrillan leaves escaped.

When fermented and dissolved in the mouth, rather than dried and smoked, shrillan kept the priestesses awake during the fast. For some, the sacred herb induced euphoria, maintaining fervour during the fast's later days.

Through the lengthy fermentation, Breeyan carefully trialled the brew. Her predecessor cautioned her to err on the weaker side, though she had never said why. Breeyan often exploited her trials to inspire visions, using it now to meditate on Amber's omen.

She reached into the barrel and pulled out a single soggy leaf. She shook off the excess moisture and placed it beneath her tongue. Chewing an old cheese rind would be pleasanter.

She lay flat on her back and waited. Nothing. Breathed in and out. Still nothing.

She was about to rise when the potent shrillan surged, tensing every muscle like a tightly strung lute. Her heart thudded in her ears, then behind her eyes. All around her, colours intensified.

She held out her hands to examine the hills and valleys of her veins. Violet fluid pumped through them. The borders of her fingers oozed, blending into each other, and then into the surrounding room. Her vestment, too, had no edges. Liquid and crystalline, it blended into the floor, while the walls melted into her flesh. No object remained discrete, certain, or still.

How easy it would be to lose oneself in these sensations.

Breeyan drew a breath. Meticulously, and with superior discipline, she constructed an image of the key points around her body. Under the shrillan's influence, they blazed, brilliant, distorting the surrounding objects and air as their magnetism sucked at her aura.

Through guttural breaths, she summoned every ounce of restraint to fight the tide of sensation.

Was Ella's unborn child in peril? Was Ella?

Amorphous clouds of blue appeared and swirled, only to recede. No danger there.

'Why this feeling of unease? The darkness?' Her voice echoed off the walls, bouncing from one surface only to sink into another, eery and distorted.

The final reverberation reflected her voice, but strangely altered.

'Unease?' the voice said. 'Darkness? Only if you let it be...'

Deadened silence.

Breeyan bolted upright. She forced the working shut, thrashing her arms to banish the key points. Shivery-sweat pulsed as she waited, sensing for any lingering, uninvited power.

For the first time in a long time, she was terrified.

Twenty-Nine

That morning, when Amber went to find Nykki to braid her hair, she found her bed empty. Her beloved wasn't far away—Amber sensed her. She followed the tug of her mind until she reached Ella's sleeping cell.

There Nykki sat, nestled behind the princess, legs straddling Ella's hips like a pair of spoons, as she braided her raven tresses. Nykki's eyes appeared soft, and Amber detected the heat of her breath—heat that travelled the length of her body to the forbidden place between her thighs.

Ella seemed oblivious, simply accepting the other priestess's help. But Amber saw it: the briefest moment where Ella turned and smiled at Nykki, and Nykki's will melted like butter.

Amber opened her god-sight. Nykki's aura lapped up the soothing waves of Ella's beguilement. She froze.

Since she'd suspected Ella, the princesses' unique and dangerous power hovered in her mind—a stubborn cloud that refused to rain—but she hesitated to draw attention to it, hoping Breeyan or someone with more experience and authority, would recognise it and take the reins. Instinct cautioned her against making the awful accusation directly to Breeyan. What if she was wrong? Gods, she hoped she was wrong.

Seeing Ella's power wind around her beloved, she needed to uncover the truth, even if it brought down a violent storm. So, when they settled into their chores later that day, she headed to the library.

Ella spent the past weeks transcribing the remaining copy of *The Lost Warriors*, the one with the missing passages, so she expected to find her in the library or scriptorium, but both rooms were empty.

Amber's focus drifted as she sought the pattern of Ella's thoughts, but found nothing. Finally, Ella remembered to shield herself. Her mind blinded, Amber searched on foot, scouring the sleeping cells, the hall of prayer, and the kitchen. She didn't expect Ella to be in the fields, but when she bumped into Meela, the priestess told her Ella was fetching eggs. Amber shuddered when Meela's eyes glazed over.

Finally, she located Ella with the carrier pigeons, and realised with sickening dread, Ella was still trying to contact Lord Venn and find a way back to her old life.

'Gods!'

Ella pivoted to face her.

'Tell me you didn't... You haven't...' What was Ella thinking? How could she risk exposing their haven?

Ella tossed her braids behind her shoulders, lifted the door to the nesting coop, and retrieved egg after egg to form a precarious stack.

'Ella.' Amber rested her arm upon Ella's, but Ella shrugged her away. She fastened her grip. Ella hefted her almost full basket to the side and shut the cage. Her former pupil stomped past. Amber trailed after and grabbed her again. Ella swung around and several eggs toppled, splattering on the ground. Amber crouched to clear them up.

'Leave it. Please.' That tone and the chill in Ella's eyes were paralysing. Power churned, fuelled by a deep, seething anger.

Amber backed away, shaking her head. She couldn't speak.

Her temples throbbed. *Unease. Darkness.* The words hovered in her mind. A warning from the god.

She turned and hurried back across the fields to the citadel, clambering up the stairs to Breeyan's study. In the shadowy corridor, she paused, steadying her breath, before creaking the door open.

Within, instead of the High Priestess, Breeyan's apprentice, Shira, poised above Breeyan's desk. Deep lines creased her forehead.

Amber wanted to turn and flee, but stuffed her panic down. Would not let Shira see her agitated.

'Oh, Amber, I'm glad you're here. You might help me,' Shira said, with a soothing welcome. Reserved and studious, Amber understood why Breeyan chose Shira for her apprentice.

With another quelling breath, she approached, mirroring Shira's quiet calm, her curiosity piqued.

A giant map covered Breeyan's desk, but instead of places, were names of people. Lines and symbols connected the names like branches of a tree. Beside the drawing sat a wax tablet with some scribbles and scratched out notes. Alongside lay several old books and smaller parchments showing other lineages, including Lord Venn of Nedran's. Shira's fingers followed the various branches.

'A genealogy map,' Amber said. 'I saw one like it at Erldan. Much grander than this, all properly illuminated.'

'A while back, Her Holiness started tracing her and Ella's shared ancestry and asked me to compare this map against our archives.'

One disadvantage of being sequestered was the limited access to public records. Elnora's priests documented significant births, deaths and the like, but the priestesses relied on messages reaching them from Ycelt, often delayed by moons or years, and with information frequently omitted.

'Given you spent time in Erldan with the princess's family, would you help me check this over?'

Amber nodded, drawing nearer. She pointed to a cluster of marks beside various names on the map. 'What are all these crosses?'

'Not crosses. X-es.'

Amber looked again. All the way down Breeyan's ancestry was at least one 'X' per row. King Rohan, Ella's father, bore no such mark. Someone—presumably the High Priestess—had drawn a line tracing back through his ancestors, marking some with crosses and others with a query. 'Do they represent magic?'

There was a cross next to Breeyan and another beside her younger sister, the late Queen Prya.

'That's what I assume.'

Amber's fingers traced the branches as Shira's had moments before. Various lines showed Ella descending from the first High King on both sides of her family. Or—wait, was that a query scribbled across the line from her to King Rohan? Someone had inked a line in its stead that traced its ancestry back to the Ancients.

Shira gathered several parchments and pushed them towards Amber. 'Do you recognise any of these names?'

'Lord Kerr of Rynwood, Lord Jonas of Nedran—these are all lords in Ella's acquaintance.'

Many lines were incomplete, a scatter of names with crosses beside them, each queried, and then scratched out. No crosses in Venn's ancestry, not even a query mark. Then she noticed the two crosses beside Ella's name and the one beside her brother, the king. She recoiled.

Shira's gaze pierced her. 'What is it?'

Amber hesitated. 'No—it's nothing.'

'You look like Xenon is about to take King Myrhan's sword and spear you.'

She shook her head, clamping down. 'It's peculiar seeing magic marked out that way... Were you aware it was Ella's brother who denounced the queen?'

'I was not. How dreadful.'

Amber twisted her braids. Couldn't meet Shira's eyes, couldn't stop picturing those cursed crosses. 'Please excuse me. I must speak with Her Holiness before the fast.' She dropped a hasty bow and practically ran out of the room.

Thirty

In the weeks that followed, Venn received several messages from the king, including one that mentioned him aiding rumoured heretics. He recalled wondering—and dismissing—that very thing. Venn evaded others' religious quarrels. Regardless of belief, showing mercy to those in need should be every-one's mission. People ought to fear harming a follower of Xenon more than upsetting a few of Elnora's priests. Everybody knew touching the Moon Sworn summoned the Curse.

In the end, he avoided corresponding with Gohran, and did not dare write to Raeyn. He could not alter the past. And now his betrothal was sealed, Ella was gone, and that was that.

Since dreaming of Ella and revisiting her grave, he didn't want to admit his foolish longing, the doubt creeping after receiving those strange letters. It wasn't merely foolish; it was childish, revivifying the torturous days, months, and years, of not knowing whether his mother was alive, before he accepted she was gone, if not from this life, then from him and his family.

Though Ella's death differed from his mother's disappearance, when he considered her letters might be genuine, the pain felt too familiar. He hadn't recognised the comfort uncertainty brought, nor how the finality of Ella's death robbed him of it. Gohran held her while she died, buried her with his own hands, leaving no room for hope.

But that morning after breakfast, when he arrived in his chamber and another bird awaited, Ella's dream voice echoed in his mind, telling him she was alive.

It couldn't be real, and yet... He retrieved the letter and read.

'For the five nights of the equinox festival, you will find me north of the temple where I have marked. This might be my sole opportunity to escape. Follow my drawing. Come alone. You must believe, my love. E. E.'

When Ella sought refuge from her brother, she feared him sending her to a temple. Women had no formal roles in the Dark Sun cult, but temples provided Her followers sanctuary from secular life. While some joined from devotion, noble families often sequestered daughters who were unlikely to find suitable husbands.

If the letter was genuine, Gohran had lied. He'd cloistered Ella, after all. But why? Though with child, Venn had agreed to marry. Gohran need not hide her.

The equinox was a few days hence. He turned the parchment over. A scrawled map directed him west and south of Nedran. He knew of no temples that way. What was she doing out there?

Assuming it was authentic and not an elaborate hoax—though he could not fathom such cruelty.

Unless someone wanted to draw him away from Nedran on his own. But who? And to what end? He reflected again on his mother's disappearance. Did he dare risk believing? Did he dare not?

His fingertips traced each word, committing the drawing to memory. Then he burned this letter like the others before it.

Those crosses haunted her, but between preparing for her trip, the fast, and Ella's solo camp, Amber had no moment to share her suspicions with Breeyan, who was almost never alone. Instead, she silently prayed Ella's pigeon flew its trained path to Crescent Mountain or The Gern, and that whoever found her message dismissed it. After all, Ella was dead. During the equinox, she would be safely out of reach, so Amber's conjectures could wait.

Meanwhile, she evaded Ella. How could she face her, knowing her former pupil would betray them? After experiencing her dark power, and suspecting a truth even darker about Ella's unborn child?

Breeyan's notations suggested King Rohan was not Ella's father, and Lord Venn might not be the father of Ella's babe. Only one man on those parchments carried the X of magic. She couldn't bring herself to utter his name. It was too awful to contemplate. Against the laws of every god. Against all decency. Yet it made sense of so much.

Now, she was to return to Ycelt to meet him: Ella's brother, the king. The probable father of Ella's child.

In near silence, Amber escorted Ella to the lookout post to establish her camp. They positioned cooking pots, stowed bags beneath a canvas sheet, and padded her bedroll with dirt and leaves covered with blankets.

Ella stood back, surveying. 'If someone told me when I was growing up that I would one day spend my nights on the hard ground in the middle of nowhere, hugely pregnant and with no husband, I would have mocked them.'

Amber said nothing.

'What if it rains while I'm out here? Am I to freeze with no shelter?'

'Breeyan has had no warnings of rain during the fast.' She handed Ella the plain dress with the let-out seams without meeting her gaze. 'In case beggars come by.' She moved to leave, but Ella grabbed her arm.

'Amber...' Those soft eyes pleading, their power churning.

She shrugged Ella away.

'I know what you think you saw. But I swear to you, I didn't send the note to hurt anyone here. I doubt Venn will even read it. He's burned all the others.'

'The others?' Amber snapped.

'Can you blame me for trying to reach him? For wanting to get away? I need to leave. You've seen what Aryon's priestesses are capable of. I'm not safe here.'

'But you're safe back there?' A flash of Queen Prya burning.

'You don't know what it's like—'

'Don't you dare. The sacrifices I've made to protect you. I've had to return, time and again. Do you imagine I chose any of this?'

'I didn't mean—I'm sorry...'

Amber shook her head. 'You haven't thought of anyone but yourself, Ella. Not once.' She pictured Nykki's legs wrapped around Ella's, heat flowing between them. The waves of blue light circling everyone in Ella's orbit. But not her. Not anymore.

She handed Ella the copy of *The Lost Warriors* she had been transcribing. 'Breeyan suggests you use this time fruitfully. You might read the story of Xarion—what remains of it after you left the complete version in Ycelt.'

Ella took the tome, confused.

'I hope you take this opportunity to reflect. To consider the people around you, how your choices affect them.'

The decisions you make affect us all, El. The voice of a man she didn't recognise slipped into Amber's mind. It must belong to Ella—some memory her words evoked. *Good*, she thought. Let her meaning land and land hard. Ella wasn't a girl anymore. She needed to take responsibility.

Ella flinched. The thought had reached her.

'I won't see you now until after the fast.' She fought the urge to reconcile. If only Ella saw and understood. She sighed. 'Goodbye, Ella.'

THIRTY-ONE

Aryon's priestesses filled the long days and eerie nights with ritualised and richly detailed processions and prayer. The fast represented the god's suffering, the lack of food, their want of sleep, descending into starvation cramps and a drug-fevered hysteria.

The first days were the hardest, as the women's bodies adjusted, but Breeyan meted out the shrillan sparingly. She was never comfortable with how readily Xenon's disciples surrendered their will. She would have forgone the herb entirely, hating the constant stream of sensations, the uncontrolled visions, but it was as the god demanded.

A novice tugged her sleeve, an acute thrill shooting up her arm. She beckoned Breeyan to follow.

Breeyan ignored the way her feet seemed to sink through the spongelike dirt and pursued the young girl's dancing hair. They stopped before a huddle of priestesses who flapped their sleeves over someone lying on the ground: Sallyn, collapsed. The priestesses eyed each other helplessly. A couple had wits enough to cool her.

Breeyan pointed to a pair of priestesses on the outer edge of the huddle. 'Fetch water. Quickly.' She knelt beside the unconscious priestess. 'Help me get her inside.'

Several clumsy attempts saw four of them heft the slight girl to the infirmary. Someone brought a pitcher of water, and Breeyan propped Sallyn up and brought it to her lips. Moisture dribbled across her cracked skin and down her neck. She pinched Sallyn's mouth open and tried again. Liquid found the back of her throat, and she roused, spluttering and gagging, opening her eyes and sucking greedily. Breeyan drew the pitcher away before she drank too much.

She sent the gawking priestesses away and kept a silent vigil, cooling Sallyn's skin with a dampened cloth, but by nightfall, she was no better. Half delirious, Sallyn flitted in and out of consciousness. Her head rolled back and forth, the fire-slap across her cheek blurring and shifting so that for a moment Breeyan saw Ella's face—or was it Prya's—aflame.

'Unease,' the girl whispered. 'Darkness.' Her head lolled to the other side. 'Only if you let it be.' Breeyan blinked, digging nails into palms. Sallyn's lips hadn't moved.

Ella watched Amber leave and travel east instead of back to Aryon. She hated knowing Amber was angry with her. Was her old tutor right? Was Ella selfish and reckless, as her aunt accused?

She ran her hands over her swollen belly. After all she'd been through, the treacherous territory she'd navigated alone, how powerless she'd been, she didn't see that she'd had any other choice. That she had another choice now. She meant what she'd said about not expecting Venn to come for her, but she needed to try.

Ella kept busy preparing food, fetching water, and washing up after herself. She picked up the book Amber handed her, *The Lost Warriors*. She flipped it open to the story of Xarion. The name resonated as though she should know it from somewhere.

The tale described a warrior priestess who influenced others' thoughts—a common gift—and altered how they felt about her, something much rarer. Xenon's army used her gifts to infiltrate the High King's men. To them, she appeared a genteel courtier, nothing more. Beneath her skirts and piled-up hair, she was a hardened fighter like them, capable of a man's malice, using magic to lure and trap, like a spider weaving.

Ella read the passage where the god's warriors assigned Xarion to shadow the High King's captain and drew breath. Wild and charismatic, the captain was impervious to Xarion's charms. For the one and only time, the sorceress experienced love willingly given and freely returned.

Oh! To experience that freedom! Not the tainted lacklustre love she'd felt with Venn after her power warped and stole free will from them both. She thought then of Jonas. The passion they shared was the closest she had come to what the book described, and she hadn't even recognised it, appreciated it. She hadn't known.

After that, the story settled into tedious, gory accounts of various battles, which Ella skimmed past. By the time she reached the gap in the narrative, her thoughts drifted elsewhere, remembering Venn, wishing he could have been like that captain instead of Jonas. She pushed the volume to one side and gave in to the weight of her weariness. She lay back, staring into the night sky, watching the shadows cast by the flames of her fire, and floated to sleep beneath the stars.

Thirty-Two

Amber traversed eastward. Shocked by her own outburst, her mind played and replayed the exchange as she rode, as if she might alter the past. She swung from wanting to rush back to the grove, craving Ella's forgiveness, to wanting to slap sense into her. Ella, of all people, should grasp the threat of discovery. And though she did not choose her strange and dangerous power, nothing would change what she was, what she had done, and what it might mean for them all.

She was not eager to see the king again, assuming he fulfilled the delivery himself. They were due to meet a few hours west of Erldan, beyond the nearest farmsteads and the watchful eyes of curious peasants.

The pounding in her temples and unease through her core had not abated. If anything, the discomfort intensified as she neared the spot designated to camp and wait. When she opened her consciousness to detect other minds nearby, the hammering grew, forcing her to shield herself from its throbbing pain.

Shading her eyes, she squinted, scanning for anyone approaching, but sensed nothing. Not even the distant jangle of a rider or thunder of hoofbeats.

Hours passed with no sign of the king or his envoy until Elnora sank towards the horizon, setting the clouds aflame, before fading into the violet of night. Still no suggestion of another soul.

Amber dozed. Gods, she was weary! She tried to focus on the twilit stars, listening for something, anything, but in the end, her attention failed, and she drifted into slumber.

These past moons acting as driver and steward to His Highness were wearisome. Jarrod honoured the king, as his father honoured King Rohan before him, but when Gohran commanded him to make this delivery alone, a weight lifted from his shoulders. The king's tirades were unpredictable, his decisions questionable. While he knew Gohran valued him, Jarrod never let his guard down entirely in his presence.

The cause of Gohran's absence was also peculiar. The High Priest had requested his help with the equinox observance—a rite with no role for a secular monarch. It was not Jarrod's place to question the king, but he worried about the shifting boundary between the king's rule and the Dark Sun cult.

'Davith arranged for a mercenary to accompany you in my stead,' Gohran told him.

Tension crept into Jarrod's shoulders and spine. 'There's no need, Your Highness. I don't mind going alone.'

'I don't doubt your capability, but I do worry about bandits.'

'Of course, Your Highness.' Gohran took his arm. A familiar giddiness came over him, as it often did in the king's presence.

'I trust you not to speak of this mission to anyone, including your guard.'

'I swear it on my father's dagger.' His most prized possession. He carried that blade everywhere.

'Good.' Gohran squeezed his arm, then exited.

The tension eased, and Jarrod continued packing his small satchel with a clean shirt, a water canteen, an apple, and a loaf of bread in case the journey dragged.

When he arrived at the stables, not one, but two hired guards, waited. For a pouch of silver, a couple of steeds, and a handful of beasts, it seemed excessive, but he welcomed the extra hands to wrangle the farm stock.

'Good day to you,' he nodded.

Both guards nodded back and motioned for him to lead the way.

Setting off with the sun low, the trio steered the stock like herdsmen. The mercenaries were gruff, silent types, glancing at one another from time to time, mostly ignoring him, which suited Jarrod, who settled into his own private thoughts as the scenery jogged by.

Several hours in, they stopped to rest and quench their thirst. It was unseasonably warm and sweat dampened Jarrod's shirt.

'Good sir, I think there's something amiss with this steed. He's pulling up lame.'

Jarrod made his way to where the guard rubbed the horse's flank. 'Let me see...' He hoped they didn't have to circle back. He examined the steed, who snorted in protest when Jarrod approached his left hind leg. 'Easy, now...' He stroked the horse, then bent to inspect its hoof.

Something heavy thudded against his skull. Shooting pain. His vision blurred. Before he could panic, arms restrained him. He shouted and thrashed. Their hold was too strong. He couldn't break free. He kicked and shoved, shoulders heaving. That grip tightened. He couldn't move.

Someone yanked on his hair. Stuffed fingers over his mouth. He bit down, jerking, kicking, but tripped and thudded to the ground. They caught his hair again, wrenched a fistful backward, head tilted, neck to the sky.

Sun in his eyes. Throat exposed. A metal glint.

No! Gods, no!

Too late.

The blade approached. Icy cold, then fiery hot. Biting through flesh. And there was not one cursed thing he could do.

Amber did not know the hour when she woke. Her temples throbbed and her skull ached. She tried to wriggle her hands and feet, but found them bound. Someone had stuffed a rag into her mouth. Her head swam, and she struggled to breathe. She wanted to shout, to scream, but couldn't move. Her sluggish body jerked, lolling back and forth. Was she atop a steed? Another jerk, another blow to her head, and then nothing.

THIRTY-THREE

Late into the fourth evening of the fast, Ella woke to approaching hoof beats. Her face tingled and her stomach fell somewhere below her knees. She sat upright, staring into the night. A single rider, a man, neared. She was about to rekindle the fire, which had reduced to embers, when she hesitated. The grey steed was not one she recognised. Her throat tightened.

Dressed in plain clothes and grubby as a farmer, the rider dismounted, steps hesitant. A shadowed face squinted towards the flames.

Then she sensed it. Anxiety, anticipation. Not hers—his, as he broke into that unmistakable proud stride. A broad grin spread over her cheeks. She hefted herself up, smoothing out the creases of the peasant's dress, and freed the tangles from her loose hair. As he neared, her chest swelled until she thought it might burst.

Venn was here. He was *here*.

Arms grasped her, squeezing. She sank against him, her body remembering his, drinking in the familiarity where his flesh resisted, where it yielded, recalling the flood of his sandalwood scent.

'I could feel you, I *felt* you…' He trembled. Her face was between his palms, and he covered her with kisses. Laughter choked with tears, hers, his. Venn ran his hands along her swollen belly. 'Gods—why?'

A hardness lodged in her chest as insects screamed in her ears. The heat was stifling. She couldn't speak.

'When I got your letters… Oh, by every demon, some I burned without opening. I couldn't believe, and yet—' A sob choked back. 'I knew you weren't gone. Couldn't be. But Ella—is this truly you? Is this another dream? I can't—Oh, gods, I can't...'

He covered her face in kisses once more, then pressed and held her to him, grasped her until she ached.

'You smell of dust and grass,' he laughed and wept. *Not like jasmine.*

His thought slipped into her mind. She brushed aside how open he still lay to her.

'Gods, why?' he asked again.

'Don't waste these moments with questions, my love. There will be time to explain. We'll have all the time in the world.'

The cry of an owl punctuated the sky.

'You were right here the whole time...' Another sob. 'I would have come for you. I would have—'

She faced him, silenced him with her lips, drew him closer and kissed away his tears. She relished the silk of his hair, the stubble of his cheeks, the powerful line of his nose, ran her hands down his jawline to his neck, his chest, as if to carve his image into her heart through her fingertips.

He grasped her. 'Ella—your hands—what happened?'

'Hush, my love...' She slipped her grip from his, and both palms savoured his shoulders, his chest, his torso, the lines of his muscled abdomen. Lips followed fingers from the hollow of his stubbled neck, down to the trail of soft hair beneath his navel. Tears streamed down his cheeks, and he trembled against her touch.

He tugged her hair, and drew her back towards his lips, as if his mouth thirsted for her, couldn't get enough of her. His hands traced the strangeness of her swollen body, but when he leaned down to kiss her belly, she flinched. He pulled away, hurt, confused.

She drew his wrists back behind her and brought his lips to hers. His hungry body responded. She slid her fingers down his abdomen to unlace his trousers, but he stayed her hand.

'Wait—There's something you need to know. When I thought you were gone... Ella, I was *sick* from losing you. I almost didn't survive... And then Gohran, he—'

'You are betrothed to Raeyn.' Of course he was. Gohran would have made certain of that.

'Always has my heart been yours, please understand that, but unless I can have the contract annulled...'

'We can worry about that in the morning, my love. Let us share this night.'

'But the babe—I don't want to hurt—'

She silenced him with her lips again. 'Let me pleasure you.' Her hands continued their journey toward his laces, slipping beneath the wool of his trousers. She sensed more than heard his grunt of desire, the tension building through his limbs, his torso, his chest. His breath quickened as she stroked the length of him. His tongue explored hers, and she savoured the heat and salt of their lips.

Somewhere in the back of his mind she sensed a small protest, hesitation, and doubt, before pleasure stifled all thought, and he gave in to her touch. Pressure built through his thighs and buttocks as he neared his climax. She eased off, slowed down, drawing out the sweet agony.

Her lips and tongue traced his chest, his belly, taking in the desire in his eyes, his parted lips, his heightened breath and low moans, pleasure tipping towards pain as he ached for his release. With her lips to his, she sped her stroking and guided him towards the point of bliss until he toppled over the brink and his release shuddered through him.

She crawled into the cocoon of his chest, listening to his heartbeat ease and slow. He held her, watching the embers flicker and dance as the stars crept across the sky. Eventually they withered, fading into uhtan in a mirror of the dying fire while they clung to one another as if afraid to let go.

The next morning, Ella woke to the aroma of brewed tea—Ycelt tea, not the acrid blend prepared by the sisters.

'Eat up, my love.' Venn handed her a bowl of porridge and a ceramic cup. 'You need your strength.'

Propped up, Ella took the offered meal gratefully. Venn sat on one of the flatter rocks opposite. His curiosity gnawed. Her letters hinted she was cloistered and needed to get away, but revealed nothing further.

It was odd. She hadn't noticed how accustomed she had become to the tickle of minds, opening, closing. Venn's mind was open, but not of his volition. Worse, he was oblivious to her comings and goings. The priestesses were constantly aware of each other's probing.

Ella also realised how weak she was. Venn's thoughts were faint, his emotions fainter. The previous night, their passion had fuelled her, but this morning, the babe sapped her strength, greedy as it readied itself for birth.

Ella sipped her tea, a scatter of leaves bobbing on the cup's surface.

Venn watched her, fresh tears falling. 'This is happening. Not some dream,' he said. 'Curse it, I feel like I've found you too late...'

She put her cup aside to squeeze his hands. 'We'll make it work, my love.'

Tension eased from his body. He'd reached a resolution. 'Jonas knows a pastoralist near here. I'm sure he would shelter you until we place you somewhere more suitable, at least until I speak to the priests...'

He seemed to mull something over. 'The babe. Gods, our babe... Surely the priests will annul my betrothal to Raeyn. Though my prior betrothal to you remains unsealed, Raeyn and I entered ours under a false premise. It would be wrong for it to proceed...' Another long pause. 'Ah, curse it. We will make it happen, even if I must line the priests' coffers with gold and silver. And Ella? If your brother tries to intervene, I will abdicate. I can't lose you again.'

She wanted to weep with joy, with anguish. Couldn't bear to tell him that, provided Gohran lived, she must remain hidden. Not yet. Let them share this flicker of hope, however fleeting.

'Ordinarily, this steed is fast,' Venn was still speaking, 'but he's not my strongest mount. If you can endure camping out another few nights, I'll return with a spare for you in a few days.'

Venn had already packed up most of her wares; they sat on the ground beside his horse. She shook her head. 'I don't have a few days. They'll be back for me this time tomorrow.'

Venn rubbed his chin. Daylight revealed the dirt crusting his nails and smeared across his unshaven cheeks. 'Then we walk. I will get you to safety. That I promise.'

A cool omen-ripple travelled the length of Ella's spine and settled in her core. Venn took her cup and dish, put them aside, and drew her close.

She managed a weak smile. 'If we are to leave, we should go.'

Venn stooped to gather her bedding. She held the opposing corners, and they shook out and folded the blankets, passing lengths back and forth. Venn grabbed the last one.

Her breath caught. 'Wait—'

Too late.

Stuffed beneath, taunting, lay her robe.

Venn dropped everything and leapt backwards. He stared as if the garment would burn out his eyes. She reached for him. He jerked aside and continued to back away. He looked to the heavens, like he feared the gods would strike him down.

'What have I done?'

'Venn—'

White as a spirit from the Afterworld, he shook his head in disbelief, palms raised to deny what his eyes demanded he see. His shoulders convulsed, fighting nausea—felt as keenly as if it lived in her body. 'Not a temple of Elnora... You're a priestess of Xenon...' *And I've touched you with lust...* 'The Curse... Gods no!'

Across the clear sky, lightning streaked, and the terrain thundered.

'Let me explain—'

All but running towards his steed, Venn clutched his bag, stumbling away from her.

'Venn!'

Head shaking, he mouthed, 'No,' over and again. He shut down. Chilled. Eyes brittle and cold. 'I've Cursed us all...'

She felt it.

And then she heard it, the thought he couldn't bear to voice. The thought she couldn't bear to hear.

Witch.

She sank to her knees.

He mounted, kick-started the grey, and galloped towards the sun, not once turning back.

PART THREE: RETRIBUTION

THE TEMPLE OF ARYON, ORDER OF XENON OF THE BLACK MOON

Autumn 797 A.S.

Thirty-Four

A hollow, fractured shell. Ella had thought there was nothing inside her left to break, but she was wrong. This ache was worse than anything she imagined. A betrayal like no other. If the goddess had poisoned her brother's heart, the god had poisoned her very soul.

And then it began. Fluids spilled down her thighs and seeped into the parched dirt. Pain tore through her abdomen, shot down her thighs, and spasmed deep in her core. The birthing.

Amber had not yet returned, and the priestesses' rites lasted for another full night. Her mind could call, but they would be dumb, deaf, and blind to her until dawn. She couldn't even scream—no one would hear her.

How long before the babe emerged from her womb? Should she attempt to return on her own, between the cramps of her labour? Or should she wait for someone to find her?

Another spasm. She clutched her abdomen, let out a cry and followed with a howl, as loud and as far as the wind could carry.

F orbidden from using magic, Breeyan and Felda hovered over Sallyn, who twitched and shuddered, while Shira stepped in to lead the final night's rites for the women outside. Tired and hungry, they waited for the sign of first light which would end the fast.

Exhausted and over-stimulated, Breeyan's hands shook, the shrillan's cumulative effects taking their toll. She encouraged Sallyn to suck on a damp rag when she was able—which wasn't often. Her skin appeared almost grey. Soon, she stopped sweating, and then she stopped twitching, and eventually, ceased moving at all.

Dawn broke, and a priestess arrived carrying a trencher. 'Food, Your Holiness. Elnora is safely clear of the horizon.'

Too late, Breeyan thought, letting go of Sallyn's limp wrist. *Far too late.* She pulled the sheet up and over the dead girl's face. 'After the breaking of the fast, let us mourn. The god has claimed one of His own.'

By the time Ella hobbled to Aryon's citadel, the clenching spasms were minutes apart. She had abandoned everything at the outpost and walked back alone, clutching her belly, pausing as each paroxysm gripped her, then shuffling on once the cramping passed.

As she arrived, a gaggle of priestesses watched on. Not with spiteful curiosity, but solemn, eyes red from weeping. What was going on? It was like they weren't even seeing her.

She staggered inside and towards the infirmary where her aunt and Felda hovered over a motionless priestess atop a slat bed, her arms folded across her chest. The High Priestess and medic sponged her flaccid limbs.

'Is that Sallyn? What's wrong with her? Why isn't she mov—' Another spasm. Ella cried out and crumpled over.

The women rushed to her side, slipped their arms beneath to support her weight, and ushered her towards an empty bed.

'Why won't she move?' Breeyan and Felda blocked her view of the other bed.

Felda hovered over her. 'Hush. Try to relax. Focus on your breathing, like when you meditate.'

Breeyan peered around. 'Where is Amber?'

Another contraction of her labour. She moaned through gritted teeth.

'Where, Ella?' That voice, commanding.

Head shaking, tears streaming. 'I don't know. She never came for me. I walked back alone.'

Breeyan faced Felda. 'Light the fire. We need something to draw upon.'

With a wave of her hand accompanied by a short, sharp, chill, Felda set the fuel in the nearby brazier alight. After a time, she retrieved a hunk of heated coal with her tongs and placed it by Ella's side.

Warmth! Immediate relief.

Felda fished out a further three hunks, placing them around Ella's limbs.

Ella sucked at their power until she felt weightless, her pain a dull ache. Her surroundings misted with the sensation of drifting through liquid far from her body. Her simulacrum seemed separated from its flesh, her physical body lying below, panting, sweating, heaving. With detached curiosity, she watched Felda and Breeyan fuss over her. They looked so far away, thousands of tiny points of light. She felt no corporeal pain, only the ebb of ethereal currents tugging at her aura.

Through the god-sight, Breeyan and Felda's auras blazed, but atop the bed beside hers, the strange empty body could have been stone.

'I didn't like the look of tonight's moon.' Breeyan's voice sounded oddly muted.

'A blood moon, sure enough.' Felda wiped her brow, head shaking.

Through mystic eyes, as though Ella hovered above the ceiling and beneath the night sky, the moon appeared low and fat and crimson.

'There's naught to say it's related to this birthing. We've had tragedy enough today.'

'True spoken,' Breeyan said, followed by an unvoiced thought: *Why hasn't Amber returned?* She dabbed Ella's forehead with a damp rag. Her concern appeared genuine.

Ella absorbed more heat and time blurred. She drifted between consciousness for what seemed like minutes, and then days, but must have been hours, while Felda and Breeyan took turns by her side.

'The babe's coming. I see it crowning.'

A sharp jolt, as though Ella's simulacrum had slammed into its flesh. She opened her eyes. Chaos. Throbbing fire. Hands fussed and prodded. A long, agonising silence, and then a piercing wail.

'Keep pushing, Ella. It's almost over.' Felda handed a flailing, gooey bundle—her daughter—to Breeyan, then placed her hands back between Ella's straddled thighs, ready to receive the afterbirth.

Breeyan drew the infant close and rinsed away the birthing gunk with a cupped hand. Water trickled over the babe's skin. With every splash, she wriggled and squirmed, eyes wide where they should squint closed. Ella had never seen her aunt move so tenderly.

Breeyan sponged the babe clean, swaddled her with a long linen strip, tucked the corners in tight, then handed her to Ella.

She sensed her aunt's emotions stripped bare as she let the newborn go. Ella held her, and she snuggled against her heart. A jagged memory tore at Breeyan, of another babe, another time. This was the most intimate regret her aunt had ever known.

Felda raised the afterbirth. 'May the god banish any remnants of Curse captured by the union of lust, Cleansed by the birthing of innocence.' She chanted in the Ancient tongue, then tossed the meaty, bloodied sack into the brazier. It hissed and smouldered. Felda's cheeks sucked inwards.

The rising vapour revealed the face of death.

Ella clasped the babe. Puckered and bluish where she wasn't cream and pink, her eyes stared. These eyes already knew. Already saw. They looked just like his. A stab through her womb, her breasts.

With a typical baby snuffle, the newborn suckled at the air, hungry and searching, her tiny fists clenching.

Eyes closed, Ella pressed her lips against that too-soft skin and wept. 'Xarion,' she whispered.

'What did you call her?' Panic in Breeyan's voice. She and Felda exchanged a glance.

'Xarion, my baby girl.'

Breeyan reached out, but Xarion glared at her with piercing ice eyes. Breeyan lowered her hands and stepped back. 'I'll return shortly.'

Ella nodded, dozing with the babe close to her heart.

Breeyan cast another look at her companion. Xarion was still watching. She shuddered, turned, and retreated, with Felda trailing after.

Thirty-Five

Venn did not stop riding until he reached Ella's counterfeit grave. Such a savage charade. Though he had seen her, held her, loved her—gods, how he'd loved her—he needed to ensure their meeting wasn't some cruel dream. That he wasn't going mad.

Her cairn mocked him. Its jasmine grown stronger and taller, crawling along the rocks, tendrils shoving between cracks, and those thorns, taunting. His body trembled, and his stomach churned. Sweat broke across his forehead and soaked his armpits.

He fell to his knees and clawed at the dirt.

Hours he dug, shovelling armfuls of soil, reaching firmly packed clumps that had never been upturned. Caked in mud, skin torn, nails snapped, he continued until he knelt inside, certain the grave was bare. As empty as his tainted soul.

Hours he'd wept here, calling to her, praying for her, his city crumbling, and all the while it was a lie.

Now, he could not weep, would not pray.

Too late, he realised why he fought for Ella against all reason, pining like a man sickens for his pipe of white smoke. Why he risked his province to marry her, to bed her. She had bewitched him. She was like her mother.

Until that moment, he never believed Queen Prya a witch. Not truly. Wasn't sure he even believed in magic—a tale spun by priests to instil fear. Now he knew sorcery was real, that Ella cast her spell over him, soul, mind, and body.

Gods, he felt it still. Yearned for her, *still*. But he could not—would not—give in to that yearning.

All those moons wasted... Years, truly, when he might have pursued a pure and righteous marriage to the Princess Elder, an alliance to benefit his province and further the interests of his people.

Now it made sense why Gohran always pushed that match. No wonder he lied and hid Ella away. His only other option would have been to denounce her, as he denounced his mother. Gods, the burden he'd carried alone.

A stab through his core. His friend watched him grieve. Lied to everyone. To *him*. How would he face the king now?

Venn climbed from the grave, brushed the dirt from his clothing, his skin. He wanted to scrub away the sensation of being soiled, corrupted. It was no good. He would never be clean again.

By the goddess, what had he done? If the Moon God had marked her... His guts wrenched, and he vomited, heaving until there was nothing left inside.

He spat on the grass, wiped his mouth on his sleeve, and straightened. What was done was done. A life with Raeyn awaited.

R elief washed over Lynden when she heard Venn's unmistakable footfalls. She set her sewing aside—not that she'd managed three stitches together—and hurried to greet him.

Grim-faced and coated in dirt, Venn clomped into Nedran's foyer. He dumped his satchel, tossed down a wilted sprig of jasmine and placed a single flattened stone on top. Fine scratches covered his arms.

'Gods, Venn! I've been sick with worry. Where have you been?'

'On a fool's errand, that's where.' He ran fingers through mud-crusted hair.

'Promise me you'll never disappear like that again. Not ever.'

'I told Mykan I would be gone for a few nights.'

'But not me. And you went alone.' Tears fell as she let her breath out for what seemed the first time in days. When she reached to embrace him, he held her at arm's length.

'Venn, what is it?'

'I want you to organise my wedding right away. You can liaise with the king's steward as to the particulars.'

'But the period of mourning—?'

'I've mourned long enough.'

The following day, Lynden presented her proposed plans. She wouldn't consult with Gohran's man until she had Venn's approval.

Venn scanned her notes, scratching out almost half the items, muttering, 'Frivolity.'

She had been wise to wait.

'The list of guests?' He held out his hand, and she passed the next parchment. 'What about Byson and Taia of Wernad? And their sons. They have kin this side of the Gythyn, too. Make sure they're invited.'

'We hardly know them.'

'It's time we got to know them better.'

Later, when Jonas returned from Lichen, Lynden showed him the revised list.

'Anyone would think Venn was making some statement about his connection to Erldan.'

'He's not prepared to back it with coin, though, is he? Does he want everyone to consider him a miser?'

'For once, I agree with him. This alliance isn't cheap. And Gohran's hardly the coin to throw around.'

'If I was Raeyn, I'd feel insulted.'

'If you were Raeyn, you'd settle for a ceremony in the stables and a plate of spoiled meat to get out from under your brother.'

Lynden pulled a mock scowl. 'Gohran might not be your favourite person, but he can be charming and eager as a yearling once you know him.'

'I'd rather not have to.' Jonas's mouth twisted.

'I don't critique your choice of bedfellows, Jonas. Kindly do me the same courtesy.'

'I can't help having a superior palate, Lyn.'

She rolled her eyes, then sighed. 'I suppose I should envy Raeyn, marrying a man she truly cares about, maybe even loves.'

Jonas squeezed his sister's shoulders. 'You'll find someone, Lyn. Give it time.'

'I hope so...'

'And he might be halfway decent.'

'Jonas!'

Thirty-Six

More elaborate than ever, Davith's equinox rites should have engrossed him, but worry crawled like insects over his flesh. Gohran could not shake the notion he should have accompanied Jarrod to deliver the dowry himself.

When he retired to his study that evening, and Jarrod still had not returned, his restlessness peaked—a fire twitching in his limbs. 'Fetch the Princess Elder,' he said to his servant.

'At once, Your Highness.' The servant bowed and retreated.

Gohran paced. This silence was unnerving.

Raeyn arrived, already in her nightdress, her copper curls combed out, and curtsied. 'Your Highness.'

'He's still not returned?'

'Who, your driver? No...' Raeyn frowned. 'Where did you send him, anyway? Why all this secrecy?'

'Some things, sister, it is better you don't know.'

'What rot! I'm supposed to act as regent, yet every time you disappear on one of your missions, I feel useless. I have kept all your secrets, brother, even from Jay.'

'Once you're settled away from Erldan, what I choose to share will be of no concern.'

A heavy sigh. 'If I see or hear of Jarrod's return, I will send word if not the man himself. Now if you'll excuse me, Your Highness, I would like to get some sleep.'

When Jarrod was not back by morning, Gohran sent men scouting. They wouldn't venture beyond the outskirts of Erldan to the west, but to direct them otherwise would invite questions he did not dare answer. Even Davith knew only that Jarrod was delivering something of value, not where or to whom.

After a few days with no sign of man nor beast, Gohran considered riding further under cover of darkness, but he had no cap or peasant's shirt to disguise his unmistakable black hair and insignia-branded garments.

Meanwhile, Davith demanded his attention, as they established henad courts throughout Greater Erldan. One matter or another always seemed to require him. But that morning, Davith arrived in the main foyer, accompanied by a neophyte, whose pale, greasy hair was slicked back and fastened with a bone clasp, a fashion the holy men lately adopted.

'Your Holiness?'

'Highness.' Davith's mouth set in a grim line. 'I bring grievous tidings.'

A lump formed in his throat, and a leaden weight settled in his stomach.

Davith signalled and his neophyte knelt, outstretched palms opened to the sky, presenting a bronze dagger.

He retrieved the dagger, its touch oddly cool. A triangle inside a wheel graved its cross guard—the mark Jarrod inherited from his father, King Rohan's driver, before him.

'Recovered from a meadow north and west of here.'

'No...' he whispered.

'Your soldiers of fortune told me bandits ambushed them, Your Highness, injuring both, but your man, Jarrod, he did not survive.'

Gohran thought the dagger might scald his flesh. He squeezed its hilt until his knuckles turned white, imagining it slicing through his fingers and palm. 'How? Did no one see them roaming?'

'Who would be out there to observe them, Your Highness?' Davith shook his head, eyes pitying.

'The guards—where are they? I must question them.'

'Gone, Your Highness. They feared the bandits returning to hunt them down and finish the job, so fled the moment their injuries allowed.'

'Those guards were the best, you told me...' Gohran angled the blade towards the priest. His voice might have been the knife's edge.

Davith rested a hand upon his neophyte's shoulder and drew him back, positioning his body between himself and the king. 'The bandits vastly outnumbered them, and I did not know they would head into wild territory, away from watchful eyes—'

Gohran edged closer. 'The delivery was *supposed* to be away from watchful eyes. Jarrod was *supposed* to be under the vigilant watch of your men!'

Davith stood as serene as if his monarch did not rage before him. Behind his back, he motioned for his neophyte to exit, and the greasy-haired youth scampered.

When Davith spoke again, his voice soothed. 'I feel your grief, Your Highness. No one could have predicted this. Perhaps if you had shared their true destination with me...'

Gohran's nostrils flared. He slowed his breathing and reined himself in. It was not Davith's fault.

'We shall find those responsible, Your Highness.' Davith approached him like a rescuer coaxes an injured wildcat. 'Let Our Lady of the Dark Sun sustain you through this hurt. I will be Her guide for you...'

Davith's voice found a crack in Gohran's shell. He shattered and dropped to his knees, weeping horrid, rusty tears. He had lost a trusted man, and Ella's dowry with him, while outlaws had seen fit to trespass his lands and follow his driver out west.

He would not contemplate what it meant for Erldan's coffers and the deal he brokered with his niece's life. Thank the goddess Venn requested he bring his wedding to Raeyn forward. He needed that alliance secured to stave off the debt collectors.

Thirty-Seven

C hanting flooded the hall of prayer for the Blessing of the Dead. The priestesses had pushed their wooden pews against the wall to create space to march in procession around an oblong slab overlaid with white cloth. Atop lay Sallyn's body, bathed in herb-infused oil until her sickly grey skin glistened. Lit candles surrounded her, their flames straight and tall, unstirred by the priestesses' movement.

Beside the slab, with her ceremonial knife in hand, Breeyan hovered over a milk-coloured foal with pinkish skin, its blue eyes staring, vacant. The foal lay limp and preternaturally quiet. Where one of its hooves should have been was a deformed stump. Marked by the gods.

The procession halted, and the women formed a series of concentric circles surrounding the corpse, beast, and High Priestess. Their chant swelled, growing fevered, almost a wail, and the candlelight elongated still more. A cool draught brushed over the dead girl. Her pale hair stirred as though the wind carried spirits, their invisible hands lifting the cloth corners to wrap around her.

With a cry in the Ancient tongue, Breeyan brought the knife down. Panicked, the beast shuddered, fighting the spell of calm laid on it. She stabbed directly into its heart, and it spasmed, then slumped, motionless.

Breeyan retrieved the knife and sliced its throat clean across. Blood flowed and oozed, and she caught the flow with cupped hands, fire behind her eyes. She scooped and poured the animal's blood over the shroud, its scarlet liquid soaking through.

A few drops reached Sallyn's lips, and they parted. Her corpse twitched, momentarily animated. The movement pulled her shroud away. Eyelids opened, her stare glassy, as she mouthed silent words. Several gasped. Studying blood-lore had not prepared them for this.

The flow of blood slowed, and the chanting faded. Sallyn's body fell still and lifeless. Breeyan closed Sallyn's eyes with her fingertips, leaving two bloodied smears. She restored the shroud to its rightful place and bid Sallyn's soul to travel safely to rest in Xenon's arms. A gust rushed through the room in answer, tousling the women's hair, tugging at their robes, and extinguishing the candles. Thick, blackened smoke lingered. Xenon had accepted her.

That afternoon, Breeyan, Shira, and two highly ranked priestesses carried Sallyn's body to a square of barren terrain. This would be her grave. Unlike those who followed the cult of the Dark Sun, Xenon's followers saw nothing sacred in burial, no need to venerate soil that held soulless shells. In Ancient times, they would have cremated her, but not now. Elnora's worshippers had tainted that rite, too.

It was Shira who later told Ella about Sallyn's death and her funeral rite, while Ella recovered in the infirmary, Xarion cradled beside her.

'Gods, how?' she asked.

Shira shrugged. 'Fever, want of food or water, a reaction to the shrillan. Only the gods can say.'

Ella looked away.

'You may consider it savage, but most of us fled for our lives when we came here. The god offers sanctuary. The least we can do is honour Him according to the scriptures. Sallyn is at peace now.'

Ella kept her eyes on her daughter. 'Did anyone from the Gern or Crescent Mountain attend?' It was customary for the orders to conduct one another's funeral rites to allow those closest to the deceased to grieve.

Shira shook her head. 'Breeyan wanted to perform the rites herself.'

Ella said nothing, wondering if there was some reason her aunt didn't want the other orders involved. Perhaps she felt responsible. The suspicion resonated. A truth, then.

Xarion stirred.

'I should feed her.' Xarion fussed constantly, wanting to be fed, to be dry, to be held. As soon as Shira was gone, Ella picked her up, grateful to be tucked away.

Felda taught her how to nurse, but Xarion wanted more than Ella could possibly give. She was fierce about it, too. It was only after Ella's true milk came in that she settled. Now, as Xarion latched on, Ella winced. She ached so much to love her, to believe she wasn't Gohran's. Yet searching that midnight hair and noontide eyes, she saw nothing of Venn in her.

Venn.

His disgust at discovering her robe tore through her core and shattered her heart anew. Since returning to Erldan she feared Venn learning of her shame, and the lie she spun to cover it. She never imagined it would be her magic he spurned.

Another tug, brutal and demanding. Ella bit down in forced silence, eyes welling again. Some days, she thought her tears would drown her.

'The lore tells us women with certain temperaments are weepy after bearing,' Felda had said. 'But I say, that's rot. I'd be more wary of any woman who wasn't emotional following her birthing. It tells me she has not grasped the truth of her situation.'

Meanwhile, Xarion almost never cried, merely watched her mother with recognition of Ella's wretched thoughts. Impossible, Ella knew. Yet that was how she felt when those familiar eyes sullied, drawing constant power.

Breeyan hovered in the doorway. 'How does she fare today?'

'Well, my thanks.' Ella pulled the sheet up to cover herself, noting Breeyan avoided using Xarion's name. 'I was hoping Amber would stop by. I haven't seen her since the grove.'

Breeyan stiffened. 'You should rest, not host visitors.'

'It won't tax me to see her.'

Her aunt paled. There was something she wasn't saying. Had Amber told her about the letters? Surely not, or Breeyan's wrath would be upon her by now. And Breeyan would be right. Such a foolish risk.

Breeyan cleared her throat. 'When your daughter has finished feeding, I can take her.' She motioned to Xarion, eyes shrewd, mouth tight.

'There's no need, Aunt. She's been quiet.' The thought of Xarion with Breeyan made her uneasy.

'The sooner she grows accustomed to being apart from you, the better. It will make it easier when you return to your usual duties.'

Breeyan reached for Xarion, grasped her close and kissed her forehead. It was the most tenderness Ella had seen her aunt display. As she carried Xarion away, the anxious twist in Ella's belly was only slightly more prominent than her acute sense of relief.

Breeyan left her niece's side with a heaviness unlike anything she had experienced. Holding the babe was exquisite. Her smell, the soft fuzz of her hair and skin! She cooed, sighing as Xarion nestled into her, those tiny eyes darting behind closed lids as her face wore the shifting emotions of her infant dreams. Breeyan kept reminding herself the babe was Ella's, not hers. *And not him.*

Xarion's heart thrummed against her chest. She wriggled and squirmed, waking. Breeyan held her close and let power bleed between them. Xarion was potent. Though barely emerged from her mother's womb, the promise of magic oozed from her.

Breeyan sensed her yearning and created a miniature diorama from ethereal substance to entertain. An image of priestesses kneeling before Xenon hovered in mid-air like a suspended sphere. Xarion watched the play of light and colours, her capability and awareness surpassing any ordinary infant who, at this age, typically experienced the world without focus.

'Those darling eyes,' Breeyan whispered. *Like his.*

Xarion stared at her, indifferent. She wanted more.

Breeyan poured power into the picture and the scene shifted. The priestesses shed robes for weapons and armour, fighting alongside their mighty warrior god. Then the temple transformed into wilderness, thick forests with wild creatures peering through leaves, shuffling along the grass.

Details grew in response to Xarion's curiosity. She yearned to see and know. Yet the image remained translucent, never quite solid, never quite real, constantly threatening to dissipate. As fast as Breeyan could build, Xarion destroyed; her desire to consume absorbing its energy.

When Breeyan looked into the child's eyes again, she felt a peculiar sadness. A darkness.

Shira approached. She sensed her before hearing her knock. 'Forgive my intrusion, Your Holiness.' Her apprentice appeared dishevelled.

Breeyan allowed the diorama to fade and Xarion glared at them both.

'Any news?' Breeyan asked, still focused on the babe in her arms.

'Not a thing. I've scoured the entire area where Amber was supposed to wait. I found remnants of a campfire and hoofprints, but they dwindle into thick grass to the north, and then nothing. It's like she vanished.'

Breeyan's connection to Amber was not strong. She had tried scrying but sensed only muffled darkness. She chewed the inside of her cheek as her nervous fingers entwined with the babe's. 'Did you retrieve everything from the grove?'

'Yes, Your Holiness.' Shira hovered at the door. 'I noticed something else out there, too. Something odd... It might be nothing...'

'Go on.'

'Did the princess mention refugees or people passing during her stay?'

Breeyan stiffened. 'She did not.'

'It's just...' Shira swallowed. 'Recent hoofprints appeared to lead up to the grove.'

Breeyan's eyes narrowed. Amber would not abandon the order, but Gohran may have persuaded her to return with him. Had he visited the outpost before he left, perhaps to see his sister, and then taken Amber with him?

She thought back to Amber's premonition and her frightening meditation. Could she have done more? If only the rites permitted magic, they could have avoided this whole tragedy. She might have used her powers to heal Sallyn, sensed Amber was in danger, and summoned her back. She certainly wouldn't have sent her alone.

That Amber's disappearance and Sallyn's death coincided with the birth of Ella's child under a blood moon had to be an omen. And then that name! Why choose Xarion? Breeyan felt she was grappling with so many loose threads, unable to weave them into a tapestry that made sense.

'Shall I return Xarion to her mother so you can update the council?'

Breeyan flinched. The irony that Sallyn's death created a welcome distraction haunted her. Priestesses rarely passed so young, and the mourning women were too absorbed to wonder why Amber had not yet returned, but she couldn't postpone informing them indefinitely.

'Leave the babe with me a little longer. There's one more thing I'd like to try before we summon a hearing.'

Much as it ached, she would spy on her lost son through the fire. He may have been the last person to see Amber alive.

Amber's muscles ached and her skin burned from being tethered. Briefly, someone removed her hood, and she spied a pock-faced lad, hair pulled back in a knot, holding a lantern. He shoved a hunk of stale bread and a leather canteen through her cage bars, then left her in darkness.

Her parched mouth watered. She tried not to lick her cracked lips as she swallowed her saliva. Her captors had bound her hands, ankles, and knees, so she shuffled her buttocks along the cage floor and nearer the bread. She shook her hair from her face, grabbed the bread between bound hands, and gnawed the hard crust like an animal, rinsing it down with canteen water. Liquid spilled along the sides of her face, down her neck, and soaked her robe. Her head still spun. She slowed her breath. Willed herself not to vomit.

Scurrying, like the patter of tiny feet. Someone moaned.

'Hello?'

Silence.

'Is somebody there?'

Another moan.

'You'll want to finish eating before they stick that sack over your head again.'

Amber took another bite of bread. She did not know whether the person speaking was the same as the person moaning. All the sounds overlapped and echoed, foggy in her mind.

Footsteps approached and the jangle of metal. She stuffed another chunk of bread into her mouth.

A bar lifted, and the door creaked open. Lantern light cast eerie shadows and her vision blurred. Crust caught in her throat. She coughed.

'Drink up,' came the voice through the dark.

She brought the canteen to her lips and savoured the last of the liquid. By the time she finished, her head whirled. Had they drugged her? Is that why she could make no sense of anything?

'Let's get you ready...'

'For what?'

A snigger.

'Ready for what?' Pitch rising.

'Oh, he's going to enjoy this one...'

More spinning. Laughter echoing. Then, nothing.

Thirty-Eight

At first light, Gohran ordered his men to scour his kingdom. Now he had an excuse to ride further west.

'Head towards the End of the World,' he commanded. 'Show the culprits no mercy.'

But an arduous day of searching uncovered nothing.

'Your Highness, shall we turn back before nightfall?' Tarraen asked. Elnora was setting behind darkening clouds, and the men hungered, slumping in their saddles.

Gohran shook his head. 'We push on. I smell a storm approaching. Once it rains, we'll have less chance of spotting anything.'

'Where are we to shelter when that deluge hits, Your Highness?'

He glanced at the wall of grey gathering. They had no bedding or canvas, for they expected to be home before now.

'You think the swine responsible will let a bit of damp slow them?'

Tarraen said nothing and signalled for the men to ride.

In the distance, lightning forked as the first bloated drops of rain fell. Static on the air like fire tingled through his veins. Lightning ignited the clouds, and amidst their shadow and light, Gohran pictured a battlefield after a war. Dead and dying strewn across an abandoned glade, vultures and crows feasting on corpses. He shuddered. With the next flash, the image was gone.

Gohran slowed, eyes narrowing as he examined the ground ahead. An area of flattened grass appeared trampled by recent livestock. The unmistakable scent of spilled blood. This must be where it happened. Yet they recovered no shred of metal, wood, or leather.

'Those villagers we passed surely saw something,' Gohran said. 'Let's circle back.'

Where Gohran burned for justice, for vengeance, his men looked resigned.

'Goddess willing, they might offer us lodgings for the night,' Tarraen said.

But when they approached the scattered roundhouses, the few stragglers retreated, slamming their doors and windows shut.

'Listen, all of you!' Gohran's voice carried across the rooftops towards curious eyes peering through doorways and window frames. 'My trusted man headed this way on equinox eve, accompanied by two guards herding livestock.' Gohran sensed their curiosity, even if they dared not come near. 'I'm told someone ambushed them in a meadow near here.' Gohran pointed toward the flattened grass they'd encountered earlier. 'The guards survived, but my man did not.' A pause, listening. 'One of you surely saw something. Heard something. Strangers passing through, or meandering stock, any kind of disturbance.'

Silence. Not even the creak of a door or window.

Gohran addressed his men. 'Search each hovel, barn, and tent. Get me answers.'

Steeds tethered, the men moved from building to hut, pounding on doors, peering through windows, and beneath canvas flaps. They inquired, cajoled, and threatened, but the villagers denied knowing anything.

Gohran spied a curly redheaded lad coaxing stray ilaks into a barn. The ilaks had startled when Gohran's men pounded on the door of the roundhouse. 'You! Boy! Come.'

The boy herded the last ilak through the doorway with his staff, then hesitated.

'When the King of Erldan summons you, boy, you come.'

'No one will hurt you, lad, provided you speak up.' Tarraen beckoned him.

The boy shuffled nearer. Gasps escaped from the roundhouse before a sobbing woman emerged, clutched the lad, and dragged him towards the house. 'Please, Your Highness. Don't hurt my Sorgan.'

Tarraen peeled the woman's arms from the boy, placating. 'We just want to ask some questions.' He put his arm around the boy's shoulders and led him to Gohran.

His freckles and the orange hair sprouting on his upper lip reminded Gohran of one of his childhood tormentors. 'Where do you graze your flock?' He nodded towards the ilaks.

'It-it dep-pends, Your H-Highness,' the boy stammered.

Gohran's eyes narrowed.

'I swear to you, Your Highness, we've seen nothing like what you describe.' The boy's mother grasped again for her son and brushed the copper curls peeking beneath her kerchief off her sweaty brow.

'M-Ma's right, Your Highness. I haven't seen aught…'

Gohran's patience thinned. He gripped the boy's collar and dragged him from his mother. The lad's face paled satisfyingly.

Onlookers gathered.

'Someone here must have noticed something,' he called.

Silence.

Gohran's fist scrunched tighter around the lad. He drew a dagger—the blade that had belonged to Jarrod—and rested it against the boy's throat.

Gasps and a quickly stifled squeal.

'Please—Your Highness!' A wiry, orange-bearded man—likely the boy's father—edged closer, his unarmed palms raised.

Nothing like the threat of violence to loosen a man's tongue, Gohran thought.

'There was a lord came through here for a time, Your Highness, but he left long before the equinox.'

'From what family?'

'I couldn't say, Your Highness. He wore plain clothes.'

'And you noticed nothing about him?'

'A good-looking sort. Brown hair and green-grey eyes. Popular with the ladies and lads who tend that way.'

'And there was that beggar woman and her children, came through around the same time, just before the lord took off. But as my husband said, that was weeks ago,' his wife hastened.

'No one recently, Your Highness.'

Gohran's grip tightened, the blade pressing into flesh.

'Please!' the woman cried.

'You've seen nothing unusual?' Tarraen asked.

The wiry man's wife stepped forward. 'That woman carried the mark of a heretic, my lord, but she didn't look like one.'

Fire flashed before Gohran's eyes, and blood thrummed in his ears. 'This woman carried Xenon's mark, and you did nothing?'

The bearded man shrugged. 'Folk here don't peek too closely into others' affairs, Your Highness. All I can say is they weren't the ones you're after.'

Gohran let the boy go, shoved him aside, and strode towards his father. The lad choked and spluttered, rubbing his neck. The man, now over-towered by Gohran, could have been his childhood tormenter, fully grown. 'It would behove you to look closely in future. It is everyone's duty to be on guard against followers of the Moon God.' He paused, holding the onlooker's attention, as he gestured to Tarraen.

Tarraen grabbed the man's arms and secured them behind his back, then yanked his bright orange curls to expose his throat.

Lightning flashed. For the briefest moment, the boy wore Gohran's frightened face, and his father, King Rohan's.

Gohran raised his dagger and addressed the villagers. 'Heresy is everyone's business.' His voice drove through the darkening sky like a nail through wood, eyes searching terror-struck faces. 'Anyone who harbours outlaws or heretics will suffer this fate.' Gohran handed the dagger to Tar, hilt first.

Tar took it, awaiting Gohran's nod, then slit the man's throat.

With grim determination, the party rode towards Erldan through the storm. Eyes closed, Gohran absorbed the chill of the wind and rain, the thunder rumbling through his torso. Opened, he savoured the lightning forking across the sky.

Alone in his room that night, he didn't need to cut. The memory of freshly spilled blood surged through his limbs. His heart pounded, echoing the final beats of life as he breathed in the vitality of vengeance. Later, he drifted to sleep, hearing the satisfying screams of those who dared defy him.

Thirty-Nine

Since Venn abandoned Ella at the grove, she might have been treading water, moving through the citadel the way a spirit roams, trapped in eternal torment. Whenever she recalled his horror, fear, and, most of all, disgust, she longed for relief from the constant struggle to stay afloat. Dreamed of tying rocks to her robe and lying face-down beneath the order's stream until her lungs emptied and her consciousness extinguished.

But then Xarion's need for her wrenched, and she couldn't follow through. She wept, brought her daughter to her breast and listened to her infant heart beating, focusing on the air filling her chest, each muscle moving, the babe's fecund scent.

When she'd held her niece Serrah for the first time, she marvelled at her tiny life. She longed to feel that wonder about Xarion. But those azure eyes and dark hair twisted.

Nonetheless, she kept Xarion close, her weight supported by a sling fastened across Ella's torso. Despite the anguish, it was for that tiny life that she dressed, bathed, breathed, and moved.

Breeyan tried to dissuade her, to separate mother from child. 'Within the order, a priestess must be loyal to Xenon foremost,' she'd said. 'Leave her in my care or Felda's if you grow too weary to carry her.'

Ella shrugged her concerns away. Using the sling kept Xarion from fussing, and it kept her putting one foot in front of the other.

That morning, after breaking her fast in the infirmary, with Xarion secured to her chest, Ella headed outside and towards the stream, in the opposite direction of the bird coops, which she couldn't bear to be reminded of.

Grey clouds gathered like a sentry, their sombre mien matched by the priest-esses as they resumed their duties following Sallyn's burial. The women spoke in hushed whispers, moving through their day habitually, reflexively, reminding her of her first trip to Nedran, watching peasants work their fields, resembling game pieces at play.

Another twist. Venn surely lodged a knife through her heart when he rode away from her, as every thought of him drove it deeper.

A ruckus nearby. Nykki gestured at Shira, tears streaming down her cheeks. 'Shira—you can't let them! I can't lose her again...'

Shira held her arms out to steady the young priestess. 'She's already lost...'

'No!' Nykki fell to her knees and sobbed. She must have noticed Ella watching them, because she looked her way with loathing. 'It's her fault. It's always her!'

Ella flinched. These past moons, Nykki had thawed towards her, though she'd hardly seen her since the fast... She'd barely seen anyone. Now she'd frosted over. What was going on?

Shira drew Nykki to rock against her and weep. Mind-murmuring between them. Though Ella stood at a distance, she felt like an intruder. She focused on Xarion and shuffled further away until she saw Nykki disappear into the citadel. Distant thunder rumbled. She should move undercover.

She hadn't got far when Shira called to her. 'Ella, hold a moment.'

She stopped and waited for the apprentice.

'It's about Amber.' Shira's dark braids wound and fastened into a neat knot at the base of her skull. Solemn eyes studied her. 'Did Amber say anything unusual when she left you at the grove?'

Ella's stomach clenched. 'Nothing, why?' Had Amber told Shira she'd tried to contact Venn?

Shira's brow buckled. 'After escorting you, she was to collect your dowry from the king.'

Ella reeled. Amber was meeting Gohran and hadn't said a word. 'Where is she? I've not seen her since.'

'She never returned.'

The ground lurched beneath her feet.

'You didn't know,' Shira spoke quietly. She never invaded Ella's thoughts like the others.

'Aunt Bree tells me nothing.'

Shira took a slow breath, her mouth a grim line. 'If there is anything you haven't told me, anything Amber mentioned. Please, it would help.'

She shrugged. 'Amber dropped me at the grove, uttered a few harsh words, and left.'

'Harsh?'

She wished she'd stayed silent. 'Just old wounds between us... When I didn't see her, I assumed she was still upset.'

Shira frowned. Another rumble across the sky, rain yet to fall.

'What is it?'

'Her Holiness and the council members plan to Sever her. I hoped you'd know her whereabouts, so they don't have to.'

She shook her head. 'It seems I know less than you.'

'I wish that weren't so. The rite will sever the parts of Amber's mind tethered to the order. Obliterate those areas of her memory.'

'Like what Aunt Bree did to Shaena and Meela?'

'Worse. Shae and Mee kept their memories intact. Severance destroys a connection entirely.'

'No. They can't...'

'Breeyan says they must. To keep Aryon safe.'

'Safe from what? There are people in Ycelt already aware of the order, and the priestesses don't go butchering their minds!' The horror of seeing Shaena and Meela's vacant stares... She couldn't let Breeyan do that to Amber. Wouldn't.

'This is different. Amber is a sworn priestess. We have no inkling where she is, or with whom.' Shira looked as if she wanted to weep. 'If you know anything that might help...'

She shook her head. 'I'm sorry…'

'What about your brother? Would King Gohran or his associates have reason to harm her?'

A hardness in her throat. 'My brother is not fond of witches.'

Shira flinched at her use of that word.

'But he wouldn't hurt Amber…' Would he? What if he was trying to get out of paying her dowry? How much had he promised their aunt? Likely more than he ever offered Venn.

Xarion fussed. She was getting heavy.

'Here, let me take her for you,' Shira reached out.

Ella lifted the sling over her shoulder and passed her across.

Shira held her gingerly in the crook of her arm. 'She's adorable. She looks just like you.' Xarion gurgled happily until the surrounding air grew chill. Shira swayed, unsteady. 'Ella—What's wrong with her? She's not—there's something not right…' Shira's voice wavered, her skin puckering like gooseflesh. 'I need to sit.'

Ella lifted Xarion from the priestess's arms. 'She's hungry.'

Shira sank to the ground and drew her knees to her chest. 'Gods, does she always do… whatever that was? Sap your energy?'

'Since the day of her conception.' Ella sat beside Shira on the ground and guided Xarion to latch to her breast.

Colour returned to Shira's cheeks. 'Why doesn't she cry like a normal babe?'

Ella shot her a foul look.

'Oh, my apologies, I didn't mean—'

She sighed.

'Do Felda and Breeyan know?'

Ella shook her head. 'And they're not going to.'

'But—'

'She's only a babe. She doesn't mean to.'

'What happens when she does that to someone else?'

'The others don't go near me or her. Only Aunt Bree, and she passes energy willingly.' She brushed Xarion's soft crown of hair with her palm. 'I don't think she's aware she's doing it.'

Shira frowned.

'When Xarion is old enough, I'll teach her to stop. Doubtless I did the same to my mother—and you to yours.'

'We've raised abandoned infants here before, and none have ever done *that*.'

'Have any had truly powerful magic?'

Shira didn't respond.

Xarion's eyes opened, and she stared directly at Shira, who shuddered. Lightning sheeted the sky, followed by the first drops of rain.

'I'll finish feeding her inside, and then speak to Aunt Bree.'

Beneath her ever-present tears, anger seethed. Venn might have spurned her, her brother might have violated her, but she hadn't finished fighting. Not yet. And if she couldn't fight for herself, she would fight for Amber.

FORTY

Within the hall of prayer, the councilwomen circled the stone idol of Xenon. Breeyan led their chant in the Ancient tongue, harmonising vocals swelling until the statue reverberated.

From her scrying, Breeyan had gleaned Gohran learnt of the ambush, but knew nothing of Amber. He had not been at the meet. When she scried for the missing priestess, even with her sisters' help, she pictured only darkness.

Protocol dictated the order's protection was paramount. If they could not determine Amber's safety—and ensure Aryon's secrecy—they must invoke the Severance. But when she informed the council Amber was lost, their objections came thick and fast.

'Please don't ask us to Sever her, Your Holiness,' said Magdelyn, a Wise whose pale braids mimicked a wispy halo framing her face.

Another said, 'At this distance, if we can't pinpoint her mind...'

'If we waver even slightly.'

Why must they challenge her at every turn?

Breeyan confronted them. 'What choice have we? We don't know where she is or who she's with.'

Pyrina stepped forward. 'I agree with my sisters, Your Worship. It's too risky. We might mutilate her mind.'

'Think of the risk if we don't,' Breeyan snapped.

'What if she's merely shielding?' asked Magdelyn.

Breeyan shook her head. 'I still sense her. It's no shield. She's blinded, and likely in peril.'

'Then we should be out there, searching for her,' she pressed.

Breeyan was regretting appointing Magdelyn to the council in Shaena's stead. 'And risk more of us coming to harm?' She pictured Ella's babe. 'What if the culprits come to Aryon?'

'Then the Curse will befall them soon enough,' said Pyrina.

'If it hasn't already,' Magdelyn added.

The Curse.

The word rippled through her, resonating like a Myan singing bowl, along with the words, *only if you let it be.* She recognised the phrase from old lore. Why hadn't she recalled it earlier?

After much wrangling, Breeyan convinced them. Severance was the only way.

Now, with hands joined, they merged their latent power. The rite forbade drawing from any external source. They could share and amplify only what they held within and between them, and with one mind, direct and funnel their energy into a single focus: the Sacred Stone.

Power hummed, and the stone glowed as if a flame burned within. Breeyan exhaled and let the energy flow. Hers, theirs, a joining of anger and fear. The god's grief-stricken features stirred. Their ancestors betrayed Him, and as the women's source poured into His replica, that betrayal pierced her heart like glass shards.

Energy swelled and bled between them, the Stone's azure almost blinding, but she did not glance away. *Picture her. Remember...*

Breeyan visualised Amber's saffron braids, her intelligent eyes—the reason Prya chose her to tutor her daughter, though Breeyan wished she hadn't. Another bright mind and astute soul, lost to the Cursed land.

The other women's images filled her mind's eye, tiny variations in perception, memory, and emphasis, all fusing to form a greater whole. And yet, their shared vision kept fogging over, as if Amber's thoughts were clouded. Had someone drugged her, rendered her unconscious?

Don't stop. Reach for her. Breeyan channelled the energy, directed their joining, careful never to defy Xenon's laws and draw another's source into herself.

The image faint, Amber's weak aura pulsed dull yellow. Breeyan drew more power and concentrated on navigating the labyrinthine twists and turns of Amber's tangled memories. It was one thing for a priestess to identify the chambers of her own mind, but quite another to recognise those segments in someone else. If Breeyan found the right entry point among her reveries...

'Call to her, each of you.'

In unison, they thought her name. If Amber turned her mind towards them, Breeyan could cut through her weakened defences and identify the segment of her psyche that housed her connection to them all.

A tremor of recognition, blurry and knotted. There was no clear border around the memories connected to Breeyan or to Aryon, but one area lit up, glowing blood-red. *An anguished smile, eyes and mouth yearning. Chestnut braids, smooth skin, heat flowing as limbs entwined. Nykahlia.*

Breeyan startled. There was no moment to consider the implications. She utilised the glow as a focal point, followed its threads and traced an ethereal boundary around every part of Amber's mind that the feeling touched.

'I need more power.' She couldn't find the edges, the substance of Amber's psyche matted and blurred together, intertwined. The lore-masters did not warn of this. Old texts told of splicing neat borders between discrete segments. Breeyan would have to encompass more of the matter that lay beyond or risk leaving traces behind.

Are you certain you want to do this? Pyrina's thought reached her. Cutting so wide and deep into Amber's mind might incapacitate her irreparably.

Please, Your Holiness...

Breeyan had read tales of bigoted men who believed themselves immune to the Curse, who sacked temples, raped priestesses, plundered coffers, and burned what remained. She imagined riders falling upon them, dragging the women from their beds, torturing or enslaving them. Cleansing them alive. Her greater fear was picturing them harming Ella's babe, her tiny heart beating, wide eyes adoring, her pouting mouth...

She had lost one child. She would not lose another. If she had to sacrifice a novice to ensure Xarion's safety, so be it.

She prepared to slice...

'Stop!'

Breeyan froze.

'Stop, all of you!' It was Ella, her raven tresses loose about her shoulders, Xarion cradled in her sling. The infant studied the idol as though she knew precisely what was happening.

A whisper in Breeyan's mind: *She should not be here.*

And another: *She is unsworn.*

'Ella! Leave us,' Breeyan commanded. Then to the women, 'Keep going. We are almost there...'

Ella strode towards the circle, tried to shove past their joined hands, but the working's blue tether of force bound them tight.

'Hold steady!' Breeyan called. She had nearly completed drawing the boundary for the first incision. It blazed like a luminous sapphire, the exact shade of the replica stone. With a touch more force, she could sever.

She began to slice...

From outside the circle, power surged, rippling in bore-like waves. The priestesses' hands blasted apart, and they hurtled backwards. Minds jarred, pain shared and amplified between them.

Breeyan's vision blurred, and her head pounded. For the briefest moment, through her distorted sight and bruised mind, the idol came to life. Xenon stood amid a battlefield strewn with corpses, and the Sacred Stone glowed the colour of blood.

Ella stepped into the centre of the circle, arms outstretched, an azure glow emanating in all directions. Cradled against her, the babe stared, almost preternaturally quiet.

'I said leave.' *You endanger us all.*

Her niece did not flinch. 'Shira told me.' She circled, catching and holding each gaze. 'You should be ashamed.'

The women cowered. Some rubbed their temples. Most were too stunned and weakened to respond.

Breeyan stood and gripped Ella's hands to force her silent. Her mind reached and clawed, but found nothing left to draw. By the gods, where had that surge come from? Was this the potency her sister promised? That she'd been waiting to see?

'Ella...'

'No, Aunt. Not this time. I won't let you break her like you broke the others.'

'I warn you...'

'Go ahead, Aunt. You won't harm me. Not now.' *You won't do that to Xarion.* Her silent message landed, and Breeyan paled.

'You imagine breaking Amber's mind will keep you safe? You call me selfish, and yet you sacrifice her, of all people. Amber would end her life before she let anyone torture your whereabouts out of her.'

The women cast their eyes to one another, to the floor, anywhere but the princess.

Breeyan addressed her sisters. 'Take your leave. Eat. Rest. Then we shall reconvene.' She did not need the entire council witnessing this defiance from her niece, while she lacked the strength to rein her in.

The women stood and shuffled out. Pyrina squeezed her arm as she passed.

They were as weary as she. First the Severance, then that surge of pure force. She ached as if its blow wrenched her simulacrum beyond her body and then slammed it back in.

Now alone, her voice barely a whisper, she confronted Ella. 'How dare you? Do you realise how dangerous that was?'

Brazen, defiant, Ella tossed her head. 'I do, Aunt. But do you?'

'You don't understand. This isn't about what Amber chooses, or how strong or loyal she is. If she falls into the wrong hands, she might not have a choice.'

'And you would cut her off before you've tried to find her, to rescue her?'

'If we don't do this, she endangers us all.' *Even her.* Breeyan nodded to the babe.

'Then I'll reach her before they do.'

Breeyan shook her head. 'Amber is sworn. Don't you understand what that means?' *The Curse.*

'The Curse should protect her. She should be safer than me in Ycelt.'

'No, Ella...' How might she explain its double-edged nature? How the Curse befalling the wrong kind of man could only ever lead to more death and destruction?

'I'm recovered enough to travel on horseback. Let me find her. Let me at least try before you butcher her.'

'What about your babe?' Breeyan asked.

'I'll take her with me.'

A spear through her heart. 'No. I forbid it.'

Xarion peered at her, eyes hard and cold. And then a sudden pinch at her mind. A craving unlike anything Breeyan had experienced.

'She's hungry...' Ella's voice strangled. Her face scrunched in pain, yet she seemed unsurprised.

Breeyan studied mother and child. There was a twist to Ella's mouth that Breeyan noticed once or twice before, usually when she examined her daughter. What darkness was she seeing there? Did she resent this child? Breeyan risked reaching for her mind, but met with fierce resistance.

The babe's hunger intensified. Ella's infant hardly ever cried, and now Breeyan understood why. She didn't have to. 'Go. Tend to her.' *But know this discussion is not over.*

Her gut wrenched as she watched them leave. What had she just experienced? That power! Gods, the brute force of it. She hugged her arms across her chest as she stared at the now lifeless idol. *Xenon, help me.*

Forty-One

'I heard of your recent encounter on the outskirts of Ycelt, Your Highness.' Davith stroked his chin with the stylus hovering above his wax tablet. He paused mid-stroke to meet the king's gaze, then peered at his notes. 'I caution against taking matters into your own hands. I worry about the ramifications.'

'What else could I do, Your Holiness? Those villagers knowingly ignored an entire family of heretics. I won't stand for it. It makes a mockery of Erldan's rule. We should establish courts beyond the towns, on the village outskirts.'

'Oh, I agree, Your Highness. Once we have the funds, you shall have as many courts as you desire.' They had established a further three outposts in the preceding weeks, taking advantage of autumn's milder weather. Already the shorter days and cooler nights hinted of winter.

'For now, your henads must make do with the coin in their coffers. When those bandits murdered my man, they stole from the king's purse.'

'As I said, Your Highness, had I known the true nature of your man's errand, I might have advised you differently.' Davith continued making notations.

Gohran wanted to knock the stylus from his priest's hands. 'A king's business is his own, Your Holiness. Your men should feel honoured to be entrusted with the monarch's work.'

'Oh, they are, Your Highness. But if we are to root out these covert heretics, we must present a united front across the region.'

'So, we shall.'

'Yet you have not confronted the dryhten of Nedran on the matter of harbouring heretics.'

Gohran ran his hands through his hair, tugging at the ends with his fists. 'Lord Venn of Nedran requested we waive the period of mourning and hasten his marriage to the Princess Elder. Between organising the wedding, hunting my man's killers and negotiating with your priests, I've had no moment to broach the subject.' He did not add Venn was yet to reply to his letters.

Davith nodded and finally put his stylus aside. 'You bear a great deal of responsibility, Your Highness.' His steady hand rested on Gohran's shoulder.

Part of him wanted to shrug it away. Another part longed to lean into the reassurance of their former bond. Perhaps Gohran hadn't provided sufficient information to equip his hired guards. He should not have relied on Jarrod alone. But who else could he trust?

As though the priest read his mind, Davith said, 'You might appoint a new adviser, and not one who doubles as your driver, or some other role. Someone whose sole focus is to serve you, Your Highness.'

'With what coin? As you said, we are scrounging to establish sufficient courts.'

'Your sister's wedding contract will ease pressure in that domain, will it not? I strongly advise that you prioritise your immediate need, Your Highness. Your role is too important. You should not concern yourself with shuffling coin and delivering livestock.'

The mention of replacing Jarrod stung like squeezing citrus into an open wound.

Davith's hand remained on his shoulder, solid and warm. 'If his Highness will permit me to help in this small way, I can source some options for you. And please—don't take my recommendation alone. Vet them according to your sound judgement.'

Tension eased from his shoulders. 'That would assist me greatly, Your Holiness.'

'**A** real life sworn priestess of the Black Moon! How archaic!'

That voice sent a chill through Amber's bones.

'Bring her here.'

The greasy-haired lad who served her bread and water gripped her arms and dragged her forward, recognisable by the acrid mix of his sweat and breath. As she shuffled, her vestment abraded the backs of her knees where rope still bound her. Beneath her loose hood, she glimpsed sandal-shod feet poking from below the hem of a fine robe, and the trailing gold-threaded fringe of a cincture. A priest.

A palm slithered around her shoulders, down one arm, across her waist, and then up the other.

'Oh, what a prize, indeed.' She shuddered. 'Remove the hood.' *I want to see her.* The thought slipped into her mind.

She wanted to kick, to scream, but her vows forbade it.

Rough hands pulled the hood off. After a moment, her vision adjusted to the dusky light, and she recognised Erldan's head priest, his twisted grin icy enough to freeze a demon's heart.

Salacious eyes ran the length of her. 'What a delightful time we are going to have!'

His fingers reached for her matted braids. His other hand caressed her cheek, as brutal eyes took in every inch of her, but carefully avoiding her gaze, his touch never lingering. He knew how to evade her influence.

Where was she? Surely these dank walls weren't within Erldan's temple. The priest continued to tug at her braids, untying and loosening, studying each strand. Her stomach churned, her mind woozy.

'That colour! Delectable.' Another tug, another braid loosened. 'To think, they locked *this* away...'

She sensed a twitch in his groin. Her breath quickened. She stared straight ahead, unmoving. Another tug. She recoiled.

He leaned in, inhaled, and whispered, 'What a delight, indeed...'

'Anyone foolish enough to meddle with a sworn priestess will know Xenon's wrath,' she said, her tone even.

'Ah yes, the Curse.' A chortle. He released her braids and wiped his fingers on a nearby rag as though he considered her soiled. 'These hands would never touch a sworn priestess in violence or in lust.' He held his palms up. 'Boy, come closer.'

The neophyte shuffled forward and bowed.

'I have many hands at my disposal. Neophytes like Grogan here. Loyal. Dependable. Expendable.' He signalled. 'Stand.' Grogan stood and Davith slapped him, hard.

Grogan steadied himself, then bowed his head. 'It is an honour to serve, Your Holiness.'

'The Curse hurts not only the violator, but everyone in their orbit,' Amber said.

'What a poor little novice you are... You misspeak your own lore. "The Curse does not only hurt the violator—it touches those around them."'

'You think that won't include you if your underlings harm me?'

'I will be nowhere near when they have their sport with you.'

'That seems a very literal interpretation. I wonder you would take such a risk.' An image played behind her eyes of priests using another body to abuse, to torture, turning a sorceress's mind powers against her. He'd done this before. But to who?

The coldest grin she had ever seen spread across that twisted mouth. 'I know you read thoughts, witch.'

Sudden knowledge seized her. Hot irons. A face thrust into a bucket of icy water. Drying scabs across a naked back. And worse, a horrid trio of lads unlacing their trousers, sniggering, and jeering.

'I may not read yours, but by the time my servants are done with you, you will have told me everything I care to learn. And if you don't, my servants will take their sweet, sweet time with you.'

FORTY-TWO

The working left Breeyan ravenous. Shira brought a plate of roast fowl scrounged from the kitchen to her study, and she gorged, ripping flesh from bone with bare hands before her apprentice reached the door.

Afterwards, she wiped her fingers on a linen strip and homed in on her unfinished genealogy work. The force Ella displayed in the hall of prayer was extraordinary, but a shadowy suspicion was forming that Ella's infant daughter had amplified it.

Shira's archival research confirmed what her sister told her years before: *There's not so much as a hint of magic among any of our acquaintances.* But if the dryhten of Nedran was not Xarion's father, who was? Had Ella let a commoner into her bed? A servant, perhaps?

When Shira returned to clear the dishes, Breeyan asked her to fetch Ella.

Her niece arrived a short time later, carrying Xarion in her ridiculous sling. Breeyan motioned to the stool opposite. 'Sit.'

Ella remained standing. 'Spare your words if you intend to discipline me. I am not sorry I interrupted the rite before you maimed Amber. She deserves your protection, but you do not deserve hers.'

That defiance! Gods, she was like Prya. 'It's not a question of discipline. It's a matter of risk. I am responsible for *all* these lives. Amber's is but one.'

Xarion peered at her with those curious blue eyes.

'The council will decide your penance in due course. Right now, there is another matter to discuss.'

Ella said nothing.

'During your birthing, I received an omen—a blood moon. At first, I thought little of it. Sallyn had passed into Xenon's arms, Amber had not returned, and you were in your labour. During the Severance Rite, I received another: a rendering of a battlefield. The warriors wore insignia long forgotten, save for the archives.'

Breeyan gestured at the papers arranged before her—the pages she removed from the order's copy of *The Lost Warriors* back when she was first granted access to the manuscripts as Her Holiness's apprentice. 'See here—these are the insignia.'

Ella moved closer, studying the illumination depicting Xenon and His warriors, men and women, slain across a battlefield. The god wore the same expression of grief as His stone idol. The blue insignia represented the azure of the Sacred Stone before it was embedded in the king's sword, while King Myrhan's emblem displayed the sword without the stone on a blood red backdrop.

'These are from the story of Xarion.' Ella sounded surprised. 'But I've never seen these pages...'

'They portray the ultimate battle fought by Xarion where she and her lover are slain. Where they slay each other. And they are the exact insignia I pictured in vision.'

Breeyan let her niece experience the chill that ran the length of her spine, watched with envy as Ella held her babe tighter. 'You can see why your daughter's name surprised me.'

Xarion frowned, one hand circling a lock of Ella's hair. She observed her surroundings the way a much older babe would.

'The name seemed fitting, somehow...'

Breeyan resisted the urge to chew her nails. 'That's what I suspected. In truth, it answered some questions for me. It confirmed you are the product of two kinds of magic: Mathildh's line, the Ancients, and the new magic imported with King Myrhan. What I don't understand is how your Xarion can be so potent. Such strength normally results from a union between two powerful mages. I can't find any trace of magic in Lord Venn's ancestry.'

Breeyan sensed Ella building a barrier around her thoughts.

'The priestesses of the Black Moon may not have to worry ourselves with the intricacies of intermarriages between close kin, as the priests do, but ancestry is still important.' She paused, watching her niece. 'While magic doesn't always breed true, magical ability has rarely skipped a generation in our family. It's usually quite potent, too. Your strength was a surprise at first, but retracing your bloodlines, explainable. I don't suppose your mother told you about our ancestors?'

'Father taught me he and Mother descended from the first High King of Ycelt.' Ella straightened. 'Father from King Raedyn's second son, who settled and was crowned in Erldan, and Mother from his only daughter.'

Breeyan nodded. Prya and Rohan's marriage reunited the original Erldan line. 'What you may not realise is while King Myrhan's children each had magic, Myrhan's second wife had sorcery of another kind.'

'Second wife?'

'His first supposedly died in childbirth, but some historians speculate it was no accident. Myrhan took a keen interest in a local chief's daughter soon after settling in Ycelt. Mathildh, her name was. Myrhan's daughter, our ancestor, was born of his second marriage. This is significant because she was one of Xenon's followers and boasted incredibly strong powers.'

'But the Old War—?'

'In the war, Mathildh and her daughter, Xarion, sided with Xenon, against her husband. Well, if you could call Myrhan her husband. Some records make clear she had no desire for marriage. Some even say he took her by force.'

Ella drew a breath, focusing on her daughter instead of meeting Breeyan's gaze.

'Xarion did not survive the war, but Mathildh arranged for Xarion's daughter, her granddaughter, to live with the holy sisters in Aryon. Her sons remained in Ycelt. She had the priests and priestesses swear they could keep their land and formal titles, the eldest as dryhten, provided they offer one daughter from every generation to serve Xenon.'

'The treaty.'

Breeyan nodded.

Ella wrapped Xarion's swaddling tighter around her.

'Xarion's daughter initially sought refuge with her uncle in Ycelt until after her grandmother's death. She was the first to be given to Aryon, her powers a dowry to seal the treaty.'

Ella said nothing as she disengaged Xarion's grip from around her hair.

'When your mother agreed to bring you here, I expected you might become my successor. Fate interfered with those plans, but then Xenon gave us a gift in baby Xarion.' Wistful. 'If we apprentice Xarion to Shira, she can learn the rites, perhaps even lead Aryon. Follow in the footsteps of our ancestors. It's a better life than an illegitimate daughter could normally expect.' A powerful, if interrupted, succession. It was fated, she was sure.

'Once Xarion is weaned and your moon-time returns, your bodies will be pure and restored, and you can take your vows.'

Ella shifted uncomfortably, as though something pained her. Was she frightened?

'I have no intention of taking any vows, Aunt, and you would do well not to force me.'

'You cannot remain unsworn at Aryon indefinitely.'

'That won't be a concern.'

'You mean to go after Amber?'

Ella didn't respond.

'I meant what I said, Ella. If you are fool enough to return to Ycelt, I can't stop you, but I forbid you risking Xarion's life in the Cursed Land.'

'I'll not leave her behind. Not with you and your vipers.'

Breeyan gripped her arm. Her strength recovered, heat spilled over and through her. 'Then you shall stay.'

Ella pushed back, her magic churning, grinding against Breeyan's. Breeyan pushed back harder, blocking Ella's power. Her head pounded and her muscles weakened, but she didn't stop.

Do you want me to use my full force, Aunt?

Ella's eyes blazed the same azure as the Sacred Stone.

With voice and mind, Xarion let out a piercing wail. Both women reeled. Breeyan released her grip and soothed her temples.

Xarion fell silent, tears glistening on her apple cheeks. Breeyan's heart melted. She would sacrifice anything, *anything*, for that tiny soul.

Ella stepped away with Xarion in her arms. 'I will stay, Aunt, but if you Sever Amber, I will leave, and you will never see Xarion again.'

Forty-Three

The journey to Erldan was slow. Venn brought an honour guard and attendants to help prepare for the wedding. Wheeled along on carts, they also carried the season's freshest produce and several barrels of ale. On arrival, servants unpacked wagons and tended horses. Banners bearing the emblems of both provinces graced nearly every wall. Though made from salvaged cloth, they appeared almost new. Within the main gates, locals bustled, while most guests wouldn't arrive until the ceremony day, or shortly before.

Raeyn was up in the women's quarters. Archaic lore had the bride undergo a series of purification rituals with her women folk to prepare for marriage. She would remain indoors, hidden from male eyes, for a full week before the nuptials. The barbaric rites that denied a woman pleasure through mutilation were long outlawed, thank the goddess. However, the customary primping and preening persisted.

Gohran greeted him on the keep's front steps. 'It is happening at last.' His hand was firm on Venn's back. 'Shall we ride tomorrow after breakfast?'

Venn shook his shoulders loose to disguise his flinch. Such eagerness in those eyes, but Venn could not stop picturing Ella's haunting smile and forbidden robe.

'My thanks, Your Highness, but I have much to tend to.' He couldn't meet that gaze.

'And a troupe of servers to help you.' Eyes narrowed, he gestured to the entourage bustling through the grounds, transporting goods inside.

'Indeed, Your Highness, and someone needs to direct them.'

'You have a steward for that.'

He wished Gohran would stop pressing him. 'I understand yours recently met with treachery. You have my condolences.'

Gohran stiffened. 'My thanks. Such a nasty business.'

'I keep hearing concerning reports of unrest, bandits, and thieves,' Venn said.

'They won't be a problem for much longer. Once I find the culprits...' Gohran's jaw twitched, the satisfaction in his imagined vengeance evident, before his features shifted, lightened. 'Let's not linger on such unpleasantness. I am glad you are here, my friend. Pleased to have you as my brother under the law at last.'

Sorrow lurked behind the king's false brightness. Desperation. A terrible burden to carry alone. First his mother, then his sister, and now his steward—likely a trusted fellow—taken from him.

'Once the chaos settles, come find me,' Gohran said. 'I should be with Davith, my head priest.'

'I will, Your Highness. Perhaps when my brother arrives. If you'll excuse me. After my servants have finished up here, I'd like to retire.'

En route to his guest quarters, a lad Venn didn't recognise stopped him. 'My lord? Lady Servan of Mornae bid me inform you she has arrived.'

'My thanks. Tell her I'll meet her in the parlour directly.'

He wanted to rest, but was keen to see his aunt again. So much had transpired since he wintered in Mornae after placing Jonas's pregnant lover, Kerryn, in Servan's service, and he could use her counsel now.

When he entered the parlour, she turned his way, face alight. 'Lord Venn! As handsome as ever!' Servan cupped his cheeks. She looked older, the parlour's subdued light and overly rich hues casting morbid shadows that washed out her features. Compared to the more modern Nedran, Erldan felt overcrowded with legacy, as if the monarch's ancestors haunted the corridors.

'Aunt. It's good to see you. I'm glad you made it so far south.'

'The High King's army couldn't keep me from my favourite nephew's wedding. Though it is odd timing, so close to winter. You'll just have to house me if the weather sours early,' she said with a sly smile, then peered down her nose at him, eyes narrowed. 'There's not some urgency around the proceedings, is there? I'm yet to meet Princess Raeyn, but I hear she is a stately and proper young woman.'

'Indeed, she is, and no, Aunt, it's nothing of the sort, I assure you.'

'I don't suppose it would matter if it was. The sooner Nedran has some heirs, the better. Your mother would never forgive me if I let your line wither.' She glanced around. A servant hovered near the doorway, eyes steadfast. She leaned in close. 'My darling nephew, I heard there was another betrothal planned in its stead. I am sorry for your loss.'

Venn felt like a hunted deer. 'How did you...?'

'Your girl Kerryn has the lay of this land still, and I'd be a poor relation not to keep abreast of my dearest sister's foals—may she rest in Our Lady's arms.' Servan turned and gave a deferential nod westward, where Elnora was sinking below the horizon. 'And may the goddess embrace your former betrothed.'

Venn blanched. He almost blurted that Ella wasn't dead. That even if she was, she would not rest with the goddess. At least Gohran hadn't denounced her, he thought. She would have some meagre existence before being eternally condemned.

Gohran had once sought exile rather than execution for a young mother within his jurisdiction. Had he sequestered Ella for the sake of the unborn child?

His child.

He recalled the shock of seeing Ella's swollen belly out at the grove, its peculiar expanse pressed against him, like some uninvited creature thrust between them. The notion of him as its father had never settled into his psyche, not like the succession that so concerned his aunt. And then it was all snatched from him.

He swallowed the wooden lump in his throat. Couldn't think about that child now. A different future awaited.

'How is Kerryn?'

'Well. Her little cherub is a wonder. He has his mother's mop of pumpkin hair, but those coal eyes are quite a marvel.'

Venn stiffened, picturing Jonas's hazel eyes—green and grey rather than brown. The what-ifs plagued him. What if he had believed Jonas when he said the babe wasn't his, and had not taken Kerryn to Mornae? What if he'd wintered with Ella at Nedran? What if Gohran never dragged her back to Erldan, if she'd never returned to him, desperate and broken, afraid for her life?

She had been afraid. Afraid of Gohran.

No wonder! Had Gohran known then what she was? Had he always known? Were there signs Venn missed? Even after Gohran denounced their mother, he hadn't suspected. Why would he?

With bitter irony, he ought to thank his friend. Had Gohran not intervened, he might have married a witch.

Raeyn was no sorceress, of that he was certain. He admired the Princess Elder, but she in no way beguiled him. Did she know her sister was alive? That she was a sworn priestess? Was he to begin his new life marred by secrets, by lies?

He choked back his tears, for he would deceive the goddess Herself if it kept Ella safe. He loved her—craved her—still.

FORTY-FOUR

This time of year, the priestesses were abustle trying to finish the harvest, stowing and preserving stores. They chopped wood, mended wall hangings, cleaned carpets and blankets, and dragged the thicker winter coverings out of storage to dust and air, ready to hang.

That morning, Shira arrived in Breeyan's study, arms laden with logs to replenish the stack for her hearth. She pushed against the heavy door with her rear. The door creaked open and Breeyan signalled for her to deposit the wood and sit, which she did, waiting for permission to speak.

Shira had barely uttered two words to her since the disrupted Severance Rite, and Breeyan let her marinate in silence while she completed her task. She need not voice her disapproval—it permeated the air between them.

The council was yet to reconvene to discuss Ella's penance, and Breeyan could not decide whether to discipline Shira as well. She should not have told Ella about the rite, but now she needed Shira's help to research alternatives to Severing Amber.

Finally, she looked up from her work. 'Yes?'

'It's Sallyn's cousin, Magdelyn, Your Holiness. She plans to return to Crescent Mountain.'

Shira's tone was even. Breeyan considered testing her apprentice's mind shield, but refrained. She would not risk fracturing their relationship further.

Breeyan sat back, eyes narrow. 'I can't say I am surprised. She only came to Aryon to be with Sallyn.'

'Belmae and Karra intend to accompany her.'

Breeyan nodded. 'They'll be safer in a group. When do they leave?'

'Two days hence. They are expecting to take at least one packhorse to ferry any goods we want exchanged.' Shira swallowed hard. 'Your Holiness?'

'Hmm?' Breeyan would not make this easy.

'I know this isn't my place...' Shira stalled, carefully plotting her words. 'If the priestesses are heading into Ycelt anyway, shouldn't they be out looking for Amber?'

A twist to her mouth. 'You are right, *apprentice*. It isn't your place. A group of priestesses may travel along the outskirts of Ycelt close to the End of the World in relative safety. It is another matter to send them into the maws of the Cursed Land.'

Shira's expression remained neutral. 'Of course, Your Holiness.' A deferential nod. 'I understand.'

'Good.'

'However, I reiterate that your niece, Princess Ella, is prepared to go, and she remains unsworn...'

Breeyan snapped. 'Ella knows if she leaves, the child stays.'

'You would have her abandon Xarion?'

A churning anguish quickly suppressed. 'She would not be abandoning her—I am her family.'

'Forgive my speaking so, Your Holiness, but I worry the others won't welcome leaving Xarion here without her mother.'

'Never would I begrudge them that, Shira. Every time we raise an infant, it reminds us of the sacrifice the god demands. Seeing Ella's child is harder still, for it reminds us that one of His blessed has birthed within these very walls.'

'It's more than that, Your Holiness. I sense an aversion in the women.'

Breeyan stiffened, ice rippling along her spine.

'At first, I wondered if it was premonitory, but I've not experienced anything as distinctive as an omen. I've heard others speaking of it. It's a feeling when I'm around the child, a sense of unease, a darkness...'

A jagged breath. Thrice now the exact words had been used to describe an ill-feeling. She had assumed it related to Amber, but she couldn't ignore the possibility any longer that it was about Ella—or more likely, her daughter.

'Forgive me, Your Holiness,' Felda interrupted, standing breathless in the doorway, Xarion outstretched in her arms as though she'd soiled herself. 'I need to speak with you about Ella's child.'

Breeyan's eyes narrowed as she took the babe. Felda exhaled, visibly relieved.

'There's something wrong with her... I'm not sure how to explain... She's drawing power. Constantly. Like you or I would eat, or perhaps breathe.'

'Of course she is. She's powerful. And a mere babe. She hasn't learnt to control herself.'

Felda blushed scarlet. 'That's what Ella said. I just thought...'

Breeyan drew Xarion to her, bouncing and cooing. 'You have my thanks, Felda. You may go.'

Felda started towards the door, then paused. 'Was Xarion's father a powerful mage, Your Holiness?'

'Not that I have found evidence for in the archives,' Breeyan said.

'Then shouldn't Ella's powers dilute, not magnify, in her daughter?'

Breeyan paled. 'Had we raised Ella at Aryon from infancy, she would have been much stronger at a younger age.'

'Yes, of course.' Felda backed towards the door.

Shira's eyes narrowed, but she remained silent. With a bow, she followed Felda's hasty retreat.

Alone with the babe, Breeyan slumped into her chair and let out her breath. So warm in her arms, Xarion's rounded cheeks blushed and her lips puckered like a tiny bow. She gurgled contentedly as Breeyan poured loving heat into her, trying to ignore the rising tide of unease. She hadn't wanted to admit her sisters might be right, that there was a darkness in the babe. There was only one thing to be done. She would summon the god for guidance. Reassurance. For surely there could be nothing amiss with this pure, divine life.

E lla stumbled through Aryon's dark corridors towards her sleeping cell. She was exhausted. Xarion woke her repeatedly through every night, for food, to be cleaned and dried, and sometimes just to torment her, she was certain. She had not recovered following her encounters with Breeyan and the council, so with an anxious twist, passed Xarion to Felda. She needed uninterrupted rest.

Along the passageway, a trio of priestesses stripped and changed bedclothes. Magdelyn, who Ella recognised from the Severance circle; Karra, a mouselike novice; and cherub-faced Belmae.

You killed her. A harsh whisper in her mind. *You brought the Curse upon us. You and that unclean child.*

She couldn't tell anymore whose thoughts reached her and wasn't sure she cared. The council had been about to destroy Amber's psyche, and for what? To protect a secret that was no true secret at all.

The women fell silent, staring as she passed. She hastened, aware of their gaze following, minds burning. They blamed her for Amber and Sallyn, though she'd had no say in either of their fates.

Once in her cell, she collapsed onto her bed, pulled the covers to her chin, and closed her eyes. She needed everything to disappear.

Blankets rustling, sheets flapping, and the women's whispers drifted through the too-thin partitions.

'Are you nervous about going?' Belmae asked.

'Not at all. I hear it's quiet in the north now,' said Magdelyn.

Karra joined in. 'I heard that, too. My sister's settled in Henctyn. It's close to the Gern.'

'Quiet doesn't make it safe. Not for us.'

'And is it any safer here? Poor Sallyn. So sudden.'

'Unprecedented.'

'I wonder...'

'You're not thinking of staying behind as well?'

'Something doesn't feel right anymore.' A wave of apprehension, but Belmae would not voice her true fears.

'You don't think it's...?'

'*She's* still here, isn't she, having birthed within these walls?'

'And the child's so peculiar.'

The Curse, that's what they meant.

'It makes me wonder if Her Holiness's judgement is clouded.' Belmae projected a picture of the foal chosen for the Blessing of the Dead. Something which spoke of the gods, yes, but hardly a sacrifice to slaughter a beast who would have died soon enough.

The others murmured their agreement.

'And now Amber is lost, too.'

Unspoken judgements followed these musings, searing her. The order's laws forbade Magdelyn from disclosing the council's proceedings, but Ella's disruption had unnerved every high-ranking priestess, and the sisters would sense that as clearly as Ella.

Exhaustion weighed heavier than their misgivings, and she let their voices and thoughts fade from her perception as she chased the void of slumber.

E lla bolted awake at a hand on her shoulder.

Shira hovered over her bed, her usual temperate demeanour having evaporated. 'We must talk,' she said.

Ella groaned and rolled over. 'Shira, please, I'm trying to sleep.'

While the rest of us work.

Ella ignored Shira's snide thought and propped on her elbow. 'About what?'

'Breeyan's little history project.'

Through the blur of half-sleep, it took a moment to realise Shira was talking about Breeyan's genealogy work.

'Has she realised yet?' Shira wasn't yielding.

'Realised what?'

'That Nedran's dryhten isn't Xarion's father?' Arms crossed over her chest, peering down.

Ella rubbed her eyes. 'Of course he is. Don't you think I'd know if he wasn't?' She'd never known Shira to be so hostile.

'Her Holiness has had me pull out every family tree of every noble family this side of the Halbar Ranges. You don't strike me as the type to have taken a tumble with someone common-born, and that only leaves one candidate.'

Snow might have melted down her back while someone lit a fire beneath her feet.

'Shira—please, I just need to sleep…'

'You know who helped me realise? Your old tutor, Amber.'

Ella shook her head. 'This is absurd. Why are you being like this?'

An image shoved into Ella's mind, of Amber examining Breeyan's genealogy notes, and Shira noting her reaction when she saw the matching crosses beside Ella and Gohran.

'Stop it! Stop it! This is nonsense.'

The vision disappeared. Shira's eyes sloped as though she pitied Ella.

'Why does it matter who Xarion's father is?'

'You might be unsworn, but such a union offends every god.' Shira loomed over her.

Ella pulled her bedclothes up tighter.

'Breeyan doesn't want you to go after Amber, but Magdelyn and the others have already provisioned one packhorse for their journey north. If we start now, we can provision another. They depart two days hence. Everything is ready. Food, bedding, utensils. You've a plain smock, haven't you? If you leave at the moon's zenith, you'll be far from Aryon before Breeyan realises you're gone.'

'You want me to leave…'

'Her Holiness's loyalty to your family blinds her.' *I won't let her sacrifice another.*

Shira, too, blamed Ella for Breeyan's choices.

'You've proved how resourceful you can be. I'm sure you'll persuade a farmer or two to shelter you along the way. Just use that beguiling smile.'

Ella clutched her blankets as the telltale prickle at her nape and the pressure behind her eyes of her power gathered.

'There's a reason Her Holiness is denying the truth,' Shira pressed.

A flash. Shira had raided Amber's memories. Seen what Amber had not wanted her to see, what she had not wanted to believe: Gohran watching Ella when he thought no one saw, and Amber recognising in that expression what Ella refused to see, time and again, until it was too late.

Shira was right. If Breeyan knew Xarion was born of incest, an abomination, she wouldn't just evict them, she would destroy them. To protect her people, she would Cleanse them as the henads had Cleansed her mother. Even Xarion.

Ella choked back a cry.

Shira was still speaking. 'Find Amber and bring her home, and I will leverage Her Holiness's blind spot for your daughter and prevent her putting those pieces together.'

She hadn't recognised her relief when Breeyan persuaded her to stay. Now that balance tipped once more. Back in Ycelt, she could no longer beg for Venn's protection. Gohran would denounce her before she revealed his shame, but if Shira told Breeyan the truth about Xarion… She couldn't stay. This wasn't only about rescuing Amber now. She would not risk her daughter's life.

'What about Xarion? She can't come with me. It's not safe.'

'I will care for her while you are gone.'

'Shira, don't let Aunt Bree sink her claws in. Don't let her be Moon Sworn.' *She doesn't belong to Breeyan. She belongs to me.*

'I swear it on the Sacred Stone.'

'As soon as I find Amber, I'll be back for her.'

When the midnight moon tide turned, Breeyan lay awake, preparing to undertake her working. She tiptoed from bedchamber to private study with an orb of ethereal light as her guide. Once there, she lit ceremonial incense and marked the required sigils with candles. On her desk, she laid a small feast of milk, bread, and cheese to aid her recovery.

She lay back and forced her breath into long, even beats. After so many years of meditation, Breeyan's simulacrum peeled away from her flesh like a dried scab. Weightless, her body might have been a lifeless lump. Her consciousness floated amid swirling mists of ethereal substance. Once, the sight of her disconnected body would have chilled. Now, she didn't glance back.

Liquid-like substance shifted and tugged at her simulacrum. She breathed into her chest, keeping one part of her mind focused as an anchor, and sent her questions into the void. Power poured behind her thoughts, travelling beyond any corporeal consciousness. *How was this child so strong? Why the unease, the darkness?*

Mists churned, forming whirlpools, then breaking waves. Within, currents flurried and shuffled, shouting, echoing. Wherever the god dwelled, her queries would reach Him.

Awaiting the reply was agony. Her deepest suspicions threatened to form pure thought to follow the others. She pushed them down and concentrated on the black and blue eddies, hoping.

Finally, a response: the image of a distant lantern light swinging, hovering, always nearing. Eventually it stilled, casting a glow across a bedroom. Closer still, she perceived a young boy playing on the floor beside a girl asleep in her bed. Both had raven-dark hair and the same azure eyes.

The boy scowled, chewing his lip, arms crossed over his chest. Asleep, the girl snuffled and rolled over. Crouched atop a rug, the boy readied to pounce on a phantom enemy, fists extended as if wielding an imaginary sword. He stepped backward and then lunged, thrusting the pretend weapon forward. Back and forth, he swung, trampled, and twisted, slashing faux opponents.

His clomping footfalls roused the girl, and she sat. Her gaze followed the boy's, seeing the same play image. The next warrior fell. She pointed and giggled, letting out an excited squeal as the boy crowed in triumph.

Air stirred. The boy hovered over the slain swordsman, one knee raised, foot rested on his chest. Both children's eyes met. He knew she had seen. Panicked, his sword and all the surrounding enemies vanished, and the entire image with them.

Breeyan stared into the blue-black void, heart flickering.

The darkness wasn't swirling as it should. She was still in vision. She absorbed the last of the room's warmth and poured heat into the working until she discerned a silhouette through the gloom. A man in profile, breathing hard into the night. Awoken from a nightmare, trying to calm himself: Gohran.

Forty-Five

Lynden woke with the sun in her eyes. Propped on her elbow, she held the bedcovers across her breasts. Gohran lay beside her, his lips slightly parted, stale breath snuffling. She had arrived at Erldan with Venn the previous day, purportedly to help the women in the lead up to the wedding. In truth, it was Gohran's bed she craved.

The king's face should have softened in sleep, but his dreams troubled him, rendering him all angles and hardness. She hated seeing him so. The empty crook of his arm taunted her. She longed to curl against his powerful chest, to twirl the dark hairs between her fingers, taste the sweat along the peaks and valleys of his abdomen, but she would not approach him uninvited.

Moisture on his cheeks. This wasn't the first occasion she'd caught him weeping. The last time, he was in the priest's temple, and she slipped away before he saw her. She never mentioned it, just as she never spoke of the burns and lines crossing his wrists, the scars like knife wounds that ran the length of his thighs, nor the strap marks across his back.

Part of her craved him allowing her into his thoughts, where she could know and understand his torment, but then she thought about unlocking his interior and terror surged, leaving her throat dry and her chest pounding.

Gohran stirred and rolled over, his features tempering at last. He scooped her towards him, arm circling her waist as his fingers twirled her hair. She savoured his warmth for the brief period she had it.

He kissed the back of her neck. An exhale tinged with grief.

'Another nightmare?' In sleep, he'd shouted Ella's name.

'Hmm? Oh, not that I recall.' He sighed again.

'I miss her, too, Your Highness.'

Gohran flinched, sat upright, and perched on the edge of the bed. A cold draught moved into the vacuum created by his absence. She had pushed too far. The slight window of vulnerability slammed shut. What torment he suffered, he endured alone.

She yearned to trace her fingers over the tree-bark-like etchings that crossed his back, to draw him to her, but he was already pulling on his shirt.

'I must tend to the morning service. But stay abed awhile. I can have the servants bring you breakfast, if you wish?'

'My thanks, Your Highness.' As a guest, she was not required to attend worship, though she should probably make the effort, given how important it seemed to the king. Lynden wondered if Gohran wouldn't have preferred priesthood to kingship. Either way, he was beyond her grasp.

He continued dressing. 'You should look over the noblemen while you are visiting. If there is a lord you favour, I'd be happy to speak to your brother on your behalf.'

Hardness in her throat. Did he want her gone from his bed, from his life?

He turned towards her, softening, as if she had spoken her fears aloud. Was her disappointment so obvious?

'A wedding always reminds one of duty, doesn't it? I'd like to know Venn will settle you with someone worthy... Though I hope you dally in my bed on occasion.' He ran the back of his hand along her cheek.

She pressed her lips to his fingers.

'Please excuse me.' He slithered away from her.

She rolled over and tucked the covers up under her chin. How much longer could she endure his oscillating fire and ice, pulling her in, then pushing her away? Sharing his bed, but nothing more? He was right. With Venn settled, it was time she found herself a husband.

G ohran left Lynden in his bed and hurried to the temple, the sour note of his nightmare persisting. He'd been a boy of perhaps seven or eight. Mother had asked him to watch Ella, who was already asleep, while she settled Jaydyn and Raeyn with their new nursemaid.

He wasn't tired yet, so created a game of make-believe while awaiting Mother's return. If he couldn't train with Father's men, he would practise here on the nursery rug. He imagined himself as the greatest warrior in Ycelt, cutting down his opponents one by one, then two by two.

At some stage, Ella must have woken. She giggled, watching him play, pointing out the approaching enemies. She saw them, too! The warriors and battlefield disappeared.

'Where did they go? Gon, bring them back!'

'Hush! There was nothing there. You're imagining.'

'I wasn't. They were right there. Gon!'

He grabbed her arm and twisted. 'Hush!'

She whimpered horribly, tears clumping her lashes, terror in her eyes. Gods, what he would have done to have taken her fear away.

Was this a dream, or a forgotten memory?

Years later, discovering Ella's magic shocked him. His anger, his fear, came not from Ella being what she was, but from forcing him to admit he was like her. A heretic.

When he woke, fire throbbed, an ache as palpable as desire mounting in his loins. He craved release, but with Lynden staying, he couldn't seek solace using the weapons stored in his secret chest. He could only use his body, and hers, to approximate relief as he swallowed his angst and prayed the goddess would forgive him where he would never forgive himself.

When he arrived in the temple, Davith was in no mood to soothe, accosting him right away.

'Have you spoken with the dryhten, Your Highness?' His neophytes bustled around the empty pews, lighting candles, straightening already perfectly laid parchments.

'Not yet, Your Holiness. Lord Venn is busy preparing for the wedding, but there will be opportunity once the dust settles on his nuptials.' After the wedding, he would be calmer, less distracted, and they could talk.

'We may not have time to wait. Were you aware there is a coven of heretics sequestered on our very borders?'

Gohran's stomach dropped below his knees as the colour drained from his face. He forced his voice steady. 'That's not surprising. The lore tells of Moon God havens to the west and north of here. It would explain why so many heretics have been passing through my lands.'

A quirk at the corner of Davith's mouth. 'Lore is often mere myth and legend.'

'And yet people act on both,' he said.

'So, they do, Your Highness. So, they do.' Davith paced. 'It might behove us to extend the goddess's rule. If a sanctuary exists so near, we should extinguish it, and any hope it represents.'

Blood pumped through Gohran's ears. If Davith was thinking of raiding Aryon, he must not realise the Moon Sworn inhabited the haven. Did he dare mention the Curse? Or would that reveal how much he knew?

He swallowed. 'I see no need, Your Holiness. Desert and wasteland lie beyond Erldan's outskirts. Anyone seeking refuge that way shall perish soon enough without our intervention. Better we expend our finite resources within Erldan's jurisdiction, and people will learn Erldan is not territory to dare trespass.' No one had sighted the outlaws who ambushed Jarrod yet, and he still needed to pay his aunt.

Footsteps crunched in the distance. Parishioners were arriving.

'Let us continue our conversation following the worship.'

Gohran took his place near the altar, but with clear access to the doors. He had no intention of lingering at the service's close. He had no desire to enter this discussion ever again.

Davith's sermon centred on the upcoming nuptials and how they created a union to solidify the goddess's rule across the southwest, though as Gohran peered around the temple, he noted Venn's absence. In fact, more than half the pews were empty. Where were his people?

When Davith invited Gohran to speak about the marriage and the henad outposts they had established within Greater Erldan, he stressed the need to bring fears and suspicions to the henads. 'No concern is beneath the notice of Our Lady's servants if we are to unhook the claws of heresy sunk into Erldan's flanks.'

Afterwards, Gohran strode across the pitted, cobbled streets towards the castle keep. Beside the road, a carter stared with eyes like stones as he repaired his wheel. *Miser*, he swore he heard the man say, though his lips never moved. More eyes glaring, bitter, resigned. Others loathing. Why weren't these folk at the morning service?

'Your Highness,' a scruffy man bowed as he passed. Beside him rested a collection pail. A beggar.

Gohran swallowed. Reflexively, he reached into his purse, then hesitated. He must not acknowledge his people wanted. Not out here, before these watchful eyes. He brushed the man's shoulder. 'May Our Lady keep you.' He dived his hands beneath his cloak and hurried on.

A woman and her clutch of hungry children stared after. *Aren't we all pious and mighty?* Her hardened gaze accused, and he could have sworn her hunger etched into his soul.

More imaginary voices in his head. He needed to silence them. He sped up, sharp wintry air rushing through his nostrils. It was one thing to be heckled away from his lands, where people did not know him or appreciate Erldan's fragile circumstances, but quite another for his subjects to revile him openly.

Thanks to the goddess, the wedding was nigh, and thanks to Nedran, it would provide a hearty feast and some free-flowing ale to distract and soothe minds and hearts, at least for a time.

Forty-Six

'How long do you suppose we have before my exacting brother summons me to take over his duties?' Jonas escorted Vera by the elbow, away from the castle and along the path leading beyond Erldan's old inner walls.

'More than this morning, I hope,' she said.

Late autumn sun shone through the chill as they strolled the grounds past the western archway, where fresh masonry afforded privacy to a picturesque glade. A scatter of stubborn daisies bloomed, determined to soak up the remnants of warmth before the crisp of winter sent them into hiding.

'If it was warmer, I'd take my shoes off to feel this lush green between my toes,' Vera said.

'That's not all I'd take off.'

Vera rolled her eyes.

He sobered. 'I'm surprised your parents let you attend, and not because it means being alone with me. Sheevan's father was singular in his disavowal of all relations between Creywmm and Erldan.'

'Ma and Pa are less than thrilled Venn is marrying into Erldan, but they also wouldn't pass up a representative from Lichen appearing at a royal wedding.'

'Tactical as always.'

'That's Ma.'

'And yet she sent you alone?'

'Pa's gout has kept him abed these past weeks, so Ma is watching over the estate. He's been grumbling around his chamber like a wounded bear.'

'Poor Teegan.'

'I'm sure it's no worse than a bee sting, but if it keeps Ma fussing...'

'I feel for her, but I'm not sorry that it's just us here.' Jonas sneaked his hand around Vera's waist.

Vera raised her eyebrows pointedly. 'With Aunty Lee to chaperone.'

Jonas peered around. They were very much alone. He leaned in close and whispered hotly. 'Lucky she's a lax one.' His palm slid lower, relishing the curve of her rear through her skirt's fabric.

'Jonas!' Vera feigned outrage, and wriggled aside, threading his wayward hand back through her elbow. 'Much as I enjoy your company, I'm here for Lyn. I will not let her endure the loss of her hopes for a love match on her own.'

Jonas rolled his eyes. 'So dramatic, Vee. Though I hope after Venn's wedding she stops loitering in the king's bed.'

'Unlikely, unless he drags her from it. She's quite smitten.'

Jonas groaned. 'Don't remind me.' He pointed to where an old elm had shed its leaves, creating a pillow of amber and cinnabar nestled between knuckled roots for them to settle on. 'Shall we dally awhile?'

'That depends on what you mean by "dallying."' Vera sidled into the crook of his arm. This was as intimate as she would let them be, he knew, in case the glade was less secluded than it appeared, but it didn't stop him aching for more when she slid her hand along his thigh.

His breath brushed her neck, but she turned to face him before his lips could linger. 'You know, I've never understood why the king insisted on the match between Venn and Raeyn. He might have secured that alliance by marrying Lyn.'

'That's an ugly thought,' he said.

'A romantic one for Lyn...'

'Perhaps he was trying to offload the Princess Elder to the one man who would do anything for him, no matter how unpleasant.'

'Jonas! Sometimes you're more outrageous than Aunty Lee... Though I suppose Raeyn's never had suitors slaying dragons for her, has she?'

'Now who's being outrageous?' he said.

'If it was only for the alliance, Venn might have married Jaydyn. At least she's not so dour.'

'Though he'd end up wondering who'd sired his sons, wouldn't he?'

'Ouch!' She laughed. 'And do you think that of me? Here we are, not even promised...' She slid her palm a little higher and squeezed.

'You don't leer after every lord who walks through the castle gates.'

'The way you do at the ladies?'

'Vee...'

'I'm not blind, Jonas.' She pulled her hand away.

'I'm here with you now, aren't I?' Jonas drew her back and kissed the delicate skin below her ear, his lips and breath teasing as her body tensed, head tilted, eyes half-closed.

She moaned.

A breeze stirred the overhanging boughs. Something metal glinted in the sunlight.

'What was that?' Vera's eyes shot open. She twisted out of his grasp and stared at the trunk behind them.

Jonas followed her gaze. Nailed near a hollow was a small plaque bearing a name and two dates. He ran his fingertips along the inscription. Ella's memorial.

Vera knelt beside him, squinted at a scrap of fabric peeking out from the tree hollow. 'What's this?' She reached inside and retrieved a pitiful-looking rag-doll. 'What a sad little thing.'

'Show me?' She handed it to Jonas, and he turned the tattered doll over, sensing they had stumbled on something private. The stuffed rags felt peculiar in his hands, and the memory of touching Ella flooded him, as if the doll was her.

'This was Ella's...' he whispered.

With a shudder, he remembered her as she'd been that final day, yearning, hostile, brittle.

Jonas stood, returned the plaything to the hollow, tucked the fabric away from view, and brushed his hands along his trousers to rid them of her haunting echo.

Vera chewed her lip as if she was fighting tears. Not for the last time he wondered if he would do her a favour or a disservice placing his betrothal brooch upon her breast.

'My apologies, Vee. Let's not dwell.' He steered them back towards the keep. 'Tell me of your dresses, ribbons, and hairpins, or whatever you ladies get up to while holed together at these proceedings. I'm imagining sheer nightgowns, brushing each other's hair, oiled massages...'

'Jonas!' She halted and faced him. 'Thank you for not thrusting it in my face. I know you and Ella were—well, *close*.'

A sharp inhale.

'I said nothing, because it wasn't my place, but when I stayed with you at Nedran while she was there, your servant told me he once caught the pair of you in the stables.' She placed her finger to his lips before he berated the servant's lack of discretion. 'He didn't want to divulge, but servants are easy to bribe. Who can blame them, living for a pittance as they do? He was so worried about tarnishing her reputation. He appeared as bewitched with her as Venn.'

She paused, and he could see her refraining from blurting, *and you.*

'I swore I wouldn't tell a soul, of course, but I'd rather we were honest with each other. About everything.'

'Vee...'

'Anyway, it seems like forever ago now.' Vera shrugged. 'She's gone.' She folded her arms across her chest, a shadow playing over her eyes. 'Just know I am not a fool. Dally where you will, but be discreet, and always come home to me.'

More and more, Vera's regard yoked him. She buried her fears in blind hope, not seeing him as he was, but some projection of who she wanted him to be. A constant reminder he would always disappoint her as he disappointed his brother. She might not be a fool, but she was fool enough to love him.

J onas wasn't ready to head indoors, and he was loath to encounter the king, so he left Vera at the foot of the keep and circled back towards town. Beggars filled the streets—more than he ever recalled seeing. Hungry eyes coveted his fine clothing, his jewelled dagger, and likely the purse tucked beneath his shirt.

Curse it, he reached within and discreetly deposited coins into caps and clutching fists.

'Thank you, my lord!' Tears welled and voices choked.

Jonas hurried past before they mobbed him. He shook his now-empty purse. Venn could advance his allowance when they returned home.

From behind, a cart crunched along the gravel, steered by a pair of neophytes with partially shaved heads. The robes were styling themselves in more obvious and extreme ways these days.

Atop the cart sat a wicker cage. Within crouched a woman with a hood covering her head, he assumed to blind her from wherever she was being taken, or perhaps to disguise her, though nothing could hide the saffron-coloured tresses peeking beneath. She wore a religious vestment, but it was a type he didn't recognise.

The scene reminded him of the heretic being escorted for execution when he was last in Creywmm, though surely Gohran's priests wouldn't conduct a Cleansing so close to a royal wedding.

The wagon slowed to navigate a series of potholes, and both pairs of eyes turned towards him, taking in his insignia.

Hurried bows. 'My lord,' one said.

'Lord Jonas,' said the other.

The prisoner jerked inside the cage, and the wagon lurched forward.

His temples pricked. They must want the prisoner removed before Erldan filled up, and the nuptials began. He wished he hadn't given the last of his coins away or he might offer a bribe to learn more.

Once through the worst of the damaged road, they sped up, and Jonas watched them veer from the surrounding township.

It was time he headed back for the noon-tea, anyway. Yet hours later, his curiosity gnawed. Perhaps he could return on horseback before sundown and track them. He shrugged off the heat prickling his mind. Following the cart was a distraction from thinking about Venn, Lynden, and Gohran—nothing more. Whatever those priests were doing with the prisoner was not his concern.

Amber woke to the ground beneath her shifting. Wheels crunched on gravel, and the movement jolted her back and forth. Voices in the distance and the murmur of unfamiliar minds told her she and her jailors weren't alone. She reached her awareness a little further, but her mind's eye flooded with gruesome horrors, and she slammed it shut.

She hadn't encountered Davith since he'd threatened her, but his servants continued their torment without laying a single finger. They circled her enclosure, leering, their crude mimes and cruder desires keeping her quiet. When they occasionally removed her hood, they knew not to look into her eyes, not to touch her, and when she didn't cooperate, they thwacked the cage bars until her head pounded.

'Want to burn, witch?' they crowed.

Some of her sisters could move objects with their minds, but Xenon had not gifted Amber so. It took all her strength to wade through the tide of drunkenness from whatever substance kept her dazed to shield her mind from her jailors' cruel and lurid thoughts.

The wagon slowed, lurching side to side over rough terrain, then halted.

'My lord,' said one of her captors.

'Lord Jonas,' said another.

She recognised that name. She had never met the dryhten of Nedran's younger brother, but knew of him, had seen him placed among the dynasties of Ella's acquaintance in Breeyan's study. Where were they? Perpetually hooded, often in darkness, she had no means to judge time passing, the day's hour, or her whereabouts.

She opened her mind again, to reach beyond her jailors' ugly thoughts, but the most she could manage was a fleeting curiosity that didn't belong to her. She grasped at the feeling, tried to amplify it, to snag the pattern of that mind, but as the wagon sped up, her strength and consciousness melted back into darkness.

FORTY-SEVEN

Venn arrived at the temple long before he needed to. Servants and holy men dressed the benches and pews with ilak fat candles and bouquets of flowers—nothing compared to the adornments happening in the main hall, he was sure.

He crept along the walls, meandered the aisles, lost to his musings. Waxy green leaves on looping vines wound around the wooden armrests, viridian claws encasing delicate cream-white buds. Jasmine. He froze.

Venn grabbed the arm of a servant fastening a vine in the next pew. 'What are you doing?'

'My lord?'

'Stop!' He tore at the jasmine, yanked it from the wood—thankfully, not the thorned variety Ella favoured. 'Get these gone!' He shoved the retrieved greenery into the servant's arms.

'What's all this?' A spindly older man with hunched shoulders nosed his way into the commotion. He must be Erldan's chamberlain.

'Sir, Lady Lynden instructed us to dress the temple with flowers...' The servant shrugged, helpless.

'Not with jasmine,' Venn snapped. 'Use anything else.' Where was Lynden?

'Very well, my lord,' said the chamberlain with an imperious sneer. He waved towards the half-decorated pews, now littered with shredded greenery and fallen petals. 'Clear this up.'

'Yes, sir. At once.' The servant bowed to Venn. 'My lord.' He gathered the remaining cuttings and knelt to sweep the floor.

'I need a drink,' Venn muttered, sinking onto the hard wooden bench seat.

'Fetch his lordship a spirit.' The chamberlain signalled to a portly middle-aged servant, who bowed and scurried away.

'Calm your nerves, my lord,' the chamberlain soothed. 'Let my staff take care of the proceedings. All will be well.'

Eyes closed, Venn inhaled until his chest swelled. The attendant was right. All he could do was wait.

On the morning of the wedding ceremony, Lynden joined the women, though she regretted it almost immediately. Carting a constantly whining Serrah, Jaydyn was in no mood to help her sister.

After the third interruption in as many minutes, she snapped. 'By the goddess, will you stop fussing for a few moments?'

Serrah broke into a high-pitched wail.

'Lyrra, can you take her?'

Lyrra looked to Lynden, eyes pleading, several twists of Raeyn's hair in each hand ready to straighten between hot flat stones.

Lynden grasped the bride-to-be's tresses, rather than the grotty toddler, who had latched onto her mother's skirt. She didn't know who she pitied more, a haggard-looking Jay, watching her sister gain all she lacked, or the handmaid forced to play her nanny.

Between the three women, they straightened and pinned Raeyn's hair to sweep elegantly from her face.

Jaydyn fastened the last pin and paused. 'It will do, I suppose, but you'll never be as beautiful as Ella.'

Raeyn's cheeks flamed purple. A slap.

Jaydyn squealed and jumped backward. The pins came with her and Raeyn's hair toppled.

'It will never stay fastened now!'

'Of course it will. Here.' Jaydyn grasped the comb and dunked it into the washbasin.

Lynden reached to stop her. Too late. She ran the wet comb through her sister's straightened tresses. All morning, they heated and stretched those wiry curls. Re-moistened, the stubborn ringlets bounced back.

Raeyn's eyes welled.

'You see? I told you it wouldn't work.'

Lynden braced herself, but the explosion never came.

Raeyn's heaved sigh reeked of resignation. 'You were right, Jay. I never should have fooled myself into thinking it would.'

Lynden guessed Jaydyn tried to counsel her sister against the marriage. She couldn't blame her begrudging Raeyn for what little happiness she gleaned living in her dead sister's shadow. She contemplated the risk she took bedding Gohran. Jaydyn's future might be hers soon enough.

The ceremony finally at hand, Venn stood rigid at the altar, wearing his grim determination like an armoured suit. Coloured candles adorned the aisles, but the pews remained undecorated. Bodies milled, pushing their way into the temple. Unsurprisingly, several key invitees failed to show, and Venn knew Gohran would perceive each absence as a blow.

Beside him, Gohran leaned in close. 'You've made the right decision.'

'You said I need to move on. And Ella's gone from this world, isn't she?' There was a catch in his voice.

Gohran seemed about to respond when the crowd fell silent. Raeyn appeared in the doorway. Her cool blue silk dress embroidered with matte-silver interlace matched the insignia on Venn's wedding shirt. The women had pulled her copper tresses into a knot at the crown of her head, leaving a sprinkling of wide ringlets framing her face.

She stepped along the aisle towards the altar. Towards him. His bride.

A woodenness settled in his stomach and chest. Once she reached his side, he held her hands in his and brushed his lips against her cheek. Lavender-scented powder mixed with thyme assaulted his throat.

Before them, Davith paced. Anticipation throbbed through the crowd. Venn was a most sought-after lord; Nedran, a highly influential province, still independent, about to be absorbed within the greater kingdom of Erldan; while Raeyn was heiress to one of the oldest dynasties, descended from the first High King in Galliarn. Blood ties to bind and bind some more. And now, blood ties tainted with heresy. A controversial match, at best.

The High Priest rode the silence, as if waiting for the expectancy to ripen. Once the air thickened with it, he stopped, turned, and opened the ceremony with a theatrical flourish.

'Children of the Sun,' he called, 'is not the binding by marriage more robust than any other?' A crowded sigh in response. 'And why is this so? Because the betrothed's vows are sacred, witnessed by Our Lady of the Dark Sun, and by each of us...'

Venn felt he hovered beyond his body, Davith's words landing beside him. Guided through the rite, his flesh undertook each necessary step, his throat uttering each required word, but he might have been somewhere else entirely.

Raeyn whispered her vows slowly, with intent, hope-filled eyes clutching. Venn rushed through his like a child swallowing medicine.

'I invite Lord Venn, the dryhten of Nedran, to seal his sacred union to the Elder Princess, Raeyn of Erldan, with the exchange of tokens.' Davith signalled for Venn to offer his brooch to Raeyn, and for her to offer him a ring.

Venn ignored the sweat on his palms and gripped the brooch, trying to steady it. Though winter approached, the room was stifling.

This was it. Once placed, they were bound, by law, and by sacred decree.

The ancient betrothal ritual he and Ella acted out hovered behind his eyes. They had been children playing make-believe. Mocking the laws. Mocking the gods. Naïve beyond measure.

A commotion at the temple's rear. A shout. 'Lord Venn! Don't marry the false-godder's daughter!'

The crowd stirred.

Venn couldn't see the caller, but it seemed to originate outside.

Someone yelled: 'Let her womb wither and rot!'

'Shut them up,' Gohran hissed to his men and the neophytes, who rushed towards the doors where a mob had gathered, trying to shove their way in.

The protestors pounded against the walls of the temple, thumping fists, sticks, anything they could carry. More shouting, then feet stomping so hard the floor vibrated.

'Bolt the doors!' Gohran commanded.

Venn thanked the goddess that no one would dare wield a weapon inside a place of worship. What was going on?

Someone hurled a rock, and the stained-glass window smashed, sending coloured shards cascading over the crowded room. Screams as people ducked and scrambled, knocking candles over. Smoke thickened where their flames caught.

'End this. Now!' Gohran shouted. He threw his woollen cloak over the fire. Extinguished, its embers smoked and smouldered.

Ash and rancid ilak fat filled Venn's nostrils. More fires had ignited where torches toppled along the opposite wall. Further scrambling to smother them.

Someone cast a moist object through the air, thudding on the floor before the altar, spattering his shirt and Raeyn's dress with crimson blood. A dead raven lay at their feet.

Raeyn choked back a horrified sob as the crowd erupted in a wave of shocked whispers, then settled into an eerie silence.

Gohran addressed the couple. 'Put those tokens on now.' Then to his men. 'Secure the doors! Nobody gets in or out!'

Venn ignored him, crouching to get a closer look at the raven. So much blood. It couldn't all belong to the bird. Something shiny poked between broken ribs, and Venn moved to retrieve it.

Gohran reached to stop him. 'This is a matter for the priests.'

Another hand on his shoulder. Davith's. 'My lord,' he whispered.

Venn stepped back.

The priest raised his palms, striding forward with eyes half closed, hands hovering as if measuring the surrounding air. He opened his eyes and spoke, his booming voice smooth, reassuring. 'Children of the Sun, I demand an end to this protest. Our Lady has offered only positive signs for this union.'

Davith's gaze darted around the temple. The doors now secured, fires safely extinguished, the riot subsided. They had made their point.

Davith motioned to a pair of neophytes who scampered towards the altar. Thick smoke smouldered as the uneasy crowd parted to let them through.

Venn couldn't rip his eyes from the raven as the neophytes removed the corpse and mopped away the blood as casually as they might clear a plate of dropped meat.

'Please, my lord, Your Highness, continue,' Davith prompted.

But Venn stood, immobilised, now staring at Raeyn, who looked equally frozen.

'My lord,' Davith said quietly. 'I sense no binding evil here, only petty malice. You may pin the brooch.'

Still, Venn couldn't move.

Gohran's hand rested on his shoulder, a warm and soothing weight. 'You can finish this,' he said.

His mind spun, and he swayed unsteadily. Gohran's eyes met his. More warmth, and the world lilted. Dazed. He shouldn't have downed that spirit earlier.

The feeling. He froze, staring at the king. He should know what it meant. Its significance. But his thoughts kept slipping away.

He clung to the priest's reassurance of the goddess's blessing, and Gohran's conviction his marriage to Raeyn would serve his province, his people, his legacy.

He pinned the brooch to Raeyn's dress and held out his hand for her to slide on his ring. Heat surged as he met the king's gaze, and then Raeyn's. His wife. He felt so heavy, yet weightless.

Davith concluded the ceremony as if the ill-omened stunt had not taken place, and the crowd's silence watching on was almost painful. At its close, they—and Venn—could not exit fast enough.

FORTY-EIGHT

It was done. Venn was his brother under the law. Despite the protest. Despite the missteps with Ella. He would renew his kingdom, feed his people, and inspire loyalty to the goddess—and to him.

Following the ceremony, Gohran invited the guests inside the castle keep, away from the remonstration, and ushered them to the main hall for the celebratory feast. His men, he tasked with arresting the protestors, save a small escort to guard the wedding party.

Gohran followed Venn's lead, stroking and soothing everyone he encountered with a reassuring patter. He didn't wait for the guests to settle before pronouncing his congratulations, brief and perfunctory. Let the drinking begin as soon as soon, feasting in the familiar—and secular—hall.

By unspoken consensus, hosts and guests kept the conversation light, but there was only so much interest the weather held.

Seated beside Venn, Raeyn twisted a knot in the skirt of her dress. Venn took her hands in his and squeezed, and the fabric unravelled, revealing a purple spatter where crimson stained its cool blue.

'Prejudice surrounds those who fear and those who envy,' Venn said. 'Do not give it another thought, my dear wife.'

'My brother is right, Your Highness,' Lynden said from across the table. 'Don't let it trouble your heart.'

'We should lead the dancing.' Venn tugged his wife's elbow. She obeyed, trailing behind, until he gripped her waist and pushed her forward. 'Smile,' he whispered, showing the mob his teeth, nodding at this one or that. On the dance floor, he held her, kissed her cheek, then beamed at their audience once more.

It was then Gohran discovered a side to his friend he had never known: the performer.

Nearby, Lynden and Jonas huddled, trying to keep their voices low, but not low enough.

'They've both gone into this with their eyes open, Lyn.'

'Perhaps. I don't suppose Raeyn had any choice.'

Jonas said nothing, but Gohran almost heard him thinking—Raeyn may not have had a choice, but he, Gohran, had.

The formalities over, Gohran slipped outside and back into town towards the temple, escorted by a handful of armed guards. He had no desire to encounter those protestors alone.

He need not have worried. Close to the keep, a couple of his men trudged their way towards him, hands and shirts bloodied, heads shaking. 'Your High-ness, by the time we found the culprits, their throats were already slit.'

A heavy sigh. They forfeited their lives before his men tortured the truth from their traitorous lips. 'My thanks. Get cleaned up and join the celebrations.'

While noble guests feasted inside, the revelry spilled onto the streets, peas-ants and servants drinking from Nedran's donated ale barrels. Children played unsupervised as mangy hounds circled, scouring for scraps. The revellers grew rowdier, unperturbed by the earlier commotion.

Once at the temple, Gohran bid his guards to wait at the doors. 'Take care of any trouble.'

Inside, Davith and two neophytes huddled around a long bench. He watched them in silence. They'd splayed the raven's corpse and were dissecting its body with ceremonial daggers.

'Is the blood human, do you think?'

'Of course not. Ilak's or boar's most likely.'

'It doesn't matter, anyway. It's this disc that bothers me.'

'Is there aught in this gesture of protest to concern me?' Gohran made his presence known.

The religious men looked up, then bowed.

'Not at all, Your Highness.' Davith's voice dripped with honey. He positioned himself to block the king's view of their work.

'Then what is all this?' He gestured to the bench.

'As you correctly identified, Your Highness: a gesture of protest.'

Gohran neared the counter, peering behind Davith's shoulders. The poor creature's wings were severed and its guts wrenched open. Inside sat the curious disc. The bird's gore hid the graved X, but cold certainty told him it was akin to the one he buried in Ella's phantom grave, and that those villagers claimed their visitor wore. It glowed. He blinked, and the light faded.

'Why protest the marriage of the dryhten of Nedran to the Princess Elder?' He moved closer.

Davith signalled his neophytes to leave. They bundled the dissected corpse into a sack and took it with them.

'May I speak freely, Your Highness? Though you make restitution with Our Lady Elnora and Her servants, there will always be individuals who dispute your family's claim to the throne.'

'How does that affect my sister and the dryhten?'

'It is a question of legitimacy, Your Highness. So far, your dynasty has no legal heirs. Any children born of the dryhten and Princess Elder will be in the line of succession.'

'Are you suggesting these malcontents hope my mother's legacy will simply die out?'

'I'm suggesting, Your Highness, that it would behove you to take a wife. The sooner you can produce incontestable heirs, the better.'

'Incontestable?'

'You would be within your rights under the High Realm's laws to adopt your niece or any child of the Princess Elder's marriage, but you should be aware their claim to the throne might be tenuous. Should that transpire, you would be wise to seek the High King's endorsement.'

'I see.' Gohran stretched his hand towards the blood-smeared bench-top. Vitality surged through him. It was hot. Not to the touch, but inside him. Human blood, he thought. Davith knew it too, he was sure.

A flash behind his eyes. Peasants stringing up a pregnant woman, slicing across her abdomen. Gods, those screams. Her contorted features. *Don't take my baby! No!* The disc hung around her neck. It glowed.

The image shifted, and he pictured the rock later hurled through the temple window, being carved with the symbols of the Ancients. They spoke in the Ancient tongue, but somehow in his mind, he understood their meaning. *A curse for the Cursed.* The child was a sacrifice to halt life. Davith was right. They wanted Raeyn barren.

A chill crept over him. 'You have my thanks, Your Holiness. I'd best tend to my guests.'

FORTY-NINE

Ella drank in Xarion's wide blue eyes framed by long, dark lashes, her silken midnight hair and puckered rosebud lips. She held her close, stroked her skin, soaked up her smell, and poured power into her. She wanted to carve Xarion's chubby limbs and the tiny heart beating behind that pink chest into her soul. A wrenching ache. How could she leave her daughter, even briefly?

Her mother's voice from inside her prison cell echoed: *Goodbye, my love.* Remembered smoke snagged in her throat.

The irony twisted and punched. What she would have given to escape Aryon's bonds and flee to her old world, but not now. Not with the memory of heretics being dragged through the streets and the henad's engulfing flames flashing through her mind. Knowing out there, no one would dare help her. Another twist and stab as she recalled Venn's rejection, his terror, and disgust, and the omnipresent horror and shame of her brother's defilement. For all Ella resented being here, Aryon was a haven, her walls thick with the static charge of magic, corridors pulsing with murmuring minds.

Now she had no choice. Breeyan's icy soul would protect her order and herself before anything else.

She must go, and Xarion must stay.

Shira had readied her stores. It would have been suspicious for Ella to do it herself. Besides, she wouldn't know what to pack for such a journey.

'Don't scry or even think about where you might travel,' Shira said. 'Not until you're safely away. And then maintain your shield.'

Already, she imagined riding into the night, beyond Aryon's pastures, and hated that a part of her felt relief. Thankful to escape the priestesses and their hostile cruelty, this life that confined her, bound her, but more, to know she was fleeing her daughter's suffocating hold.

Shira and Breeyan forcing her to leave Xarion behind was like relinquishing a responsibility thrust on her against her will. She never wanted motherhood. Never had the chance to choose. This relief was a freedom, and she hated herself for its existence.

A deeper loathing came from sensing what the priestesses experienced around her daughter. There was something profoundly amiss about Xarion. Some compulsion to devour and consume no one could ever fill. Ella hoped by leaving her daughter, she might be free of that need, too.

Already she yearned to pull away, to sever her maternal bond, and protect from losing the part of herself she had grown and sustained in her womb and birthed into painful existence, but Xarion would not let her. Her daughter's tentacles clawed, her heart demanding the flood of nurturing that ran so deep she couldn't breathe.

If only having a child had been her choice. If Xarion didn't remind her every moment of what Gohran had taken from her, she might have luxuriated in that warmth. Cared for her daughter as selflessly and unguardedly as Aunt Bree.

That night in her cell, Ella fed Xarion one last time, and left her sleeping in her crib. She choked back her tears and stuffed her anguish deeper than she had imagined possible, as she and Shira sneaked past their slumbering sisters towards the stables where her steed and packhorse waited.

They hadn't reached the stables when Xarion's need screamed through her mind like a violent storm. Its force was paralysing. She couldn't think. Couldn't move. Couldn't speak. She clutched her temples and heart, anguish surging through every morsel of her. Her knees buckled, and she collapsed.

'She knows. Shira, she knows...' A guttural growl, her voice choked off.

'Who?'

'Xarion...'

Shira's face contorted, and she pressed her fingers to her temple. She felt it, too. 'Gods! How?'

That force! Ella's limbs might have been weighted in lead, her torso chained, but that searing in her heart, psyche, and breasts was as if Xarion poured acid into her soul.

'Fetch her, Shira,' Ella's voice strangled.

'You can't take her,' Shira said. 'Not into Ycelt…'

Ella shook her head. 'Don't bring her to me. Take her to Aunt Bree. She's the only one who can calm her.'

Shira hesitated, as if she wasn't sure whether to stay and help Ella or answer that cry.

'Hurry, Shira…'

Shira faced the citadel and her entire body visibly eased, satisfying Xarion's demand, a desperate thirst quenched. She swung back to Ella. 'Go before Breeyan realises. Go now, Ella!' She hitched up her robe and ran.

Ella clambered along the ground, crawling away from her abandoned child. Her knees and palms scraped across hard-packed dirt, jutting twigs and stones stabbing and abrading. Pain speared its talons into her, dragging her back, but she crawled on. She needed to reach her steed before Breeyan discovered her leaving.

Cold air surged through her nostrils, shoved its way down her throat, and burned her chest as she drew all the warmth from her surrounds. The sobbing in her mind intensified, a high-pitched banshee wail, amping to an excruciating crescendo.

Let me go, Xarion. Let me—

The rusty squawk of a nighthawk sounded in the distance. Another crawl forward. Another inch closer.

So cold. So heavy.

Above, Xenon's light cast an eerie glow, the god watching on. She was a mere plaything.

She dragged her torso and limbs by her forearms. *Let me go…*

Another squawk and then blessed silence. The sobbing eased, enveloped in soothing warmth—not hers. *Breeyan.*

Ella gasped divinely warm air. Her flesh tingled with heat and weightlessness, her body propelled forward, as though the tether she struggled against tore free, binding chains falling away. She knelt and then stood, her muscles quivering.

There was no time to linger. She scrambled for her steed, its breath snorting white puffs into the night. She untethered it and the packhorse, then mounted and steered them east into the dark.

Freedom—and quiet in her mind—at last.

The full force of Xarion's piercing screams hit Breeyan's mind long before Shira reached her. She realised immediately what that anguish must mean: Ella was gone.

It took hours to settle her, though *settle* was not quite the right word. Eventually, Xarion slept from sheer exhaustion.

Breeyan wished she could join her, disappear into the black void of unconsciousness for a time. She shut her chamber door, sank into her chair, and breathed.

How long would she have before Xarion awoke? Not long enough. She ripped her chewed nails from her lips, flexed her fingers, drew her shoulders back, and with an extended exhale, summoned Shira.

Moments later, Shira entered, her expression unreadable, mind shut tight.

'Did you honestly believe I wouldn't know what you planned?' she said, though until those screams, she'd had no idea. How had Ella hidden it? How had Shira?

Tired and rusty, the tragedy of the preceding months—years, really—etched themselves into her mind and onto her body, the threads of her machinations unravelling before her. Xenon help her, she was weary.

Another breath. Distant bleating and the low of disgruntled herd beasts carried across the night.

'Ella has gone to find Amber, Your Holiness,' Shira said. 'I tried to stop her.'

Breeyan straightened her torso, stiff and tall, and lashed her mental whip until Shira winced. 'Don't lie, Shira. Not to me. Not now.'

Shira turned slowly and crossed her arms over her chest. She met Breeyan's gaze, unflinching. 'I sent her.'

'You did what?!'

'Someone needed to. She is unsworn, and Ycelt is her realm. She has a better chance than any of us to find Amber and bring her home. Forgive me, Your Holiness, but you would not see reason. Your priorities lie elsewhere.' She glanced at Xarion asleep in her crib.

Breeyan was about to speak.

'Discipline me if you choose, but when I accepted the role of apprentice, I vowed to remain loyal to the *order*.' Not her. 'That includes every soul who resides here.'

She opened her mind and Breeyan read her recent memories: Magdelyn, Karra and Belmae discussing their increasing unease around Ella and her babe, deciding to leave because they had lost faith in Breeyan's rule. Another image toppled unintended over the first: Nykki, begging Shira to protect Amber.

Nykki.

Breeyan recognised Nykahlia and Amber were close—friends since arriving as adolescents. But when she reached Amber's mind during the Severance, she discovered their connection deeper and stronger than a friendship bond ought to be. She knew what she must do.

'Fetch Nykahlia,' she said.

'Your Holiness?'

'You may be right, Shira. Ella is better gone from here. Much as I hoped my niece would settle into this life, she came to us far too late. If she can find Amber and bring her home, that is all to the good.' It was their only option.

Shira nodded and went to wake Nykki.

Breeyan stood over Xarion's crib, reached for that tiny soul, inhaling her skin, cradling her warm heart. Now there was no one to take the babe from her.

FIFTY

Dressed in her silk nightgown, bedclothes pulled to her chin, Raeyn stared at the ceiling's wooden beams. Her tight breath seemed loud and laboured as a sprinting steed. Jaydyn told her some of what to expect on her wedding night as the women bathed and oiled her skin before she retired to the bedchamber.

'So, Venn will enter me, then thrust about like an ilak ram mounting a ewe, and this culminates in spilling his seed inside my womb?'

Jaydyn almost spat out her drink. 'Well, yes, to put it crudely. But that's only as the priests describe. If he's any taste for the sport, it should be a little less cursory, and provide a lot more pleasure.'

Raeyn blushed, thankful Venn's sister Lynden had not joined them for this ritual.

'Don't forget, I've only experienced Sheevan's fumbling. Venn will be more generous, I'm sure.'

Raeyn recalled her sister boasting of her lover's prowess, but sour experiences had a way of tarnishing memories.

'Likely the dryhten will be a skilled lover, Miss Raeyn,' Lyrra reassured.

'Though sometimes you have to direct a man to tend to your pleasure, Your Highness,' another serving woman added.

'A disappointing truth.' Jaydyn let out an exaggerated sigh, and the women tittered.

But as Raeyn lay waiting for her new husband to seal their marriage in her bed, she stiffened, frozen. She couldn't rid the blood-soaked bird from her imagination, and wanted it finished. Thanks to her brother, her family was reviled, but she hadn't expected dissent at her wedding, not when people throughout Ycelt loved and respected the dryhten.

Now, as Venn snuffed out the lantern, his approaching footfalls echoed. In the near blackness, he might have been a stranger.

He leaned over the bed. 'May I?' His voice cracked.

She nodded, unable to speak.

He peeled back the bedclothes and climbed atop her, clutched her wrists, and kissed her, hard, not seeming to care that she was frightened, that this was her first time. He shoved her nightdress above her waist and pushed himself inside her. The sensation wasn't pain, exactly, but it wasn't comfortable. It was a strange intermittent fullness. Different from her self-ministrations.

Above her, Venn's eyes were open but unseeing, his hands groping but not finding, and in his desperate, almost violent thrusting, Raeyn sensed him searching, expecting something from her. Something she couldn't give. Didn't know how to give.

Afterwards he left her, door barred, to sleep in his own room.

She rolled over and curled her knees to her chest, hugging her blankets around her. She should feel relief. Married at last, soon to be settled at Nedran. Head of her own household, removed from the memories of her mother's execution, gone from her brother and his people's condemnation. Secure. And while Venn wasn't the most handsome or charming man she encountered during her period of courtship, she had known him to be gentle, honourable, and kind. A man who would treat her well, show her every respect, even without love. She might have grown to love a man like that.

But that night, there was no sign of such a man. No matter if he was gentle and loving hereafter, the damage was done.

V enn ought to have stayed the night in Raeyn's bed, but he needed to get away. The vacuum of her body and hollowness of her kisses were a painful reminder of what would never be. An emptiness akin to caressing a lifeless doll. Yet she wasn't lifeless. Raeyn was someone he respected, wanted to grow fond of, but his involuntary resentment seethed when she couldn't give him what his flesh and spirit required. What the gods and their priests forbade.

He recalled drinking Ella's essence into him, her warmth more exquisite than the purest opium, and thought he might be sick. It wasn't love or even lust he craved. It was her beguiling power.

Ella left him broken. A cracked vessel nothing could ever fill.

He forcibly reminded himself she did not choose to be born with magic, cursed by a fate beyond her dominion. But he'd had a choice. He chose to touch her with lust, though he hadn't known what she was.

She concealed it from him.

And if she hadn't? Had she come to him with the truth, might he have helped? He wasn't sure. He may have sent her packing as he intended before she persuaded him to defy his prudence and the will of the king. His only certainty was knowing he would not have taken her to his bed.

He shuddered. He would never scrub his tainted soul clean.

A knock at his door.

Venn groaned. What did somebody want at this unearthly hour? It was still dark. He pulled on his shirt and trousers and shuffled to the door.

There stood his aunt, already dressed, carrying a warm wash basin.

'Has something happened?'

Servan strode past and placed the basin on his dresser. 'Hurry and ready yourself. We're attending the dawn worship.'

'Whatever for? It's not the day of the sun.'

'Your new wife will be there, and you ought to be, too.'

'On the morning after my wedding?' He yawned.

'You can return to your bed later.' She folded her arms, with no sign of giving him privacy. 'After that little incident yesterday, you need to be on your guard. Assume the robes are always watching. Whatever you believe behind drawn curtains, be certain the priests notice you observing their rites. I'll not let you end up on the wrong side of the holy men like your father.'

He finished dressing, scrubbed his face, and tidied his hair.

With a frown, she glided her palm over his stubbled chin. 'It will have to do.'

'If you weren't my mother's sister...' he said.

'We should hurry.' She led him downstairs and into the crisp morning.

Sun peeked over the horizon through the grey of uhtan as people from all directions hurried towards the temple. He'd never seen Erldan at this hour.

Inside, people crowded into pews and hovered against walls and in the aisles. He spotted Raeyn seated near the front and slipped in beside her. Charred wood and spilled wax mingled with the stronger fragrance of incense, but nothing disguised the wintry draught seeping through the broken window. He reached for Raeyn's hand and offered a smile, but she kept her eyes forward and shoved her palms beneath her skirt.

The priest droned. Something about honour and the divine rule of monarchy and he stifled another yawn, rubbing the unfamiliar gold band adorning his finger. So strange to have uttered vows inside these walls only one day earlier.

Where Raeyn would not meet his gaze, Gohran smiled with affection, as though nothing was amiss.

'Brother.' He touched Venn's shoulder. Familiar warmth surged.

Warmth like Ella's. His mind skipped.

The metal disc the protestors stuffed inside the raven flared behind his eyes. It resembled the exact one he uncovered in Ella's mock grave. The one that now sat on his nightstand beside her string of pearls and a wilted sprig of jasmine. His surroundings closed in.

'Excuse me.' He pushed past the parishioners and hurried outside, the briskness soothing his flaming cheeks. He gasped for air.

Memories of the wedding ceremony inundated. Gohran's hand upon his shoulder. That feeling of drunkenness. So familiar.

He never understood why Gohran denounced Queen Prya at Ella's birthday ball, what he'd seen that evening in the great hall. But something in his mother's actions had stirred Gohran to accuse her of heresy. Something invisible to every other person in that room. But not to Gohran. What if it was precisely what he experienced just now?

Queen Prya, Ella, and him—Gohran.

Venn didn't wait for the service to finish. He hurried back to the castle. He had to get away. Raeyn could accompany him or join Lynden and Jonas after the week's festivities. He didn't care. He needed to be gone.

'Venn!' Servan called, running to catch him up. She fell into step beside him, panting. 'What happened?'

'You don't want to know, aunt.' What could he tell her? That the king himself was as much a heretic as his mother? 'Curse it!' Servan was right. Piety was the best disguise of all. No one—least of all him—suspected the man who outed his mother to the priests.

'Watch over Lynden and Jonas for me and have them return to Nedran as soon as is polite.'

'You're leaving already?'

He swallowed, hating the lie he was about to tell. 'I can't keep pretending, aunt. I thought I was done grieving my first intended, but it seems I acted with haste. I need to be in my own city, my own home.' He would make it up to Raeyn, somehow.

'Of course. I understand.' She rubbed his shoulder, an ordinary stroke of human warmth. He recognised the difference now. 'I'll have the servants ready the princess's belongings. She should return with you.'

Venn nodded. 'My thanks.'

The carriage ride to Nedran was excruciating. Venn's bleak thoughts consumed him. He pushed himself to show Raeyn affection, extending his hand and planting a kiss on her cheek, but his new wife seemed as unyielding as a carved stone. The entire way, she sat angled towards the window, away from him, staring into the distance.

He hadn't the capacity to decipher her frost. She insisted she was glad to leave, so it couldn't be him dragging her to Nedran before the nuptial celebrations concluded. 'I've been waiting a long time to start my new life,' she assured. In truth, so had he. He just expected it to be a life with her sister.

At least Raeyn didn't resemble Ella. Didn't sound like her, smell, or taste like her. If they didn't share their mother's smile, he would have sworn they were unrelated. For that reason alone, he was thankful Raeyn rarely smiled.

Venn supposed she had little to smile about. Married to a man who cherished her sister. Orphaned, like him, but with her mother, it was at her brother's hands.

Raeyn never spoke fondly of Gohran. He'd assumed it was challenging to watch her younger sibling step into a role denied her because of her sex, but now he wondered if she saw Gohran as others seemed to. Harsh. Irascible. Tyrannical.

A side of his friend that always existed, but that he had never seen. That Gohran prevented him from seeing.

With magic.

He wanted to ask if Raeyn was privy. Had she known about her mother? About Ella? But each time he tried to speak, his words snagged in his throat. He couldn't utter his thoughts aloud. Wouldn't make them real.

And if she didn't know, and he revealed the truth, would she denounce him as he denounced their mother?

When they finally reached Nedran, he helped his bride from the carriage and welcomed her to her new home. The entire scene was too reminiscent of Ella's arrival, following her mother's arrest. He choked back a sob. Raeyn either didn't notice, or she ignored it.

'Mykan, have Bess show Princess Raeyn to her quarters.'

He left Raeyn with the servants and retreated to his study.

Raeyn felt cheated. Even if Venn didn't desire her, he had always been attentive and kind. But the way he bedded her on their wedding night, she might have married a stranger. And since fleeing the temple and demanding they return home, he seemed like an enemy.

In the carriage, she couldn't sit far enough from him, flinching each time a pothole bumped their thighs into one another. At least his dark thoughts preoccupied him, and he did not force conversation.

When they arrived, she immersed herself in new surroundings. With its open, light-filled rooms and modern furnishings, Nedran was a world apart from Erldan. She understood why Ella enjoyed staying away so long. How suffocating it must have been to return.

Bess showed Raeyn to her bedroom, prattling about the household. Efficient and friendly as Nedran's other servants, Raeyn warmed to the lady's maid, hoping to find a ready home among the staff—they would be her company now.

Her airy bedchamber housed a polished dressing table, a silk-covered armchair, and an expansive bed. Sheer curtains strung from carved bedposts, the mattress dressed with fresh blue linens, and a silver-trimmed silk coverlet.

The servants had left the internal door adjoining the master bedroom open, making the room appear even larger. Venn must be in his study, because his chamber was empty.

She closed the door. 'I'd like some privacy.'

'Of course, Your Highness,' Bess said.

Raeyn examined the door latch. 'Is there no bolt on this side?'

'Not on either side, Your Highness. There's never been a need for one.'

A weight lodged in her throat. 'Then I shall sleep in a guest chamber until one can be fitted.'

Bess looked stricken. 'Of course, Your Highness. I'll have the chambermaids ready the room where your sister stayed while she visited—may Our Lady keep her.'

Raeyn was weary, but she couldn't rest while that door remained accessible. She wished Lynden and Jonas had returned with them, so she wasn't alone with her strange husband. She hovered uncertainly.

'Let me show you to the women's hall, Your Highness,' Bess said, and she nearly wept with gratitude.

FIFTY-ONE

That evening, Lynden arrived at dinner to find Jonas and Vera huddled at one end of a table, while Cousin Moyra and Aunt Servan joined Vera's aunt, Leena, at the other. Minstrels played quietly in the background of the near-empty hall, but no one danced.

Lynden half expected Princess Jaydyn to appear, but perhaps with her sister gone, she had retreated upstairs. It's not as though she was vying for a husband among the remaining guests. Many returned home following the strange protest, and the few who lingered spoke in subdued murmurs, staying out of politeness or to mingle.

'I didn't expect you to favour us with your company, Lynnie,' Moyra said.

Ever the peacemaker, Servan sat between Moyra and Leena, who abraded one another with their contrasting backgrounds. Where Servan and Lynden's mother had married great lords, their cousin Moyra's late husband was a commoner, and Leena had no love for the common-born who failed to elevate themselves.

Lynden wasn't sure if Moyra realised how conspicuously she resembled the peasants feasting outside. Perhaps it would have been kinder not to invite her. Born into an older dynasty, Vera's aunt could be scathing, and she could tell by Moyra's flushed cheeks she bolstered her confidence with free-flowing wine.

Lynden groaned theatrically and sank into her chair. 'Gohran has been in a mood since the wedding. He wanted to visit the temple again before dinner.' She rolled her eyes. 'I wonder if he would be more content as a priest than a king, but I can't imagine anything duller!'

'Not everyone can be as entertaining as us, Lyn.' Jonas chuckled.

'If only conceit was a more attractive quality,' Lynden said.

Jonas arched his brow. He would not bite.

Lynden reached for the wine. 'Distract me, please! What were you two whispering about?' she said to Vera and Jonas.

'Just politics, Lyn. You'd be bored,' said Jonas.

'If it was politics, you'd be bored, too,' she retorted, filling her glass to the brim. 'Let me guess. Prospective suitors for the rest of us? With the pair of you sorted—'

Vera winced.

'My apologies, Vee, I forget my scoundrel brother hasn't made an honest woman of you yet. But Jonas, you've no excuse not to seal your betrothal now. Tell him, Aunty Lee.' Lynden had referred to Vera's aunt as hers since she was a girl.

'Lyn!' Vera's eyes popped.

'If you must know, we were discussing Venn and Raeyn,' Jonas said coolly.

'They must have been eager if they've left for Nedran already,' she said with a sly smile.

'This is earnest, Lyn,' Servan said, her tone staid. 'Venn was quite agitated when they departed this morning.' Servan's solemn brow was concerning.

'Most alarming, Lynnie,' Moyra said. Eyes watery and overbright, she nearly toppled her wine, reaching for more.

Beside her, with a withering glance, Leena steadied Moyra's glass and the carafe before pivoting to address Lynden. 'Have he and the king quarrelled, do you know?'

'Not that Gohran mentioned to me,' she said.

'Pity.' Leena's eyebrow raised, salacious lip quirked. 'Now we might never find out. Anyway, we're heading to Lichen tomorrow. With the nuptials over, I need to get Vee home.'

'Why don't you travel with us?' said Vera. 'There's room, and you won't have to borrow the royal carriage.'

Panic in her throat. She wasn't ready to leave Gohran's bed. 'Can't we see out the week? Jonas, please?' She squeezed her brother's arm.

'I thought His Highness was boring you,' Jonas said.

'Not when it counts.'

'Lyn!' Vera feigned outrage, glancing towards the older women.

'Oh, Jonas, let your sister stay. She won't have these kinds of opportunities once she's under a husband's rod,' said Leena. 'But make sure you keep us all updated.' She winked at Lynden. Vera's aunt was forever living vicariously. Gods, she hoped that wasn't her some day.

'I agree with young Jonas,' Moyra interjected. 'You can't be too careful, Lynnie. Tongues always wag, and you don't want to end up like you-know-who.' She glanced towards the royal bedchambers.

Servan reached across the table to squeeze her hand. Eyes soft, she gazed first at Jonas, and then at her. 'Stay and let the newly wedded couple settle in at home. But Lyn, make this your last visit. Don't lose all sense to your loins.'

One relation was plenty; three were overwhelming. 'Please, can we talk about something other than my *private* liaisons?'

Those cursed protestors may not have cost Gohran his alliance, but their stunt again soured his relationship with Venn. His brother-in-law's expression in the temple that morning haunted. When he offered his arm in greeting, Venn seemed to fear him. Was repulsed by him. Venn left the service abruptly, and by the time Gohran returned to the keep, he and Raeyn had already departed for Nedran, without farewell or explanation.

Once, Gohran believed if he honoured and worshipped Elnora enough, and brought Her sufficient souls, She might take this poison from his blood, his heart, and rid him of his torment. But now, his suffering seemed inexorable. Even if the truth stayed buried from his people, his mother's heresy tarnished him in their eyes, and Venn saw it, too.

His subjects tried to hex his bloodline, but maybe they were right to. His mother, his aunt, Ella, and him. The goddess had forsaken them all.

As darkness fell, he returned to the temple, seeking comfort in the only other means of soothing: Davith's presence in Her holy temple.

He arrived to find Davith's neophytes scurrying, tidying, and laying holy implements with precision. Someone had scrubbed the bloodied bench and removed all traces of the dead raven, but there was no sign of the High Priest.

'What have you done with the carcass?' he asked.

'Gone, Your Highness.'

'Burned.'

Cleansed, more like. He caught the eye of one lad. 'Where is His Holiness?'

'On urgent business, Your Highness. He didn't say where.'

The neophyte was hiding something. He probed deeper. The lad's eyes drifted out of focus, as though he daydreamed. He knew exactly where Davith was.

Released, the boy blinked repeatedly and rearranged his shirt front. 'I will inform him you stopped by, Your Highness.'

'My thanks.' A sourness on his lips. Davith was hiding as much from Gohran as Gohran hid from them all.

Fifty-Two

It seemed an entire moon cycle before Ella calmed her nerves. Riding through the darkness, she barely noticed her burning thighs, the aching cold, and biting reins, as Xarion's absence sliced her heart and tore her psyche. Had she not needed to rest her steed and packhorse, she would have kept riding, but eventually, she stopped and made camp.

Shira packed a bedroll and blankets, and a trio of poles to secure her canvas coated with ilak fat to shelter her from the elements. She rummaged through her stores for some flatbread and an apple, along with nose bags of grain for the animals. She used her power to ignite a fire and prepared a meal of boiled grains.

Her stomach satisfied, huddled in a blanket, she risked using her magic to search the flames for Amber. Even if Breeyan sensed Ella now, she could outrun her, and without a clear direction, she might wander and never find the lost priestess.

Breeyan's scrying had not located Amber, but she didn't know modern Ycelt like Ella did. She peered into the flames, drawing heat, using their dance as a focus, and pictured her old tutor. Imagined the pattern of her thoughts, stretching to the farthest edges of her awareness. The faint flickering of thought, barely discernible, and then only embers.

She wanted to weep. Didn't want to be out here alone. A deep breath. She added dry fuel from her stores, coaxed the flames higher, then refocused her scrying.

A mind tugged at hers. Not Amber, Breeyan, or Shira. Was that Nykki?

She followed the tug and stared into her blaze until her vision wavered, then resolved into three faces peering into a fire on the other side.

A jumble of thoughts cascaded over hers—sparks of knowledge toppled over one another and dropped into her mind. Breeyan was letting her go. Not just letting go, but helping her. And using Nykki and Shira to do so.

Hands clasped, the women directed her attention back to Amber. She held steady as their joint force surged, a blue net cast out to sea, its strength and distance amplified by Nykki and Amber's bond. As Ella joined them, Breeyan leveraged Ella's relationship with Amber, too, sending their net further, sucking at Amber's mind like iron filings to a lodestone.

Through the fire, Breeyan shifted, and Ella glimpsed Xarion's sling fastened across her chest. Her heart wrenched. She wanted to howl, to scream. Xarion! Oh gods, her babe!

Focus, Ella. Breeyan's thoughts were as stern and commanding as her voice. *I need you both calm.*

Breeyan was right. With Xarion settled, her power was a weapon. Distressed, it was a liability.

Ella inhaled from deep in her belly, allowing air to fill her lungs and still her heart. She continued until her blood pulsed slowly, evenly. Focus adrift, she followed the blue net, sensing loss and longing, fear and fire.

In the distance, consciousness flickered like a lone candle. She recognised the pattern of Amber's mind, but that pattern drifted, like drunken lilting. She concentrated until her vision of Amber came into focus, almost as if she could reach out and touch her.

A stroke—not hers—travelled the length of Amber's cheek. Large but smooth hands twirled strands of her saffron hair. She wanted to recoil.

Stay focused.

An oil-slick voice gloated, taunting. Ella recognised that timbre, let her recognition draw her nearer.

The voice said, 'Still, you have not told my servants why the King of Erldan consorts with heretics...'

'Why would I be privy to any of the king's business?' Amber spat.

'He was meeting with you.'

'Like your novices, I do as instructed, and I don't question my superiors.'

Another tug at her hair. Ella experienced Amber's flinch through the fire, but it wasn't she who felt it this time—it was Nykki.

'Take your time, little sparrow, I am in no rush...'

'And yet I can't tell you what I don't know.'

Those tepid fingers released Amber before she could grasp a hold and use her influence. Her mind skipped again, and her head lolled. She forced herself upright, but she still saw muffled darkness. They must have a hood over her.

'Perhaps if you stop drugging me, I might remember more...' she said.

'And give you an opportunity to use your powers? I think not, little sparrow.'

A flash behind Amber's eyes of torturous violence. Not done to her, but experiences fed to her. *A young girl with golden eyes, whimpering, screaming.*

'You know what my servants are capable of,' the oily voice said.

'If you were going to touch me, you would have already done so,' Amber retorted. 'You *do* fear the Curse.'

'I fear nothing but the wrath of the goddess.' Why did Ella recognise that voice? 'But tell me, sparrow, why do your people carry these?'

A tug as someone removed the hood. Amber blinked, eyes half blinded by the sudden light. She kept her gaze lowered, would not look at her captor, would not meet his gaze. In his palm rested a disc graved with an X. He drew it closer, and it glowed, then dulled when he pulled it away.

'The mark of Xenon. His followers believe it will guide them to safety,' Amber said, her tone even.

He brought it close again, and it blazed. 'Why would it light up like this when I hold it near the king?'

Amber looked up, and Ella saw him. Davith.

Her vision broke off. Ordinary campfire flames flickered against the night. Frantically, she tried to rejoin the working, but terror gripped her. Her mind raced, heart pounding, and she couldn't calm herself to focus. She thought she might be sick.

Erldan's head priest, Davith, had Amber. He'd captured a sworn priestess—her friend—and now he knew Gohran had magic, and there was nothing she could do.

Shira sent Ella into Ycelt as the safest option for them to recover Amber, but it was not safe for her. If she ventured into Erldan or Nedran, or went anywhere near Erldan's head priest, her life was forfeit.

Gohran woke, drenched in cold sweat, dread pounding his throat. Absolute certainty gripped him. Something terrible was to happen.

Instead of the usual owl calls and animals mewling, the night was eerily quiet. Asleep beside him, Lynden's chest rose and fell in a steady rhythm. He longed to draw her close and still his fears, yet he needed to push her away, to hide.

He lay back, closed his eyes, and tried to calm the foreboding. But beneath his eyelids, he envisioned Ella's tear-stained face, her bitter hatred. Then he pictured his mother tied to the stake, screaming as her flesh burned. The illusory smoke cleared, and behind her stood his father. He searched Rohan's expression for any sign of affection, of approval, but his father's eyes wore the frost of winter.

'My son, a heretic. An abomination,' Rohan's words boomed before he smacked Gohran's face. He knew it wasn't real—couldn't be real.

He clutched his cheek. 'Father! Please!'

Arms entangled him, as someone whispered, 'Hush, my love...'

Not his father. A woman's voice. He shoved and slapped, needing to be free of that grip. Shouted: 'Get off!'

A shriek, and then that voice again, now cold, firm. 'Don't touch me ever—*ever*—again.'

It was Lynden. Oh, by the goddess. He'd struck Lynden.

Then, as though she remembered who and what he was, she said, 'Your Highness, please excuse me.' Through the dusky light, she straightened, pulled on her nightdress, gathered her other belongings, and, with chin raised, retreated from his room, slamming the heavy door behind her.

Her footfalls slipped into the darkness. Gohran sat dumbfounded. The moment he lashed out, he was unaware it was Lynden. All he saw were the relentless images that came unbidden. That he needed to stop.

He should follow her and make amends, but froze. What had she witnessed? What had he revealed?

He stared into his empty room, utterly alone. He missed Ella.

His mind skipped, and he closed his eyes, searching. She wasn't at Aryon. The knowledge gripped him. Panic. By the goddess, where was she?

Dream images danced before him, like ghostly shadows cast across his walls. He could not control them. Could make no sense of them.

Why did the visions persist? Why was he this monster? He did everything the priests demanded and more. He didn't ask to be this way.

He needed to exorcise them in the only way he knew how.

He bolted his door from the inside, then reached beneath his bed for his private chest. The only person who witnessed his scars was Lynden, and she never mentioned them. It was one reason he trusted her, one reason he was reluctant to find a wife or bed any other woman.

His secret, his shame.

Clouds gathered, covering the moon on the eve of winter, as he forced his strap to cut through his flesh again and again, until the pain and energy expelled through his blood left him at peace.

Fifty-Three

On his way from seeing Vera's carriage off, Jonas encountered Gohran striding across Erldan's grounds. Too late to change direction, he waited, head bowed, hoping the king would greet him promptly and move on.

'Lord Jonas,' Gohran said, blocking the path. The gods did not smile on him that day. 'I see you're finally venturing outdoors for a bit of sport.' Gohran's voice grated.

'I find it oppressive cooped within these walls, Your Highness.'

'I expected you would return home with your brother.'

'Please forgive the disappointment, Your Highness. Lady Lynden wished to remain a while longer, and it would be unseemly to leave her unchaperoned. Though now Venn is safely bound to your sister, I assume you'll bid your last farewells.'

'I assure you I've no intention of doing such a thing—not that it's any concern of yours.'

Jonas shot his eyes to meet the king's. 'You won't have a simple time finding suitable betrotheds, then.'

'The lady won't, certainly.'

'And is that why she's in your bed? One spoiled sister for another?'

For an answer, Gohran smiled, a cold, gruesome grin, before he turned and strode towards the castle keep.

Jonas swore under his breath. Why had Venn ever befriended such a swine?

On the way to his guest room, Lynden met him on the stairs. A pair of servants trailed after, carrying her trunk. 'I'm ready to leave the moment you are.'

'I thought you wanted to stay...?' Perhaps she had finally seen sense, even if Gohran wouldn't.

Moisture hovered in the corners of her eyes, and she drew her lips in tight. She was trying not to weep.

'I'll collect my belongings,' he said.

Soon they bustled into the king's carriage, which Gohran loaned to drive them home, and they were safely on their way.

Lynden tried to hide her puffy-red eyes, but when Jonas laid a comforting arm across her shoulder, her tears burst free.

'Come on, Lyn, it can't be as bad as that. I saw at least two men at the wedding who weren't repulsive.'

Lynden shot him a foul look.

'My apologies. I shouldn't tease.'

She didn't respond, and they rode on in silence.

Some hours out of Nedran, Lynden squirmed in her seat. 'It's odd. Sitting in this carriage makes me feel like spiders are crawling over me.'

'Because of Ella?'

Lynden nodded. 'This is likely where she died.'

'Lyn, you've been to places where people died before.'

'I know... It was just strange seeing Venn with Raeyn instead of Ella, knowing she'll be living with us.'

'She'll run her own estate, too.'

'Gohran says not.' A catch in her voice.

'Oh?'

'She'll keep her title, but Erldan hasn't the resources to support another property.'

'Where has Erldan's coin gone?'

'Gohran donates generously to his priesthood.'

'Only a blind man would miss the gold dripping from Erldan's robed. But he should have funds saved from Ella's dowry.'

'That's a morbid thought.'

They fell back into silence.

Outside, the carriage wheels squeaked as they bounced along the worsening road. With their provinces sealed, Venn and Gohran might spare the coin to repair it.

Jonas pushed the curtains aside and peered out. Grey clouds livened the autumn colours of the rolling hills and meadows, while spindly branches lay bare, ready to catch the winter snows.

His throat caught. It had been almost two years since the snows trapped Venn up north, leaving him to winter with Ella at Nedran, and when, tarrying for hours in her company, he'd realised it was more than lust he felt.

He dropped the curtain back down and smiled wryly at his sister.

'You miss her,' she said.

'I do.'

'So do I.'

He slipped a comforting arm around Lyn's shoulder.

After a moment, she edged forward and rapped her knuckles on the carriage roof.

'What are you doing?' he asked.

The driver slowed. 'My lord?' he called.

Lynden opened the carriage door and popped her head out. 'Lady, you mean. Can we take a slight detour?'

The driver halted. It wasn't Erldan's usual man, who Jonas heard had recently passed under grievous circumstances.

She squeezed Jonas's hand. 'We might as well pay our respects while we're out this way.'

Jonas sighed. He was eager for a bath and a solid night's rest in his own bed, but he agreed. He'd never experienced the connection to her grave Venn had. To him, it was a mound of dirt and a pile of rocks. Ella lived on in his memory.

The carriage veered off the main road and drove on.

When the path narrowed to a deer trail, the carriage pulled up, and Jonas and Lynden journeyed the last stretch on foot.

Lynden spotted wild snowdrops peeking through the long grass and stooped to gather a posy. 'I rarely see them growing this far south,' she said. 'It seems like an omen.'

'Come on, Lyn.' He wanted it over.

Eventually, they crested the hill to the mound where Ella's grave should have stood.

Lynden gasped. Someone or something had demolished the cairn. Stones lay strewn and the surrounding terrain had been dug up. Atop the disturbed dirt, the jasmine-bush, once so carefully tended, sat upturned, now a spill of dried and curled leaves clinging to a pile of lifeless branches.

He hardly believed what he was seeing. Graves might seem futile, but he did not condone their desecration. It dishonoured the dead and living alike.

He swore. 'Who would do such a thing?'

Lynden remained silent, her snowdrop posy trailing by her side.

'You know, don't you?'

She glanced towards the carriage. The driver was out of earshot. 'A while back, Venn disappeared for several nights, and when he returned, he was covered in dirt and scratches, and acting so oddly. I didn't know what to make of it...'

'You think he did this?'

Lynden shrugged.

'But why?'

She shook her head. 'It was right before he brought his wedding to Raeyn forward.'

'Grief will turn a sane man mad soon enough,' Jonas said, drawing his sister to him. She buried her face against his chest and wept, shoulders trembling, her tears moistening his treasured shirt—the one Ella helped him mend—while he stared at the desecrated mound.

Lyn had never grieved, he realised. Not properly. Not when Venn was such a mess. And he hadn't been there, had he? Curse it. How much he would change given the chance.

'Come stay with me in Lichen, Lyn, while Raeyn and Venn get settled. Vera would love to host you. You can help me plan our wedding.'

She nodded, dabbed at her eyes with her handkerchief. Turning away, she knelt to arrange a few stones into some semblance of order.

J onas intended to confront Venn when they arrived at Nedran, but Lynden's maid, Bess, stopped them in the foyer.

'His lordship does not wish to be disturbed,' she said.

'I don't give two coppers what Venn wants.' His brother was going to provide some answers.

'I'm only relaying the dryhten's wishes, my lord,' Bess said, head bowed.

'Of course, my apologies.' Jonas sighed.

'It's fine, Bess,' Lynden said. 'Leave us.'

Bess curtsied. 'Thank you, my lady. Before I go, may I give you this? The maids found it when they were clearing out the late Princess Ella's old room.' Bess handed across a strange-looking tome.

Lynden took it. 'My thanks, but Bess—why were they cleaning out that room? Are we expecting a guest?'

'The Princess Elder requested a separate chamber, my lady.'

Jonas and Lynden exchanged a glance. 'Thank you, Bess. Where is the princess now?'

'In the women's hall. She's been taking her meals there or in the guest chamber, but I'll tell her you're back and have supper served in the dining hall.'

What was going on? 'Show me that book?'

Lynden passed it across. *The Lost Warriors.* The cover displayed an embossed ring that resembled a full moon, encircling a large 'X'. Jonas flicked through the dusty pages.

Lynden peered over his shoulder. 'Ynad of the Gern... That sounds positively heretical, doesn't it?'

Jonas continued browsing. 'Lyn, you may be right. Look here, this story contains priestesses with magic.' He flipped over a few more pages and a parchment fell out. He read the scrawled text. 'Did Ella ever talk about someone named Amber?'

Lynden shrugged. 'Not that I recall, but Venn might know who she is.'

Jonas slammed the volume shut and tucked it under his arm. Another of the many puzzles he'd like his brother to solve.

'Jonas—' Lynden reached out, but then lowered her hand. 'Be gentle with him.'

Upstairs, Jonas thumped on the door of Venn's study. He didn't wait to be invited in.

In the shadowy light of a single lantern, Venn slumped over his desk, an almost empty bottle of spirit beside him. 'I left word not to be disturbed.' Alcohol flushed his cheeks and wet his mouth.

'So you can play the part of a drunkard? What is going on?'

'Leave, Jonas.'

'Not until you answer me.'

'I said leave!' Venn stood and his chair toppled over. Sweat stained the armpits of his half open and untucked shirt and beaded around his uncombed hairline.

He'd never seen Venn like this, eyes bloodshot and wild. Swaying, Venn raised his bottle, swigged the last of its contents, and hurled it across the room. Jonas ducked aside just in time. The bottle shattered against the wall beside him.

'I told you to go.'

Footsteps scurried towards the sound of smashed glass.

'My lords?' Mykan appeared in the doorway.

'If you want to keep your post, you'll go, Mykan. Now!'

'Ignore his lordship,' Jonas said to Mykan. 'My brother is not himself.' He glared at Venn. 'I'll not stand by and let you threaten our loyal staff. What, by every demon, has got into you?'

'I thought you'd be gone for the rest of the week,' Venn said. 'Was the king's hospitality not to your liking?'

'Mykan, give us a moment.' He nodded to indicate the steward should step outside, but not wander too far. He turned back to his brother. 'Gohran loaned his carriage for the ride home. Lyn and I just returned from Ella's grave.'

Venn looked up. A smirk spread across his face, cold and terrifying. 'What a mockery of the gods, that was.'

'What do you mean? Why is her grave destroyed? Her cairn—it's gone.'

'She's gone, yes, but not from this life.' A chortle.

'Come, Venn. Sit down.' Jonas placed Ella's book on the desk and righted his brother's chair. Venn slumped into it. Beside the book, a coin-sized disc glinted beneath the lantern light—a token of some kind, attached to a chain. Was that an X in its centre? He peered at the volume's cover. The symbols matched.

Venn's rambling continued. 'When I thought she'd died, it almost broke me.'

'You're not making any sense. Why don't you sleep this off and we can talk when you've sobered?'

'I saw her, Jonas.'

'Who?'

'Ella. She's alive. Ella is alive.'

Had his brother returned to having his strange dreams and talking to Ella again? Their aunt had told him he was struggling with grief, but this was becoming absurd.

'You imagine you see her sometimes, and still talk to her, and that's understandable, when we lose someone we love...'

Venn shook his head, met Jonas's gaze and gripped his arms, hard. The lantern cast shadows across his unshaven cheeks, making them seem sharper, hollowed out. Haunted. 'I rode to her. Saw her. Touched her. Jonas, I laid with her, as best we could manage. She was heavy with child.'

'No, Venn. She lost the child, remember? She died.'

'You don't understand. Gohran lied. The cairn is gone because I dismantled it. Her grave is empty. She's alive, and she may have birthed the child by now. My child...'

'Come on, you've drunk far too much...'

'No, Jonas—she's a priestess. A sworn priestess of the Black Moon.'

Jonas froze. The book. The disc. 'You're talking nonsense. If that were true, Gohran would have denounced her.'

Venn gripped him harder. 'Gohran lied to spare her. She's a heretic, a witch, but he hid her. Not like their mother.'

'If Ella is alive, why isn't she here, under your protection? You've never believed in any of that heresy folly.'

'It doesn't matter what I believe. How do you imagine the priests would react to discovering I harboured a heretic? I won't have them disappear you or Lynden, as they did our mother.'

'Are you implying the priests thought our mother was a witch?'

'I don't know, Jonas. I don't think so. Gods—how would I know? But Aunt Servan is convinced the priests took Mother to leverage power over Father.'

'Venn—you're not making any sense.'

'Nothing makes sense. Not when Ella is still alive.'

Jonas had never considered that sorcery might be real. But the more he contemplated it, the more the idea of Ella having magic fit.

It was the smallest things. Odd occurrences surrounding her. The way she intuited people's thoughts and feelings. Her suspicious fortune playing tiles. Vera's mother had said it, hadn't she? *What was so special about the younger princess, besides a pretty face?*

He closed his eyes. Recalled the one and only night they shared. How she infused his senses. How alive she made him feel. What had Vera said about Ella bewitching the servants? Curse it. He'd accused her of bewitching Venn himself. He felt sick.

And yet she beguiled him utterly. Beguiled them all.

Even her brother.

Ella was right when she said the kingdom was filled with ugly, foetid rumours. People always whispered that Ella and Gohran were closer than siblings ought to be. That Gohran was possessive and favoured her. Ella insisted they were playmates, that they'd only had each other growing up. But what if that wasn't it? What if he had cause to protect her? What if he knew her secret?

Jonas paced, mind reeling. 'If you speak the truth, Ella has been alive all this time. Curse every god and demon. I'll kill Gohran for this.'

'No—Gohran spared her, kept her safe.'

Jonas recalled that refugee woman and her children passing through the outskirts of Ycelt, and her son who didn't make it, his corpse abandoned as a feast for the ravening birds. That could have been Ella. Could be her, still. 'How long have you known?'

Venn shook his head.

'How long?' His voice cracked. 'Was it back when you brought your marriage forward? Why? If you knew Ella was alive, why did you marry Raeyn?'

Venn threw back his head and laughed again. That cold, ugly chortle.

'Where is she? You said Gohran hid her. Where?'

Venn's brittle, broken laughter continued. 'Cursed. I'm cursed. I touched her and now I've cursed us all...'

Venn was too inebriated to continue this conversation. 'Come find me when you're sober,' Jonas said, and left his brother to marinate in his dark, obstructive mood.

He nodded for Mykan to attend to Venn and marched down the corridor to his room. His servants had already prepared a bath, and he stripped off and steeped in the heat and soap.

What had become of his brother? How long had he carried this secret? Did Ella have magic? A sworn priestess of the Black Moon. If that were true...

Venn wasn't the only person who had touched Ella with lust, though Jonas hadn't bedded her.

Even if she was a priestess, the Curse was nonsense. A tale told to frighten men into keeping their hands to themselves—a just measure, judging by some fiends he'd encountered.

And even if Gohran believed Ella was a witch and hid her rather than expose her, he was still a brute who denounced his own mother!

And Venn knew. Venn knew, and still he'd entangled them with that monster.

But if Ella was alive, if she'd carried Venn's babe, and he could find her, the priests must annul Venn's marriage to Raeyn. They could sever Erldan's noose around Nedran's neck, and they would all be free. Except he would have to convince them she was no witch...

Gods. If Ella was alive... He inhaled, imagining her scent, her taste, her lips on his... Through the rising steam of his bathwater, his chamber's walls might have been closing in.

He scrubbed, rinsed, and dried, and pulled on his last clean pair of trousers and his least sweat-stained shirt, stuffed a spare shirt in his bag, and went to locate his sister. He would have to leave Lynden and Mykan to watch over Venn.

Witch or not. If Ella was alive, priests and his brother be damned. He would find her.

PART FOUR: UPRISING

THE KINGDOM OF ERLDAN, YCELT

Winter 797 A.S.

Fifty-Four

Ella flitted in and out of sleep, her breath forming ghostlike puffs in the grey as her fire dwindled beneath the stars. Anxious minds tugged at hers, but she swatted them aside, facing the night. Did they not realise they were ordering her to her death?

She concentrated on her mind's chambers. Tried to isolate the segment connected to the order and build a wall against them that would allow her to open her senses to potential danger. But Xarion was there, clawing, nagging, so she shut off entirely. It hurt too much to remain exposed.

At the false light of uhtan, shivering against the icy air, Ella fed her steed and packhorse from her stores, packed up her camp, mounted and led them on.

With every jog, her breasts ached, heavy with milk. Xarion hungered. Even at this distance, her body responded with grief as sharp as shattering glass. To gain some relief, she held her reins with one hand and supported and massaged her breasts with the other. What did women who handed their infants to a wetnurse do when their bodies continued to produce? What did mages do when that child put power behind their hunger?

She wished she had learnt more about motherhood. About magic. About so many things.

Scattered tree shadows told Ella she headed east, but several hours into her journey, clouds overhead gathered and thickened, threatening rain. She didn't know where to go.

What was Davith doing with Amber, and behind her brother's back? Breeyan must have known it was a risk to keep sending a priestess into Ycelt. And if his servants still lurked, might they come for her? It wasn't safe to continue towards Erldan, or anywhere someone could recognise her. Not without a solid plan. She wanted to flee, away from Aryon and Ycelt, but if Shira revealed Xarion's father's identity, her aunt would Cleanse them both.

The sky darkened. No one was going to rescue her. She must do this alone.

She located an oversized tree with exposed roots, her best hope of shelter, and set up camp. Better to wait out the storm than travel into it. She lit a fire and willed it to survive long enough to thaw out her muscles and boil some gruel and left her pails out to collect rain.

Thunder clapped. Her steed snorted and whinnied. She hoped it wasn't storm-shy. The packhorse grunted, resigned, and sought shelter beneath the boughs. She hunkered into her bedding, listening to the rainfall until, exhausted and sleep-deprived, she fell into oblivion.

'Who was that man?' Shira asked.

'I do not know,' Breeyan said, silently cursing the limits of her scrying. That he was a man was all she gleaned.

The women encircled Breeyan's hearth, surrounded by sacred sigils, incense burning in censers at key points. Even combining their abilities, they saw only what their flesh and psyches had experienced directly.

'Then how will she find Amber?' Nykahlia's voice rose in desperation.

'It does not matter that we don't recognise him. So long as Ella does.' Ella's reaction indicated a person she knew and feared. Not Gohran, but someone using Amber to leverage him.

Had Prya focused less on Ella, she might have equipped her heir and not left him vulnerable to predators. Breeyan hated how powerless she was to influence her son's fate.

With a frustrated sigh, she rebuilt their fire, and the trio tried to restore their link to her niece, but Ella had shuttered her mind like a fortress that even

Xarion's yearning couldn't penetrate. Breeyan drew some of the blaze's heat to soothe the babe, who suckled warm ilak's milk through a cloth nipple.

When they couldn't reconnect, Nykahlia—not Xarion—grew inconsolable, her wail reaching a fevered pitch. 'Ella can't cut us off! I need Amber back!' *My beloved.*

Nykki's sobs continued and Breeyan eyed her sharply. Had she and Amber acted on their lust? A tingle travelled her spine. *Unease. Darkness.* The Curse hovered.

She steadied her breathing against the rising tide of panic, tempted to order Nykahlia to follow Ella into Ycelt, help her find Amber, and send the trio north. Have them gone from here.

Shira watched her, silent, guarded. Her apprentice saw into her heart. She drew a further breath and steeled her mind shut.

Shira scooped Nykki to weep into her chest. 'Come, let us rest for the night before we try again...' Glancing back at Breeyan, she shepherded Nykki away.

Let them judge her. They did not share her responsibilities. She cradled Xarion close and stared into the waning flames, recalling her working, the god's warning, and, with a stab, her lost son.

An arm grabbed Ella, startling her awake. She squealed and a callused hand covered her mouth. They'd come for her. They would take her like they took Amber!

Panicked, instinct claimed her, her body remembering Jonas's training, even when her mind couldn't. She kicked and scrambled, shoved an elbow into her opponent's gut, rolled over, and followed with a knee to his groin.

The man doubled over, grabbed his crotch, and groaned. 'You little witch!' He groped for her wrists and pinned her down.

Leveraging his weight, she used her thighs to flip him over and straddled him. Jonas taught her to run away at that point, but he didn't know of her forbidden weapon. For the first time, Ella was unambivalent. She did not hesitate to wield her magic.

Untethered from her babe, free from emotional entanglements, she caught the man's gaze and held it. Her power tingled. Their struggle generated heat—his anger, her fear—and it flowed like a syphon. Intoxicating.

Her opponent's focus drifted, jaw softening, muscles relaxing, until his grip eased, his mind stripped naked as his fury transformed into fear. And then, as her power surged, something akin to adoration. As he took in her lithe body, her long, dark hair, and the fire behind her eyes, she sensed the faintest quiver in his loins. He had wanted to capture and maybe kill her, but now he wanted her alive. Wanted—

'I'm so sorry, my lady.' He scrambled to ingratiate himself. 'I presumed you were an outlaw.' Her power coursed, and his toppling words responded to her unspoken curiosity.

Her lips curved, half grin, half sneer, as she relished his will melting and bending beneath her.

He was hers.

'Please, let me up. I swear I won't harm you.' His greying beard bounced as he spoke.

She narrowed her eyes. The man was perhaps three score years, though his weathered skin added to her estimate.

'We've had so many bandits raiding...'

'I am no bandit, thief, or outlaw,' she said, hearing the hauteur in her voice.

'I see that now. Please...'

She lessened her grip.

'Let me offer you shelter and a hearty meal to make amends.' His features softened, desperate and pleading.

She stood and stepped off him, brushed the damp leaves from her clothes, then offered her hand and helped him up. She surveyed her sodden camp. Her steed was gone, its broken tether dangling. Thankfully, the packhorse was too stupid to follow.

'Let's get you to my homestead before the next downpour.'

Daylight revealed a scattering of farmsteads in the distance. How had she camped so close to this quasi-village? She must have veered north when she lost Elnora's direction behind the approaching rain.

'Thyss is my name,' the man said, leading the packhorse and steering them on foot.

'I'm Nessa,' she offered a common peasant's name.

What were all these people doing living so far from the major towns? She wondered if they owed fealty to her brother, or if they were outside his jurisdiction. Hopefully, they were beyond his notice.

When they reached an Ancient-style mud brick roundhouse, Thyss bid her to wait outside. 'I'll let my wife know you're here.'

Soaked and freezing, she hovered near the small hut's entrance, willing the rain to hold off.

When a woman with wispy hair and rounded hips emerged, she eyed Ella warily, then introduced herself as Mara. 'What brings you this way, girl?'

'Nessa,' Thyss said. 'Her name is Nessa.'

Ella offered her hand in greeting, but the woman kept her thick arms crossed over her chest.

'Pa drank a few too many ales, good lady, and I thought it wise to stay away until he sobered, but with the storm, I lost my path.' She let her warmth flow, but there wasn't much left. The air was still and cold, and the woman would not touch her.

She glanced at Ella's packhorse. 'And you need an army's worth of goods for an overnight sojourn?'

'When Pa goes on a rampage, I never know how long it will last.'

She grasped for a source of energy. Distant static crackled, the storm brewing another batch of rain. It might be enough.

Through her god-sight, its vibration hummed. She netted and weaved, caught the woman's gaze, and let her power flow. 'I'll be gone soon. I only need shelter until the storm passes.'

The woman swayed, slowly nodding. 'I'll set up Thymm's old bed for you tonight.' She was picturing a stocky blond lad who must be their son. 'I've no food to spare, but if you've grain in your stores, you may use my stove.'

Ella didn't want to sacrifice her meagre supplies until she knew how long she would have to rely on them. But once indoors, warm and fed, with her power restored, this couple would do anything she asked. 'Of course. My thanks.'

Thyss helped tether her packhorse beneath a thatch-roofed structure, more like a marquee than a stable, then ducked inside after his wife.

Ella rummaged through her bags for some grain, setting aside enough for her horse. With little to graze heading into winter, she used it sparingly, then retrieved carrots and tubers to pad out their stew.

Damp soaked her leather shoes and numbed her toes. She wrung the bottom of her dress where it had dragged through the mud and grass. Hovering outside the hut, she listened, munching on a carrot for what little energy it provided.

Within, the woman hissed, 'She smells of sour milk.'

'What of it?' Thyss said.

'She's had a babe. So where is it? And who is the father? It's all well for you to invite a stranger into our home, but I'll turn her over if someone comes looking for her.'

Ella swallowed the last of her carrot, drew her shoulders back, and stepped across the threshold. Loudly, she said, 'I've brought enough for each of us.' Her smile inviting, she raised her cooking pot and approached the hearth built into the curve of the wall. 'If I can trouble you for some fuel, I'll start the fire and make us a meal.'

The woman addressed her husband. 'Fetch some wood and dung, would you?' Once he was out of sight, she leaned in close. 'Where is your babe, lass? And who is the father?'

What was usual in these circumstances? What would she believe? 'The babe is with his father's family—a king's man. Pa was drinking the king's coin.'

'Don't lie to me, girl. As if King Gohran would hand over his precious coin to anyone but Elnora's priests.'

Eyes cast down, she scrounged for any iota of energy in her surrounds. 'Have you met the king, good lady?'

'Ha! As if royalty would take an interest in the likes of me. But I don't have to meet a man to know his ilk, girl.'

Faint charge in that disgust—but not enough. A deep breath. 'The babe is with its father's family,' she said quietly. 'You're right—I wasn't waiting out Pa's drunkenness. He's arranged a marriage for me, but the man treats his hounds better than his servants, and I've seen him kick the poor beasts till they pissed blood.' She waited for her words to land, for the faintest sign of sympathy—a way in.

The woman's lips pursed, unconvinced.

'Please—I can't go back.' Ella sensed Mara's emotions roiling. She drew upon their charge, met Mara's gaze, and with a touch to her arm, weaved her power.

The woman wavered. She had known such men. 'What kind of father marries his daughter to a brute?' she tutted, shaking her head.

Thyss returned, laid fuel in the hearth, and crouched to light it.

'Could I borrow some clothing while my dress and shoes dry out?' she asked. They must notice her shivering.

'I'll see if Thymm left anything behind.' Thyss ducked behind a cloth partition separating their beds from the main living space.

She willed Mara to follow.

'I had best help him. My husband can never find ought,' she said, eyes rolling. With the partition's cloth raised, she hesitated, glancing back, as if she didn't trust leaving Ella alone.

Ella smiled with a tingle of warmth, and Mara let the curtain drop behind her.

With them both out of view, Ella captured the fire's heat, returning some to the flames to coax the blaze along, and greedily sucked in the rest.

Through the screen, her hosts continued their whispers.

'That accent—I tell you, she's noble born.'

'What if she is?'

'Do you want some high and mighty lord to come looking for her?'

'We'll hide her.'

'Not with that strange dark hair...'

By the time they returned, the fire blazed. Ella located a kitchen knife and chopped tubers and carrots to toss into the pot with the simmering grain, all the while drawing upon the excess heat.

'Here, lass.' Mara passed her a pair of woollen trousers and a coarse linen shirt. She smiled her thanks, directing and winding her will. Without Ella asking, Mara took over the cooking while she undressed.

Embarrassed, Thyss ducked back outside, muttering something about collecting more wood.

Ella hid her smirk. Embarrassment, disgust, desire. It was all fuel for her magic. Let the air thicken with it.

'Those clothes should warm you, lass. And a hearty meal will relax that gooseflesh.'

She pulled on the trousers and shirt, but slowly, letting the woman's mixed emotions seethe.

Mara glanced down, where Ella's leaking milk dampened her shirt. 'That must be uncomfortable. Have you any winter cabbages in those packs?'

'I don't think so...'

'Once the rain eases, I'll see what's ready to be harvested.'

Puzzled, Ella frowned.

'Cabbage leaves, lass. They'll help with the weaning.'

So it went, the pair fussing to make her comfortable and cared for. Ella had no cause to fear or doubt them now. They were utterly within her thrall. And as she wound and threaded her power, she wondered if this strange elation was what her mother experienced as Erldan's queen.

Fifty-Five

Jonas didn't wait for Venn to sober. Gohran's carriage had already departed, so he mounted a fresh steed and rode directly to Erldan, his heart in his throat beneath the darkening sky. He only stopped when threatening clouds obscured Xenon's light, seeking shelter with villagers, before setting out again at uhtan.

The worst of the rain shed, his steed's hoofs churned clomps of mud and veered around potholes until he neared the kingdom's outskirts, when he slowed, letting the beast pick its path.

Erldan's inner gates loomed, and the steam of his conviction dissipated. He had not thought this through. He couldn't confront the King of Erldan and demand he reveal where he'd hidden his heretic sister. Gohran would arrest him before he finished his first sentence.

He would need to select his words with care, for he would not leave without answers.

He rode on, pulling up outside the closed gates.

Palm raised, a guard said, 'His Highness is not accepting visitors.'

'Tell him it's Lord Jonas of Nedran, and that I have news of his sister.' He didn't specify which.

'Yes, my lord.' The guard signalled to a footman, who bowed and marched towards the keep.

There was no evidence of the nuptials a few nights earlier. The sodden streets surrounding the castle seemed hollowed out, as though the rain evacuated straggling revellers. Further away, a ladder rested against the wall of the temple where the ceremony and protest had taken place. A pair of artisans worked to repair the window's shattered pane, while another couple of lads carried brooms and pails towards the front steps. No women, he noticed.

'Lord Jonas of Nedran?' The footman had returned.

'Yes?'

'His Highness bids you leave your message with me.'

That coward wouldn't face Jonas on his own. 'I have ridden all the way from Nedran. I can shelter in the town and wait until His Highness's next hearing.'

The footman nodded.

'You might wait a while, my lord,' said the guard. 'The next public hearing won't be until the moon is waxing gibbous.'

Jonas ran his fingers through his hair. 'I'd wager if His Highness knew what news I bring, he would seek an audience sooner—and in private. It's about the late Princess Ella.'

With backs turned, the men spoke too quietly for Jonas to overhear, before the footman addressed him again. 'Very good, my lord.'

The guard opened the gate and let him through. Jonas dismounted and handed his reins to a second footman. The first escorted him to the keep. When they reached the foyer, he instructed Jonas to wait.

When the footman reemerged, he ushered Jonas upstairs towards the parlour. More waiting. Jonas puffed his cheeks in an exaggerated sigh. Gohran's stalling felt like a ploy. He paced, examining the miserable wall hangings and grim carpets. He doubted a complete refurbish and addition of brilliant chandeliers could rid Erldan's interior of the gloom imprinted from its foundations up.

Eventually, the footman returned, and led him along shadowy corridors that reeked of burning oil from dim sconces until they reached a carved heavy door.

The footman opened it and bowed. 'Your Highness, Lord Jonas of Nedran.'

Gohran perched behind his oversized desk. Jonas entered and waited for Gohran to invite him to sit, but the offer never came.

'What matter is so urgent?'

'Your Highness, I bring news of your sister, Princess Ella of Erldan.'

Gohran's eyes narrowed. He signalled for his man to leave, and sat poised until the door latched shut behind him. 'The late princess, you mean?'

'Not late at all, Your Highness.' Jonas ran his fingers along the pommel of his sheathed dagger. 'My brother told me Princess Ella lives, Your Highness.'

Gohran stood, temples reddening. 'What?'

Jonas took a slow, steadying breath. 'It's not my place to question His Highness's decisions. However, I wish to know where the princess resides.'

'Whatever spurious nonsense your brother spouted, I assure you, I buried my youngest sister with my own hands.'

'Then why does her grave lie hollow?'

Gohran's entire body tautened, and Jonas hid a smirk.

'If Lord Venn or anyone else treats sacred ground with such impiety, then the gods will punish them soon enough.' Gohran faced him, employing that same mesmerising gaze. Obdurate, Jonas stared straight back. Gohran would not budge on this, but nor would he.

'I'll find her, Your Highness. And when I do, the priests will annul my brother's sham of a marriage to the Princess Elder on the grounds his prior betrothal was consummated, even if it was never sealed.'

Gohran paled before rising blood flushed his skin. His simmering eyes appeared black in the low light.

'That sounds like a baseless threat, *my lord*, but a threat nonetheless.'

Wood in Jonas's throat. His hand slid from his dagger, and he held his palms open. 'Not intended so, *Your Highness*, I assure you. I merely seek information as to her whereabouts.'

'She is gone from this world, and to suggest otherwise is to accuse your king of deception.'

'*A* king, Your Highness, but as yet, not *my* king. I've sworn no oath of fealty.'

'And yet you enter *my* kingdom with your accusations.'

'I came bearing news that your sister's grave lies bare and that my brother believes she lives. There is no accusation here, merely information and a question, Your Highness.'

Gohran rapped his fist upon the desk, and the doors opened. Two burly guards entered.

It took Jonas a moment to realise what was happening. They approached slowly, footsteps heavy, armoured chest and shoulder plates encasing barrelled torsos, closing in on either side. Approaching *him*. He peered around. A further guard stood in the doorway with halberd raised. Gruff arms seized his elbows and yanked him tight.

'Lock him up while I decide what to do with him.' Gohran's words ground between clenched teeth.

'Your Highness, this is false arrest and imprisonment. I have done you no harm,' Jonas said.

'Shut him up.'

A slap, followed by a punch to his guts. He doubled over. Rough hands straightened and dragged him from the king's study.

'If you arrest me, you'll be answering to my brother.'

Callused hands cupped his mouth, pinched his cheeks, and squeezed his jaw.

How had he been fool enough to think he could query Gohran with any other result?

Servants stopped and stared as the guards hauled him through the corridors, down winding stairs, and towards the bowels of Erldan's keep, leaving him to moulder in the corner of a musty cell.

Mindful of his rank, his jailors delivered a stretcher for a bed, clean blankets and water, decent food, and a chamber pot.

The prisoner in the cell beside his was not so fortunate. A girl of perhaps thirteen, huddled without a bed or bedding. Legs pulled to her chest, she trembled. Was she accused of heresy? When he approached her cell, she faced away and hugged her legs tighter.

He sank back and stared at the ceiling. This was going to be a long night.

Curse his self-righteous tongue. He should have stayed silent about the annulment. He supposed a stay in a dungeon while Gohran contacted his brother was a fair price to pay for his stupidity.

But he saw the lie in Gohran's eyes. The king was afraid. And if he hadn't told Venn about Ella, how had Venn discovered her?

Gods, his thoughts could churn all night. Venn wouldn't let harm come to him, surely. And Gohran wouldn't be foolish enough to take any action that might lead to irreparable conflict between the two provinces.

He just wished the crawling in his stomach would subside, that creeping fear that Gohran would act without considering the consequences for his relationship with Venn and Nedran, and the deeper fear that with Venn in his current state, he might sacrifice Jonas to maintain that relationship.

FIFTY-SIX

'How do you fare in your new situation, Your Highness?' Lynden passed a trencher across the dining table to Raeyn.

Venn was absent, and despite his promise to take Lynden with him to Lichen, Jonas rode out alone without explanation the moment he'd bathed. 'Watch over Venn, Lyn,' he said. 'I'll be home as soon as soon.' He planted a forehead kiss and strode away, carrying a lone saddlebag.

He warned her to leave Venn be, but she'd been foolish enough to poke her head through his study door. Seeing his inebriated state, she did not linger. He seemed half mad, worse than when he first grieved over Ella. What had got into everyone?

Mykan assured her he would monitor Venn and sent her to tend to Raeyn.

She wanted to weep. But when she looked across the table, Raeyn appeared so miserable that she mustered a cheering smile.

'I'm settling well, my thanks,' Raeyn said, not smiling in return.

'Bess told me you are sleeping in the guest chamber. Are the furnishings in the master rooms not to your taste?' She couldn't imagine anyone would prefer Erldan's styling to Nedran's, but perhaps Raeyn wanted something more familiar around her.

'No—they're fine...' her voice trailed off.

'If there's anything you need...' Lynden realised how ludicrous she must sound. This was Raeyn's home now. Raeyn was the household's head. She had already instructed the servants to accommodate her. She didn't need Lynden's assistance, and she certainly didn't need her permission.

Their conversation stalled into oppressive silence. The scrape of cutlery, chink of glass and crockery bounced off the hardwood floors, and Lynden wished they had a high king's wealth to hire minstrels for ordinary meals. Anything to distract from this prickling discomfiture.

A servant hovered, surveying the table.

'Has someone taken Lord Venn his meal?' she asked.

'Indeed, Lady Lynden.'

'Wonderful, my thanks.' She dismissed the servant and then turned back to Raeyn. 'Will you and Venn try for an heir right away?'

Raeyn looked stricken.

'I mean—well, my apologies, I just assumed...' She hadn't meant to be tactless. Insensitive. Not when Ella's pregnancy stole her life.

Raeyn cleared her throat. 'I intend to honour my duty to bear the dryhten heirs.'

Lynden topped up her wine and signalled for another carafe. She itched to ask Raeyn what passed between her and Venn. Wanted to ask after Gohran. But Lynden might have dined opposite a wood-carved statue.

Raeyn's own thoughts absorbed her, more detached than vulnerable, as if a part of her wasn't even there. When she addressed the servants, it was with quiet command, and Lynden saw the queen she would have become, had the laws allowed her to inherit the throne.

She brought her glass to her lips, and Gohran's ice-blue eyes flashed in its reflection, his violent hand whipping across her face. She cupped her cheek to soothe the invisible bruising. Beneath the surface, his sting echoed, and deeper still, shame marred.

A sigh and another swallow of wine. She was naïve to assume Gohran would be any different with her. Despite witnessing terror in the eyes of his servants and sisters, she imagined breaking through that protective shell, entering where others couldn't. As if he would soften for her alone. As if she could reach him. Heal him.

Too late, she discovered the barbs upon his casing. His claws did not retract, and he left her wounded.

She needed to be alone.

As soon as was polite, she excused herself.

'You're not retiring to the parlour?' Raeyn's eyes sloped, almost pleading, before flattening to her even mien that offered no hints, her request devoid of warmth.

'I assumed you would want to head to your chamber,' Lynden said, hoping she didn't look as pleading. Raeyn did not seem a games woman, and if dinner was any indication, they would have little to discuss. Jonas had better return soon. If she had to sit with Venn's new bride for another meal, she might develop a taste for over-imbibing to alleviate her boredom from the dourest woman she had ever encountered.

'I wondered if you might share your local knowledge. Help me become acquainted with Nedran,' Raeyn said.

Lynden glimpsed the barest smile and sighed. Raeyn may have stumbled upon the one thing she could not resist. She signalled to a servant. 'See if a guard can escort us into town.' Heading out must be preferable to brooding alone in her room with her dark thoughts.

They did not dally but headed straight for The Red Rose—the perfect place to unveil Nedran's secrets. Settled in her usual table inside the lady's tavern, which was quiet for the hour, Lynden slipped into the rhythm of sharing intimate knowledge of her home.

Raeyn said little, sipping her wine, observing and listening.

Lynden surged ahead, encouraged by the tide of mulled wine, and the illusion of privacy amongst lush, cushioned furnishings and strangers.

'When you and Venn have your first babe, you'll have to fend off my relations,' she warned, her grin wicked. 'My aunt, and our cousin, make our family's business theirs.'

'The lord would need to attend to my bed first.' A bitter edge as Raeyn's voice cracked.

Lynden was used to her acquaintances sparring, returning her salacious banter, but perhaps Raeyn's sombreness provided an opening. She wondered how far to venture.

'I hope Venn and Gohran haven't quarrelled. Their relationship seemed mended with your betrothal. But after that strange commotion at the wedding... Do you know what troubles your new husband?'

A wry twist at the corner of Raeyn's lips. 'Your brother is a stranger to me.'

'Venn is usually more affable, I assure you. He hasn't been himself since...' She stopped from mentioning Ella. 'Well, for a while.'

'You need not protect me. I'm aware he pines for my sister.'

Lynden said nothing, and looked for a server to fetch more wine, though her goblet was still half full. She drank deeply, warmth flooding her chest and flushing her cheeks, then cleared her throat. 'You must miss her as much as Gohran does. Ella meant a great deal to us all.'

'Indeed.' Another catch in Raeyn's voice.

Lynden couldn't imagine resenting her siblings. Venn and Jonas butted heads like rutting ilaks, but beneath their bluster, they cared deeply—even through the rift Ella caused.

She floundered, trying to steer the conversation back.

Raeyn rescued her by finishing her goblet, and standing to announce, 'It's getting late. We should return.'

Fifty-Seven

The room spun, and Venn's stomach lurched. He couldn't recall a time when he'd felt so wretched. How much had he drunk? He willed his surroundings to stop moving so he might survey the damage. Shattered glass littered the doorway, empty carafes and half-drunk skins lay strewn. A toppled lantern had mercifully smothered itself before catching alight.

He threw off his blanket and untangled his limbs from his sheets. At least he made it onto his bed to sleep—or had Mykan carried him? He didn't remember.

What was the last thing he recalled? Jonas. Jonas shouting about Ella's grave. Oh gods. He'd told Jonas. He reached for his chamber pot and hurled his guts.

He dragged himself back to bed, crawled under the covers, closed his eyes, and tried to ignore his head pounding.

Hours he flitted in and out of sleep, only for his realisations to panic him awake. He'd allied his people to a liar and a heretic.

Servants tiptoed to clean around him. They brought water and food, and some horrid concoction to ease the pain.

'Don't sniff it, my lord. Just swallow it straight down.'

He did as instructed, trying not to empty his guts again, then buried his head back beneath his blankets.

He remained abed for the rest of that day, save for a brief outing at Mykan's insistence, to absorb some fresh air.

That night, a servant brought him dinner—no wine, only water.

'Please send my apologies to the princess and my siblings.'

'Yes, my lord. Though Lord Jonas is not in residence.'

Venn groaned. Hopefully, he'd taken refuge at Lichen. Selmyra and Teegan would calm his brother if Vera couldn't.

Venn struggled through the next few days, but welcomed the distraction of his regular duties. He had much to catch up on following the wedding. As he sobered, it was like a fog lifted and he saw with renewed clarity.

He forced himself to preside over his people's hearing, though his stomach was still sour, and despite the residual pounding in his head. Seated behind his bench on the dais, his scribe beside him, his citizens crowded into the room and huddled before him. One by one, he invited them forwards to voice their concerns.

At first, attendees sought his verdict on minor squabbles, such as settling disputes over grazing rights. Venn listened with measured patience and made rulings he considered firm but fair, his justice one reason his people honoured their dryhten.

But then the hearing took a sharp turn. One man stood, hands at his hips, and boomed his question. 'My lord, must we attend worship daily now that Nedran and Erldan are allies?'

Venn reeled. 'I should think not. Citizens of Nedran have always been free to worship or not, as they choose.'

'King Gohran makes all his citizens attend,' called another.

'The henads come for those who don't.'

'How will we tend to our farms if we're always in services, my lord?'

'And our trades!' someone else shouted.

'Yes—and trades.'

Others joined in, their concerns toppling one another.

'Will his henads raid our homes?'

'What about the protest?'

'And that dead raven!'

'I heard King Gohran made a deal with the moneylenders from Myan. Is Nedran in debt now, too?'

'Is it true King Gohran murdered a villager out west?'

Venn held up his hands for silence, but the crowd didn't stop, their voices growing louder, feeding off one another's uneasiness, until all Venn heard was a cacophony of angst.

He rapped the pommel of his dagger on his bench until the rabble fell silent.

'Good people. I appreciate your concerns and assure you my ties to the kingdom of Erldan do not extend to the loss of your privacy and your freedoms. I will take these matters to the king to establish a formal proclamation protecting your rights.' *And mine*, he thought.

Following the hearing, he rode through Nedran's grounds to clear his head, listening to the rhythmic clomping of his steed's hooves thudding through winter grass, thankful the snows and ice hadn't yet set in.

The chill of rushing air stung his heated cheeks. This alliance was supposed to improve Nedran's situation, not worsen it. Gohran assured him it would quieten the rising unrest around the hallit trade. Too late, he realised the alliance benefited Erldan, not Nedran.

When he arrived back, Mykan informed him Jonas had not returned, and Lynden was tending to his new bride.

'Will you dine in your study again, my lord?'

'Yes—wait, no. I'll take my meal in the dining room.' He couldn't avoid Raeyn forever.

When he entered, he was relieved to find Raeyn and Lynden talking quietly. Strikingly dissimilar, he hoped they would get along. Though he supposed it wouldn't much matter once he settled Lynden away from Nedran.

He wanted her married soon after Jonas—or sooner, if he couldn't wrangle a betrothal contract out of his brother within the coming moons. But that would leave him spending each evening alone beside Raeyn. Was there truly any hurry to settle his siblings now?

He sighed. Given his people's rising angst, there was more urgency, not less. He needed Nedran allied to Lichen before Teegan and Selmyra changed their minds.

He forced a smile, took his place at the table's head, and inquired after the women's day. A servant brought wine, but he covered his glass. 'Water is fine, my thanks.' He never wanted to imbibe again.

The meal dragged, the trio chatting about the coming winter, wondering how intense the snows would be this year. Lynden eyed him curiously, Raeyn, warily, and he continued to converse as politely as if entertaining emissaries from a rival province.

The servants had just laid the last course when a courier arrived.

A knot formed in Venn's chest when he saw the insignia. What more could Gohran want from him?

He broke the wax seal, opened it, and read.

'What does it say?' Lynden asked with forced nonchalance, eyes on her meal as she tore a chunk of bread.

Raeyn studied her glass, running her fingertips around its base.

'Jonas has been arrested.'

'What?!' Lynden stood.

Raeyn's fingers pressed against the glass until her fingernails paled.

'The letter doesn't say on what grounds. The king merely writes to inform me there will be a hearing to determine the matter.'

The room closed in around him. His sister shouted, while his new bride sank stonily into her chair. The courier awaited a response, but he couldn't think. Their questions clamoured.

Louder still were the questions he asked himself.

Jonas must have ridden directly to the king shouting accusations—but what accusations, exactly? What had he revealed to Jonas in his drunken stupor?

He cursed his brother for being so rash, so foolish. Then cursed himself for being more so.

Venn closed his eyes to block out the room, to stifle his thoughts, but one memory rang through his mind like a Myan singing bowl: Jonas's low voice, threatening, *I'll kill Gohran for this.*

Fifty-Eight

Thyss and Mara strove to accommodate Ella within their village and home. The couple sheltered, clothed and fed her, while she pondered how to retrieve Amber without risking her life. In exchange, she helped prepare for the coming winter, spreading manure, harvesting cabbages and leeks, planting and pruning, and readying supplies.

The villagers lived communally, sharing crops and livestock. Older folk contributed their knowledge and expertise when their bodies weakened. When not working the land, youngsters shepherded ilaks and herd beasts, including Ella's packhorse, to the surrounding pastures. Children played between errands, basking in the milder weather. Soon, the cold would force the inhabitants to shelter, feeding themselves and their animals from stores.

As in Aryon, this far west and south, winters often saw only a scatter of snow. Semi-nomads who roamed further north over summer camped alongside the fixed homesteads in a patchwork of canvas tents. More bodies to help, more mouths to feed, and more eyes on the quiet young stranger dressed in lad's clothes who hid her hair beneath a borrowed cloak.

Thankfully, these folk kept to themselves, grateful for another body—anybody—to share their labour.

Settled in her temporary shelter, Ella made excuses to scry for Amber, fetching water, tending their fire, but the village was so small, she was rarely unobserved. More than once, someone accused her of dallying, or commented on her odd habit of staring into a void when she should be working. She retaliated with a disarming smile, savoured their transforming disdain, as her power flowed.

In those rare moments she touched Amber's mind, she saw only muffled darkness. Amber's captors kept her covered, her thoughts fogged, unreachable. And whenever Ella detected another voice, she broke her vision off, petrified of encountering Davith's contempt staring back.

Behind the far reaches of her awareness, Xarion's need was constant, overlaid with a stronger sense of her daughter safe and cared for, Breeyan attuning and attending to her babe as Ella never could. Focused on her work, she soothed her breasts with harvested cabbage leaves and shuttered her mind and heart. It was her only means of keeping them both alive.

That day, she collected dung pats in a wicker basket. Alongside her, a lad with dusty brown hair and blue-grey eyes spread some of the manure to fertilise their fields. Whatever was leftover they would dry to supplement their meagre firewood.

The boy was a head shorter than she, and the fuzz across his freckled cheeks hadn't yet darkened, but he glanced at her through thick, pale lashes, and blushed when she aimed her gaze straight back.

She smiled and beckoned him closer. Face like a ripened tomato, he approached, wiping his hands on muddy trousers. She sensed the heat radiating from his shoulders.

'You're Thomys, aren't you?'

He nodded, sucked on his lip, studying his shoes.

She didn't need him to look at her. He was completely in her thrall. Not bothering to disguise her sly satisfaction, she let her lips widen; her smile opening, welcoming. Inviting.

'Do you know where your village lies in relation to the Kingdom of Erldan? To the province of Nedran?' She had seen Thomys herding stock, and riding atop a wagon to deliver taxes. Or perhaps tithes.

He cleared his throat. 'Of course.'

'Could you draw me a map?' She pointed to a mound of dirt. Flattened it with her shovel. She wasn't entirely certain where this village lay, having lost her bearings during the storm the night Thyss found her.

Brow creased, the lad's bottom lip slipped back between his teeth as he took his hoe and traced lines across the dirt. 'There's no proper road until you get to here,' he said, marking a point a hand's span from the village.

'And from which direction does Elnora rise?'

He drew an arc from right to left. 'That's where She starts,' he said. 'And that's the End of the World.' He squiggled a border along the left of the drawing, joining with Elnora's path. Where the initial trail ended, he scratched a line extending from top to bottom, with two points marked. 'Nedran and Erldan. If you take that first track, you can't miss the main road. Then you turn north to the dryhten's city or south to the king's.'

'And how far to travel from point to point?'

'That depends.' He shrugged. Blushed again, eager to satisfy her curiosity.

'Thom, get back to work!' someone called.

'My thanks,' she mouthed.

Another flush, and he scurried to his row.

Ella crouched to study the map. Even without distances, it helped her find her bearings. She stood. Tried to establish where the first trail began, relative to the sprawl of village buildings. Looked up to track Elnora. A blinding flash. She'd shaded her eyes too late. Squinting, she cast her gaze back down towards the boy's etching, but a purple-black sphere eclipsed her vision.

A tug and a tingle radiating from her spine. Her mind was falling, peeling away from her flesh. Then flying, floating along the drawn path. Like viewing the map hidden between the pages of *The Lost Warriors*, her god-sight rendered the boy's sketch in three dimensions. Not as a tunnel, but a carrier pigeon's passage across the sky. Its drifting currents mirrored the sensation she'd experienced visiting Venn through her dream state, and again when she'd birthed her babe. Her simulacrum hovered above her body, only now it traversed an imaginary path. Free.

Memories crowded. What each place meant to her. Guiding her, propelling her towards—

'You too, Nessa!' The villager's voice cut through her working, dragging her back with an icelike blast. 'We need to get that manure spread.'

She winced as her simulacrum slammed into her body. Recoiled as though struck. She swayed, limbs trembling, gooseflesh puckering, head woozy.

She blinked herself steady, the ground solid beneath her feet and the air chill against her skin. The scent of tilled soil flooded her nostrils, and she rubbed her shoulders warm, pressed her temples to soothe, then collected her shovel, and set to work, hugging this strange new discovery tightly to her chest.

FIFTY-NINE

Jonas lost time waiting for word from his brother, oscillating between acute panic and excruciating boredom. A pair of sconces offered dim light. His was one of several cells, separated by iron bars within a cavern dug beneath the keep and reinforced with ageless stones. Stale air carried the scent of clay and refuse, periodically flushed anew when guards arrived with fresh bread, water, and occasionally meat, and replaced his chamber pot.

The lass in the next cell sobbed intermittently. She looked half-starved. Hunted. Haunted.

'Want some of this food?'

She refused to answer, but shuffled nearer to accept his offering through the bars, her peculiar eyes a luminous gold. No wonder she hid them.

The priests warned witches all bore some stain of their heresy. Ella's azure eyes and raven hair were uncommon for this region, but not sufficient to arouse suspicion when her mother's and brother's colouring was identical.

Behind his eyelids, he pictured her, remembered her body against his, what his hands and mouth experienced.

Nothing heretical, only bewitching.

He sighed. He could no longer deny she was alive. Gohran would have mocked and sent him away were his accusations baseless.

He looked again at the gold-eyed girl, now nibbling bread with her back to him. 'Do you know what's to happen to you?'

Silence.

Another sigh. 'Me either.'

The quiet between them grew onerous, but the food eased the girl's tears.

Jonas drifted into his thoughts, finding sleep, only to wake with his heart in his throat, Gohran's imagined face in his as he pronounced Jonas guilty of treason.

More time passed. He didn't know how much. More food and water arrived. He offered some to the girl, and what she refused, he left untouched, stretching the hours by savouring each morsel. Gods, this was tedious! Why hadn't his brother intervened already? He rolled back over, chasing sleep.

When next he woke, it was to the sound of chains. Not guards, but robes, using a staff and shepherd's crook to prod and steer a hooded prisoner, as though to keep her at a distance. Another door opened. They shoved the prisoner inside and slammed it shut. She drooped across the cell floor as if she had drunk too much ale. Through the obscure light, he was slow to recognise the religious vestment and saffron hair beneath that hood: the heretic the robes carted through the city before Venn's wedding.

Was she awaiting execution? Or her trial? Though one assured the other. Everyone knew heresy trials were a sham. To the priests, a lone accusation was a death sentence. He hoped the same was not true for him.

He waited until the robes were gone. 'Hello?'

A moan.

'Are you hurt?'

Another moan and a muffled, throaty rasp, like she struggled to breathe. Behind her back, her hands writhed against their bindings.

'If you manoeuvre this way, I can help,' he said.

She alternated swinging her legs and torso and shuffled along the ground as he stretched his hand between the cell bars.

Footsteps outside.

'Curse it.' He retracted his arm and retreated to the shadows, rubbing his flesh where the bars bit.

Murmurs, before the footsteps fell away.

He edged back and whispered to the woman. 'Can you come closer?'

She shuffled nearer. He grasped the hood—a burlap sack—and pulled it off. Her captors had stuffed a rag into her mouth, and her eyes watered, blinking through the dim light. He removed the gag, and she sputtered, heaving juddering gasps. Gratitude spread across her face. In silence, she eyed his bread.

He held it out, and she tore off chunks with her teeth. He offered his water and tilted the cup so she could drink. Liquid dribbled into her mouth and down her chin, and she nodded with thanks.

'If you turn around, I'll try to loosen those ropes,' he said. More shuffling, until her back was to him, and he could access her hands. Her skin was raw from where the bindings had abraded. 'I'll be as gentle as I can.'

'Put the hood back on...' she said, her voice raspy. 'In case they return.'

He complied, then continued working at loosening the knotted twine.

More footsteps. She rolled away from him, and he retreated to his cot.

The door creaked open. A wiry man and a robed lad entered the dungeon. He recognised Erldan's head priest from Venn's wedding.

Still and quiet, he feigned sleep.

'How fares my little sparrow this evening?' The priest's slow, measured steps echoed. 'What delights my servants have enjoyed with that fragile mind.' A snigger. More footsteps, pacing. He reached to pick something up—the gag—and tutted. 'Do I need to bind this in place?'

Silence.

He tossed it aside. 'You could have made this easier. Swifter. Less painful. But if you won't speak, I shall savour my amusement.'

More footsteps, keys jangling in a lock, feet shuffling. 'Then we have this tiny finch.' He entered the cell of the other prisoner, the girl with golden eyes. 'Most entertaining for my servants...'

The girl's snivelling returned, louder, more insistent.

'Look at those yellow irises. They say you've shown not an inkling of witchery, and yet the Moon God has marked you.' His slick voice oozed. 'Sorcery or not, when I do *this* to you, my sparrow over there twitches...'

Jonas felt queasy, grateful he couldn't see what that robed roach did.

'Stop...' the saffron-haired prisoner murmured. 'It's me you want. Stop using her.'

'Now she speaks.'

'Please—'

More shuffling, more snivelling.

'Water—I need water... Please, I need...' Her rasping trailed off.

A thump, then silence.

'Sit her up, lad,' said the head priest. 'But don't touch her.'

Jonas risked propping on his forearms. The robed lad hovered over the saffron-haired prisoner, who lay sprawled, unconscious. The lad tried to rouse her with the end of his crook. She didn't move.

'I think she's stopped breathing,' the lad said. He leaned closer, hovering his hand an inch above her chest and throat at the opening of her hood.

The prisoner jerked her wrists free and clutched the lad's arm. He froze, her grip paralysing. She ripped the sack from her head. Grabbed his jaw. Forced him to meet her gaze until his limp body sagged. Collapsed to the ground, his keys and crook clanged beside him. A cold draught rushed to fill the void where he'd crouched.

Jonas had no moment to process what he'd witnessed: magic wielded like a weapon.

Near the door, the head priest hovered. He wore a peculiar blank expression, and the prisoner—a sorceress—winced.

Jonas scrambled to retrieve the fallen keys, but they landed beyond his reach. The robe's crook was closer. Face turned aside, he mashed his cheek into metal, and extended his fingers until he brushed against its wood. He pedalled his fingertips, trying to gain purchase, urging it closer. It was there... So near... One more pedal... His fingers slipped and pushed the rod away. He swore.

The robed lad roused, groaning.

Eyes fixed on his, the sorceress forced him to the ground.

She pivoted to the head priest. He stared towards, but not at her, wearing that same blank expression, staff poised between them.

Jonas reached again for the fallen crook. If only she could kick it...

As if he'd voiced his thought, the sorceress pushed the rod nearer. He grabbed and leveraged its crook towards the ring of keys.

The head priest raised his staff, angled to block the sorceress from reaching him. Touching him. She stood tall and firm, gaze aimed at his.

The priest laughed, an icy chortle that quivered through Jonas's bones. 'I know your ways, little sparrow.' His staff pushed into her chest. He held it crossways, arms outstretched beyond her grasp, his sheer size preventing her from connecting with him.

In the cell beside his, the gold-eyed girl, previously silent, emitted a piercing wail. Her cry continued, escalating in an anguished, violent crescendo. The head priest winced and covered his ears with his hands.

The sorceress lunged close and gripped his wrists.

As if his limbs had turned to gruel, the priest lurched.

Slow, deliberate, each word a blow landing, she said, 'Open. The. Door.'

His movements wooden, the priest did as she commanded, then stepped aside and slumped to the floor. Both men dozed like drunkards.

Near the dungeon's exit, the sorceress hesitated, swaying, shaking. She leaned against the wall for support, her breathing laboured.

'Can you get her out?' Jonas nodded towards the gold-eyed girl. Still wrangling the crook, he tried to nudge the keys within reach.

The sorceress staggered over the fallen lad and kicked them towards Jonas's cell. He retrieved the keys, cycling through each until one fit his lock, and his cell door swung open.

'Pass me your food.' The sorceress trembled.

Groaning from the floor, the robes stirred.

'We need to get her out first,' Jonas said. The yellow-eyed girl must be gone before their captors roused to their feet. Hands shaking, he tried the same key on her door, without success. He tested another. And another. None fit. He swore again.

'I won't leave you,' he said, and the girl's wail faded to a whimper.

Movement behind him. Jonas risked a glance over his shoulder. The sorceress towered over the collapsed robes, gnawing on a half-eaten joint of roasted meat salvaged from the rations inside his opened cell.

He tried the next key, willing his hand steady. The lock clunked, and the door swung open.

'We need to go,' the sorceress hissed, grabbing her hood. 'The regular guards will return soon enough.'

He tugged the gold-eyed lass's arm, urging her towards the door, and she squealed, flailing.

The sorceress stepped between them, clasped the girl's hands and directed her gaze.

The girl shuddered, then fell silent. Terror transformed into a docile, childlike smile—a nightmare, soothed, followed by an aching, biting chill.

The sorceress faced Jonas. 'Take her. I'll follow.'

The girl appeared awake, yet unconscious. Golden eyes open but unseeing. Standing but resting. He slipped his arms beneath her chest and knees and carried her—a dead weight—leaving the sorceress to hold the robes back.

Once they were clear of the dungeon, she followed, slammed and bolted the door behind them.

The trio shuffled along the dank passage. The sorceress seemed to know where she was going.

'If someone comes now, I can't stop them,' she said, tossing the stripped bone aside. 'I've nothing left to draw upon.'

Jonas realised she didn't eat from hunger. She needed sustenance to fuel her magic.

The dungeon corridor opened into the root cellar beneath the main keep, as though, when built, it had been expedient to dig a shared underground space. A staircase led up to the kitchen, which was blessedly empty.

In his arms, the gold-eyed girl roused and squirmed.

With a touch, the sorceress lulled her, then stumbled. 'I can't continue doing this.' She paused, resting against a bench, the surrounding air like ice. 'Get her outside and away before she wakes enough to scream. I'll grab some stores and meet you.'

Jonas nodded.

'Hurry.'

He wasn't familiar with this part of Erldan, but most kitchens had a rear entrance. A small door against one wall opened, but it led back to the root cellar beside the dungeon. 'Curse it!'

'This way,' the sorceress hissed, carrying her former hood, now laden with produce.

Jonas could not discern the hour, but marvelled when the sorceress led them confidently through the dark and into the frosty night.

'My steed...' he said when she headed for the city gates.

The sorceress shook her head. 'It's too risky to go near the stables. We need to leave on foot.'

She was right. The girl grew heavy in his arms. 'I have to set her down...'

'Not yet.' The sorceress peered along the quiet streets. She tugged them behind an abandoned wagon, and they crouched next to a row of discarded wine barrels, their sour, vinegary aroma assaulting his senses.

Ahead loomed the city gates. 'How are we getting past the night watch?'

'Hush. Let me think.'

Still cradled in Jonas's arms, the gold-eyed girl stirred. The sorceress rested a palm on her, and she shuddered, then wilted into a stupor. Chill blasted into the space between them. The sorceress reached her other hand into her stolen hood and retrieved an apple. Jonas had witnessed no one so ravenous. She followed with a skin of ilak's milk, devouring the entire thing, then wiped her mouth on her ratty sleeve.

The sorceress looked down at her robe. 'Give me your clothes.'

'What?'

'If I'm to get close enough to use my magic, I need a disguise. The guards will spot my vestment the moment I approach.'

He was about to suggest she swapped attire with the lass, but the girl's dress was far too small.

'Hurry,' she said.

He set the girl down and undressed, while the sorceress slipped off her robe. He tossed her his shirt and trousers, which she pulled on, stuffing her saffron hair beneath so it appeared cut off at the neckline, then passed him her robe.

Jonas drew the scratchy vestment over his head. It smelled of excrement, blood, and vomit. He nearly gagged, but it was better than standing naked in the cold.

'I think I'll have enough strength to influence them now,' the sorceress said. 'Wait for my signal.'

Jonas didn't even have a dagger to defend them if something went awry. Gohran's guards had confiscated his saddlebags and everything but his shirt, trousers, and boots, when they arrested him.

The sorceress hobbled towards the night watch with a stiffened gait, noticeable now in his trousers.

The watchmen were on their guard as she approached, but quickly relaxed and opened the gates. She turned and waved for Jonas to follow. He hefted the gold-eyed girl and slung her over his shoulder like a hunted carcass. With the other hand, he grabbed the food sack, then strode to join the sorceress, moving awkwardly in her strange robe.

A shout from the rear. He picked up speed. Once they were through, the sorceress used her peculiar powers on the watchmen who shut the gates behind them. He still couldn't quite believe what he was seeing.

Not far along, they veered off the road and into the brush. The sorceress spotted some deeper scrub where they crouched to rest.

Hoofbeats thundered, accompanied by shouting, as riders neared. Jonas's heart thundered to match. He tried to quiet his breath, hiding vaporous puffs beneath the putrid robe as the trio laid low and silent.

Another shout, and the riders steered away, their hoofbeats fading in the distance.

Jonas peered through the dark at the sorceress and the gold-eyed girl as his racing heart slowed and his stampeding breath eased.

What had he done?

Prior to his escape, Venn might have argued for his reprieve on the grounds that Jonas was brash—foolish—not treasonous. Venn would have appealed to their kinship, and Gohran would show his gracious mercy, flexing his dominance, before Jonas slinked home, chastened, to his brother's berating.

But now? He'd made himself a fugitive.

The gold-eyed girl whimpered again. Those monsters tortured her. Tortured them both. He'd had no choice but to act. No one deserved to be treated as they had.

A hand touched his, and then a mind. *Worry about getting justice later. Right now, we need to survive.*

By all the demons in the Afterworld, he wanted to slice Gohran's throat, and then the throat of every last robe. But the sorceress was right. In that moment, he needed to focus on staying calm and remaining alive.

Sixty

Amber did it. She was free. Tears sprang, but she choked them back. There wasn't time to weep. Not yet. They needed to press on. The priest's men would keep hunting, and now they had the king's riders trailing them, thanks to the prisoners she'd freed.

That poor girl… What the priests did to her… She itched to scratch out their leering eyeballs and stab their vile hearts. Their torments flared in the girl's mind, flashing her back there bodily, as if she relived her torture. Only someone of Breeyan's magical calibre might heal psychic wounds so severe. Meanwhile, Amber used her novice skills to still her wild panic.

The male escapee was a complication. Each time the tortured lass became aware of a man nearby, her terror erupted. If she didn't need him to carry the girl to safety, Amber would abandon him. She was safer on her own.

The trio traversed west and slightly north, resting often. They avoided the road and farmsteads, keeping to the scrub, which thinned the further they travelled.

'We need horses,' the man said. 'And shelter before we freeze out here.' He pointed to her vestment, which stopped mid-calf, leaving the bottom of his legs exposed.

She opened her senses. They were alone for now. 'Here, swap. Quickly.'

He peeled off her robe, shivering, every hair on his body raised.

She poured power through her touch to prevent the tortured girl rousing while the man was undressed. Such a sight would reignite her screaming.

'What's your name?' he asked, handing over her robe.

She wished she wasn't as cold as he appeared, but her magic stole any remnants of warmth from the surrounding air. 'Amber,' she said. Angst staved off the chill somewhat, but though she needed its strength, its heat, they couldn't risk a fire.

'Wait—Ella's Amber?'

She froze, the soiled vestment halfway over her head. She scanned his thoughts, but couldn't reach him. Did he know who she was? 'I once worked at the castle.' Hastily, she added, 'For the queen.' Her trembling fingers worked to remove his shirt from beneath her robe.

'That would explain the note.'

'Note?' She passed him his shirt.

'The one I found in Ella's book.'

A sharp glance. *The Lost Warriors.* 'Where is it?'

'Back home.' He slipped his shirt on.

'Which is...?' Her cramping fingers struggled to unlace his trousers.

'Nedran.'

'You're Lord Jonas of Nedran?' She stepped free and passed the trousers across.

'The very man.' Naked from the waist down, he gave a mock bow.

What was he doing being held captive by Ella's brother?

'You might call me a political prisoner,' he said, pulling his trousers on.

Had her thought reached him?

'Do you know where Princess Ella is?' he asked.

'Nowhere you'll find her,' she snapped.

He fastened his trousers. 'The king told everyone she was dead.'

'Gohran was always shrewd.'

'Please.' His arms gripped. 'I need to see her. She's the reason I came back to Erldan.'

'And look where that got you.' She willed him to release her. He didn't move. Penetrated his gaze. No response.

'I risked my life and probably my brother's too, helping the king's prisoners to escape. Tell me where I can find her. Please.' Eyes beseeching.

She shrugged him off and hugged her robe around her. It reeked. She reeked. But it was warm. 'I'm fairly certain *I* just helped *you* escape. King Gohran is not aware I was a prisoner, and I would have eventually freed myself.'

'It may not appear that way to the king.'

'Then you should have stayed behind,' she said.

'How would you have carted her?' He nodded towards the girl, who had curved herself into a ball like a sleeping cat beneath the sliver of moonlight.

Amber said nothing.

'I've come this far. Tell me.'

'Ella doesn't need you to rescue her any more than I did. She's more powerful than you or I.' Why couldn't she stop him?

'I don't want to rescue her. I need to see her.' *Now I know she's alive.*

She shook her head. 'It's too dangerous. She's better dead to everyone in Ycelt.' How could she make him understand?

'I'll take her far from here. By the demons, we'll travel to Myan if we must. No one will find her there.'

'I said, leave it.' Power gathered behind her words, but it was like blustering at a rock. He was immune. 'I'm not telling you this to protect Ella. I'm protecting you. She's dangerous. Her power is dangerous. She can't help it. You think her brother wanted to do what he did?'

'What did Gohran do?'

'Oh gods. You don't know...' Why didn't she keep her mouth shut? She'd resisted that demon priest's torture. Surely, she could hide Ella's secrets from this ordinary man. Yet he was so open and guileless that she yearned to trust him.

He wasn't giving up. 'I know Gohran hurt her. He's a brute.'

'He can't help what he is any more than she can.'

'You're defending him?'

'His magic is broken. *He's* broken...'

'He is a monster.'

She could not disagree. 'Please trust me, and leave Ella where she is. For her sake and yours.' Nearby, the girl roused. 'Let's keep moving,' she said.

'We should veer north.' He pointed. 'There's nothing further west except The End of the World.'

She didn't correct him.

'I know somewhere we can shelter, but it's another day's travel without transportation, and if I have to carry the girl…'

'Let me try something,' she said, grateful he'd stopped badgering her about Ella. She crouched beside the dozing girl, cast her focus adrift. If she wound a temporary shield around her mind, Amber might wake her, have her walk on her own. She searched for the hum of energy. There wasn't enough. Her surrounds were cold and still. And she was weary. Gods, she was weary. She barely sourced power to quiet the girl where she lay.

'What if I go ahead and then double back once I've borrowed some steeds?'

She shook her head. They might freeze before he returned. If he didn't abandon them.

'I don't have a weapon, or I would hunt us a meal… Not that we've anything to cook it on.'

Lighting a fire was too risky, but an animal would provide warmth. Blood. Life force. With that kind of power, she might protect them, persuade anyone who came for them.

But Xenon forbade it.

She wanted to howl at the waning moon. *Why gift us tools but prevent us from using them?*

The temperature was dropping. 'We can't stay out here. We need to keep moving,' he said. 'It's our only chance.'

Amber studied the poor, broken girl. 'I'm sorry. I can't—I don't have enough power. The moment I let go, she's going to rouse and start screaming. I'm fighting her constantly.'

Brow scrunched. Mouth tight. He was wrestling with something. 'Then I'm sorry. I must continue alone. If I stay, we'll all die out here. I promise to hurry back, but I can't guarantee it will be soon enough.'

She nodded. 'I understand.'

He hesitated. 'You're certain there's no other means to source power?' He nodded towards the sack of food.

'Not enough. Not now.' Eyes to the moon, she prayed, but the god remained silent.

She could die now, or she could die later. 'Give me your arm.'

Confusion crossed his features, but he did as she asked.

She sucked on her bottom lip, caught his gaze, and rolled up his shirt sleeve. 'This may hurt.' She drew him close, pressed her nail into his flesh until it broke through his skin, and whispered, 'Xenon, forgive me.'

A sharp inhale. He winced, but remained calm.

Breath poised, muscles tensed, she waited. His blood welled, but she felt nothing. No thrill coursing through her. No fiery, intoxicating charge. His source might have been tepid, stagnant water. She sensed the barest tingle—natural warmth from the heat of his body. Not enough. It wasn't working! Why wasn't it working?

Riders in the distance. They needed to get away.

'What's happening?' he asked.

'Nothing! Nothing is happening.' She swore under her breath.

He looked at her, panicked. 'How can I help?'

She inhaled to steady her heart. 'Brace her and keep her from seeing what I'm doing.' She was loath to abuse the poor girl's body further, but if she didn't, they would die out here. Amber positioned her torso between the girl and where she cradled her arm, hoping to minimise her exposure as she dragged her nail and broke the girl's skin.

Pure force surged. Her limbs and heart blazed.

'Ah...' There it was.

Amber's pupils enlarged until her irises almost disappeared. The landscape brightened like daylight, save for the lack of colour, and her focus sharpened. Static tingled where fabric touched her skin, and icy air rushed through her nostrils. She resisted soaking up that power, basking in its heady bliss, and directed the force into the lass.

Davith had been right. The girl was born with unfortunate-coloured eyes, but no magic to show for it.

Amber used her amplified gifts to explore the girl's wounded psyche. Aggravated and inflamed, the distressed region resembled a friction burn with jagged, irritated edges. She constructed a casing, flooded its margins with soothing power to lock the horrifying memories away.

The enchantment wouldn't last, its barrier gradually eroding without constant fuel, but it should get her beyond their pursuers' hearing if her panic broke through.

We need to go. Amber fed the thought into the lass's open mind, hand encasing her wound, keeping it hidden. She kept the girl close, drawing and pouring energy in equal measure, standing between her and Jonas.

She nodded to Jonas, and the trio hastened west and north. The lass limped with them, slow and docile, but supporting her own weight to relieve Jonas. Huddled together for warmth, they ducked behind vegetation and kept out of view of the road and any wider trails where their hunter's steeds might follow and set further into the night.

Sixty-One

Though she had not located Amber, Ella did not give up. And now she had a new possibility to explore—using her mind to follow a drawing to a distant point. When she travelled along the tunnels in the scriptorium, she assumed her simulacrum following its passageways was a property of the map. Magic imbued by a powerful sorceress. What if it wasn't a magic *map*, but a magic *process*?

She needed to experiment, to learn more, and so volunteered for tasks away from prying eyes, or out in the fields, where she etched lines anew, but couldn't replicate her experience. When the tingle of magic began, she pictured floating, but her mind couldn't source sufficient power to follow. Running water and fire weren't enough. Nor riled emotions.

The one time her mind peeled away, she lacked fuel, her simulacrum like a tether stretched so thin it would break, and she feared it might shatter, leaving her flesh to perish. Heart racing, breath gasping, she scrambled to reconnect and ground herself in her icy surrounds. What if her mind and body separated and could not rejoin? Would her mind wander, an untethered haunt, her flesh an unsouled ghoul?

Afterwards, she dared not test the limits of this strange power. Not unless she sourced ample, potent power.

A few days later, she stumbled upon a possible source. Two women hefting a hunted deer, its haunches sliding off their shoulders, passed her in the fields. Freshly killed, gore soaked its coat and smeared their shirts.

'Can you help us, lass?' one called.

She dropped her hoe and scurried to take some of the beast's weight. Power surged. Eyes closed, she inhaled as it tingled through her heart, her limbs, her loins. When she reopened her eyes, fire burned behind them.

Her smile weaved, the women's thoughts clear in her mind. One found Ella alluring. Hoped her husband wouldn't notice. The other reflected how much she enjoyed having Ella around, though Ella barely interacted with either woman.

The animal's source seeped through her, and she absorbed its electrifying thrill. Felt her magic gather. Its tingle no longer frightened her, but exhilarated.

'We'll carry it to Willun's hut.' Willun was the village butcher, who carved and distributed their kills.

Harnessing power like that...

She recalled reaching Venn through her dreams. Those times they almost connected, flesh to flesh, fuelled by the bite of thorns. Thought back further to the thrill of his shirt and hands soaked in animal remains. And later, to her wounded arm, wrapping its magnetism around her brother.

Blood.

Potent enough to warp and bind, and perhaps travel using will alone...

A source Xenon forbade.

There was no moment to contemplate further. As they neared the butcher's hut, someone shrieked, 'Riders headed our way.'

One of the women turned to Ella. 'Hurry inside, lass!'

Ella stalled, transferring the flank slung over her shoulder.

'Leave that and go!'

Hoofbeats and the jangle of riders approached. She couldn't tell how many. She ducked within a mud brick hut, through the cloth partition to its beds, and sought a place to hide, but the furnishings were too sparse.

'Search the buildings,' someone shouted.

Growing up, when she and Gohran hid from their sisters, or the children who tormented Gohran, she learnt to keep moving, and sneak to where their pursuers had already hunted. She emerged from the hut and crouched low, keeping the building between her and the rider's line of sight, waiting for an opportunity to circle back.

'We're looking for a robed woman with yellow-orange hair,' one rider said.

Did they mean Amber? Had she got away from Davith?

'And a lass with pale yellow eyes,' said a husky voice.

'No one would mistake those eyes,' the first added.

'They were last seen travelling on foot with a man with light brown hair, green-grey eyes, about this tall.'

If it was Amber, who was she with?

From behind the roundhouse, Ella observed the men invade and explore each building, lean-to, and tent. If they came from Erldan, it wouldn't take them long to recognise her.

Out of view, she slipped into a neighbour's barn. Inside stood a large haystack the villagers used to insulate the cold ground. She buried herself under it, and hunkered, waiting, breathing, hoping.

Beneath the false darkness of the hay, she tried to picture her drawn map, to will her simulacrum to separate from her flesh so she could disappear, but she had no focus, nothing to follow or move towards. Though her power churned, her mind stayed stubbornly fixed to her body.

Resigned to remain hidden, she listened to the muffled sounds that would indicate it was safe to surface. Footsteps neared, then fell away, then neared again. Muted voices questioning, shouting. The wait was agonising.

Finally, the men addressed the villagers. 'If you see these folk, or anyone like them, send word to His Holiness.'

'Are these heretics?' someone asked, though Ella couldn't hear the reply.

Hoofbeats faded into the distance, but she only emerged once Elnora's light dwindled to dusk. Hay covered her hair and face, clinging stubbornly to her clothes. She coughed, spat, and brushed the straw away, then stumbled to Thyss and Mara's hut.

That raid was close. Too close.

When she stepped through the doorway, Mara looked up from where she prepared their evening meal, her face alight.

'We thought we'd lost you,' Thyss said, brow creased and eyes soft. He dropped his mending to clasp her arms.

Seeing them tear up, her eyes welled.

'I imagined that awful betrothed coming for you,' Mara said, whomping her cleaver through a chicken carcass until its bones snapped.

'Were they holy men?' she asked.

Mara nodded. 'Robes who can't hold on to their prisoners.' She pictured men with partially shaved heads, stony eyes, and a greasy, pimpled lad. No one Ella recognised. Perhaps new recruits.

'You should stay hidden a while longer, lass, in case they camp nearby and keep watch,' Thyss said.

'Shall I start the fire?' Once ablaze, she would risk opening her mind to sense for danger and scry for Amber. Confirm it was her they sought.

Mara finished chopping, wiped her hands on her pinafore, and, with a frown, pulled a stray straw from Ella's hair. 'Here—finish this.' She pointed to the quartered bird. 'I need to fetch something.'

Mara disappeared outside, and Ella heard banging and rustling as she fried the portions of chicken. When Mara reemerged, she carried shears and a dye pot and placed them beside Ella on their only bench. 'Once you've set the pan to simmer, let's see what we can do with your hair.'

Ella almost wept as Mara grabbed fistfuls of raven tresses and hacked them with her shears. The slicing blades reminded her of cutting fabric, the silken black strands pooling at her feet.

Afterwards, her fingers explored the blunt ends, cropped just below her ears, where the cool air brushed her neck.

'Let's fix that colour.'

The reek of stale urine assaulted Ella as Mara slopped the stinging cold paste through her remaining hair and along her scalp.

'I've stirred in some madder, but I'm not sure how it will take. The black may end up yellow.' Mara frowned. 'Hold still and I'll wrap it in some linen for the night.'

Over dinner, Ella tried to ignore the pungent waft, but said nothing. She wanted it done, and the foul gunk rinsed off.

With all the fussing over her appearance, she had no moment to scry. That would have to wait until morning. And as she lay awake in another man's bed, another couple's home, her strange new hair marinating, for the first time, she felt grateful for her powers. Without them, the holy men might have captured her in the wilderness—or worse, the villagers would have turned her over.

The next day, hair rinsed and dried, Mara ushered Ella towards the water trough to inspect her reflection. She braced. They could disguise her hair, dress her in lad's clothing, but what good was that, when she wore her mother's face?

Yet, when she studied her mirrored image, Mara and Thyss standing behind her, she gasped, for she did not recognise herself.

Sixty-Two

Days passed since Gohran's courier carried news of Jonas's arrest. It was a rare morning when Davith did not require him, so he settled into his study to tend to his affairs.

'Has there been word from Nedran?' he asked his guard. He still lacked a page.

'None, Your Highness.'

Gohran could not believe the gall of Venn's younger brother. To barge into his kingdom, his castle, and accuse him! A few nights in his dungeon should dissolve the smirk from that charming face.

But if Venn didn't intervene and call Gohran's bluff soon… He couldn't risk Jonas making his assertions in open court. Needed to silence him.

He could not fathom how Venn discovered Ella. The dryhten seemed distant prior to his nuptials. Formal. Due to nerves, Gohran imagined. And when he'd left so abruptly the next day, Gohran assumed he was reacting to the protest. What if it wasn't nerves or unease? What if he already knew?

But how?

Apart from his aunt and Aryon's priestesses, no one knew Ella was alive but him and Jarrod, and Jarrod was dead. Unless his driver revealed the truth before those bandits murdered him.

Gohran presumed the bandits' motive was mercenary. But what if it was political? After all, they wouldn't have known Jarrod carried a copper worth stealing, and it was unusual to risk ambushing a king's man for stock alone. Hijacking animals required planning and bore the penalty of death.

'You should not concern yourself with shuffling coin and delivering livestock.' Davith's words returned to him. He did not recall informing his priest that transporting stock was part of Jarrod's mission.

Davith vouched for those guards. Davith was the only person who knew Gohran required hired swords. But why would Davith betray him?

'Had I known the true nature of your man's errand, I might have advised you differently…'

'Tell His Holiness I wish to see him,' he said to his guard. 'Immediately.'

By the time Davith arrived, trailed by his entourage of neophytes, Gohran was ready to erupt. Strewn parchments littered his desk, mostly scratched through, along with several broken quills.

When his servant announced the holy men, Gohran bid the neophytes wait outside, and had his servant join them.

Stiff-backed, Davith entered. He surveyed the walls, crowded with tapestries, eyes narrowed, before he faced Gohran, and his features tempered. 'Your Highness.' A bow. 'You seem troubled.'

That lilting voice once soothed. Now it prickled with deceit.

'It was you,' Gohran hissed.

'Your Highness?'

'Jarrod, my driver. They were your men who accompanied him.'

Davith's jaw tightened. Barely discernible, but Gohran saw.

Outwardly, Davith heaved a sigh, brow furrowed in a mockery of fatherly concern. 'Your Highness, I appreciate this incident has you preoccupied, but you must move on. It's not fruitful for you to… *obsess.*'

Once Davith's patronising tone would have shredded, but now his disapproval wafted like mist. He confronted the High Priest. 'You were the only other person aware of the meet, Your Holiness.'

'Nonsense. Raids are a fact of our existence. Your man might have told a dozen people himself. For your own sake, I caution you to let it go.'

Gohran shook his head. 'Jarrod was the most loyal man I've ever known. He met my gaze directly when he swore his oath of silence. I would know if he lied.'

Another sigh, almost bored. 'What of the person he was going to meet? He wasn't dropping your goods to an unmanned void.'

It couldn't be his aunt's priestesses—Xenon forbade aggression. Besides, what motive had they? His aunt was already getting everything she wanted.

'No. They would never be violent.'

'"They", Your Highness? You mean, the priestesses who live in that Black Moon haven on your border that you refuse to acknowledge?'

Gohran thought he might catch alight where he stood.

'Interesting that you trust a man by whether he meets your gaze...' Davith stroked his chin, half-covering his mouth, but Gohran witnessed his sneer. 'I see your special gift, Your Highness. Your *knack* for persuasion.'

The terrain beneath might have trembled. Chest tight, temples pounding, fire swept along his torso, up his neck, until his face was ready to burst aflame.

He needed that persuasion now, reached for his priest, his mentor, but Davith's staff blocked him.

'Dare you move to strike a king?'

Dare you attempt to bewitch a priest? Davith's lips never moved, yet Gohran heard him like he'd heard the unspoken words of his peasants outside the temple.

Shame they don't make daft men kings, Ella once said.

Was he going mad?

Gaze aimed at Davith, Davith's focus wouldn't resolve upon his, as though he looked through, but not at his king.

Davith broke away, lowered his staff, and turned aside with calculated nonchalance. 'Never would I threaten a monarch. You are my trusted ally and king, *Your Highness*.' He trod slowly, deliberately, contemplating the tapestries.

Why wouldn't Davith look at him?

Davith rubbed his chin, settled his attention on a tapestry that depicted Erldan's first ruler. 'Such a longstanding and powerful dynasty. Were you aware your ancestor bedded a witch? All those generations ago. And here you are, a son of a heretic.'

Why was he drawing this out?

'There have always been questions about that union's legitimacy, and therefore, their descendants. Some accounts say the priests never sealed the betrothal. After all, it is within the remit of Elnora's priesthood to refuse a marriage where a king's fitness to rule is in doubt.'

'What has any of that to do with my man's murder?'

'Should the true purpose of your man's mission become more widely known, the priesthood may come to doubt His Highness's fitness to rule. It would be a shame to see such an enduring dynasty perish.'

Gohran forced his reeling mind steady. 'Whether I marry is of no concern. Princess Jaydyn already has a babe in arms, and Raeyn is sure to follow.'

'Provided the raven's curse was barren.'

Gohran stiffened. 'You said that gesture was petty malice, nothing more.'

'Petty words to soothe petty fears, Your Highness.'

What did Davith want from him? He must know. Just denounce him and be done with it!

'Your man's fate is a mystery to me, Your Highness, but with further funds, we can extend our enquiries...'

Blackmail. 'I've already told you Erldan has no coin to spare.'

'But with Erldan tied to Nedran...'

'Any additional wealth from that alliance will barely cover Erldan's debts. My man was repaying a debt that day, and those funds were forfeit. That doesn't erase Erldan's liability.'

'If your coffers are as empty as you claim, perhaps it would behove His Highness to call upon the charity of his priesthood.'

The gall! Erldan's priests grew fat on the wealth of Erldan's donations. *Bribes. They were always bribes.*

'I can recommend several trusted men to assist in your duties—both here and in Nedran.'

'Trusted like the men who slayed Jarrod?'

A sneer. 'You may refuse my offer, Your Highness, but I cannot guarantee finding your man's killers. Nor can I dissuade any challenge to your dynasty's legitimacy. Were it to emerge that you consorted with heretics... Of course, if

His Highness were to make circumspect appointments to appropriate posts, he could assure his continued legacy...'

From the time he was a boy, Davith advised him. Nurtured him. Gohran trusted him like a father. Had it always been a lie? Had he always known the truth?

Elnora cursed him. Created a loathsome monster. He hurt everyone he cared about. Father. Mother. Sister. Friend. Lover. He was poison. Eventually, they all uncovered the truth. Despised and abandoned him.

Now his mentor, the person who replaced his father in his esteem, hadn't just abandoned him. He was using him. Using him the way his mother had wanted to use Ella.

His love of Davith shattered. Its distorting lens dispersed, revealing the bitter truth: Davith wanted control of Erldan and, through his alliance, Nedran.

Clarity, at last.

He thought back to establishing that first henad outpost when Davith had him persuade the local priest. This entire time, Davith used him to let the priests infiltrate. Gohran even pushed to increase their presence and authority. He'd suggested it.

Had Davith always known he was as much a heretic as his mother?

Thunder rumbled. Mounting static that begged for release. He yearned for its charge to surge and blast through every morsel of this man who betrayed him. Become the abomination his father believed him to be.

Energy roiled and burned. Throbbed and oozed. Within and around, as though apart from him.

It would only take one glance, one step, one touch, and he could strike Davith down.

'Your Highness?'

Gohran froze. Closed his eyes. Unclenched his fists. Swallowed.

If he struck now, if he inched closer, Davith would denounce him. His life and his kingdom, forfeit.

Davith knew. Davith owned him. And there was nothing he could do.

Powerless.

'Leave me.' His words choked from his throat. 'I shall consider your advice.' He needed Davith gone.

Alone, he had no moment to think, to breathe, before a servant thundered up the hall, panting.

'Your Highness! Your prisoners have escaped.'

'What? How?'

'We went to serve their meals and found the dungeon empty. All three doors were open.'

Who were they holding besides Venn's brother? Had someone freed them? A traitor? 'What are you waiting for? Hunt them down. Don't let Lord Jonas get away.'

The man bowed and turned.

'Wait—'

'Your Highness?'

'Don't bring him back.' If he revealed Gohran's shame… 'Find him and kill him.'

'But—Your Highness…' The man's terror ground across his face and body.

'Tell the men, if they value their lives, it must look like an accident.'

He didn't need to speak the word. If Venn suspected they killed his brother, it would mean war.

Sixty-Three

'I don't dare light a fire. Not yet. We're still too close,' Amber said.

Weakened and weary, the trio made it through the night. They stopped in a clearing to sit and rest. Not for long enough to sleep.

'I need to draw more power, and I can't keep using her,' Amber nodded towards the younger girl. 'She's depleted.' *And she's suffered enough.*

'Try me again,' Jonas said, rolling up his sleeve.

Head shaking, she pushed his shirt back down. 'It won't work. There's something about you... I don't know how to explain...'

Hadn't Alina said something similar when he'd asked to try her potions? That there was something peculiar about the way his mind worked.

Alina's tales of hypnotic, drug-induced visions were nothing to what Jonas witnessed over the preceding day. This saffron-haired sorceress read minds, bent the will of others, stupefied, practically paralysed, and sucked power out of people.

Could Ella do those things? Amber had said Ella was stronger, more powerful. Excitement tingled. Anticipation. He longed to experience that with—

'I said leave her,' Amber snapped.

He startled. 'How can you read my mind, but not use my blood?'

She drew her fingers across her heart and body in a gesture resembling the devout warding off witchcraft. 'Xenon help me—I shouldn't use anyone's life force,' she said. 'And I don't know. Sometimes our thoughts exchange, but I can't influence you and I can't draw from you.' She peered into the distance. 'We don't have time to explore your limitations. We should keep moving.'

'*My* limitations?'

'Come.' She stood and led them deeper into the undergrowth.

Bare, spindly branches reached across their trail like spider webs. Fallen leaves blanketed the spongy ground, slippery and moist. Elsewhere, thick foliage surrounded mud-crusted pools. Keeping to the main trail would have been quicker and easier, but too risky.

The lass walked between them, shaking, whimpering.

'Poor thing, they've shattered her mind,' Amber said, as though the girl wasn't right beside her. The sorceress's periodic touch eased the girl's distress and kept her quiet.

'Did those priests have magic?' Jonas ducked and weaved around exposed branches and tree roots.

Amber scoffed. 'Most definitely not. But a tortured body will damage a mind soon enough.'

'Those demon spawn,' Jonas spat. 'And they did that to her, to get to you?'

Amber flinched.

'My apologies. I didn't mean...' his voice trailed, but his next question nagged, unspoken. *Why aren't you like—that? Like her?*

A wry smile. Amber tugged her robe from a clinging vine. 'You expect me to trust you with that knowledge?' *After I've seen it warped and perverted?*

Curse it! He wished she'd stop eavesdropping on his thoughts.

Another twist to her mouth. 'How much further is this village?'

'I've never travelled there on foot, but I'd say we'll be near enough by nightfall.'

Jonas's first instinct was to head to Tymot's farmstead, for shelter, and to borrow steeds. But then he remembered he was a fugitive, and these escaped heretics. He had no desire to expose the villagers to Gohran's ire, or to attract the attention of the priests. But without steeds, they were slow and weak.

'We'll have to steal some,' Amber said.

Jonas blanched. Every iota of his being protested the idea of thieving, especially from those with so little. But she was right. They could not enter the village openly, so they must arrive by stealth.

Jonas's legs and back ached. Trekking through uneven terrain activated dormant muscles. He preferred the familiar straddle of his steed's gait.

Better to move on foot than not at all.

'Would you kindly stay out of my head?'

'Stop thinking so loudly, then.'

Elnora hadn't begun her descent when they stumbled across a lad herding a flock of ilaks.

The lass saw him first and shrieked. Amber grabbed her arm and hushed her cries to a low, shuddering whimper.

Instead of fleeing, the lad froze, startled like a hunted deer.

Amber turned to Jonas and the girl. 'Stay back.' She dropped her food sack and approached the boy with outstretched arms to show she wielded no weapon. 'Hush, lad,' she crooned, as she had spoken to the girl moments before.

Within reach, she stroked his arm, clasped his hand, and he swayed, dreamy-eyed, as if drunk on shrillan smoke. Amber moved in close, spoke too quietly for Jonas to hear. The boy nodded slowly, waved his crook to round up his ilaks and herded them towards his farmstead.

Jonas was about to call after when Amber raised her palm for silence. She trudged her way back. 'I've solved our transport,' she said. 'He'll meet us after dark with a pair of steeds. Meanwhile, we had best camp far from here.'

Slapped awake, he saw why the priests sought to round up and destroy these powerful women. Recalled teaching Ella how to defend herself, as if she would ever need his help. Not if she could do—whatever *that* was.

Pulled from his reverie, Amber's faltering voice reached him. 'I-I need fuel...' she stumbled. Another step, and she slumped to the ground, shivering.

Jonas crouched and drew Amber close. She was ice cold. 'Give her your arm,' he said to the girl, who watched with wide, hunted eyes.

Her muscles grew taut, terror breaking through Amber's enchantment. Like a half-starved wildcat, she leapt, clawing him off Amber. He caught her wrists, twisted and pinned her against him. One arm wound around her emaciated body, the other stifled her screams.

'Hush, or they'll find us!'

She bit down hard, bucking and kicking. At least she'd stopped shrieking.

He loosened his grip, tempted to release her, let her flee into the forest. She may not get far, but she would be free from the likes of those priests. Free from any man.

'Don't,' Amber said. 'She won't survive out there. My High Priestess can heal her. I just need to get her home.' Amber's skin grew alarmingly grey, the edges of her lips tinged blue.

The tortured girl writhed against him.

'He's safe. I'm here,' Amber said to the girl, her voice the barest whisper.

The girl's fight petered out, and Jonas removed his hand from her mouth. He drew both women close, holding them firm, keeping them warm. The girl squirmed, but when she realised Amber was with her, safe, she settled.

'I'm going to risk that fire,' Jonas said, extracting himself, leaving them huddling for warmth and security.

He sucked at the wounds on his fingers. For a tiny lass, she was fierce.

By the time he returned with enough dry kindling to burn, Elnora was sinking below the ochre-tinged horizon, his companions nestled, dozing. He stacked the fuel—fallen branches and dried leaves—and dropped Amber's hood containing their remaining food nearby.

Amber roused. 'I'm not sure I've energy enough to start the fire…'

'And I'm not much of a hunter, so we'll need to supplement this.' He presented a small squirrel carcass.

Amber's face lit up. 'Pass it here.'

Puzzled, he handed it to her, tail-first.

Eyes closed, Amber clutched the poor dead creature, as if praying, her hands covering the open wound where he'd struck it with a rock. Her cheeks restored to a fleshy pink, her lips to a plump crimson, and when she opened her eyes again, they glimmered. She waved towards the kindling, sparking their fire alight, and tossed the carcass back.

Jonas weighed it, expecting it to feel different. Drained. It was colder, but otherwise, unchanged. He skewered its scrawny torso with a stick and held it over the flames to cook.

When the herder eventually returned, leading a pair of steeds, the fire had dwindled to glowing embers. As he approached, Amber said, 'One for you, the other for me and the girl.'

'I thought we'd travel together...' *To find Ella.* His voice fell away. She'd already told him she would not help.

'From here, we travel alone.' *Do not follow, or you'll risk my home.*

'Never would I—'

The lad interrupted. 'You were right to stay away. Yesterday, the priests came searching, and now, the king is on his way. Take the steeds and go. Quickly.'

'My thanks,' Jonas said. 'I will return your generosity with interest as soon as soon.' He didn't know how he would explain this to his brother...

Venn.

Gods, what had he done? He couldn't beg for protection and forgiveness. Not now. Not while Venn was bound to Gohran, a poisonous ruler with dangerous ideals and an unhinged temper.

A monarch.

Who he defied.

Treason.

With one rash action, he'd shattered his life.

He needed that contract annulled. Voided. But without evidence that Venn's marriage was invalid, the priests would not dissolve the alliance. He had to find Ella. Not for himself, but for his brother, and his brother's people.

If Amber wouldn't help him, he would search alone. Finding her alive was the only way to disentangle them all.

Sixty-Four

Following the robed men's search, Ella hunkered down, waiting until she knew their attention had moved on. With her changed appearance, and the villagers' protection, she told herself she was secure until she could locate Amber and get away.

But where Xarion's presence stalked, an open wound that would not heal, Ella had not detected her erstwhile tutor. Occasionally, she sensed Venn's thoughts upon her, even now, and Gohran's, always, despite her efforts to shut him out. But she and Amber were not bound by the intimacy she shared with her lover, her brother, her child.

She could only cling to the hope that when the holy men described their robed escapee having yellow-orange hair, it was Amber they referred to, and that her companions were benign.

Away from her daughter, among strangers, her power blossomed, thrummed, beguiling the villagers, who strove to keep her hidden. Wanted her safe. She need only smile, touch an arm, or aim her radiant gaze, and those around her glowed warmth right back. With no prior ties or emotional bonds, she didn't mind knowing her magic bound them. A temporary hiatus from Aryon, her daughter, and her former life in Ycelt.

That evening, she asked Mara to fetch grain, and Thyss to chop kindling. Out of their sight, she scrounged the fortitude to scry yet again. She cast her gaze adrift among her hearth's flames, expecting that same muffled darkness to taunt. But this time, she sensed a familiar tug, unaccompanied by the intoxicated lilting. A clear, solid pull. At last, an image formed.

A woman crouched before a fire; palms raised to its heat. Ella steadied her breath and homed her gaze. Distinctive saffron hair hung matted and greasy about the woman's shoulders. She looked up, peered into the flames. Amber. Her old tutor was unencumbered, her mind no longer clouded. Encircled by wilderness, she had got away from Davith and evaded his robes. Free.

Ella widened her vision. The straggly bare trees and wild long grass surrounding her might belong anywhere between Erldan and the parched barren lands of the End of the World.

A man spoke to her. Ella recognised that voice. Not a person Amber knew, but someone Ella knew all too well. His light brown hair fell across green-grey hazel eyes. Brow arched. Lips curved.

Jonas.

Her stomach tilted, and her breath stopped. For a moment, she was everywhere and nowhere.

Throat clogged, her vision broke off, leaving dwindling flames, and a painful void.

Jonas. With Amber.

'Are you well, Ness?' An arm on her shoulder. She startled. Thyss had returned with kindling.

'Oh! Yes,' she said with a cough. 'Just reflecting on all you and Mara have done for me.' She smiled, her power flowing reflexively, as she added another log to replace the heat it stole.

'You've breathed some life into these musty walls, lass.' He chuckled. 'It's been an age since Mara laughed at my terrible jests.'

Whatever his feelings in private, Thyss kept his attentions fatherly, but Ella sensed the current of desire that ran beneath. How long before Mara noticed his hungering eyes, his quickened breath, before her presence tainted their lives and this haven, too?

As though she heard her name, Mara pushed through the door, panting. Her voice rose in panic. 'The king's men are coming.'

'Now?' Dark cloaked their village.

She nodded. 'A lad returned from the city. Overheard them preparing. The king thinks we harbour an escaped prisoner.' She eyed Ella. 'A man.'

Jonas.

Thyss swore.

Images rushed behind their eyes. *Gohran's men invading their homes. Shouting. Accusing. Terrorising. Dragging villagers to question. A boy and his father, a woman screaming, a blade slicing across a throat. Voices keening into the night.*

Gohran was coming.

Before Mara uttered the words, her bones felt it. Her reprieve was over.

There was no time to plan. Once Gohran realised the village folk helped her, his men would burn every man, woman, and child alive.

'I must leave,' she said.

'Nonsense, no one will recognise you. Not now.' Mara brushed the ends of her cropped yellow hair fondly, reassuring.

'We'll hide you, lass.'

Concealed from Gohran's guards, but not from him. Not when he would feel her presence long before he reached her, just as she sensed him. Eternally tethered.

'Let me think,' Ella said, stoking the hearth.

Her focus drifted. Amber had abandoned her fire and was travelling on horseback towards the rising moon. Gods willing, on her way back to Aryon. She didn't need Ella to rescue her. Not now. With Amber safe, Ella might retrieve her babe and flee.

Heart wrenching, she felt more than saw Xarion's smile, snuggled securely in her aunt's arms. Breeyan returned that warmth with a kind of untainted love Ella could never provide. Even if Breeyan let her take Xarion now, what life would Ella offer when, each time she looked into her daughter's eyes, her brother stared back?

Her image shifted until Breeyan came into focus. On the other side of Xarion sprawled her genealogy map. Breeyan's fingers traced the various lines, coming to rest between Ella and Gohran, their matching crosses taunting. If her aunt hadn't recognised the truth, she would soon enough.

Her mind sought to envision Venn for the first time since he discarded her at the grove. Her hearth's flames flickered, and his image sharpened. She gasped. Seated opposite Raeyn, he appeared shattered and broken, his mouth curved in a tight sneer, eyes shadowed and embittered. A mess. Lynden sat beside them, wearing a strange, haunted expression. Quiet, stifled, lonely.

She broke off her vision. Knew what she needed to do.

She turned to Mara, channelled heat. 'Stuff whatever you can fit from my stores into a saddlebag.'

'But Ness—'

Hand raised, she shook her head. 'If the king finds me here, I risk all your lives.' She was a danger to everyone in her midst. 'Hurry. Please.'

Mara did as she asked.

To Thyss, she said, 'Where is the safest place beyond Nedran and Erldan? Somewhere the priests don't bother.'

He scratched his beard, brow scrunched.

'Think. Quickly.' Drawing more heat, she gripped him. Eyes pleading. Pictured their little village, tucked beyond any town, and until now, beneath the notice of the local overlords.

His eyes grew soft, focus hazy. 'I know folk who live in the forests behind Rassit,' he said.

There was no way to reach Rassit without cutting too close to Nedran. To Erldan. West lay Aryon and then, wasteland.

She crouched, grabbed a hunk of charcoal, and swept a space on the floor. 'Draw it for me?' *Show me the path as a bird's passage across the sky.*

Confusion played along his brow, his mouth, before he took the blackened coal and dragged.

She stoked the flames, sourced more power, and urged him to picture this place as though he were there. Its people, its buildings. Anyone he knew or cared about.

Translucent images formed: *a blond young man, a weathered face, a whining child, a crooked-eared pup, tail wagging, snout barking. Comfort. Familiarity. Warmth.*

'That's it,' she coaxed, peering at the door, willing Mara to return.

She thought again of Amber. Hardness in her chest and throat. It was Ella's fault the priestess was out here. If not for her, her old tutor would have remained tucked at Aryon, quietly studying to become a member of the council. Had she not sought Venn's protection, he may have lived content with her sister. Had Gohran not uncovered her magic that day in Erldan's glade, he might never have challenged their mother, but found a devout wife and inherited the throne when it was due. Jaydyn could have married Sheevan, and raised Serrah at Creywmm, the first of a brood of children. Jonas would have wed Vera and settled on one of Lichen's estates, and Lynden some handsome, pampering lord.

Instead, her Curse warped their fates. Poisoned them all.

Brief though her stay with Mara and Thyss had been, she had proved she could survive. Provided she stayed hidden, her powers kept her safe. But her loved ones were not safe while she was near. She had to be gone, far from everyone she cherished—especially Xarion. Her heart lurched.

Mara passed the bag. 'Here, lass. I packed what I could spare and saddled a steed. It's tethered outside.'

Gohran's men were pressing in. She sensed them. Sensed *him*. He knew she wasn't at Aryon, but didn't know where. He wasn't looking for her. Not tonight. But if she stayed, he would find her. Feel her soon enough.

She shook her head. 'They'll spot me on horseback if I leave now. I can't outrun them.'

'Then don't leave, Ness. You'll freeze on foot out there tonight.'

She swallowed. 'I can't stay.'

'How will you get away?'

A cold, gruesome grin, compelled into warmth. 'Do you trust me?' she said to Thyss.

He nodded, eyes unfocused, swaying gently.

'Mara?'

Another nod.

'Pass me a knife.'

She took the handle, brought her gaze back to the drawing made from charcoal and dust, willed Thyss to keep remembering, to continue imagining. Invited Mara's thoughts to join him. The fire dwindled.

Her brother's eyes, his cruel sneer, getting closer. She was running out of time.

She shoved his image away. Thought again of every person she'd cared about. Loved. They needed her far from here.

She addressed her hosts. 'Give me your hands.'

And they did.

She sliced the blade across one palm, and then the other. A grunt. A cry. She ignored their sharp inhales; faces scrunched as their blood welled.

Power gathered. She inhaled its exhilarating thrill. Felt her eyes glow.

The drawn path beckoned. *Voices laughing. Bickering. People peered and dogs barked. Before a hearth, a grey tabby purred.* Memories that didn't belong to her. She squeezed more blood. Let it surge. Channelled the passage across space, through time.

Her simulacrum peeled from its flesh. She drew more strength and slid along it, her mind floating, drifting, mystic eyes observing her crouched body huddled beside Thyss and Mara far below.

Gohran's thoughts pressed in.

Their bloodied hands gripped, she squeezed, willed Mara and Thyss to imagine a face known intimately to them, if not to her, and continued to follow the path.

Ethereal currents swirled and tugged, her vision shrouded in dark, in light, with the sensation of swimming, floating, flying. The fire of blood coursed through her body, propelling her forward. Her fogged vision cleared, like clouds of magic parting. Outside, snow blanketed thatched rooftops, crisp and clean. Homogenous trees—varieties common around Ycelt woodlands, not the straggly monsters near her village, near Aryon—creaked under its weight.

She continued, past the woodlands and towards a cottage. Within a lantern lit room, beside a hearth, a face formed. A stocky blond lad. His aura dull, but his image clear and strong. His smile was oddly familiar. He smelled like her pillow, her borrowed clothes. His name whispered across the ethereal currents: Thymm.

Through her hosts' imaginations, she saw his blond hair as she'd once viewed Venn atop a mound of grass, peeking through the clouds. The man's face had grown rougher than in their favoured memories, age etched around his eyes and mouth. Memory and reality blurred. His image wavered.

Don't stop, she pleaded, unsure if she spoke with voice or mind.

Her simulacrum was so close now.

If she failed to transfer mind and body, her life was forfeit, but if she stayed, she would die anyway, and so would Mara, Thyss, and every person living out here. She carried her Curse wherever she went.

She must do this. No one could rescue her, but she had a chance to rescue them.

A final surge of power.

She summoned her flesh to follow that blond lad's face, the tenor of his voice, surrounded by laughter and animals. His smell, an odour she'd grown accustomed to, wearing his clothes, sleeping in his bed.

Her simulacrum pulled at her flesh, a hungry, wrenching force, like someone ripping the meat from her bones.

Thyss and Mara shouted after her, their voices calling, fading. So far away.

She looked down. Her hands were empty. Her cloak and clothes were gone.

Another tug, another jerk. A scythe-like pain through her temples and spine, and then the searing jolt of flesh slamming into spirit.

A sudden, biting chill.

Darkness.

Naked and alone, the song of unfamiliar insects, the call of alien birds. Stars winked as the moon smiled above. She had carried her Curse into the quiet, eerie night.

Sixty-Five

Beneath the sliver of Xenon's smile, Breeyan rocked Xarion in her arms, humming an Ancient hymn. Her study's hearth ablaze, she soaked up the warmth, feeding the babe all the power she craved to soothe the rupture from her mother's absence.

She recalled her erstwhile High Priestess: 'Xenon will make many demands of you. Your priestesses will not always favour your decisions. At times, they may dislike you. But it falls to you to protect Aryon's lore, her location, and her people.'

Since she had leveraged Shira and Nykahlia to reach Ella and search for Amber, her scrying met the cloak of Ella's resistance, but on this night, her niece's guard was down as she peered into a fire of her own.

Ella's thoughts touched hers, the barest brush, before she shuttered her mind, and Ella turned to speak to someone. A limitation of her scrying, Breeyan couldn't see who. Merely sensed their presence in Ella's mind. No sign of fear or malice. These were folk Ella trusted.

She widened her vision, tried to picture Ella's surroundings, but the image fogged over. She drew more power and moved her focus back. Though she could not discern Ella's location, one thing was frighteningly obvious: the churning blue light emanating from Ella and winding around her companions.

Not a line of influence. A binding force.

Beguilement. It had to be.

She banished her vision and turned towards the parchments still sprawled across her desk: her family's genealogy map and the stolen pages of *The Lost*

Warriors, which, spurred by an omen, she'd hidden all those years ago. She ran fingertips over the names, traced hers and Prya's lineage alongside Ella's.

Unease prickled.

She pushed the map aside, drew the old story closer, and read.

When Xarion looked up, her lover had come. Their eyes met, and nothing else mattered. Weeping, they clutched one another as steeds thundered nearer. Xenon, leading her sisters. Betrayal shadowed the god's luminous eyes. From the other direction came King Myrhan's men. An ambush. Their last chance to flee. But Xenon's disappointment—and her shame—haunted. With a forced breath, she faced her lover and drew her sword.

A snuffle. Baby Xarion snuggled into Breeyan's chest, breathing, dreaming. Breeyan kissed her soft raven hair, tears moistening those black curls, her creamy skin. She didn't stir. Breeyan turned to the story's end and read on:

Under the blood-hued sky, the warrior-god Xenon raised his powerful arms.

'It is over.' His voice thundered across the clouds. Sweat trickled down his battle-hardened body, collecting blood from each wound, the blood of each enemy slain. Arms dropped by his side, head bowed, he stepped over strewn corpses, and met the eyes of the king. 'It is over,' he repeated.

Behind stood the few surviving warrior priestesses: armour-clad, armed, and waiting.

King Myrhan's men gathered around their leader, anxious, watching the king's bejewelled sword even now at the ready.

Eyes ablaze, Xenon clasped Myrhan's sword with both hands. The blade bit into his palms, but he did not flinch. Clamped harder. Blood welled between his fingers and plunged to the ground. The blade curved and strained, and finally snapped, freeing the stone embedded in steel. The clang of splintered metal pierced the thick quiet, but the stone hung silent in mid-air.

Xenon intoned a sacred chant, a bittersweet song that spoke of regret, and the gem drifted towards him. With a word, it shattered. Xenon absorbed each miniscule fragment within his flesh, leaving an unfamiliar void.

'If it is war that you want, it is war you shall have. Eternally...' Xenon cast his mournful eyes upon the men who betrayed him. Then, head shaking, he turned

away. His back to them, he spoke. 'Do not touch my people. To them, a simple life, a pure life—eternal peace.'

He strode towards the twilit moon. Turned back one last time. 'My Curse be upon you.'

Breeyan pictured the scene, the god leaving the mortal plane to inhabit the Afterworld ever more. He bid his followers eternal peace, but there was a price to pay. No violence, but no lust. No war, but no love. No *passion*.

When Xarion and her lover slayed each other, their armies followed to their deaths. The captain was impervious to her powers, but his army was not. Each soul entirely in her thrall, her beguilement fuelled their intractable belief.

Xenon watched each side grow more enamoured, more beguiled. More entrenched.

And when He surrendered to end the war, He forbade his followers from wielding their magic in this way ever again. To ensure no man fell victim inadvertently, He rendered his followers' bodies sacrosanct. None could enact violence or lust without summoning the Curse. None could draw power from another life. Not animal. Not human.

She often wondered if, descended from that Ancient warrior priestess, her sister Prya possessed remnants of her Ancient power. So rare. Her sister charmed and seduced their parents, their acquaintances. Their lover.

She pondered it again when she met Ella, sensed a strange force winding and churning throughout her damaged aura, but had not witnessed it while Ella's growing babe syphoned her magic. In truth, she had not searched for it. Had not wanted to find it. Not when Xenon bid if those gifted with beguilement could not be isolated, they must be destroyed.

Xenon did not gift Breeyan so, but she seduced King Rohan, nonetheless.

Betrayed her sister as her sister had betrayed her.

Vengeance, yes, but also a taste of the life denied her. A sample of freedom before her life at Aryon stole it for eternity, for even in this haven, she wasn't free.

Her sister had wanted the throne. She had wanted the man.

Rohan was not an easy man to love. Brutal. Savage. Proud.

Theirs was not a sweet bardic romance. When Rohan thrust her onto his desk, shoved her skirts above her knees, and tasted the salty sweet between her thighs, he'd demanded she grip fistfuls of his hair, force him deeper, call his name. Worship him.

Oh, how she worshipped him.

The Curse had seemed so abstract. She had not taken final vows, a barely inducted novice, when she escaped her unwelcome home, and savoured Rohan one last time.

Though Prya beguiled him, he didn't hesitate to satisfy his lusts with his wife's sister's body. How Breeyan craved his forceful hands, his rough mouth, the weight and power of him.

She recognised that violence in their son. Gohran was not an easy man. And when she witnessed his aura, twisted back on itself, she hadn't wanted to contemplate what it might mean. Convinced herself it was his repression, perhaps a disturbance from his mother's death. Her abandonment. Something—anything other than what was becoming so evident.

She eyed the genealogy map again, noting the marks and lines she had drawn. Like her, Gohran possessed no beguilement.

But what about Ella? If what she saw through the fire was Xenon's forbidden gift, Ella's dose was potent.

When Prya first told Breeyan of her daughter's magic, she had examined their ancestry, started to question whether Ella was not the product of Rohan's seed, but Prya's vengeance, for every morsel of her former lover was devoid of magic. Discovering Ella's potency, she was certain Rohan was not Ella's father.

Similarly, when she observed Ella's power amplified in Xarion, she knew Lord Venn of Nedran could not be Xarion's.

Breeyan pulled the babe close. Did not open her god-sight. Refused to view Xarion's aura.

Xarion's power wasn't merely strong. It was strange. Even without seeing, she sensed its peculiar, inverted currents roiling.

She had only witnessed one aura like it.

Gohran's.

It made sense of her omens. Her visions. Her dreams. The scars marring Ella's aura. The darkness when she studied her babe.

She choked back a sob.

Xarion was her granddaughter. Her grandniece. And she was Cursed.

Unease. Darkness.

Since Ella arrived at Aryon, misfortune had spiralled. Amber and Nykahlia bonding not as friends but lovers. Sallyn's death—the first recorded from the equinox rite. Amber's kidnapping. What if the Curse was spilling onto everyone in Ella's wake?

Only if you let it be.

But what if Xarion's darkness wasn't Ella's Curse? What if it began a generation before, when King Rohan satisfied her every lust? What if the tragedy started when Prya was the first woman of their line outed for her magic?

Not Ella's Curse, but hers.

It is said the Curse brings horror thrice over... Sister, Niece, and Son. Gohran's magic, twisted on itself, denounced his mother, defiled the woman he believed was his sister, but it was she, Breeyan, who started it all.

Unease. Darkness. Only if I *let it be.*

Thunder rumbled. A flash behind her eyes. That same battlefield, those ancient insignias of red and blue. A broken sword. A blood moon.

And from the corpses rose a girl with azure eyes and midnight hair.

Xarion.

To be continued...

THANK YOU

Thank you for joining me on this journey

Loving the series so far?

Rate and review Christine's work wherever you get your books and book recommendations. Your support helps bring this work to new readers.

Connect

Subscribe to Christine's newsletter for new releases, bonus content, and more:

christinepriestly.com/newsletter/

Website: christinepriestly.com

Connect: linktr.ee/christinepriestly

DISCOVER

Need more?

Dive deeper into the world you love with this bonus prequel:

Breeyan's Betrayal
A Lost Warriors Novella

'*...He could never give her the thing she craved most: his heart.*'

Forced from her home, a sworn priestess of the Black Moon, Breeyan seizes the chance to revisit her former life and the throne her sister stole. But while Queen Prya recovers from yet another miscarriage, she leaves Breeyan to entertain her first love: the king. A novice priestess, Breeyan should pose no threat. After all, King Rohan belongs to her sister, and she to the god. But can you ever trust someone you once betrayed?

Subscribe to receive your copy of Breeyan's Betrayal FREE:

christinepriestly.com/newsletter/

ACKNOWLEDGEMENTS

They say writing the second book is the hardest, but my greatest challenge has been finding balance. The Lost Warriors world has existed so long within my psyche that my urgency to get it onto the page, and into your hands, has been overwhelming. Almost like a precious window finally opened, and I'm terrified circumstances will slam it shut at any moment.

Since rediscovering my writing, I have lived, breathed, dreamed, and moved with and through my characters, and it's sometimes difficult to come up for air, so I want to apologise—and thank—everyone in my life who I have annoyed, frustrated, and neglected with my obsession.

Along the way, my incredible alpha and beta readers have offered their sage advice and insights, helping uncover my blind spots, and getting this sequel where it needed to be. Lisa Witten, Imogen Reed, Rebecca Ciezarek, Marnie Johnston, and Samantha Starling. I couldn't have done this without you.

An extra special shout out to Kelly Richter, who in addition to alpha and beta reading, has been my sounding board, my sanity check, and my cheerleader.

With thanks to my editor, who supports my vision in the best way.

To my beloved readers, just wow. Your support and belief have blown me away.

And to Mr Lee, always.

Here's hoping my characters will play nicely and not blow up my plot again in Book Three!

With love and endless gratitude,

Christine Priestly

ABOUT THE AUTHOR

Christine Priestly is an Australian author with a penchant for sipping tea, cuddling cats, spinning stories (and poles!) in her spare time. By day, she's unravelling the mysteries of human desire as a sexologist and hypnotherapist, but by night, she's weaving tales of enticing characters to leave you breathless and entertained. Her work has appeared in magazines and anthologies over the years, adding a dash of darkness and a pinch of spice to the literary world. So, grab a cuppa, pet your feline friend, and get ready to dive into Christine's world of words.

Follow Christine's journey and see upcoming titles:

christinepriestly.com

www.ingramcontent.com/pod-product-compliance
Lightning Source LLC
Chambersburg PA
CBHW051318190726
48290CB00001B/204